THE WEALTHY FRENCHMAN'S PROPOSITION

BY
KATHERINE GARBERA

Katherine Garbera is a strong believer in happily-ever-after. She's written more than thirty-five books and has been nominated for *RT Book Reviews* career achievement awards in Series Fantasy and Series Adventure. Her books have appeared on a bestseller list for series romance and on the *USA TODAY* extended bestseller list. Visit Katherine on the web at www.katherinegarbera.com.

This book is dedicated to Rob Elser
who is my knight in shining armour.

Acknowledgements

I have to acknowledge my children Courtney and Lucas who were wonderful while I was writing this book during their summer break. They were extremely understanding in letting me plan events for them around my writing schedule. I know that every mother says she has the best kids in the world—but I really do!

One

"*Bonjour,* Sheri. Did the interoffice pouch arrive yet? I have sent something special in it for you!"

Sheri Donnelly smiled into the phone at Lucille Dumont's greeting. She loved her job at the Sabina Group. She'd been unsure what the future would hold six months earlier, when the small magazine company she worked for had been purchased by the large French conglomerate. But the change was working out beautifully.

Lucille was Sheri's counterpart at the publishing company's Paris office. Though they'd never met, Sheri always pictured Lucille as a chic Parisian. Partly because of the way she sounded over the phone and partly because their boss, publisher Tristan Sabina, had said that Lucille was nothing like her when she'd asked what his other assistant looked like.

"No, why?"

"I sent you the latest copy of *Le Figaro*." Lucille was a devoted reader of all tabloid magazines. She often sent Sheri the French tabloids and loved to receive the gossip rags from the U.S.

"Tristan hates it when you do that."

"He doesn't have to know. And he's on the cover with a gorgeous woman."

"I might be interested in it," Sheri said. Tristan had become kind of an obsession with her. Not anything unhealthy that bordered on stalking, but more of an unquenchable curiosity. She wanted to know all about him. So far, she'd learned that he was demanding but gave praise easily. Plus he was extremely cute. And a widower.

"I thought you would be."

Sheri grimaced. Was she that transparent, even over the phone? "Was there anything else?"

"Yes. I want to know about the woman. She's a

blond American actress, Kate or Jennifer or something. Do you know if he is seeing her?"

An actress? She'd been jealous of the coffee girl from downstairs whom Tristan flirted with every morning. No way could she compete with a beautiful blond actress. Sheri personified plain and dowdy, two things she knew about herself but had never been able to change.

"I don't have any details," Sheri said, smiling at the office mail guy as he dropped off the pouch. Now she was curious to see exactly what was in there.

"See what you can find out when he gets in to the office. You have the inside scoop on this one."

"I'm pretty sure that Tristan will fire me if I start gossiping about his personal life."

"You are right about that." The deep, velvety cadence of Tristan Sabina's voice made her start guiltily.

She gulped and looked up into his steel-gray eyes. "I've got to go, Lucille." She hurriedly said goodbye and hung up the phone, still holding Tristan's gaze.

His thick brown hair was longer in the front than in the back and his face had the healthy glow that came from spending time outdoors and not on a tanning bed. This morning he wore a blue pin-striped shirt, open at the collar, and a tailored navy suit. The sight of him made her want to stare dreamily, which was *so* not like her.

"Talking about me again?"

"Lucille and I have to talk about you," she said, trying for the cheeky tone she usually pulled off easily. "We're your assistants."

"True, but that did not sound like work."

She shrugged, unable to stop her speculative thoughts. Was he dating a Hollywood starlet? And when had it happened?

"What was Lucille calling you about?" he asked as he reached for his messages, and began thumbing through them.

"Oh, you know how she is, always thinking there's something exciting going on here in New York," Sheri said, looking down at her computer screen and hoping he'd just go into his office. She couldn't look at him and not tell him the truth.

"Ms. Donnelly?"

"Hmm…?" she said, still not looking up. Her computer screen was infinitely fascinating at this moment. *Please let him go away.*

"Look at me." She finally did. "What did Lucille ask you about?"

"I told you," she said, dropping her gaze to his open collar.

"Why will you not look me in the eye?" he asked, his accent very pronounced.

"Because I don't want to lie to you."

"Then do not lie to me."

She shrugged again. The last thing she wanted to talk about was his personal life. *Liar.* "It was something she saw in *Le Figaro.*"

"About me and a woman?" he asked.

She nodded.

He didn't say anything else, just stared down at her, and she started to feel really self-conscious. What if, somehow, he could read on her face that she was attracted to him? What if he picked up on that and it made working for him awkward? What if…?

"You have a conference call with Rene in fifteen minutes, and he just sent a lengthy e-mail that you should at least glance at before you talk to him," she said, holding out a copy of the e-mail, which she'd printed out for him.

For a moment she didn't think he was going to let her steer the conversation back to business.

"You are right, of course," he said, taking the papers.

"I highlighted the topics for you and jotted down the information I had on each one."

"Thank you, Ms. Donnelly. I don't know what I would do without you."

She flushed at the compliment. "You're welcome."

She watched until he walked into his office. She was going to kill Lucille. Not that the other woman could have known that Tristan would arrive while they were talking about him, but still....

She reached for the interoffice pouch and opened it. The magazine spilled out. The cover featured Tristan's publicity shot but inset was another picture. The paparazzi hadn't gotten a very good photo, but he looked very amorous, as did the woman wrapped around him. Sheri traced her finger over the line of his eyebrows, ignoring the headline and just concentrating on Tristan.

She was careful never to stare at him at work, that wouldn't be appropriate, but—

"Ms. Donnelly?"

"Yes."

"Put that magazine away."

She blanched and opened her bottom desk drawer, tossing the tabloid in there. "Was there something you wanted?"

"I need the book for the *Global Traveler.*"

"Yes, sir. I think that Maurice has it down the

hall," she said, standing and leaving the office before he could say anything else to her.

Oh, man, this was so not good. Twice in less than ten minutes, he'd caught her slacking on the clock. One of his big no-nos. To be honest, she didn't do a lot of it. But she had a feeling that wasn't going to matter. If she wanted to move up the managerial ladder, perhaps someday become an associate publisher, she'd better not get fired.

She grabbed the book, the big mock-up binder of the issue they were currently working on for their *Global Traveler* magazine, and hurried back to Tristan's office. He was on the speakerphone with his brother, Rene. The conversation was in French and she understood only about every third word they said. Tristan gestured for the book and she handed it to him before leaving the room.

She got back to her desk and saw an instant message from Lucille.

[L.Dumont] Did T walk in while we were talking?
[S.Donnelly] Yes.
[L.Dumont] Did you tell him what we were talking about?

She thought about filling Lucille in but then decided better of it.

[S.Donnelly] I really can't IM right now.
[L.Dumont] OK. Ping me when you can.
[S.Donnelly] Later.

Later, she thought. If she still had a job. She doubted that Tristan would fire her for talking on the phone, especially to Lucille, but she knew he wouldn't hesitate if she gave him enough reason to believe she was more interested in his personal life than in her job.

"Do you need anything else before I go, Mr. Sabina?" Sheri asked right at five o'clock. Not that she had anything really interesting to go home to. But she'd made it a point not to stay late since Tristan had become her boss. She found she liked the office a little too much when only the two of them were still there.

Tristan glanced up from his phone, which he'd been staring at in…amazement? His bangs fell over his forehead, making him look devilishly handsome.

He looked at her assessingly, making her

more nervous. "Actually I do have one more thing to discuss with you, something that has just come to my attention. Please come in and shut the door."

Sheri tried to school her features as she entered the office but guessed she'd failed when he gave her another odd look. Was the tabloid conversation going to come up again?

She walked across the Italian marble floor to the thick Arabian carpet that lined the area in front of his desk. The Sabina Group was a first-class outfit all the way. No cheaply made faux-wood desks or cubicles for their offices. And Tristan's office was a lush as they came. She took a seat on one of the leather wingback chairs that he had for guests.

"Before you say anything, let me apologize for looking at that magazine earlier. Sorry about that. I couldn't resist seeing what Lucille was talking about."

He shook his head. "No need to apologize. I think I let my temper slip a bit when I saw what you were reading."

"Why?"

"The paparazzi are always following me around. They can be a real nuisance," he said.

He sounded almost bored, an air she knew he

used to hide his anger. "You've been making the headlines a lot, lately," she said.

"Our family always has. My grandmother was a famous actress in France, and my grandfather was a director. My family always generates a lot of interest."

"I'm sorry. I wish there was something I could do."

"Well, actually, there is."

"What?" She hoped he wasn't going to ask her to be some kind of paparazzi lookout. "I'm not sure the celebrity photographers who follow you are going to disappear if I ask them to."

"No?" He arched one eyebrow at her in a totally arrogant way, giving her a half smile that melted her brain.

"Maybe you should stop partying," she said before she thought better of it.

His lips twitched and he shrugged one of his shoulders in a very Gallic way. "Unfortunately it is too late for that." He rubbed the back of his neck. "I have a proposition for you, Ms. Donnelly."

"And that is?"

"A personal one."

"How personal?"

"Pretty personal."

"I thought it was important to you to keep things strictly business among everyone at the office," she said.

"Well, this is personal business. What would you say to an all-expenses-paid trip to the island of Mykonos in Greece?"

Her breath caught. "Tell me more," she said.

"One of my best friends is getting married there next week."

She stared at him, confused. "Do you want me to go in your stead?"

"No. I'm asking you to come with me and be part of the bridal party."

Come. With. Him. Oh, God, she wanted to jump up, say yes and leave before he changed his mind. Maybe he had noticed the real Sheri beneath the plain clothing. But she wasn't that naive. There had to be more to this than any kind of latent attraction.

"Why me?"

"The bride, Ava Monroe, is American."

"You know other Americans," she said, thinking of the actress.

"It's short notice and I want to bring someone I am comfortable with. Someone who won't be nosing around in Christos's business."

This wasn't the most flattering invitation she'd ever had. It reinforced something she knew but hated to face. That she wasn't a forever kind of girl. That men moved on, always leaving her behind. Starting with her father, the pattern had repeated again and again over the course of her life. She tried not to dwell on it or mope around, but sometimes she forgot and hoped...hoped that those little-girl dreams of a white knight would become reality.

She still wanted to say yes.

"Christos Theakis?"

"Yes. Do you know him?"

"Only what I've read about Christos and the Theakis heir in the papers." The Greek shipping tycoon had recently come to America and been photographed with a lovely woman and a young boy. The tabloids had speculated that the child was his secret son.

"What did the scandal rags say?"

"Not too much," she said, taken aback by the vehemence in his tone. She should change the subject. "What exactly does this proposition entail?"

He pushed to his feet and walked around his desk. He leaned back against the polished walnut surface, crossing his legs at the ankle.

"I want you to be my date for the week during

the wedding activities. They need a few women to round out the bridal party. The bride has one close friend she has asked, and she and Christos would like the groomsmen to invite the other attendants."

She stared at him for a minute, unsure she'd heard him right. She shook her head and opened her mouth, but no words came out. Then she closed her eyes. "Okay, did you say *date?*"

"That is correct."

Her eyes popped open. "Are you crazy?"

"Maybe. But I am serious about this."

"Serious about taking me to Greece for a week." She crossed her arms over her chest and settled back into the chair.

"Actually, ten days. And I already told Christos that you will be there."

"Shouldn't you have asked me before you started announcing that?" she asked, not even trying to keep the surprise from her voice.

He lifted one eyebrow at her. "I apologize. There wasn't time to discuss it with you. Christos just called to ask me and wanted a name to include in the wedding program. As my assistant, you were the first suitable woman to come to mind."

"Mr. Sabina—"

"Call me Tristan."

She stared at him. "Are you asking me because one of your lovers might get to thinking that marriage to you might be in the cards?"

He shrugged.

"Don't you care for any of them?"

"I care for all of them, but that isn't the point. I've had my once-in-a-lifetime love. Marriage is something I won't share with anyone else."

She'd heard through Lucille that he'd deeply loved his first wife, and that she'd died, but knew few other details. "Why not?"

"That's irrelevant. The only fact that concerns you is that I'd like you to accompany me to Greece for this wedding. It is a proposition, Sheri," he said in that low-toned voice of his. It was the first time he'd said her first name. He always addressed her as Ms. Donnelly.

"Like a business deal?" she asked.

"Yes, exactly. You do this for me and then I do something for you in return."

"What kind of favor?" she asked.

"Any. Your choice."

He seemed to have given this some thought. "I don't know. I'm not really that good at social stuff."

"I'll show you. That will be part of my favor to you."

"I'm still not sure… I can't make a decision like this so quickly."

"There is not much time. I'm leaving at 8:00 a.m. tomorrow on my jet.

"Sheri, I need you," he said, walking over to her and putting his hands on the arms of the chair. He leaned in close, and she shut her eyes as she breathed in the delicious scent of his aftershave.

He needed her. Oh, man, there was no way she was going to say no. Ten days of just her and Tristan… She couldn't resist the opportunity to get him to see her as more than just his assistant.

Two

The marriage of his best friend was a good reason to celebrate but, since Cecile's death, weddings had become painful for Tristan. Still…on this day, with the sun shining brightly in the Greek sky and the champagne flowing freely, he wasn't focused on the past.

In fact, as the reception progressed, he was becoming more and more obsessed with *Sheri*. He'd invited his assistant because he knew that bringing a real date to a wedding always made the woman start looking at him like he had the potential to be a husband.

He wasn't going down the aisle again.

Yet…there was something about Sheri that he found comforting. She was fun to work with, she was pleasing to look at it. Not a world-class beauty, but so unassuming about her looks that it was refreshing to be around her.

But today she looked exquisite. The pale bridesmaid's dress made her skin glow and the subtle makeup that someone had applied to her face gave her an understated beauty that he couldn't keep his eyes from. Seeing her move lithely through the stately, beautiful Theakis home and grounds where the wedding was being held had put her into a new light.

"You're staring at your secretary," Gui said as he came up behind Tristan.

"Am I?"

Gui arched one eyebrow at Tristan but said nothing more. Count Guillermo de Cuaron y Bautista de la Cruz was one of his two best friends, Christos Theakis, the groom, being the other member of their triad. They'd met at boarding school in Switzerland when they'd all been ten, three young hell-raisers who had nothing in common except being second sons, boys who'd grown up with no pressure or expectations.

In their twenties, they'd started a business called Seconds, a string of nightclubs in posh hot spots all over the world. The exclusive clubs were *the* place to see and be seen the world over, and every night the bouncers turned away more celebrities, wannabes and hangers on than they let in.

He heard the husky sound of Sheri's laughter and Lucille's familiar snort and smiled to himself. Lucille, who knew Christos well from working with Tristan for so long, had also flown up for the wedding, and the two women had hit it off in person. He wasn't really surprised, because Sheri was one of those women that everyone got along with, and she and Lucille had already been friendly via the phone.

He didn't examine too closely why he'd asked Sheri, and not Lucille, to be his companion for the wedding.

"You're staring again…are you falling for her?"

"Falling for who?"

"Your secretary."

"You know how I am. She's pretty and available."

"And that's enough for tonight," Gui said.

Tristan shrugged. He didn't like to talk about his attitude toward women. He had two sisters and had been married to the love of his life. If he'd been a different man with a different sex drive, he would have lived the rest of his life as a celibate. A part of him had died with Cecile.

But he had never been able to turn off his attraction to the opposite sex. Six months after her death, he'd found himself starting a string of one-week affairs. Sex was the only thing he'd ever take from the women he became involved with.

He suspected that would not be enough for Sheri. She also worked for him, and that complicated things. He shook his head and signaled the waiter for another glass of wine. The vintage was a very nice one from his family's vineyards.

"Tris?"

"Hmm?"

"She's not like your other women—"

"I know that, Gui."

Gui nodded. "I can't believe that Christos is married."

"It's not the death sentence you think it is." Though he'd never admit it, Tristan envied Gui his attitude. Gui had never been serious about one woman, and he moved through life with a kind of light charm that Tristan admired.

The music changed and a sweet, slow song came on. Couples filled the dance floor with Ava and Christos in the center. They seemed so… He shook his head, not willing to go there.

"I have to go," Gui suddenly said.

"Why?"

"Those men are too old for Augustina," Gui said, acting the protective older brother to his sister, who had been Gui's companion in the wedding party. Tristan bit back a smile as he watched his friend wedge his way between Augustina and her suitors.

He felt a small hand on his arm and glanced down at Sheri. "Having fun?" he asked.

"Yes. I can't believe I was reluctant to come," she said. Her breath smelled faintly of champagne. She held a half-empty glass in her right hand. She tucked her left hand between his arm and body.

She closed her eyes and swayed to the music. Just a little movement and humming under her breath.

"Are you enjoying the reception?" he asked.

"Yes, I am. Ava's so sweet. Thank you for inviting me to join you this week."

"You're welcome. I believe I owe you something."

"What do you owe me, Tristan?"

There was a dreamy quality to her voice. From the first it had been obvious to him that she was attracted to him. But she was careful to keep that attraction to herself and had put a barrier between them. Put him into a box, so it seemed. But tonight…tonight, with the trio playing romantic music and the wine flowing freely, none of that mattered.

"Dance with me, *ma douce?*"

She smiled up at him. "I'd love to."

He had never seen that exact look in her eyes before. "You seem different."

"Maybe that's because we're not in the office."

"No, we are not. What difference does that make to you, Sheri?"

"It makes all the difference in the world, Tristan."

She wrapped her arms around his shoulders and leaned up on tiptoe, brushing her lips against his neck. "This is so nice."

Tristan knew he should pull away and let her go but instead he leaned down, put his hand under her chin and tipped her head up toward his. His lips found hers easily and she sighed into his mouth as their lips met.

The wedding that she'd been nervous about participating in had taken on a certain dreamlike state. The champagne was good. Very good. There really was a difference between that stuff she bought in the grocery store and fine French champagne.

The music was chic and sexy and, as Sheri

leaned closer to Tristan, she realized that he was, too. His cologne was one of a kind and smelled delicious. She'd never get enough of it. Even at work the scent lingered in his office when he was away.

She knew it was partly the alcohol she'd drunk that gave the evening the magical quality that it was taking on as she danced with Tristan, but just this once she felt as if she was woman enough for him.

The right kind of woman for Tristan Sabina, international playboy, her boss and the sexiest man she'd ever danced with.

"What are you thinking?" he asked, his French accent nearly as appealing as the strong line of his jaw.

"About you."

"Really?"

"Um…yes. What are you thinking?"

"That maybe I should pull you closer," he said, suiting action to words.

She rubbed her cheek against his shoulder and closed her eyes. She knew this was another part of the wonderful dreamland she'd been in for the last week. Being on Mykonos was like being in a fantasy world.

Tristan and his friends were wealthy in every sense of the word and, when she was with them, she was living a life that was far removed from everything she'd ever known.

"Okay?"

"Yes," she said, her words a sigh. "Though I thought we'd decided that…um, we'd just have a professional relationship."

"Did we? I think we can both be forgiven for making the most of this moment, on a night like tonight."

She looked up at him, trying to judge if he was sincere, and she saw something in his eyes. Something she'd never seen in them before.

Lust.

Everything feminine in her clenched at that expression. Here was what she'd dreamed of. And how sad was it that she wanted to accept whatever he had to offer?

"For just this night?" she asked, to make sure she understood what he was offering.

"That's all I have in me," he said, but in his eyes she saw the hint of something more.

Some kind of emotion that intimated that he did feel more, but why did she care? Being in Tristan's arms was enough for her. This moment dancing together was better than she'd ever imagined it could be. She kept breathing deeply, trying to imprint the scent of him in her soul. She ran her hands down his shoulders and back, feeling the strength of his body under her touch.

If she were braver she'd press her body closer to his so she'd have the imprint of him against her to recall when she was back in the office and they were simply employer and employee again.

His finger under her chin startled her into opening her eyes and when he tipped her head back and their eyes met, she realized that there was more happening here than just a dance. She saw something else in Tristan's gaze. There was such sadness there, she thought. A kind of pain that she recognized all the way to her lonely soul.

Tristan Sabina, lonely?

The thought was ludicrous.

She shook her head. What the hell was she doing? This was her boss. She pulled back, put a respectable few inches between them, and he let her.

She got the message loud and clear. There *wasn't* more to this than Tristan feeling lonely at the reception and wanting…what exactly?

She tipped her head to the side as he brushed his finger along the line of her jaw. "Why are you looking at me like that?"

"I never realized how beautiful your eyes are."

She caught her breath. She wasn't beautiful and

she knew it. Her eyes were brown. Not the kind of luscious chocolaty color that poets wrote about, just plain brown. She shook her head.

"Yes, gorgeous. I could get lost in them."

"Tristan—"

He rubbed his thumb over her lower lip and her thoughts dissolved. She felt a tingling from that contact that spread down her neck and shoulders. And she realized that the safe little way in which she'd been obsessed with Tristan had turned into a dangerous and exciting attraction.

She knew that he wasn't himself tonight. That Monday morning, when they were back at work, they would return to the relationship they'd always had.

A sane person would turn around, walk off the dance floor and go back to her room.

But she'd been alone in her room for much of her life. In a box of her own making where she was safely insulated from pain. From the men who always left her.

She looked up at Tristan. He stared at her lips. His own parted as he stroked hers. And she wondered if knowing he was leaving, figuratively speaking, after one night would somehow lessen the pain of being left once again.

And she didn't kid herself that it wasn't going to be painful when he left. It was always painful, but being with Tristan…being in his arms and experiencing the things she'd dreamed of since the first time he'd walked into her office…well, that might be worth it.

Wouldn't it?

She didn't know and didn't want to analyze it. For once she wanted to forget that she was a plain-Jane kind of woman. That she was the kind of girl who usually went back to her room alone. For tonight, she was the woman that Tristan Sabina was looking at with lust in his eyes.

He and Sheri danced together for the rest of the evening and once Christos and his bride left, Tristan thought of leaving, too. But he glanced over at Sheri and was unable to walk away.

He drew her back out onto the dance floor, moving their bodies together. Feeling the rightness of the way she fit in his arms and against his body.

If she pulled back, of course he'd let her walk away. He had never had to coax a woman into his bed. But with Sheri, he was tempted. He was tempted to ply her with champagne and kisses.

Kisses.

He'd tasted her lips once, and now that was all he wanted to do. Stroke his tongue over the seam between her lips until she sighed and opened her mouth. Let his tongue sweep into the softness of her mouth. She would taste sweet…of champagne and something else that was uniquely Sheri.

He could not resist. He lowered his head, and she rose to meet him. She moaned into his mouth, wrapping her arms around his neck and leaning up on her tiptoes to keep their mouths together. He held her waist, lifting her against him. He felt the impact of her breasts against his chest and wanted to groan out loud. How could he ever have missed the fact that Sheri was a damned attractive woman?

He pulled back and looked down into those deep chocolate eyes of hers. They were wide and dreamy-looking. She brought one hand from his shoulder to her mouth and traced her lips with her forefinger.

"Sheri?"

"Hmm?"

"Would you like me to kiss you again?" he asked.

"Oh, yes," she said, licking her lower lip and leaning her weight on him as she stretched up toward him.

He bent lower and as soon as his lips brushed hers she opened her mouth and her tongue met his.

Just a soft, tentative touch, and then she made that little moaning sound and he felt the gentle edge of her teeth against his lower lip as she sucked him into her mouth.

He opened his eyes and saw that hers were closed and she was absorbed totally in the moment. He realized things were going too far for a public dance floor. Sheri's burgeoning passion was for him, and him alone.

Damn, he'd never felt this possessive about a woman before.

He lifted his mouth from hers, tucked her head into the curve of his neck and shoulder. Rubbed his hands down her back until he thought he could walk without each step being painful.

The crowd at the reception had thinned. The photographer from the Sabina Group was still there, but otherwise the event was paparazzi free. The guards that Christos had hired had provided an environment where his bride and his guests could relax and not have to worry about being pursued.

"Sheri?"

"Yes, Tristan?"

He couldn't ask her to stay with him tonight, he thought. This was his assistant. The woman he counted on to be cheeky and funny and to keep his

New York office running efficiently. Yet he wanted her, and he wasn't in the habit of denying himself anything he wanted.

"Did you like that?"

"Kissing you?"

"Mmm, hmm."

"Oh, yes. Very much. And dancing with you," she said, her eyes sparkling as she shimmied against him in time to the slow jazz number playing. "Did you enjoy it?"

"Kissing you or dancing with you?" he asked, just to tease her.

"Both."

"Yes."

She arched both eyebrows at him. "Really? I know you're used to more sophisticated women."

"How do you know that?" he asked. He never discussed his private life at the office.

"I searched you on Google. I read the *Post*. And Lucille sends me the French tabloids with pictures of you."

"Why?" he asked, realizing that Sheri was a lot more talkative when she drank. Normally, she'd try to play off her interest in him, but not tonight.

"You're my obsession," she said, her tone airy and breathless.

"Obsession?" he asked.

She flushed and pushed out of his arms. Her hands came up to cover her face. "Oh, my God. I can't believe I said that."

Tristan cupped her elbow and led her from the dance floor. Sheri grabbed a glass of champagne from a passing waiter. Taking a delicate sip, she drew to a stop.

"Will you please forget I said that?"

Not in a million years, he thought. She was totally unique in a world of women who fawned over him. There was a freshness to her. An innocence that he'd never experienced. Not even with Cecile, who'd been ten years his senior.

"Tristan? Did you hear me?"

"Yes, I did."

"And?"

"No, Sheri, I will not forget you said that."

"Why not?"

"Because I like being your obsession. What have you obsessed about doing with me?"

She shook her head and he wondered if she'd back down now. Instead she took a sip of her champagne and smiled up at him. "I'm not sure you're ready to know about that."

"When do you think I will be?"

She shrugged. Her delicate shoulders moved underneath the pretty silk straps of the bridesmaid's dress. "I'm not sure you'll ever be ready."

"Why not?"

"Because of what I said earlier."

"And that was?"

"You're not used to a woman like me."

"*Ma petite,* that I may not be, but I'm definitely ready for a woman like you."

Three

Sheri kept her hand in Tristan's as they walked toward the front of the mansion, where the valet was stationed, to get his car. Suddenly she hesitated, realizing that this was going to change her life. She forced herself to look around and acknowledge that, if she kept walking, her life *would* change.

"Sheri?"

She bit her lower lip, wondering if she was going to pass up the chance of a lifetime. And the answer was…she had no idea. She was torn between what she wanted—the man she'd wanted for so long—and self-preservation.

"Yes?"

"Would you like to stay here?"

No, she thought. But now she couldn't say that she was swept away by the moment. He was putting the onus on her, which was exactly where it should be. Clearly, he was leaving…and the thought of watching another man walk away was too much for her. The decision was made that easily.

She had no idea what the future would hold, but on this night she was going to be with Tristan. And it could only be this night, because she was flying back to the States in the morning.

"Where are you taking me?" she asked.

"My villa."

"You have a villa on Mykonos?"

"Yes. I own property all over the world," he said.

"Why? There's no real reason for you to be here for the magazine."

"One of my best friends lives here. Plus, in the summer, it's a nice place to holiday."

She nodded. "I don't own any property." She was very lucky that her brownstone in Brooklyn was a fixed-price rental. She'd taken over the lease upon her aunt's death.

He arched one eyebrow at her. "Is that important?"

She shrugged and realized that, to him, it wouldn't be. And unless she wanted to ruin the wonderful attraction that was flowing between the two of them, she needed to stop being so mired in who she was.

"It's not. So where is this villa?"

"Not far. Ready to go?"

She nodded.

She started forward but he stopped her with a hand on her arm, drawing her back against his chest. He leaned down and whispered something in French that she couldn't understand and kissed her neck.

Tingles of arousal spread down her body, tightening her nipples and making her breasts feel fuller. He wrapped his arms around her from behind, one hand at her waist, one hand right under her breasts.

She tipped her head to the side to give him better access to her throat. He whispered her name and kept her close to him before biting her softly and lifting his head.

He took her hand in his and led the way out of the building. They waited for the car. Tristan kept his gaze on the night sky. But Sheri couldn't help looking at him and marveling that, for tonight, he was hers.

Tristan Sabina is going to be mine. The future didn't matter at this moment, because she wanted him with the kind of keen longing she'd never experienced before with a man.

He turned to her and lifted one eyebrow as if he were asking her what she was thinking. She flushed and shook her head.

He smiled then lowered his head and kissed her, his lips feathering over hers and his hands skimming down the sides of her body. His fingers brushed against the curves of her breasts and came to rest at her waist, pressing her up into his body.

She liked the way he felt against her. His height made her feel delicate and very womanly. His hands were large enough to span her waist and she felt them wrap around her. Everything else dropped away.

There was just her and Tristan. His lips on hers, his hands on her body and the very essence of him seeping into her cold and lonely soul.

She suckled his lower lip, drawing it into her mouth. His hands tightened on her and his erection brushed against her lower belly. She swallowed hard and pulled back, looking up at him.

She had a little sexual experience, but nothing that had made her feel like Tristan was.

"What is it?" he asked, bringing one hand up to cup her cheek. His thumb stroked her skin and she looked up into his warm gray eyes and felt something shift inside her.

"Why me?"

"Why not you?"

She shook her head and realized that, if she asked questions, she should be prepared to hear an answer that might not be what she was searching for.

But she'd never been a coward, and this night with Tristan…well, she wanted to make the most of it. Be someone she'd never been before.

"Seriously, why are you making a move now?"

"That sounds so crass, *ma petite*. I have no ulterior motive. I have a beautiful woman in my arms and I don't want to let her go."

"I'm not beautiful," she said, because she knew it was true. There were truly beautiful people in the world and she wasn't one of them. She was more apt to be described based on her sterling personality. It wasn't that she was unattractive, it was just that there was nothing that really made her stand out.

"Tonight you sparkle," he said.

She felt her cheeks heat up with a blush. He lowered his head once again, kissing her, and in his arms she realized she did feel beautiful. She felt worthy to be on his arm as they got in his black Lamborghini and drove through the narrow streets of Mykonos.

He kept her hand on his thigh and his hand on top of hers, moving only to shift gears, and occasionally to lift her hand to his mouth to kiss the back of it.

She leaned her head back against the leather seat and turned to watch him. Tristan Sabina…she couldn't believe she was alone with him at last.

Tristan parked the Lamborghini behind his villa and got out. Sheri had her door opened before he got there. He offered his hand to help her out of the car. He saw the surprise in her eyes as she took it.

He realized that no one had ever been good to her in the way that men should be toward women. He wanted to change that, at least for tonight.

When she was standing next to him, he tucked a loose curl behind her ear. He couldn't get enough of touching her. He led the way into his house, tossing his keys on the kitchen countertop and hitting the light switch. She stood awkwardly just inside the doorway. Was this the moment when she'd change her mind?

He wouldn't pressure her into staying, he thought.

Then she nibbled on her lower lip and his entire body went on point. God, he wanted her. Why now?

He'd had a few inconvenient fantasies since they'd arrived here on Mykonos. Away from the office, Sheri had dropped her barriers and started to relax. He'd always liked her cheeky attitude, but seeing her in shorts on Christos's yacht during the week and tonight in this dress that actually fit her…well, it got to him.

He tried to remind himself that she was his assistant and that this was the kind of situation that Rene always warned him against. Fraternization was firmly frowned upon at the Sabina Group, especially by the CEO, Tristan's older brother, Rene.

And frankly, now that she was here in the villa, she seemed nervous. Not at all like the sexy woman he'd held in his arms on the dance floor.

"Would you like a drink?"

"No thank you," she said. "I… Show me your place."

He shrugged out of his tuxedo jacket and tossed it on the bar stool at the kitchen counter. He led her out of the kitchen into a formal reception room and up the stairs to the living room. He'd put on some music and dance with her again. That would relax her like nothing else would.

And he'd have her back in his arms.

"Look at the view," she said as they stepped into his living room. One wall was all windows, showcasing the view of the city of Mykonos and the Aegean Sea.

"It's even more spectacular from the balcony. Would you like to see that?"

She nodded.

He put his hand on the small of her back and lowered his mouth to hers and kissed her slowly. She shifted in his arms, turning to wrap her arms around his shoulders.

Blood rushed through his veins, pooling in his groin. He lifted his head. Her lips were wet and a little swollen from his kisses. "Come, let me show you the view."

He led her outside and the cool evening air surrounded them. She rubbed her hands over her arms. He brushed her hands aside, caressing her and pulling her back against his body.

He kissed her neck and shoulders as she stood still under his touches. Then she turned around and rose up on her tiptoes, taking his mouth with hers. Her tongue teased his and he realized that, though she was a little nervous, she was with him right now.

Wanting him the way he wanted her.

He felt her fingers at his neck, loosening his bow tie and then tossing it away. "Can I unbutton your shirt?"

"Yes."

She did with slow touches. "You have a great body, Tristan."

"How do you know?"

"I saw it in *People* magazine's spread on you last summer. A photo of you at the beach."

He growled deep in his throat when she leaned forward to brush kisses against his neck. Her lips were sweetly shy as she slowly unbuttoned his shirt. Then she nibbled her way lower, and he felt the edge of her teeth graze his skin.

He watched her, his eyes narrowing and his pants feeling damned uncomfortable. Her tongue darted out and brushed his nipple. He arched against her and put his hand on the back of her head, urging her to stay where she was.

She put her hands on his shoulders and eased her way down his chest. She traced the muscles that ribbed his abdomen and then slowly made her way lower. He could feel his heartbeat in his erection and he knew he was going to lose it if he didn't take control.

But another part of him wanted to let her have

her way with him. When she reached the edge of his pants, she stopped and glanced up his body to his face.

Her hand brushed over his straining length. "I guess you like that."

He muttered the French equivalent to the American "Hell, yeah," and pulled her to him. He lifted her slightly so that her breasts brushed his chest. "Now it is my turn," he said.

Blood roared in his ears. He was so hard, so full that he needed to be inside of her body *right now.*

Impatient with the fabric of her dress, he drew it up over her head and tossed it out of his way. No bra. He caressed her creamy thighs. God, she was soft. She moaned as he neared her center and then sighed when he brushed his fingertips across the *V* of her panties.

The cotton was warm and wet. He slipped one finger under the material and hesitated for a second, looking down into her eyes.

They were heavy-lidded. She bit down on her lower lip and he felt the minute movements of her hips as she tried to move his touch where she needed it.

He was beyond teasing her or prolonging anything. He pressed her panties aside, slipping two fingers into her humid body. She squirmed against him.

He pulled her head to his so he could taste her mouth. Her lips parted and he told himself to take it slow, that Sheri wasn't used to him. But one touch and he was out of control.

He held her at his mercy. Her nails dug into his shoulders and she pressed upward. He pulled away from her mouth, glancing down to see her nipples pushing against his chest. She closed her eyes and held her breath as he ran his finger over one nipple. It was velvety compared to the satin smoothness of her breast. He brushed his finger back and forth until she shifted on his lap.

He caressed her back, scraping a nail down the length of her spine to the indentation above her buttocks.

He wanted to give her so much pleasure, because he suspected she hadn't experienced true passion before.

Women were vulnerable when it came to sex. Not just in a physical way, but in an emotional one, as well, and Tristan made it a point to make sure that his lovers knew how sexy and beautiful he found them.

She moaned, a sweet sound that he captured in

her mouth. She tilted her head to the side immediately to allow him better access. She held his shoulders and moved on him, rubbing her center over his erection.

Gently he scraped his fingernail over her nipple again and she shivered in his arms. He pushed her back a little bit so he could see her. Her breasts were bare, nipples distended and begging for his mouth. He lowered his head and suckled.

He held her still with a hand on the small of her back. He buried his other hand in her hair and arched her over his arm. Both of her breasts were thrust up at him. He had been with many women, but he knew that he wanted Sheri more than he'd wanted any other woman in a long time. What the hell? This was sex, not about wanting her.

He wouldn't let this be about anything other than the physical. One night together.

"Tristan?"

"Hmm?"

"Okay?"

Damn. He didn't want her out of the moment. "I'm fine. Just enjoying you, *ma petite*."

Her eyes were closed, her hips moving subtly against him, and when he blew on her nipple he saw gooseflesh spread down her body.

He loved the way she reacted to his mouth on her breasts. Her nipples were so sensitive, he was pretty sure he could bring her to orgasm just from touching her there.

The globes of her breasts were full and fleshy, more than a handful. He licked the lily-white valley between them, suckling at her to leave his mark. He wanted her to remember this moment, what they had done, when she was alone later.

Soon her hands clenched in his hair and she rocked her hips harder against his length. He lifted his hips, thrusting up against her. He bit down carefully on one tender, aroused nipple. She cried his name and he hurriedly covered her mouth with his, wanting to feel every bit of her passion. He was so hard he thought he'd die if he didn't get inside her.

He glanced down at her and saw that she was watching him. The fire in her eyes made his entire body tighten with anticipation.

Since he'd always prided himself on being a conscientious lover, he knew he should ask about birth control, but that could be a mood killer with some women. So instead he reached for the condom he'd put in his pocket earlier before leaving for the reception. He'd planned to get laid so he could assuage the memories of his own wedding but he'd never anticipated he'd be here now with Sheri.

"Tristan." She said his name with the hint of shyness he'd noticed in her earlier.

"Yes," he said.

"I'm not…really good at this."

"You will be in my arms."

She shook her head. "Don't wait for me to… well, you know. It's hard for me."

"It won't be with me."

"Tristan—"

"Shh," he said, pulling her back into his arms and setting about arousing her again to the point where she would forget that she supposedly couldn't orgasm. Because of her cheeky attitude, he hadn't realized how innocent Sheri was. She seemed like a confident woman, comfortable with who she was, and only here on the balcony with her in his arms did he realize that she was as big a fraud as he was.

"Come to me now."

She reached between his legs and fondled him, cupping him in her hands, and he shuddered. He needed to be inside her now. He eased her panties off then shifted and lifted her thighs, wrapping her legs around his waist as he leaned back against the wall of the balcony. The sky was full of stars and the lights of Mykonos spread out below them. Her hands fluttered between them and their eyes met.

He held her hips steady and entered her slowly, deeply, pulling her down on him until he was fully seated. Her eyes widened with each inch he gave her. She clutched at his hips as he started thrusting. He leaned down and caught one of her nipples in his teeth, scraping very gently. She started to tighten around him. Her hips moved faster, demanding more, but he kept the pace slow, steady, wanting her to come before he did.

He suckled her nipple and rotated his hips to catch her pleasure point with each thrust, and he felt her hands in his hair clenching as she threw her head back and her climax ripped through her.

He varied his thrusts, finding a rhythm that would draw out the tension at the base of his spine. Something that would make his time in her body, wrapped in her silky limbs, last forever.

He turned them around so that she was pressed against the wall, then he tilted her hips, giving himself deeper access to her body. She scraped her nails down his back, clutched his buttocks and drew him in. He tightened, and his blood roared in his ears as he felt everything in his world center on this one woman.

He called her name as he came. She tightened around him and he looked down into her eyes as he kept thrusting. He saw her eyes widen and felt the minute contractions of her body around his as she was consumed by another orgasm.

He rocked his hips against her until she stopped moving. She wrapped her arms around his shoulders and kissed the underside of his chin.

"Thank you."

"For what, *ma petite?*"

"For giving me this night. It's like something out of one of my dreams."

With those words she brought him completely out of himself and into a place he'd been only once before. A place of vulnerability that he'd hoped never to find again.

Four

Tristan carried her back into the villa. Sheri didn't get a chance to look at the place though, as he carried her straight to the bedroom.

He put her on her feet next to the bed.

As she stood naked in front of him, he traced the strawberry birthmark on her right hip. She felt so vulnerable, standing with him looking at her. He'd refastened his pants and his shirt hung open, but he was still essentially dressed and she was naked.

She crossed her arms over herself, one across her breasts, the other over her lower body.

"What are you doing?" he asked, his voice deeper than normal, his French accent more pronounced.

"I'm not…"

"Not what?"

"I look better with clothes on," she said at last.

He shook his head. "Not those baggy frocks you wear in the office."

"You don't like the way I look at work?"

He traced his finger over the edge where her right arm covered her breasts. His finger dipped beneath her arm to caress the upper curves of her breast. "I like the way you look. It is those frumpy clothes you wear that I don't like."

"Frumpy?"

"Yes."

"I'm not good with fashion," she said, not sure why she was telling him this. In the darkened bedroom, with her body still tingling from the incredible orgasms he'd helped her achieve, she felt oddly relaxed. If only she was wearing something. "Why don't you take your shirt off?"

"Would you like me to?"

"Yes, definitely."

He shrugged out of it, and she reached for it before he could toss it aside. She put her arms in the sleeves, but he held the two sides open. "I like you naked."

"I feel too exposed."

"Why?"

She felt more vulnerable now than she had just a second before. She just shrugged.

He didn't say anything else, just bent to trace her birthmark with his tongue. Could he want her again so soon?

She couldn't think as he stood back up and lifted her onto the bed. He slipped off his pants and underwear, then bent down to capture the tip of her breast in his mouth. He sucked her deep, his teeth lightly scraping against her sensitive flesh. His other hand played at her other breast arousing her, making her arch against him in need. Yes, he could.

She reached between them and took his erection in her hand, bringing him closer to her, spreading her legs so that she was totally open to him. "I need you now."

He lifted his head. The tips of her breasts were damp from his mouth and very tight. He rubbed his chest over them as he slid deep into her body.

She moved her hands down his back, cupping his butt as he thrust deeper into her. Their eyes met. Staring deep into his eyes made her feel as if their souls were meeting. She felt her body start to tighten around him, catching her by surprise. She climaxed before him. He gripped her hips, holding her down and thrusting into her two more times before he came with a loud groan of her name.

He held her afterward, disposing of the condom but then pulling her into his arms and tucking her up against his side.

She wrapped her arm around him and listened to the solid beating of his heart. She fought to remember that this was just for one night. Men leave, she reminded herself firmly. But, lying in his arms, she felt as if this could last forever. She burrowed closer to him, holding him tightly to her.

She wished she could say that she understood him better now than she ever had before. But she had the feeling that she'd simply revealed her own weaknesses. Showed how little she felt she was worth.

"Are you sleeping?" he asked.

She felt the vibration of his words in his chest and under her ear. She shifted in his embrace, tipping her head so she could see the underside of his jaw.

"No. Too much to think about." This had been the most exciting day of her life. She felt as though, if she went to sleep, she might wake up and find none of it had happened. He traced his fingertips over her body, starting at her forehead and moving slowly down. She felt him linger on the birthmark, tracing over it again and again.

He tipped her head up so that their gazes met. "Thank you for coming to Mykonos this week."

"You're welcome. I enjoyed it."

"Was the vacation what you thought it would be?"

She pushed herself up on one elbow, looking down at his dark features and tracing her finger over his brows. "I can safely say it wasn't at all what I expected it to be."

"Better?"

"Yes." She paused. "Thank you for wearing a condom," she said. "I'm not on the pill."

"No problem."

It bothered her that he'd had condoms on him. That spoke volumes about the differences in their attitudes toward sex and sex partners.

"I don't think either of us wanted to deal with an unexpected pregnancy."

"You're right." His words were a stark reminder to her that this was a one-night stand. No matter that he hadn't said anything; she could read between the lines. Though his attitude toward pregnancy was one she shared. When she was eighteen, she'd vowed she'd never have children. She'd been too young to make that kind of decision, but the emotions behind it had been real.

Sheri still slept in his arms. Tristan glanced at his watch. They were flying back to the States later this afternoon. Because he wanted to linger, he pushed himself out of bed. He wanted to pull her into his arms and hold her tightly to him so that he knew she'd stay right by his side. And he'd only ever wanted to stay in bed with Cecile.

"Tristan?"

"Right here," he said. He sat on the side of the bed with his back to her, because if he saw her in his bed one more time he'd make love to her again. And he needed to start building a distance between them again. Last night was fine, but this morning he needed to get her dressed and out of his villa.

"Is it morning already?" she asked, leaning up to kiss his shoulder blade.

He shifted away from her on the bed, putting some distance between them.

"Yes."

In the silence that followed, he sensed her confusion.

Her stomach growled, breaking the tension, and he laughed. "Hungry?" He dared a glance at her.

She buried her red face under the sheet. "Yes. I was too nervous to eat last night."

"Why nervous?"

"Ava wanted her wedding to be perfect and I didn't want to screw it up. And Augustina is gorgeous, as is Ava's maid of honor, Laurette. I was the only weak link in the wedding party."

"You were gorgeous, too," he said glancing over his shoulder at her again.

She was this morning, too, with her thick hair hanging around her shoulders. She didn't have a speck of makeup on, but the beauty that he'd somehow never noticed because of her ugly clothes now shone through.

She shook her head. "I'm not, but thank you for saying that."

She wrapped the sheet around her torso and leaned up, embracing him from behind. She kissed the junction where his neck and shoulder met. "Thank you for last night."

To hell with restraint. He pulled her around on his lap. Felt her hips brush his morning erection. He kissed her forehead. "Thank *you*, Sheri."

She hugged him. Just put her arms around him and held him close. And he knew that no matter what happened he didn't want to hurt her. He wanted to believe that he could find a way to make sure she didn't regret being with him.

"Have you thought about doing anything else at the magazine?"

She pushed away from him, sitting on the bed next to him. "I can't work for you anymore?"

He got to his feet and found his pants, pulling them on quickly. "Of course you can continue to work for me. But I wondered if you'd ever considered an editorial job, or sales?"

"Tristan?"

"Hmm," he said without turning to face her.

"Look at me please."

He turned, hands on his hips. "Yes?"

"I don't expect anything from you after this. This was just two people who hooked up at a wedding reception."

He doubted she was aware of how transparent her face was, or how she'd flinched when she said *hooked up*. He scrubbed his hands over his face. The morning sunlight seeped in under the wooden blinds that covered the windows, painting the room in cheery colors. But instead of seeing the promise of a new day, all he felt were last night's regrets.

He knew better than to take Sheri to his bed. She

wasn't like the women he usually dated. "We were friends before this."

"We were acquaintances," she amended. "And we'll go back to being them again. Don't worry about me. I might not be as used to this situation as you, but I can handle it."

He had no doubt that Sheri could handle anything that came her way. She was strong like that. "Very well. Would you like to take a shower while I see about breakfast?"

"You can cook?" she said, with the cheeky grin he'd come to know so well.

He flushed at the way she said it. "No, but my housekeeper can."

"What's on the menu?"

"Whatever you like," he said. Mrs. Thonnopulus was very skilled in the kitchen and he had no doubt she'd be able to fix anything that Sheri asked for.

"Raisin Bran and some coffee would be great."

He nodded. "We'll have breakfast on the balcony. I'll use the guest bathroom down the hall."

She shook her head. "Don't be silly. I can use that one." Then she turned bright red and looked around his room. "I'm going to need something to wear."

"I'll bring in some clothes for you. You wear a size six in the States?"

"Yes, I do. But…whose clothes are they?"

"My sister's." Thanks to Blanche, he had grown up in a household where discussions had routinely centered on fashion. He knew equivalent sizes. "Go and shower. I'll leave the clothes on the bed."

She nodded and tugged the top sheet completely free from the bed, wrapping it around her. She looked small standing there, and vulnerable.

He turned away before he did something else he'd regret, or said something he knew he couldn't possibly mean, because he never dated a woman for more than a week. He usually only took them to his bed for a night or two and then moved on.

Sheri was no different.

He wondered exactly how many times he was going to have to say that before he started believing it.

Sheri stood on the threshold between the living room and the balcony. Looking out, she saw the place where she'd made love with Tristan for the very first time. Her body was sensitive this morning, remembering the feel of him against her— inside her.

She shook her head, trying to force the images

of Tristan making love to her from her head. She wished she could forget him easily. Get the distance she knew she'd need before they were both back in the office on Monday morning.

Yet, at the same time, she didn't want the feeling of having his body inside hers to fade.

Tristan stood by the railing. He was on his cell phone, and he gestured for her to sit at the wrought iron table that was set for breakfast for both of them. He wore a pair of black dress pants and a short-sleeved, casual shirt. He looked suave, debonair, and she felt… Well, even in the sophisticated clothing he'd provided for her, she still felt a bit frumpy.

There was a plate of croissants with jam and butter, the cereal she'd requested but in European packaging with a different name than she was used to in the States, and a small French press coffeepot.

She fiddled with her hair, tucking it behind her ear, waiting for him to look back at her. And when he did, she wished he hadn't. There was too much knowledge in his eyes. It was clear that he knew she wasn't herself this morning.

Tristan put his hand over the phone. "I have to finish this call and I'll join you in a moment."

"No problem. I can take care of myself."

He gave her that steely-eyed look of his, but she ignored him as she seated herself.

"I'll be right back. Wait for me to eat?"

"If you'd like me to," she said, but inside a panic was starting. She wanted to forget about breakfast and get away as fast as she could. She also wanted to linger. Wanted him to be sitting here waiting for her. Maybe kiss her when she'd come out instead of being on the phone.

But that was just more of the fantasy she'd always wanted, and this was reality. One-night stands weren't the beginning of a romance. They were temporary.

Temporary.

Maybe if she said the word enough times she'd start to realize that her reality wasn't with Tristan.

Too bad she remembered the way he'd held her last night even when they were sleeping. There was some kind of closeness between them that she didn't want to let go.

"I would."

She nodded as he walked away. Watch him, she told herself. Watch him walk away and know that he's not the kind of man who'll stay. Temporary, she reminded herself again.

But dammit, she wanted him to be. Last night she realized that she'd been trapped in a box of her own making, that she'd let the men in her life dictate how she moved through life.

Last night she'd stepped outside of that box.

Instead of feeling unworthy of a man's attention, she'd felt as if she deserved to be with Tristan. She wasn't kidding herself that he might be the man for her. Their lives were too different. But he had changed her, and as she poured a cup of black coffee she realized she didn't want to go back to being the woman she'd been before.

It was time she started living.

She took another sip of her coffee and felt that nervous anticipation that came from waiting. It reminded her so clearly of the times she'd sat in front of Aunt Millie's house, waiting for her dad to show up. And he never did.

God, she was pitiful. She pushed to her feet and walked away from the table, taking her coffee mug with her. She went to the railing and looked down at the street. It was crowded this morning with cars and people. Strange for a Sunday.

A man glanced up at the balcony and took a photo. She shook her head, knowing he was capturing the architecture of Mykonos and not her.

She stepped back from the railing so that he could get a better picture.

"Come inside," Tristan said, and something in his tone put her on edge.

"What? Why?"

"We have to talk."

Man, she hoped he wasn't going to fire her. If he did, she could find another job as an executive assistant somewhere else in the city, but starting over was always hard.

"Let's talk here," she said.

"No. Come inside now."

"Why are you—"

"Sheri, inside now."

"Tristan, you can't speak to me like that. I'm not your pet or slave."

"I don't think of you that way. Things have happened. Come inside and I will explain."

"Is it Christos and Ava? Are they okay?"

"Yes, they are fine," he said, reaching for her elbow and drawing her into the living room. He closed the door behind her and then clicked a button on the remote in his hand. The blinds slid slowly down, covering the windows.

"If this is how you always behave the morning

after, I finally understand why women only stay with you for a short while."

"Sheri, this is serious."

"I was being serious," she said, knowing that she had to find a way back to being his humorous assistant.

"You are being cheeky and another time I'd appreciate that, but not right now."

He was starting to scare her. "Tristan, I can… Listen, it won't be weird at work. I'm not going to be all clingy or anything."

"I know you won't be."

"You're going to fire me?"

He crossed his arms over his chest and gave her a narrow look.

"I can handle it, honestly. I just need to know what I'm facing."

"You're not facing anything," he said, tossing her a newspaper. A Greek tabloid. "We'll face this together."

She saw the photo of herself naked in Tristan's arms as they were kissing on the balcony.

Five

Sheri had never wanted to be famous. Unlike other kids who dreamed of celebrity, she'd preferred her natural anonymity, so as she stared down at the newspaper in front of her, skimming the headline written in a language she couldn't read, she saw only her picture.

Her face got hot as she blushed harder than she ever had before. She was going to die. That was it. There was no way she was going to live through this.

It was bad enough that she'd made the highly questionable decision to sleep with her boss. But now the entire world would know… Hell, *Lucille* would know, and she wasn't going to let Sheri forget about this.

"Oh, my God."

"I don't think praying will help," Tristan said in a quiet voice.

"What do you recommend?" she asked, desperately wishing she could go back in time.

He put a hand on her shoulder. It was big and warm and as he squeezed so slightly, she felt a little better. Not much, mind you, with her face and the ecstasy she'd felt in his arms clearly on display for the world to see.

Tristan's expression wasn't visible, as his face was buried in her hair. Her hands shook as she looked at the picture.

"I don't look like myself," she said, tracing a finger over her face. Her eyes were half-closed and she was clutching at Tristan as he kissed her. Thank goodness his broad shoulders covered her naked chest fairly well.

He reached around her to take the paper. "You look like a woman in the arms of her lover."

"Yeah, ya think?" Sheri said, unable to help herself. She wished she could get good and mad. But this wasn't Tristan's fault. It was only that fact that was helping her keep it together. That and the strong belief that if she let go of her control she was going to crumple to the floor and never get up.

"Cheeky is cute, Sheri. Sarcastic is not," he said, his accent very strong and pronounced.

She hated when he did that arrogant thing. Actually it was attractive at times, but right now, while she was grappling with the shock of seeing her scandalous picture in a major newspaper, it wasn't.

"Sleeping with you was fun while it was our little secret," she said, mirroring his tone. "Having the entire tabloid-reading world know about it is not."

"Sheri—"

She cut him off and turned away, walking farther into the elegantly appointed living room. She stood underneath a painting, a large oil by someone famous, she was sure, but she didn't know art. Her aunt Millie's taste had run more to prints of the Brooklyn Bridge than real art.

"Sorry, was that too sarcastic? I'm not used to dealing with the paparazzi the way you are."

"You're right," he said. "This is my mess. I will take care of this."

"How, exactly?" she asked.

"Leave it to me."

"Do they know my name?" She pivoted to

face him. The morning sunlight streamed through the glass doors behind him, keeping his face in shadow.

Tristan lifted the paper and read the article.

"You haven't read it yet?" she asked.

"Not all of it."

"What does the headline say?"

"'Snagged. Elusive bachelor found in love nest.'"

"Oh, my *God*."

"If you're going to pray, you should at least ask for something."

"Tristan, I'm going to ask for lightning to strike you."

"Not a wise course of action," he said.

"You don't think so?" she asked, trying to keep the panic she felt rising inside her from her voice.

He wrapped his arm around her waist and drew her into his body. "I don't. You need me, Sheri Donnelly, and I'm going to get you out of this mess."

This close to him, it was hard to keep the distance she'd been struggling to maintain since she came down for breakfast.

"I can't believe this," she said.

"What?"

"I took a chance last night… Man, I knew that leaving the reception with you was a bad idea, but

I was only thinking about what you might think when you saw me naked."

Tristan drew back and tipped her head up toward his. "What I might think when you were naked?"

"Yeah, you know, stuff like, 'she's a lot flabbier than the women I'm used to….'"

"*Ma petite,* you were perfection in my arms last night."

"You don't have to lay it on that thick, Tristan. I look in the mirror every day and what I see staring back at me isn't perfection."

"Your mirror is not the best. Otherwise you'd never leave your flat in the clothes you wear."

"Um…are you trying to make me feel better?" she asked.

He gave her a quick pat on the backside and stepped away. "I was, smart-ass."

"So how are we going to deal with this?"

"*We* are not. I am."

She shook her head. No way was she going to leave everything to Tristan. Thus far he hadn't exactly been successful in getting the paparazzi off his own tail. And she wasn't like him. She couldn't afford a security detail, or a chauffeur. She took the subway to work and walked seven blocks from the station to her office.

"Tristan—"

"Enough. I said I will deal with it. Trust me."

Tristan wasn't surprised by the flash of temper in Sheri's eyes. But he was surprised that she backed down. She crossed her arms over her chest, and he saw tears gleaming in her pretty brown eyes.

He was angry. At himself for not anticipating that photographers would be bold enough to take advantage of an intimate moment. At Sheri for looking up at him with wounded doe eyes that made him realize he *had* to fix this. She simply wasn't as sophisticated as the heiresses and actresses he usually brought to his bed, and laughing off this kind of scandal was beyond her.

And mostly he was mad at the tabloid that had decided to print this picture. He suspected it was because the publisher, Gabrielle Damienne, was an ex-lover of his and they hadn't parted on the best of terms.

"Sheri?"

"Yes."

"Will you trust me?" he asked.

Distantly he heard the doorbell ring, but knew the housekeeper would answer it. He had the feeling that anyone who came to the door today he wasn't going to want to see.

"I'm not sure."

Was her trust really important to him? She was more than a one-night stand, she was a woman he cared for, but he wasn't going to love her. So was trust really that important?

Yes, he thought. He wanted her to say she trusted him to handle this for her. He wanted to demand it. To make her admit that she would rely on him to handle this media mess.

"You seemed sure last night."

She narrowed her eyes and then tipped her head to the side. "Last night was lust. Surely you knew that."

He felt the burn of her words and that sickly sweet tone she used. He knew he'd been rushing her out the door until he'd seen the paper. He hadn't really cared if she'd picked up on that fact earlier. But now, hearing those words come from her lips…he realized he already cared more for Sheri than was prudent.

She was dangerous because she made him feel way more than lust for her sexy little body, which she kept hidden under the ugliest clothing he'd ever seen on a woman.

Today, dressed in his sister Blanche's blouse

and trousers, she looked…almost beautiful. Actually, the only thing detracting from her beauty were those wounded eyes of hers. She was hurting, and a different man, a man who still had a romantic heart, would soothe her.

There was a rap on the door. "Mr. Sabina?"

"Please come in."

Mrs. Thonnopulus opened the door. "I'm sorry to interrupt, sir, but Count de Cuaron y Buatista de la Cruz is here to see you."

Gui. He must have seen the paper this morning. And Tristan was glad to have his friend interrupt this situation with Sheri, which was going from bad to worse.

"Send him in."

Less than a minute later Gui strode through the door. Wearing jeans and a designer one-of-a-kind shirt, Gui looked relaxed and casual. Not like the aristocrat he was, but more like the second son he also was.

"Ms. Donnelly, Tristan, please pardon my unscheduled visit. But I need a word with you, Tris."

"About?"

"A sensitive matter," Gui said.

"Does it involve the photos of us in the newspaper?" Sheri asked, all blunt American.

Tristan wanted to order her from the room so he could have a discussion with Gui without her sarcasm.

"Indeed. So you've already seen the papers."

"Papers?"

"Reuters picked up the photo. It's in every tabloid I've been able to put my hands on this morning," Gui said.

Sheri started trembling. She turned her back on both men and dropped her head down to her chest. Tristan watched her, knowing she was dealing with the pain and unable to make himself walk across the room and comfort her.

He'd done enough of that this morning. He needed to keep a distance between them.

Gui arched one eyebrow at him and nodded toward Sheri. Tristan shrugged his shoulders and shook his head. Gui rolled his eyes and went to Sheri's side. He wrapped one arm around her shoulder and handed her a snowy-white handkerchief.

And Tristan saw red. It was that simple. He knew he'd just dismissed her, but he couldn't stand to see Gui touching Sheri. She was his. *His.*

He was across the room before he realized he was moving. He nudged Gui aside and pulled

Sheri into his arms. She put her head on his shoulder and he felt the warmth of her tears sinking through the cotton fabric of his shirt.

A wave of total helplessness swamped him. How was he going to fix this? He'd spent the last eight years since Cecile's death moving forward, never stopping to answer questions or challenge the paparazzi that followed him and the scandals he wove effortlessly.

He wrapped his arms around her and held her the way he hadn't held a woman in eight long years. He held her to give comfort. He felt the shackles he'd tried to wrap around his heart shift.

He lifted her face to his, aware that Gui had stepped out to the balcony to afford them some privacy at this moment.

"*Ma petite,* stop your tears."

"I… Yes, I will. It's just, I have no idea how to handle this," she said, sniffling delicately.

Damn those big doe eyes of hers, he thought. He wiped her cheek with his thumbs, brushed them down her face until the tracks from her tears were completely gone.

Step away, he told himself. Comfort was one thing, but kissing her now would be the kind of mistake he was too smart to make.

He'd started to lower his head, wanting to taste her one last time, and she rose on her tiptoes, eyes closing, and leaning into his body. And he knew that for her sake, so that he didn't hurt her any more than he already had, he couldn't kiss her.

So instead he brushed his lips against her forehead and stepped back. He turned away, but not quickly enough to miss the disappointment and hurt on her face.

Sheri had to get out. When Tristan turned his back and walked to the balcony, where she saw Gui waiting, she grabbed her handbag and made a beeline for the door. Enough of staying here. She was clearly not wanted.

And she had experienced more than enough of that in her life. She needed to move. She checked for her hotel-room key and her passport. Both were in her handbag. She also had enough money to pay for a cab.

She wondered if she should take the time to ask the housekeeper to call one for her or just take a chance at flagging one down on the street.

She heard the rumble of Tristan's and Gui's voices and knew that hanging around wasn't going to work for her. She was probably going to cry again, which was a stupid "girl" reaction to the situation, but she was tired. And she'd made love—no she'd *had sex*—with a man she'd been fantasizing about for too long. And now the entire world would know.

The only silver lining she saw was that Aunt Millie was dead and wouldn't see the picture.

She walked down the stairs to the ground floor and paused in the kitchen, looking around and remembering how excited she'd been when she'd followed Tristan through this room.

How very much she'd wanted that man.

And he'd wanted her, she thought. At least for one night.

She opened the kitchen door and stepped outside into a perfect February morning. Or at least, perfect on the island of Mykonos. It was a resort town. A place the trendy visited.

She should have felt out of place all week but there had been something very welcoming in Tristan's group of friends. Ava had made her feel so at ease, but then again the other woman was an American and had somehow recognized the attraction that Sheri felt for Tristan.

"Mademoiselle?"

"Miss?"

"Hey, lady?"

The cries came at her from every corner as a group of photographers moved closer to her. She scrambled backward, reaching for the handle on the kitchen door. She tried to open it but her hands were sweating and she couldn't get a good grip.

She covered her face with her hands, took a deep breath and then opened her mouth and screamed the way she'd been taught to in self-defense class. A deep-throated loud sound that actually stopped the questions that the photographers were throwing at her in every language imaginable.

Asking her name. What kind of lover Tristan was. Did she think she'd finally snagged the elusive bachelor?

The door opened behind her and she felt Tristan's arm come around her waist as he drew her back into the kitchen and slammed the door closed.

She glanced up, thinking to thank him, but he looked so angry. So…not in the mood to be teased. She'd had no idea he could ever look that mad.

"What were you thinking? Why would you leave the house without my permission?" he asked.

She backed away from him but he put his hands on her shoulders and held her in place.

"I want answers, Sheri. This isn't a game. The paparazzi are going to be all over you until this blows over."

"I needed to get away," she said.

"From me?"

She nodded. "I…I like you way too much to be your plaything."

Tristan cursed under his breath, using the few French words she'd become very familiar with since he used them regularly in the office.

"*Merde* is right. I'm trying to be cool about this whole thing but…I'm not ready to this morning. I'm tired and my body still tingles from the last time we made love, and you were pushing me out the door this morning."

She tucked a strand of her curly hair behind her ear and looked up at him from under her eyelashes. His expression was unreadable.

"So I was trying to leave," she said, concluding as quickly as she could.

Tristan turned away from her, leaning back against the wall and crossing his arms over his chest. "First of all, I'm not expecting you to be blasé about sleeping with me."

"Well, that's good. Because I'm not."

He started to speak, but she held up her hand. She couldn't bear to hear him say that she was one of many to him. "I don't expect you to feel the same."

He shook his head.

"I can still feel you on my body, *ma petite*. The remembered feel of your sheath clasping me is making it damned hard for me to let you go."

"Oh."

"Yes, oh. Maybe you don't know quite everything."

She looked down. "I never meant to imply that I did."

He nodded. "Good. Then stop trying to manage this on your own. We need to deal with this together, or else you're going to get hurt."

She wrapped her arms around her waist before realizing what she was doing. The move was a dead giveaway that she felt vulnerable, and Tristan already had seen her with tears in her eyes. She knew him well enough to know that weakness wasn't something he understood.

He was immune to that flaw. And if he wanted her by his side, wanted them to be a team, she wanted to be worthy of staying with him.

This was the first time a man had come after her

and brought her back. The first time a man hadn't walked away from her, or simply let her walk away.

She knew better than to read too much into it, but she felt her heart beat a little faster.

Six

The getaway was simple. Gui, Sheri and Tristan left together via Tristan's dark-windowed Mercedes sedan, which the housekeeper drove to the private airport where the Seconds corporate jet waited for them. They had decided that Sheri would accompany Tristan to Paris and then back to Manhattan instead of getting on the commercial flight straight back to New York that he'd booked for her return.

She'd lost that wounded-doe look and smiled at him whenever he looked at her—which wasn't as often as he would have liked, but ignoring her was the only way he could even pretend to himself that he wasn't starting to care for her.

In that moment when they'd heard her scream, he'd felt fear for another person for the first time in eight years. And the fact that he'd wanted to first protect her and then rip apart the photographers who had threatened her, had been a warning Tristan couldn't ignore.

Despite the fact that he knew Gui was right and the only way to protect Sheri was to keep her by his side, another part of him—the man who'd experienced the crushing blow of losing the only woman he'd ever loved—wanted her far away from him.

"Have you been to Paris before?" Gui asked Sheri.

"No, never. This trip to Mykonos was the first time I've been out of the U.S."

"You should travel more," Gui said. "Tristan, you should make sure that Sheri has the opportunity to see the world. Do you know she still lives in the same brownstone that she was raised in?"

Since he wasn't deaf and the corporate jet wasn't a jumbo one, he'd heard the details of her life as Gui pried into her past. He knew it was Gui's way, but he hated the attention that his friend was giving to Sheri. And hated even more the way she soaked it up. She was hungry for a man to talk to her.

"I heard."

"It's in Brooklyn."

"Thanks, Gui. I know where my assistant lives," he said.

Sheri flushed and he saw her sink deeper into her chair. He'd crossed a line with that comment. He didn't need to put her back into the employee role at this moment.

Gui gave him a sharp look and turned back to Sheri, telling her about his latest escapade with one of his cousins who was at the Spanish royal court.

She laughed, but the sound was hollow and he knew he'd done that. Taken away her joy by being a complete ass. He should apologize but, when she was ignoring him, he knew that they were both moving apart. The way they needed to.

But dammit to hell, if Gui didn't move away from her, he was going to leap across the aisle and strangle his friend. "Sheri, when you have a moment I'd like to discuss a few things with you."

"What about?"

"Work. Our delay in returning to the office will mean rescheduling some appointments."

"Of course. I didn't bring my laptop with me…."

"You can log in on mine," he said.

"Surely that can wait," Gui said.

Sheri patted Gui on the arm. "No, it can't. I don't mind working. It'll give me something to occupy my mind."

Sheri moved across the aisle so that she was sitting in one of the captain's chairs and she turned it to face him. He turned his laptop around on the built-in desk. She leaned forward, a lock of her hair slipping free and brushing against her face.

She concentrated on typing her log-in to the network and then her password.

He leaned back in his leather chair and watched her work. Since this was the corporate jet owned by Seconds, there were three distinct areas. Gui's area, where Sheri had been sitting, was decorated in a classic style very much befitting an aristocrat. There was something quite traditional about Gui underneath his rebel exterior.

Christos's area was modern and sleek. Eschewing anything traditional due to a severe disagreement with his father when he was eighteen, Christos always chose things that wouldn't fit the traditional Greek way of life that his father, Ari, wanted for him.

Tristan's area was a blend of modern and classical. His desk had been handed down to him by his grandfather. It was old, though well polished, and except for two marks, looked to be in perfect condition. There was a small ink stain near the hole where an inkwell was once kept, and under the blotter was a series of initials. Each Sabina who inherited it added theirs to the line.

For all that he was a second son, he wasn't like Christos, who hated his family's traditions. He liked knowing his place in the Sabina line. But then, he had sisters and a large pool of cousins. Christos had recently lost his only brother in a plane crash.

"When do you anticipate being back in Manhattan? You have two video conferences scheduled this week. Rene could handle them in your place."

"I saw those e-mails, too. I think we need to get Maurice on the phone to talk through the book for *Global Traveler*. The new layout is supposed to start in the next issue, and I'm still not satisfied with the changes."

Sheri typed as he talked. He knew she was jotting down notes. He did like how efficient she was. Even before they'd been lovers, he'd liked watching her work. Her fingers were long and elegant. He would have said they were the most attractive part of her, before he'd seen her last night.

Her body was exquisitely formed with generous curves, but not overblown. And she'd been—

"Tristan?"

"Hmm?"

"I asked if a conference call will be fine? We can get the book scanned into a PDF and have it available this afternoon."

"Yes, that is fine," he said, and turned his attention to work. It was the one safe thing they had between them, and he knew that, when they landed at Le Bourget airport in Paris, he'd once more be focusing on the woman and not his executive assistant.

Tristan's sister Blanche waited for them in the chauffeur-driven Mercedes at the airport. Sheri immediately wanted to hide back on the plane. But that was cowardly and she'd… Well, she wasn't going to do it, no matter how tempted she might be.

"*Bonjour,* Tristan," Blanche said, embracing him. She continued speaking in French, which Sheri couldn't follow at all when the speaker was talking as quickly as Blanche was.

It was clear from her tone that she was upset with Tristan and reading him the riot act. Sheri stood in the shadows and watched the two interact. She saw the affection beneath the lecture.

And Tristan smiled down at his sister indulgently. Sheri watched the two of them longingly. She'd always wanted a big family. Not necessarily blood relatives, but a network of people who cared deeply for her and let her do the same for them. It was clear that Tristan had that.

Watching him with Gui and Christos over the last week had given her a glimpse into that world. Seeing him with his sister added another dimension.

"Why are you hiding over here?" Tristan asked, coming back to get her. "Blanche wants to meet you."

She took a deep breath. "I wasn't hiding. I wanted to give you a moment alone with your sister."

"I appreciate that."

"It looked like she was lecturing you. I didn't think you'd tolerate that from anyone," Sheri said, without really thinking.

Tristan smiled, and for the first time she realized that he usually had a practiced smile for business, because this one lit up his eyes. He loved his family, she thought. She couldn't help smiling back at him.

"She's eleven months older than I am and thinks she can boss me around."

"Not many people can do that because of your arrogant attitude."

"Arrogant?"

"Um…I think you know what I mean," she said, blushing a little because she'd never meant to say that out loud.

"I really do not know. Explain it to me."

She shook her. "I'm not myself today. I didn't mean to say that."

Tristan tucked a loose strand of her hair behind her ear. She tried not to react to his touch. But everything feminine in her came to attention. She almost sighed, but that would have been too revealing. So instead she took a deep breath.

"Looks like she does a fairly good job at it. Bossing you around that is," Sheri said.

"Well, she is not the only one," Tristan said, arching one eyebrow at her as he led her across the tarmac toward the waiting car.

"I would never try to boss you around," she said.

"I might let you in bed," he said, and they were at Blanche's side before she could respond.

"Blanche, this is Sheri Donnelly. Sheri this is my sister, Blanche Sabina-Christophe."

Sheri held her hand out to the other woman but Blanche leaned forward and air-kissed her cheek. Sheri did the same but felt kind of silly. Blanche smiled kindly at her.

"Your name is familiar to me. Have we met before?"

"She works for me in the New York office," Tristan said.

Blanche's eyes narrowed as she glared up at Tristan. Sheri took a step back as the affable woman of just seconds before was replaced by someone who definitely resembled Tristan when he was angry.

"I don't think we've had the chance to meet before, Mrs. Sabina-Christophe."

"Please, call me Blanche."

Sheri nodded. There was renewed tension between brother and sister and she had no idea what to say to break it. As Tristan's assistant she was used to stepping in and smoothing over awkward situations but this…there was no way she could interfere.

"Um…I guess you saw the tabloids."

"*Oui.* The entire family is gathering to discuss it."

Sheri took a step backward, longing to hide back on the jet. Even more, she yearned for her small, comforting brownstone. The one place in the world that had always been her constant. The one place in the world where she felt safe.

"Can you give us a moment, Blanche?"

"Certainly."

"Why don't Blanche and I take the second car

and give you and Sheri some time alone on the drive to your parents' house?" Gui said.

"I need to talk to Tristan about some family business," Blanche said.

"I don't mind riding with Gui," Sheri said, thinking that would be the easiest solution.

"I would mind. Blanche can go with him. We need to talk."

Sheri realized that his indulgent attitude toward his sister only lasted for so long. The commanding man Tristan normally was had come back to the surface.

"Tristan—"

"Blanche, this is not open to discussion."

She shrugged in a way that Sheri thought was distinctly French and turned to Gui. "I suppose that will be fine. You must be on your best behavior, Gui."

He lifted Blanche's hand to his mouth and brushed his lips across the back. "With you that will be easy."

"I'd be flattered if I didn't know you were always trying to charm anyone female."

Gui laughed and said, "You always say the nicest things."

"Your ego can stand it."

"Indeed," Gui said, leading her away.

Tristan led Sheri to the car, and she slid inside.

She started to move across the seat to make room for him, but he closed the door behind her and walked around toward the other side. She sat there for a moment feeling as if she'd stepped into someone else's life. And realized that she wanted it.

Tristan wasn't sure that coming to Paris was the best idea he'd ever had. But he needed the resources of his family and he'd wanted to take Sheri to the safest place he could think of. The Sabina house on the outskirts of Paris was just that.

His *grandmère* had been a famous actress in Europe, and his *grandpère,* a director twenty years her senior. They'd had a scandalous love affair that had resulted in a marriage that lasted for fifty years, until his *grandpère's* death. And the paparazzi had hounded them all their lives.

Tristan's mother had grown up with the photographers following her and the world being interested in everything she did. Tristan and his siblings had done the same.

They were used to the attention, but there were times like this when he resented it.

"Are you okay?" Tristan asked, looking at Sheri.

She'd be so easy to care for. Hell, he already cared more for her than he should. But he had to keep his focus, his distance from her, because he knew that she was barely holding herself together and a full-blown affair with him wasn't going to help her.

"I'm fine," she said, but she was clutching her purse to her stomach and staring out the window.

"Sheri, look at me."

"Not now, Tristan."

"Yes, now."

She shook her head and turned her body away from his as if to emphasize her determination.

He simply took her chin in his hand and turned her toward him. She had that wounded look in her big doe eyes again and he felt the impact all the way to his cold and lonely heart. She kept her gaze fixed at his chest.

"What is wrong now?"

"Um…I work for you. Everyone in the world knows I slept with you. Figure it out."

He bit the inside of his cheek to keep from smiling. There was the sassy girl he knew. The one that he'd been attracted to and hadn't understood why.

But now it all made sense. There was a real fire and passion in Sheri that she kept deeply buried.

"What happens between us is our business, *ma petite*."

"That's easy for you to say. Guys will slap you on the back and say, go, you. But everyone will look at me and think…"

"Sheri, please look at me."

She turned to face him fully and lifted those beautiful brown eyes of hers to meet his gaze.

"You are never going to be able to control what anyone thinks about you but you can control how you feel about what happened. Do you regret becoming my lover?" he asked.

She nibbled her lower lip and then sighed. "No. I don't. Being in your arms was incredible."

"Then don't worry about the photos or the press or any of it."

She arched one eyebrow at him. "That'd be a little easier to do if I hadn't met that lot head-on this morning. It was a little scary."

"It is irritating. I will install you at my parents' house and then take care of the paparazzi."

"You keep saying that. And I don't like it."

"What don't you like?"

"You taking care of everything. I'm not some doormat. Despite how I might act at the office."

"You're borderline insubordinate at the office." He smiled to show that he was joking.

"Only borderline? I'll have to work on that," she

said, and he saw the spark of her personality peeking through the sadness that had engulfed her for most of the day.

He knew it was a mistake to want to cheer her up. To care so much about her happiness, and about seeing her smile, but he did. He wasn't going to be able to offer her anything else, so his protection and her happiness were it.

"I'm not above using discipline to keep you in line."

"Like what? You going to spank me?" She shook her head and covered her mouth with her hands. "I can't believe I said that."

Immediately he had a vivid image of her sweet, bare ass as she lay over his lap. He hardened, then shifted to relieve some of the pressure at his inseam.

She flushed, and he knew that he wasn't going to be able to keep his hands off her. He wanted her again. If he'd been able to distance himself in Mykonos, take her to the airport and put her on a commercial flight, it would have been different but now…he was going to have her again.

He needed to get her out of his system.

Seven

As her words echoed between them, Tristan leaned forward, took her face in both of his hands and kissed her. She closed her eyes and surrendered to the feelings he drew from her effortlessly. She'd been craving this for so long. It felt as if a lifetime had passed, instead of just hours, since he'd touched her like this.

She opened her mouth for his tongue, which teased hers. He ran it along the roof of her mouth and then drew back, catching her lower lip between his teeth and suckling her.

She shifted closer to him on the seat, needing more of him. Shivers of desire coursed through her body. She put her hands on his face, touched his jaw and then slid her fingers into his hair.

It was thick and silky. She tilted her head to the side and he drew her even closer to him as his mouth continued to explore hers.

He drew back from her and she opened her eyes, staring up at him. "I can't get enough of you," he said.

"Is that a bad thing?" she asked. Her lips were tingling from the contact with his.

"Of course not. I am French. We live for physical love."

"And romantic love?" she asked, because she knew deep inside that she was falling in love with him. The seeds had been planted long before she'd known him as anything other than an attractive man who was her boss.

"Romantic love…what about it, Sheri?"

"Do you believe in it, or just lust?"

"I believe that we all get a once-in-a-lifetime chance at romantic love."

"Once in a lifetime?" she asked. That sounded good to her. "I believe in that, too."

He gave her a little half smile. She thought about what she knew of Tristan. How he was rumored to still be mourning his deceased wife even though she'd been gone for a long time.

"Did you— Never mind."

"Go ahead and ask."

She knew she was prying, but after all they'd shared, and given the fact that she was vulnerable to Tristan in a way she'd tried to not let herself be to any man, she had to ask.

"Did you have that with your wife?"

He looked at her then, and the expression in his eyes made her realize there were layers to Tristan she might never understand. The pain in his eyes took her breath away.

"Yes."

She nodded. There really wasn't anything else to say. His one-word answer in that monotone told her everything she wanted to know about where this relationship was heading. Ha, she was kidding herself to call it a relationship. It was a one-night stand, except…he'd just kissed her like he wanted her again.

So she had to decide right now. Was she going to be an affair for him? Could she really deny herself Tristan just because he couldn't love her?

"Have you ever experienced that?" he asked her.

"Would I be here if I had?" she asked, careful

not to let on that she suspected he could be that once-in-a-lifetime love for her.

"I guess not," he said, stroking his finger down the side of her face and then down the length of her neck. "Why haven't you?"

She swallowed hard. "I don't know. I don't trust easily."

"But you trust me," he said. "You came to my bed last night."

"It wasn't easy," she said. "But you wanted me…."

"And you wanted me, too."

"Yes, I did."

"Did? And now you do not?" he asked. He traced the scoop neck of her blouse and then moved his fingertip lower, to the upper curve of her breast.

She shifted her shoulders and had to force herself not to follow his touch when he pulled his hand away.

"Do you still want me, *ma petite?*"

"You know I do. One night…it doesn't seem like enough time with you."

"What would be enough time?" he asked.

She doubted a lifetime would be, but she couldn't say that. So instead she shrugged.

He smiled down at her. "I want more time with

you. Are you willing to continue what we started last night?"

She thought about that. Her first instinct was to say yes. But what would that be like? Hell, she was going to be miserable when things ended between them anyway. Now or later…and later sounded much better than now. So…

"Yes."

He smiled at her. "Good."

"You are *so* arrogant."

"You say that as if it is a bad thing."

He leaned over and kissed her so deeply that she knew she'd made the right decision. Tristan might think all he had to offer her was lust but she sensed so much more swirling under the surface.

And he'd stayed, she thought, as she wrapped her arms around those broad shoulders of his and hugged him as close to her as she dared. She wanted to hold him even tighter, but she didn't, afraid he'd realize how much he meant to her. That might be the trigger that finally made him leave.

Rene waited for them under the portico at the side entrance of his parents' mansion. Tristan took one look at his older brother's face and knew that he was facing a long afternoon. And he also knew it was nothing that Sheri needed to be a part of.

His family was overbearing at the best of times. Today, with his face once again splashed on the pages of every gossip magazine, it would be even worse.

"You have two choices," he said, turning to Sheri as the car came to a stop. To the driver he called, "We need a minute, Tollerman, before we'll be getting out."

"Yes, sir."

Tristan curved his arm around Sheri's shoulders and drew her close to him.

"What are my choices?"

"I can have Tollerman take you to the Ritz and you can use the suite I keep there, but there is a chance that the paparazzi will be there."

"For me?"

"No. They wait there for a chance photo of anyone of interest. And I can call and ensure that you have security and can go in the back entrance."

"What's my other choice?" she asked.

"Come inside with me and sit by the pool while I deal with my family."

She sighed. "I'll stay with you."

"Good." He smiled at that. "We're ready now, Tollerman."

"Very well, sir."

The driver got out and opened Sheri's door first. As she slid out of the car, he noticed the way the fabric of her trousers pulled tight across the curves of her butt. The image of her across his lap flashed through his mind again. Dammit, he wasn't into anything kinky as a matter of routine, but he couldn't get the idea of spanking Sheri out of his head.

She glanced back at him just before the door closed and he realized she'd caught him staring. He rubbed his hand against his thigh and she giggled a little. He knew her thoughts were along the same line as his. That she'd found humor now made him feel good.

He climbed out of the car as Sheri came around to his side.

Rene pounced. "It's about time. We need to talk before you go inside."

"Blanche already delivered the news."

"Tristan—"

"Not now. Sheri, this is my brother, Rene."

She held out her right hand and wrapped her left arm around her own waist, something he noticed she did when she felt insecure. He didn't have to be a mind reader to tell that she felt vulnerable now.

It compounded his desire to make her safe. To take care of her. He was good at taking care of people, he thought. He didn't have to love her, but he could make love to her and take care of her until this storm blew over.

"*Enchanté,* Mademoiselle Donnelly. It's a pleasure to meet you in person."

"For me, too, Monsieur Sabina. Please call me Sheri."

"And I am Rene."

Tristan led her up the stairs away from his brother. He sensed she regretted saying she'd stay with him. He didn't give her a chance to change her mind, just ushered her into the house and found one of the downstairs maids.

"Nathalie, please escort Mademoiselle Donnelly to the pool area," he said in French.

"*Oui, monsieur.*"

"There's a cabana stocked with leisure clothing. I'll be a while, so you should eat lunch. Just tell Nathalie what you would like."

She glanced around the large foyer where Rene stood waiting for him and then she took his wrist and drew him aside. "Look," she said. "I think I've changed my mind about sitting by the pool."

"Too late."

"We're not at work. You can't just give orders and expect me to do what you say."

"Yes, I can. And I have. Go relax by the pool while I sort out my family."

"I don't like taking orders in my personal life."

"Too late. I'm a bossy kind of man, which you already know."

"Yes, but I thought—"

He bent and kissed her, because he knew Sheri would keep arguing and he needed to get her somewhere safe before Blanche and the rest of the family came out and started questioning him in front of her.

If he was going to protect her, he needed her safely tucked away.

He lifted his head, turned her toward Nathalie. "Go." He followed his command with a smack on her backside. She gave him a quick glance over her shoulder. "I will now, but this is the last time I'm going to be tucked away while you deal with a problem."

"We can discuss it the next time we're in this situation," he said, fairly confident that they'd never be in this situation again.

She shook her head, and he wondered if she regretted going with him last night. He watched her walk away, trying to make himself regret that he'd taken a nice young woman and put her in this situation, but he couldn't. There was something about Sheri that drew him. For safety's sake, he should back away, but he'd always lived for danger and this woman seemed like a challenge he could handle.

"An employee! Tristan, honestly, you've gone too far this time."

"Rene, it's not as it seems."

"Good luck explaining that to the board."

Tristan felt very much the wayward son as he leaned against the mantel in his father's den. It was funny to him that, outside of this room, he was considered to be a forceful man. Inside, he was always keenly aware that he was his father's son. And that he'd never lived up to the expectations Louis had for sons. Rene did it exceptionally well but he'd been the eldest and the expectations for him had been different than the expectations for Tristan, which were pretty much that he simply stayed out of trouble.

"This can't continue," his mother said.

"Maman, it's not as if I seek out this kind of publicity."

"We know that, Tris. But you have to admit your behavior is out of control," Blanche said.

"Out of control? I'm trying to have a normal life."

"We want you to settle down," his father said. "That's the only real solution to this problem. Until you do, the paparazzi aren't going to lose interest in you."

Tristan shrugged one shoulder. He wasn't marrying again, something he'd promised to Cecile on her deathbed. Their relationship had been so intense, even in those last moments when he'd held her fragile body in his arms and watched her slowly slip away from him.

"The press have always been interested in our family," he said.

"The rest of us don't do anything that gives them a reason to photograph us," Rene said.

"What are you getting at? I can't control their actions."

"That's right, you can hardly control your own," his father said.

"*Père,* I'm grown. I don't answer to you."

"Do you answer to Ms. Donnelly?" Blanche quietly interjected into what would have been a very heated argument between him and his father.

"Why do you ask?" Protecting Sheri had been on his mind since she'd screamed outside the villa on Mykonos. He'd brought her here thinking that together the entire Sabina family could help him keep her out of the glare of the spotlight, but he realized now that he didn't want to leave her in their care. Not that the option of doing that was open to him now.

"Because she's not used to being followed by tabloid photographers, and she works for us."

"Tristan, you slept with an *employee?*" his mother asked.

"Enough. I'm not discussing my personal life with any of you."

"This isn't personal. It's business."

"How do you figure, Rene?"

"If it involves someone who works for the Sabina Group, that does involve us. She's not some heiress used to the paparazzi and she would never have been exposed to them if not for Tristan," Rene said.

"I agree. We're going to have to do something. Maybe transfer her to the London office," Louis said.

"We're not transferring her anywhere. She's always lived in Brooklyn and I don't want her life disrupted," Tristan said.

"It's a little late for that," Blanche said.

Everyone joined in the discussion on what should be done with Sheri and how Tristan should have shown more sense, and he shook his head. He was tempted to grab Sheri and leave. Just walk away from his family and his position at Sabina Group, but he liked the magazine he'd started. And he wasn't a quitter. Never had been, even when the odds were stacked against him.

So he pushed away from the fireplace and waited until everyone stopped talking at once.

"Sheri isn't your concern, Rene."

"How do you figure?"

"She's my fiancée, so I'll be the one to look after her." The words came out of nowhere and stunned everyone into silence. He heard his mother gasp, and Blanche's expression—a cross between disbelief and shock—was comical.

"Fiancée? You're going to marry this girl?"

He felt trapped by circumstances and his own desires. He wanted Sheri and wasn't ready to let her go just yet. But he knew he had to do something to protect her from the tabloid press. As his fiancée, she'd be in the society pages for the right reasons.

He rubbed the back of his neck as he thought of the last time he'd told his family he was getting married. Cecile had been standing at his side, but otherwise the stunned disbelief of his family was exactly the same.

He tried to find the humor in it, but it was difficult. "Now that everything is settled about Mademoiselle Donnelly, I'm going to my townhome in Paris."

"Everything isn't settled, Tristan. Bring your fiancée in here so we can all toast the new couple," Rene said.

"And I want to talk to her about planning a party," Blanche said. "We can do it in conjunction with the launch of our summer fashion guide. I think that will be the best way to introduce her properly to the world at large and as one of us, don't you think?"

Tristan shook his head. "She doesn't have time to plan a party. She's my assistant."

"Nonsense, Tris, she's your fiancée now, that takes precedence."

"No, Blanche, it doesn't. You and Maman can plan a party for us if you want to, but Sheri will continue working for me."

"Why?"

"Because that is her desire. That's the reason we've kept our engagement secret all this time."

Eight

Sheri had changed into a red-and-white maillot and a wraparound sarong. She sat in the dappled sunlight that filtered into the glass-enclosed pool. There was a sense of peace that reminded her of the quietness of her own small backyard garden in Brooklyn, although the indoor pool was heavily landscaped and looked like paradise, while her own garden was little more than a few fruit trees, bare now that it was the middle of February.

Aunt Millie had been a big believer that being

outside could soothe the soul as nothing else could. When Sheri had been upset by her father once again missing a birthday or scheduled visit, Aunt Millie would lead her to the backyard and tell her stories of fairy princesses who lived in the garden under Sheri's bedroom window.

She closed her eyes, reaching out with her mind to her aunt. She wished she could feel Millie's arms around her once again. She was so tired of being alone. Of facing every situation on her own.

She heard the sound of footsteps and glanced over her shoulder as Tristan approached. He looked grim, and she wondered if the paparazzi had followed them and were now camped out on his parents' doorstep.

She stood up. "Is something wrong?"

He shook his head. "Sit down."

She sank back down onto the lounge chair. It was thickly cushioned, probably more comfortable than the old mattress she slept on at home.

"What's up?"

"I've decided the best way to handle the paparazzi is to take charge of the situation."

She liked the sound of that. "Good. Running away seems cowardly to me."

He gave her a faint smile. "You never fail to

amaze me," he said, and for once that arrogant tone she associated with him wasn't there.

"How am I doing that?" She usually glided through life being dependable or invisible. Which, she realized, was why the photographers had shaken her. She'd never stood out from the people she worked with or dealt with on a daily basis. How could she handle the attention of the world?

"By being calm about the photographers and my family. A quick flight out of Greece to Paris hasn't seemed to upset you at all."

It was sweet of Tristan to say that, but she was anything but calm. "I guess we're going to pretend that moment at the airport where I almost bolted didn't happen. And the time when I started scream-ing in front of the photographers," she said in a teasing tone.

That startled a laugh out of him, and she felt bet-ter for it.

"*Exactly*. The solution I propose may sound a bit odd to you at first. But let me explain every-thing before you comment on it."

"Okay," she said, taking a deep breath. What was he going to say? Well, what could he say? *The board and I think you need to find a new job. And I want you to deny ever being with me.*

His touch on her shoulder startled her out of her thoughts and she looked up into those deep gray eyes of his. She loved his eyes, and had often imagined him looking at her just as he was right now.

"Breathe," he said.

"I am," she said, with a long exhale.

He took her hand in his and held it loosely in his grip. "You have such pretty hands."

Of course he'd notice her hands. Considering she wasn't beautiful like the women he normally surrounded himself with, her hands were probably the only thing he'd found good-looking about her.

He lifted one of them to his mouth and kissed the back of it, then tucked his fingers around it. She smiled at the way he did it…linking them together.

She felt a bit of calm steal over her. This didn't feel like the big brush-off. And she'd had enough experience with being shown the door that she'd know if a man was doing that to her.

In fact, her stomach wasn't a tight knot like it had been the day that her father had sat her down to talk. She realized suddenly that her dreams were still alive. All this time, she'd thought she was a cynic and a realist but, sitting in this beautiful solarium filled with the sound from the waterfall at the end of the pool and the scents of Eden around her, she was holding her breath not because she felt like something bad was about to happen, but because she anticipated something good.

Tristan made her feel like the kind of woman for whom a man would make a grand gesture to keep in his life. And in the car, he'd all but said he wanted to continue their affair. So what could this be about? What was he going to say to her now, in this paradise?

"So what did you come up with?"

"I want you to be my fiancée," he said.

Sheri was sure she'd misunderstood him, because she knew he wasn't the marrying kind, but she thought he'd said *be his fiancée*.

"What?"

"I want you to be my fiancée for the time being. Just until the furor of the press dies down."

She felt the blood rush from her face and closed her eyes. Of course, it was temporary. She had forgotten the one truth of her life—she was meant to be alone.

Sheri pulled away from him and got to her feet. Moving a few yards away, she wrapped one arm around her waist and then a few seconds later turned back to him, putting both hands on her hips.

"Why would I agree to that? That's a crazy solution. Who's going to care that we're engaged?"

"The Sabina Group board, for one. They wanted to transfer you to the London office where you could hide out until this blows over."

"Why wouldn't that work?"

"Because I need you in the New York office," he said. He wasn't giving her up. She was one of the only two assistants he'd ever had that didn't annoy him and actually made him want to go into the office, Lucille being the other.

"I'm still not following why you came up with this solution," she said. She wasn't belligerent or demanding, which he would have brushed aside.

"The only thing that will get the press off your back is if we take control of what they are covering. A wedding is the kind of thing they eat up."

She tipped her head to the side and gave him a long, level stare. "So, we're getting married?"

"No, just planning a wedding."

She shook her head. "Do I seem that desperate to you?"

"No, you don't seem desperate."

"Well, then why do you think I'd settle for being your pretend fiancée?"

"Because you aren't going to be able to stay here at my parents' house the way I'd hoped. And your home in Brooklyn isn't going to offer you any protection from the paparazzi. They'll follow you from the second you leave until the moment you return. Are you ready to deal with that on your own?"

She shook her head and then turned away from him. He let her have a moment of privacy, but he could sense her weakening and he'd already decided this was best for both of them.

And he wasn't backing down. Sheri was going to be standing in his parents' den really soon, toasting their engagement with a smile that would convince the world that they were the real deal.

He went over to her, touching her shoulders. How he'd never noticed her before last night still amazed him. She had an incredible body. He lowered his head, dropping a soft nibbling kiss against the back of her neck. He ran his hands down her arms and drew her back against his body.

"I want what's best for you, *ma petite,*" he said, unable to resist kissing her collarbone.

Her skin tasted faintly sweet, something he'd never noticed in a woman before. But she tasted good to him. And he brushed his tongue against her smooth skin to take a little more of that taste into his mouth.

She shivered in his arms, arching against him, tipping her head back against his shoulder. Her eyes were wide as she looked up at him. So very wide and vulnerable.

Her mouth trembled and he knew she was on the cusp of giving in to him. He leaned down and kissed her. Not softly, but with all the passion inside of him. He kissed her like a man who was hungry for his woman and wanted everything that she had to give.

He broke the kiss only when he needed to breathe and immediately came back to her again, sucking her lower lip into his mouth and drawing on it. She moaned and turned in his arms until he felt the curve of her breast brush his upper arm. Her nipple was hard; he felt it through the fabric of her maillot.

He felt a twinge of conscience at pushing her now. But in the end, he knew what he had to do to take care of her. This was all that was in his control.

"Tristan?"

"Hmm?"

"I… Why don't you want to really marry me?" she asked, her voice so soft it was hardly a whisper.

He closed his own eyes. "I told you I had my once-in-a-lifetime love, remember?"

"Yes, of course I do. But what has that got to do with marriage?"

Tristan turned her in his arms and tucked her up close to his body, trying not to remember how perfectly they'd fit together when making love despite the differences in their heights. Once he'd been buried hilt-deep in her body, he'd felt the perfection of it.

He drew her back into his arms, lowering his head once more, wanting to take her mouth and stop her questions.

But she pulled away. "No more. I want you, but I want answers, too. I don't understand why you won't really marry me."

"It is not you," he said, the words spilling out. "I will never marry again."

"Then why pretend to be engaged?"

He pushed his hands through his hair and turned his back on her. He couldn't look at her and lie. When she'd said she couldn't lie to him, in the office a few short weeks ago, he'd had no idea what she felt like. Now he did.

And he wasn't giving her up. He hadn't gotten Sheri Donnelly out of his system yet and he wasn't going to let her go until he did.

"It's the only way I can protect you the way I want to, *ma petite.*"

"Why do I need protecting?"

"Because this is my world and I seduced you without thinking of the consequences."

"You didn't force me to sleep with you," she said, cheeky tone in place.

"I know that, Sheri. But you weren't aware of what it is like to be hounded by the press and I should have taken steps to protect you and your identity from them."

Even if she'd known how things would turn out this morning, Sheri doubted that she would have not gone with Tristan last night. Even now, sitting in a well-appointed formal living room surrounded by the entire Sabina family, she didn't regret her decision.

Tristan sat next to her, his arm resting casually over her shoulders. He toyed with her hair, something he did a lot. Sitting there she felt a sense of rightness all the way to her soul and she knew she'd said yes to his outrageous proposal for one reason and one reason alone. She was going to find a way to make Tristan Sabina fall in love with her.

She was going to do everything in her power to keep this man who'd stayed. And she was coming to realize that Tristan gave her clues all the time about what it was that he enjoyed about her.

If she paid attention, she could be what he needed her to be for him to fall in love with her. It didn't have to be the all-encompassing love that he'd had with his late wife. She'd be satisfied with just some kind of deep caring from him.

She settled into the curve of his body as Rene lifted his champagne flute and said something in French that she couldn't understand. Tristan squeezed her shoulder and lifted his own flute. So she did the same, taking a delicate sip of the delicious French sparkling wine.

Tristan leaned closer to Sheri and whispered directly in her ear. "Rene said that he wishes us happiness and laughter all the days of our lives."

She smiled up at him. "Well, I want that, too."

Tristan's eyes narrowed a bit but he dropped a quick kiss on her nose. She realized that he was going to fight her the entire time. Try to keep her in the role of pretend fiancée. And the only way she was going to get him to think of her as anything else was to make him need her.

He needed her body, but was sex enough? Could she hold him with sex when she'd never really tried to keep any of her previous lovers…? Okay, there hadn't been that many, but she had to look at it from a historical perspective.

Blanche stood up next. Tristan's sister made Lucille look like a country bumpkin. She was simply elegant and sophisticated. She spoke in a sweet tone, smiling indulgently toward Tristan.

Again the toast was in French. Tristan didn't lift his glass this time. Instead he put it on the table and stood up, leaving the room without a comment.

Sheri felt awkward. "I'm sorry, my French isn't good enough to know what you said."

Blanche shook her head. "I just said that we were happy to see him moving past the pain of heartache and moving into a new love."

But the way they were all staring at her, she realized they knew what she'd known all along. That Tristan wasn't in love with her. It was fine for the two of them to know that lust was all they had between them. But his family…

"I'm not the love of his life," she said.

"I'm not so sure about that, Sheri. You're the first woman he's brought to meet us in eight years."

Sheri took small comfort in that. "Will you please excuse me?"

"Of course. If you are looking for Tristan, try the third floor. Fourth door on the left."

She left the room without another word. Walking slowly through the house, she was reminded again that there was a huge difference between her and Tristan. This one—the material things—didn't seem as big a deal as their difference in willingness to love.

Tristan was such a dominant, arrogant man, she had a hard time imagining that he was afraid of anything, especially falling in love again.

But those rumors about his first marriage… about his first wife… She needed to find out exactly what she was up against.

She climbed the curving staircase, looking at the huge portraits hung on the walls. Pictures of men who resembled Tristan, and some portraits of people who were vaguely familiar to her. His famous grandparents, she thought.

He'd grown up surrounded by a rich history, whereas she had only what she took with her. Aunt

Millie's warm memory and the cold emptiness of her father's desertion.

She got to the third floor. At the landing there was an upholstered chaise centered under a dominant portrait of the Sabina siblings when they were younger…probably late teens, she thought.

Blanche was seated in the center and Rene and Tristan stood on either side of her. Blanche was elegant even as a teenager, smiling beguilingly out of the portrait. Rene was serious and even then looked as if he were all business. And Tristan. Her heart caught in her throat. He was laughing, very much the rebel in his casual rock T-shirt, whereas his siblings were dressed to the nines.

She had never seen an expression like that on Tristan's face and she thought that this is the part of him that died when his wife did.

She reached out to touch his face, letting her fingers hover over the curve of his mouth. It felt like what she'd done so many times in her apartment late at night. Lusting after a man she couldn't have.

And now that she had the Tristan she'd thought she wanted, she realized he only was giving her half of himself. The part he thought she'd accept without question.

And she knew now she wanted more. She was

falling in love with Tristan Sabina, and she wasn't going to be satisfied with merely keeping him from leaving.

She needed him to fall in love with her. Not just to care for her, but really fall head over heels in love. She turned to walk down the hall and saw the gilt-framed mirror and the reflection of the woman there.

She was going to have to make some serious changes if she was going to win Tristan's love.

Nine

Two weeks later, Sheri wasn't sure who she was anymore. Despite the fact that Tristan wanted their lives to remain the same, they had been changed by the "engagement." Blanche had even taken her shopping before allowing her to leave Paris. And Sheri had enjoyed her time with Blanche.

She found herself interested in clothing for the very first time. Standing in front of her closet in the brownstone in Brooklyn, she realized that it might be a bit small. It never had been before.

But then, she'd never had a closet full of outfits

for every type of event known to man. She'd turned into a socialite without even trying. She was exhausted, because Tristan had been extremely serious when he said that he still wanted her to work for him.

Her phone rang while she was in the middle of getting dressed in a Chanel linen-and-cashmere strip tunic that ended well above her knees, showing off her trim calves and ankles. She'd never really thought about her body, but Tristan's lovemaking and comments left no doubt that he liked hers. Her legs were slim because she'd always lived in the city and walked everywhere.

"Hello?"

She was getting better at accessorizing, but had been keeping the outfits put together the way Blanche had arranged them for her. Trying to make Tristan fall in love with her, trying to remember how to be fashionable and avoiding the paparazzi were a lot to add to her life. Most of the time she felt as if she was juggling and dropping most of the balls.

"*Bonjour, ma petite.* I'm downstairs in the car waiting for you."

"Good morning, Tristan. I'm almost ready."

Propping the phone between her ear and shoulder, she paired the tunic dress with a pair of lizard-

and-lambskin sandals and a calf-skin belt in white with a distinctive Chanel belt buckle. She had a chunky bracelet that she put on her right arm and then she carefully opened the box with the diamond watch that Tristan's parents had given her as an engagement present. They'd had her initials and the date of their engagement—the date she and Tristan had made up—engraved on the back.

"This would be a lot easier if you'd just move in with me."

"No, it wouldn't."

"Why wouldn't it?"

"Because then I'd have to move out again when the engagement was over. This way, I'll never have lived in your house."

"Or slept in my bed for an entire night," he said.

She always came back home after they made love at his apartment. And he never stayed the night at her place. She was doing everything she could to insulate herself against the pain of heartbreak, but she had the feeling that no matter what she did, it was still going to hurt her if he left.

"Well…"

"Well, what? Why are you so stubborn about this one thing?"

"Because I'm your pretend fiancée, Tristan. If

I were really your woman and you were going to claim me in front of the world, then I'd be living with you in a heartbeat."

He said nothing, as she'd suspected he would. "I'll be down in a minute."

She hung up the phone and turned back to the mirror. Her dark brown hair now had highlights and she knew how to put on makeup so that she looked like all the other women who had always surrounded Tristan. A part of her was amazed at how she looked, another part disgusted. She was changing every part of herself for a man who was her *pretend* fiancé, and she was no closer to figuring out how to make him fall in love with her.

She stared down at the engagement ring on her left hand. Tristan had wanted something big and flashy but she'd stubbornly refused. If he really loved her and was buying her a ring that symbolized his love, she would have bowed to his wishes, but he'd been buying the ring for others to see and she had dug in her heels.

She liked the understated platinum ring she had on. It fit her hand and her finger. And unlike a more costly ring, it didn't make her feel as if she'd sold herself to Tristan.

The clothes she knew she'd donate to Dress

for Success when she was done pretending to be his fiancée—if she didn't turn the pretend part into reality.

"Why did you hang up on me?"

She yelped and spun around. Tristan stood there, gorgeous as always. "Why are you in my house?"

"You gave me a key, remember? I am your fiancé."

She made a face at him in the mirror. "Just for pretend."

"Sheri."

He said her name in a stern tone that told her she was pushing too hard. But she didn't want to back down. She was tired of pretending, and the only way for that to stop was for Tristan to see her as more than a lover and an assistant. She was pretty sure that's all he saw when he looked at her.

"What?"

"What is the matter with you this morning?"

She shrugged. If he'd demanded an answer or kept pushing her, she could have gotten angry and then used her anger to keep the truth at bay.

"Answer me. Please."

"No."

She reached for a pair of platinum bangle earrings and slipped them into her ears. Tristan came up behind her, rested his hands on her shoulders and leaned in low so that his gaze met hers in the mirror.

"What is wrong?"

She bit her lower lip, afraid of saying too much. But suddenly she realized that the changes she made were all superficial and deep inside she was the woman she'd always been. And that woman wanted more.

"I don't want to be your fake fiancée. And frankly, I can't understand why this isn't real."

Tristan would be damned if he was going to have this conversation with her. He'd been dodging the same questions from Gui, who had warned him that toying with a woman's emotions was only going to lead to trouble. And Christos, who didn't know the engagement wasn't real and thought that he had made a great decision. Since Christos's marriage to Ava, the man thought all anyone needed to be happy was a wife.

But Tristan knew better. He wasn't toying with Sheri's emotions, and he sure as hell wasn't going to really marry her. He knew himself well enough to know that there were only certain things he could control. And surprisingly Sheri was one of them.

He bent his head to nibble on her neck in the spot he knew was sensitive. She undulated under his hands and reached back to put her arms around his neck, turning her head to the side until their lips met.

He hated not waking up with her every morning. He suspected that was why he still wasn't ready to move on from her. He had yet to spend an entire night with her, save for that first one on Mykonos. And he hadn't appreciated it then.

"I thought you were in a hurry this morning," she said, turning in his arms.

"Just to see you." Her dresser surface was clear except for a small jewelry box. "Are you wearing panties?"

"Yes," she said. "I tend to wear them when I'm going to work."

"Take them off."

"Ask me nicely," she said.

And Tristan leaned down to take her mouth with his, kissing her slowly, thoroughly. He caught her earlobe between his teeth and breathed into her ear as he said, "Please."

She shivered delicately, her hands clenching on his shoulders before she stepped back half an inch. "Okay."

She tugged the short hemline of her dress higher

and lowered a pair of whisper-thin white cotton panties. She balanced herself by putting one hand behind her on the dresser as she stepped out of her underpants.

The movement thrust her breasts forward. The high, round neck of her tunic didn't show nearly enough of her chest for him. He reached for the belt at her waist and unhooked it, letting it fall to the floor.

He lifted her up on top of the dresser and pushed her tunic dress to her waist. She parted her legs and he groaned her name. Blood rushed through his veins, pooling in his groin.

She continued smiling up at him as she leaned back on her elbows. "Was this what you had in mind?"

"Almost," he said, pushing her dress even higher until her breasts were bared to his gaze. The bra she wore had thin lacy cups and he could see the distended nipples peeking through the lace. He leaned down and licked them both.

Her legs shifted restlessly around his hips. Though it had been just last night, it felt like an eternity since he'd last held her in his arms.

He'd been aroused since he'd entered her house. She reached up and pulled his head down to hers. Her mouth opened under his and he told himself to take it slow, but slow wasn't in his programming with this woman. She was pure feminine temptation and he had her in his arms. He slid his hands down her back, finding the clasp of her bra and undoing it.

He grasped her buttocks, pulling her forward until he was pressed against her feminine mound. He felt the humid warmth at her center through the fabric of his pants and reached between them to caress her. She shifted more fully into him.

The fabric of her dress, bunched under her arms, just covered her breasts as she breathed heavily. He saw the hint of the rosy flesh of her nipples and lowered his head, using his teeth to pull the loosened fabric away from her skin. He ran the tip of one fingertip around her aroused flesh. She trembled in his arms.

Lowering his head he took one of her nipples in his mouth and suckled her. She held him to her with a strength that surprised him, but shouldn't have.

Her fingers drifted down his back and then slid around front to work open the buttons of his shirt. He growled deep in his throat when she leaned forward to brush kisses against his chest.

She licked and nibbled and made him feel like her plaything. He wanted to let her have her way with him, but there was no room here, no time for seduction or extended lovemaking.

He pulled her to him and lifted her slightly so that her nipples brushed his chest. Holding her carefully, he rotated his shoulders and rubbed against her. Blood roared in his ears. He was so hard, so full right now that he needed to be inside of her body.

He caressed her creamy thighs. God, she was soft. She moaned as he neared her center and then sighed when he brushed his fingertips across the entrance to her body.

The area was warm and wet. He slipped one finger into her and hesitated for a second, looking down into her eyes.

She bit down on her lower lip and he felt the minute movements of her hips as she tried to move his touch where she needed it.

He was beyond teasing her or prolonging anything. He needed her *now*. He swept her dress over her head and tossed it on the floor. She shrugged out of her bra and he lifted her off the dresser, turning her to face its mirror.

"What are you doing?" she asked, looking over her shoulder at him.

"I want you to watch us as I make love to you."

She murmured something he didn't catch. "Bend over slightly, *ma petite.*"

She did as he asked, her eyes watching his in the mirror. "Take your shirt off, please. I want to see your chest."

He smiled at her as he shrugged off the shirt she'd unbuttoned. His tie was tangled in the collar, but he managed to get them both off. He took out the condom he'd put in his pocket this morning and donned it quickly.

"Hold on and keep your eyes on mine in the mirror."

"Yes," she said.

He covered her with his body. Their naked loins pressed together and he shook under the impact.

He cupped her breasts in his hands then slipped one hand down her body, finding her wet and ready. He adjusted his stance, and then entered her with one long, hard stroke.

She moaned his name, still holding his gaze. He bit softly at her neck and felt the reaction all the way to his toes when she squirmed in his arms and thrust her hips back toward him.

A tingling started in the base of his spine and he knew his climax was close. She writhed more frantically in his arms and he moved deep with each stroke. Breathing out through his mouth, he tried to hold back the inevitable. He slid one hand down her abdomen, through the slick folds of her sex, finding her center. He circled that aroused bit of flesh then scraped it very carefully with his nail. She screamed his name and tightened around him. Tristan pulled one hand from her body and locked his fingers on the dresser over her small hand, then penetrated her as deeply as he could. Biting down on the back of her neck, he came long and hard.

Their eyes met again in the mirror and he knew that he wasn't going to find a way to live without her while he kept making love to her. And that meant he needed to come up with another plan. Something that didn't involve her being his pretend fiancée.

Ten

Two weeks later Sheri was still no closer to getting the answers she wanted from Tristan. But plans for the engagement party were going forward. The Paris branch of the Sabina Group was prepared to launch a new magazine on weddings and was using their engagement party as the first big glamorous event they'd cover. She'd promised Tristan that she'd stay with him until the engagement party was over.

A part of her worried that what she'd found with him was going to end too soon. Another part was afraid that it wouldn't end soon enough.

The one thing she didn't doubt was that she was in love with Tristan.

"Sheri, have Maurice come to my office in ten minutes."

"He's going to want to know what you need to see him about."

Tristan glanced up from the folder in his hands. "I'm going to fly your suggestion for the Travelogue column at the back. See if we can use celebrities instead of travel writers."

"Really? It was just an idea to boost readership."

"I know. I like it. I'll make sure that Maurice knows you came up with it."

She smiled. "I don't care about that."

Tristan leaned one hip against the side of her desk. "What do you care about?"

"World peace," she said, completely deadpan. She didn't want to have a serious discussion at work, but this was the only time when Tristan really opened up to her. It was almost as if he knew she'd only let things go so far in the office.

"*Ma petite,* are you going to leave me for a beauty pageant?"

"Not my scene."

"I know. This is your scene, isn't it?"

She nodded. "Working with you suits me to a tee."

"Just working?"

"Well, we don't live together."

"And whose fault is that?" He sounded almost huffy.

"Yours."

"Mine? I asked you to move in with me."

"More like ordered." She smiled. Take that.

"It didn't do me a lot of good."

"You wouldn't want a woman who just said yes to your every whim." That she knew.

"Try me."

"Try you? How?"

"Move in with me. Stop making me take you back to Brooklyn every night."

"What would change if I did that?" She was so tempted to say yes. Had been since the first time he'd told her to move in with him.

He leaned in close. "We'd be together all the time."

"But just temporarily."

"Is that what's stopping you from saying yes?"

She wasn't going to answer that question. She'd have to reveal too much of herself, too many things she'd long kept hidden. She glanced down at her computer screen and clicked on the instant messenger button to summon Maurice. The sooner they had someone else in the office, the better it would be for her.

"Sheri?"

"Hmm…"

"Look at me."

She glanced up.

"I want to know why you haven't moved in with me. The truth this time."

She folded her hands together on her desk blotter and then pulled them apart. "It is the temporary thing."

"I don't understand how it's any different if you move in with me," he said.

Sheri pushed her chair back from the desk and got up, walking around so that he wasn't leaning over her. "The difference is I've never lived anywhere but that brownstone."

Tristan stood up from where he'd been leaning against the desk. "The brownstone is your home."

"Yes. It's my home. It's the one constant I've had in my life since I was eight, when my mother died and my father dumped me at my aunt's, and, as you pointed out, what we've got going is only temporary."

Tristan didn't say anything else and Sheri wanted to curse at herself for letting the conversation get so personal. She really tried to be cool and breezy whenever she talked to him. Always tried so hard to keep her emotions bottled up and a secret from him.

"Is that it?"

"No…I'm also afraid that, if I move in with you, I'll start to buy in to the fantasy you've written for us. I might start to really believe that I'm your fiancée, and that would be devastating for me when you leave."

"All relationships end."

"How do you figure?"

"Even the strongest and most loving relationships end with death. So no matter what, everything is temporary."

"Tristan, that's sad."

"What is?"

"That you view life that way."

"It's realistic, Sheri. Hell, if you were to admit it, you see things the same way."

She shook her head. "No, I don't."

"Even though you won't leave your little brownstone?" he asked.

"That's different. I don't see relationships as temporary. I see them as unbalanced."

"I'm not following."

Sheri crossed her arms over her chest and stared at Tristan. His eyes were misty gray today because of the shirt he had on. He was so handsome, sometimes she worried that he'd wake up to the fact that there were a million gorgeous women in the world who'd gladly be his pretend fiancée and do whatever he asked of them.

"My reality and that brownstone are tied together. I see relationships as unbalanced because I've always been the one to care more than everyone else. And in the end, they've all left me behind."

Tristan didn't say anything and she felt like an idiot for revealing what she had.

"I'm going to run down and get Maurice."

She walked out of the office and down the hall, trying to pretend that nothing had changed, but knowing that everything had.

At the end of the day Tristan was tired. Sheri had made excuses to be away from her desk for most of the afternoon and he'd let her. There was work to do and he didn't need the distraction that she presented.

But in the back of his mind all he thought about was what she'd said about people leaving.

He thought in terms of temporary because his life had always been in constant change. The only thing he really counted on was his friendship with Gui and Christos.

And even that was changing, with Christos's marriage. He was happy for his friend, but at the same time concerned for him. Christos had never allowed himself to love a woman before, not the way he was in love with Ava. Tristan hoped they had a lifetime together, but his experience had taught him that they probably wouldn't.

There was a knock on his door.

"Enter."

The door opened to reveal Sheri. "I need your signature on these papers before I leave for the night."

She was all business. Until this afternoon, he hadn't realized how much of her personality she hid when she was in the office. It was only because of the last three weeks, when he'd seen so much more of her, that he now knew that.

She handed him a folder and he opened it up. He glanced at the papers and realized he wasn't reading them, so he closed the folder and pushed it aside.

"Please have a seat, Sheri."

"Is something wrong?"

"Yes. I have decided that I can't allow you to

continue living in Brooklyn. I have arranged for you to move into my place immediately."

She shook her head. "We've had this discussion."

"Exactly the problem. You need to be living with me." The engagement was working exactly as he'd hoped it would. The tabloid press was being very kind to Sheri and everyone he knew was excited for him. For the first time since Cecile had died, he felt as if his life was on the right path. He wasn't just running and trying to keep distance between himself and his life. And Sheri had given that to him.

And their conversation earlier had made him realize that he hadn't done the same for her. And that was not acceptable to him. Though he would never admit it, he liked the feelings she evoked in him. He knew they couldn't be love, because they felt nothing like the emotions he'd had for Cecile. But he did care for Sheri, and her happiness was important to him.

She nibbled on her lower lip. "What did I say that made you think that I'd agree to this?"

"It was what you did not say. Our engagement has given you a chance to change things about yourself. And I realized today that they were all surface changes. You need to move out of that brownstone if you are ever going to see yourself in a different light."

"Tristan—"

"No, listen to me. I know what it is like to be stuck in one place."

"That's a complete lie. You never stand still. How could you possibly know what I'm like?"

"That's precisely why I know. I have been always focused on the future to keep from dwelling on the past. Whereas you just stay there, stuck in time."

"I'm not sure you're qualified to be talking to me like this."

"Qualified?"

"Yes, qualified. You don't really know me all that well."

"I know you intimately, *ma petite.*"

"So did two other men and they didn't have a clue about what made me tick."

He hated the thought of anyone else having been with her. She was *his*. He didn't know exactly when he'd started thinking of her in those terms. But he did now. He wanted to tell her that he'd be the last man to know her intimately.

Where the hell had that thought come from?

"Those men weren't me. And I'm not taking no for an answer on this."

She stood up and walked over to him. She pushed her finger into his chest. "You're being a bully."

"No, I'm not. I'm being a man and taking charge."

"This is the twenty-first century, in case you'd forgotten. A time of compromise and 'working things out.' Women don't need a man to take charge," she said. The flash of temper in those big brown eyes of hers made him hard.

He was so tempted to lean down and kiss her. But she lifted her hand and put two fingers over his lips. "No, Tristan."

"No?"

"Don't kiss me, because then we'll be making love and I'll find myself living with you."

"I do not see the problem. You like making love with me, and you are going to be living with me either way."

She shook her head. "I don't want to live you."

"Give me one good reason why."

She wrapped her arms around her waist and took two steps back from him. "I...well, let me just say that I have a really good reason and leave it at that."

He crossed his arms over his chest and arched one eyebrow at her. "That might work if you had plied me with sex, but since you declined...I'm feeling stubborn."

She just stood there, and he wondered if he was pushing too hard. Why was this so important to him? He wasn't one hundred percent sure, but he guessed he wanted everything that Sheri had to give. She gave so willingly of her body, but she kept a tight rein on her soul. On the secrets that she guarded for herself. And he hated that there was a part of her that he didn't know. He wanted to know everything about her. He wanted to possess her completely.

"Tell me."

This had been the longest day of her life. And the most stressful. She had no idea what was going on with Tristan, not that she ever really had. She only knew that if he wanted to know what was inside her head, then they were both in trouble.

Tell me.

He wasn't asking nicely, he was demanding. And when it came to Tristan, she had absolutely no willpower. She wanted him to know her secrets because she loved him. Because no matter what her mind tried to tell her heart…her heart still believed that if he knew all her secrets, he'd fall for her, too.

Which was so stupid. He was the man who'd told her that all relationships were temporary. That all relationships ended. And heck, she knew that. Everyone she'd ever cared about was gone. Even Aunt Millie, through death, just as Tristan said. Though that's where she and Tristan differed. She knew the difference of having lived a life with someone you loved in it and having that person taken from you in death, versus having someone leave you because they couldn't love you.

"Why is it important to you? Why do you care?"

"Because I'm not the type of man who would let my fiancée live in another house. I would want her in my bed every night."

"You'd want *her* in your bed every night?" she asked.

"I want *you* in my bed every night. I want to wake up in the morning and see your face."

Suddenly Sheri wasn't sure what she knew anymore. Was Tristan simply afraid to admit his feelings for her? She knew he wanted her. No man had made love to her as often as he had. No man had ever said the things he did to her, whispering in her ear about how sexy she was and how much he wanted her.

But a part of her was afraid to believe it. She simply wasn't the kind of girl who inspired that feeling in a man like Tristan. Yet now, here he was, saying he wanted to wake up with her every morning and… "Tristan, I want that, too."

"Then why won't you move in?"

She looked at him. Just stared at the face that had graced the cover of more magazines than she'd ever dreamed of. And realized that at some point in time, he'd become so real to her. The Photoshopped perfection of those magazine photos wasn't the man she loved. *This* was the man she loved.

The man with a small scar under his left eye. And five-o'clock shadow on his jaw. The man who looked at her with exasperation at times, but always with honest emotion. Even if she couldn't always identify that emotion.

The man she loved.

"I haven't wanted to move in with you, because I love you, Tristan."

He took a step back. His arms fell from his chest and he looked at her as if she'd surprised him.

What had he expected?

"Should I not have said that?"

He shook his head. Then rubbed a hand over his forehead. "I was not expecting that."

"You weren't? Everyone knows how I feel about you."

Sheri felt so incredibly vulnerable right now.

She wrapped both arms around herself, holding herself as tightly as she could.

"Everyone?"

"Well, Ava noticed, and she hardly knows me at all. I'm pretty sure Lucille knows. She picked up on it the first time we spoke on the phone. Even your friend Gui knows. And I didn't have to tell him, either, he just guessed."

She didn't expect Tristan to love her back. Oh, man, what if that was what he was afraid of? "I don't expect you to love me."

He shook his head. "I don't believe in more than one love in a lifetime."

"I know that. I think that's part of the reason I love you so much. I want to fill up that emptiness you have."

Tristan walked over to her then. He took her shoulders in his hands and drew her toward him. His mouth came down on hers, heavy. He kissed her so deeply and with so much passion she couldn't help but respond.

She wrapped her arms around his shoulders and simply held on to him. He was in complete control and he made her forget everything. But she felt so much more now. It was as if, in admitting her love for him, she was finally free to let go of all the barriers she'd been keeping between them.

His tongue brushed hers and she moaned deep in her throat as shivers of awareness spread down her body. She moved closer to him. Needed to feel his body pressed up against hers.

Tristan lifted his head. "Thank you for loving me."

She couldn't help but smile at the polite way he said that. "You're welcome."

He brushed a strand of hair from her face and stared down at her with such seriousness that she felt a pang deep inside.

"There isn't a lack of love in my life, *ma petite*. There is a burned-out hole where my heart used to be, and I'm afraid no amount of love will ever bring it back."

Eleven

"**I**'m home," Tristan said as he walked into his apartment a little after ten o'clock one week later. He'd had a late dinner meeting and, for the first time since Cecile's death, he was coming home late not to servants and an empty house but to someone.

Sheri came down the hallway with a book in one hand and a pair of reading glasses on. She smiled at him. "How was it?"

"Not too bad. I think we will be launching a cooking magazine in the early fall next year."

"Good. I think that's great. Do you have any meetings you're going to need me to set up?"

"Yes, but I do not want to talk about that tonight."

Her smile turned suggestive. "What do you want to talk about then?"

"My woman."

"*Your* woman?"

She was sassing him and he had to admit he enjoyed it. He'd been unsure what living with Sheri would be like, but after the first night he'd realized that he made a good decision. He'd made love to Sheri twice last night, and then again in the morning before they'd left for work.

Having breakfast and then heading into the office together underscored to him what a great companion Sheri was. She suited his life perfectly. And the fact that she loved him made it all the sweeter.

"Were you waiting up?"

"Sort of."

"Why?"

She shrugged and he was starting to realize that's what she did when she didn't want to answer. It was her way of not lying about anything, of hiding when she felt that answering would leave her vulnerable.

"Will you come into the kitchen with me?" he

asked, shrugging out of his jacket. He hung it in the hall closet and then loosened his tie.

"Yes," she said. "Are you hungry? Mrs. Ranney made a pie."

His New York housekeeper was a whiz in the kitchen.

"Did you have any?" he asked, following her down the short hallway into the kitchen.

"No. I wasn't hungry earlier."

"Will you have a piece with me?"

"Maybe a small slice. I try not to eat after seven."

"Why?"

"Because unlike you, I don't work out every day."

"You could," he said, settling at the breakfast bar while Sheri moved around the kitchen. She found plates and cut them both a piece of pie. She was more at ease in his house than he was.

"You don't need to work out, *ma petite*. You look lovely as you are."

She arched one eyebrow at him. "Really?"

"Honestly. You have a sexy little body that I can't get enough of."

She blushed and smiled at him. "Then I should keep doing what I've been doing, and that's not eating late at night."

"Milk, coffee or some kind of after-dinner drink?"

She leaned over the breakfast bar to slide his plate in front of him. He took her chin in his hand and kissed her long and slow. Now he felt as if he was home. The home he found in her eyes and in her arms.

She pulled back, looking bemused, and he smiled inside. He loved that she was so guileless about how attractive she was and about the effect she had on him.

She turned away, grabbing a napkin and fork for him. "Did you want a drink?"

"Yes. Milk, please."

She poured him a glass and then brought her plate around to his side of the counter and sat down next to him.

He realized he wasn't interested in food. He'd forgotten what it was like to have a woman in his home. To have a woman take care of him.

"Mrs. Ranney said that strawberry-rhubarb was your favorite."

"It used to be."

"Do you want me to get you something else?" she asked.

"Yes."

She started to hop off her stool, and he lifted her up and settled her on his lap. "What are you doing?"

"Having something sweet."

"I didn't realize I was sweet."

"You're tongue is sharp, but your kisses, *ma petite,* they are very sweet."

"So are yours," she said. She wrapped her arms around his shoulders and held him close. "I missed you tonight. Your apartment is so big. I felt very lonely without you."

Lonely. That was a word he'd learned to ignore for a long time.

He thought about the future, and for the first time he realized he was *looking* at the future. One that he wanted with Sheri. Not as his wife, because he'd already given his name to the one woman who'd owned his heart.

But he did want her to stay with him. Wanted Sheri to be in his life, and not just at work.

"You're staring at me," she said. "Why?"

"Because I like the way you look at me."

"Ah, ego. I should have known."

He just shook his head. Then kissed her one more time, because he couldn't resist her mouth when it was this close.

He lifted her in his arms and carried her down the hall to his bedroom. Laying her in the center of his bed, he came down over her, bracing his weight on his forearms so that there was a small gap between their bodies.

"I want you to live with me."

"I am living with you," she said.

"I mean, even after the engagement party and my family goes home."

"Am I here for them?" she asked.

"No, *ma petite*. You are here for me, and I'm asking you to stay."

Sheri held her breath as Tristan lowered himself over her. She would never say it out loud, but she loved the feel of him on top of her. It made their relationship real when, after they made love, she'd wrap her arms and legs around him and just hold him, pretending she never had to let go.

But now, she thought, she might not have to let go. She didn't know what he meant by asking her to stay, but it sounded positive. She couldn't believe she'd waited so long to move in with him. Granted it had only been for a little over a week. But their lives had meshed together.

She liked living with him. For the first time in her entire life, she felt like she was in the place where she was meant to be with the man to whom she belonged.

"What do you mean?"

"That I want you to stay with me, and not just as my temporary fiancée. I want this to be permanent."

She felt a rush of joy and she tipped her head back, blinking so he wouldn't see the tears in her eyes. She took a deep breath and felt the gentle stroking of his finger against the side of her cheek.

"So what do you think?"

Her gaze met his and she tried to read the emotions there, but as always she had no idea what he was feeling. But she knew what *she* felt. She loved this man. She wanted nothing more than to say she was his and live the rest of her life with him.

"I think yes. I'd love to spend the rest of my life with you."

He gave her a tight smile and kissed her. "Great."

"Great? That's all you can say?"

"It seemed more appropriate than 'get naked.'"

She laughed and hugged him tightly to her. "Get naked would work."

"Really?"

"Yes!"

He laughed then, and she felt a sense of rightness deep down in her soul. In that empty part that had been hollow since her father had left all those long years ago.

He started to unbutton her blouse and she put her hands in his thick hair, rubbing the back of his scalp as he undressed her. She thought of the wedding plans she'd put off making, because planning a wedding she wasn't going to follow through with had seemed like torture. But now she could stop putting off Blanche and really start thinking about the kind of bride she'd be.

"When do you want to get married? I know we'd been putting off picking a date because of the pretense, but now that we're going through with it things are different."

Tristan stopped unbuttoning her blouse and lifted himself off of her body. "Married?"

"Isn't that what you meant, Tristan? If we're going to live together permanently…"

He pushed completely off her and sat on the edge of the bed, his back to her. And she realized he hadn't meant marriage. "What were you thinking?"

"That we'd live together," he answered.

"What's the difference in living together and being married?" she asked. "Everyone already thinks we're engaged."

"I don't give a damn what everyone thinks. We both know that we aren't really engaged," he said, glancing over his shoulder at her.

She shook her head, fiddling with the ring he'd given her, and realized that her shirt was unbuttoned and she was still laying in the middle of his bed. She sat up and quickly refastened her shirt.

"I don't know what to think anymore," she said, climbing off the king-size bed. "I never know what to expect from you, Tristan."

"I do not understand," he said.

And for the first time, she realized that he really didn't understand what she was talking about. Because Tristan was always looking out for himself. For his own desires, his own safety. She had been thinking that because he showered her with attention and gifts, he was caring for her.

"I love you. Do you remember that?"

He stood up and walked over to her. He touched her so softly, tracing the lines of her face with his fingertip. "I do remember it. Hearing you say you love me is something that I think about a lot."

"And…?"

"And that's why I want us to continue living together."

She staggered back away from him. "Did you ask me because you feel sorry for me?"

He shook his head. "I asked because I'm tired

of being alone. And you bring something to my life that I never thought to find again."

"Love," she said. "I bring love to your life."

"No, you bring that to yourself. To me you bring companionship and friendship…an end to the loneliness I've felt when I'm around other couples."

She didn't know what to say. Because she had the feeling that he'd asked her to live with him out of pity. She realized for the first time that her father had done her a huge favor by leaving. Because Tristan staying with her out of guilt or pity made her feel worse than being left behind.

"What are you going to do?" Tristan asked Sheri. He could tell that things weren't going the way he wanted them to. If there were a way for him to go back ten minutes, he would have kept his mouth shut.

"I don't know what I'm going to do. Obviously I gave you my word that I'd stay with you until the party and that's…in two days, right? So after the party I'll move back to the brownstone."

He knew he shouldn't be mad at Sheri. But he was. If she wasn't so stuck in her bourgeois American idea of what a relationship should be, then he'd have everything he wanted. "Running back to your favorite hiding place?"

"I'm not running," she said, crossing her arms around her waist and staring up at him with those big wounded doe eyes.

But this time he didn't let the eyes affect him. He knew better. She was as manipulative as the other women he'd dated. The ones that had always wanted to be Mrs. Tristan Sabina and had schemed to get there. Sheri was the same, she just went about it differently. "It sure seems that way from where I'm standing. You said you loved me, and now that I won't marry you…you're going back to the same place you've always run to."

She dropped her arms and stalked over to him. "Well, you'd know all about running. Of course, you hide out in the public eye. Dating a bunch of different shallow women. Acting like nothing in life affects you."

Tristan couldn't argue with that. "What do you want from me?"

"I don't know."

"Don't hedge, Sheri. Tell me what you want. How can I make this right for you?"

She turned away and then glanced back at him. "You could love me."

He didn't know how to answer that. "I'm…I can't do that."

She nodded. "Then you have nothing I want."

She walked to the bedroom door and he realized that she was leaving. That she was going to walk out that door and he wasn't ready for her to go.

"Sheri."

"Yes?"

"I really want you to stay."

She looked back at him. "I want to. But for the first time in my life, I realize that I can't keep settling for the least bit of attention. You changed me over the last few weeks. Made me into a different woman. And the one constant through all of that is how much I love you.

"But tonight, I realized that loving you isn't enough for me, and it's not fair to you. You need something more. Something I can't give."

He didn't know what she was talking about, but could tell that it made a lot of sense to Sheri. "Are you leaving tonight?"

"No. I gave you my word I'd stay through our pretend engagement party."

"Very well. Thank you for that," he said, gathering his facade around him. He always knew how to put on a good face. And it wasn't like he really loved her. She was his *pretend* fiancée. "I'll sleep down the hall."

"Okay."

He walked out of his bedroom. In the wide, long hallway he heard her footsteps behind him. "Tristan."

He looked back.

"I thought you were different," she said, her voice sad and low but still audible.

"Different how?"

"I don't know, just different from the other men in my life."

"I am sure I am different."

"On the outside you are very different. But inside, you're the same."

"Same how?"

"Hollow and empty. Unwilling to let your guard down for a second and accept the gift of my love."

Her words were heartfelt, and to be honest, he did feel an ache deep inside at her words. He'd thought for a long time that he wasn't exactly the man he used to be.

"I have a full life. After you break our engagement I will be back to my busy schedule and the life that I have become accustomed to."

"That doesn't mean that you're happy."

He saw the tears in her wide brown eyes and

knew he was going to remember that look on her face for a long time.

"Happiness is a fool's notion."

"No, it's not. Unless you think it's foolish to take a risk. To put yourself on the line. And I know you don't, because you take risks every day in business. At the Sabina Group, and with the nightclubs you own with Gui and Christos. It's only in your personal life that you refuse to take a chance."

He pivoted on his heel and walked back to her. "Studying me in magazines and tabloid stories does not mean you know who I am and what makes me tick."

"No, it doesn't," she said. "What makes me an expert is having fallen in love with you. And living with you this week has shown me a man that few people really see. I do know the real you."

"Do you? Who is the real me?"

She took a deep breath and looked up at him. In her bare feet, he felt like he towered over her. "The real you. Are you sure you want to know?"

"I asked, did I not?"

"That's right. You did. Well, the real man I've seen, Tristan, is a coward. Someone who's felt a deep pain, and I'm not discounting that. But because of one loss, you've cut yourself off from ever loving again. And that seems cowardly to me."

Tristan didn't answer her, just walked away. And this time he wasn't coming back. He wasn't a coward, and he wasn't about to let Sheri Donnelly use those words to make him do something he knew he'd regret.

Twelve

Sheri left early and arrived at the office before Tristan. He called from the limo and asked her to join him going to the airport to pick up his family. She made an excuse about being too busy, and he let it go.

She knew she would have to see him again tomorrow night at their engagement gala, but until then she was hiding out. She had never had a broken heart before. She wished she could fall out of love with Tristan, but it simply wasn't that easy.

He'd been the embodiment of every romantic

fantasy she'd ever had. The lover she'd always wanted. He'd made her feel as if she was the sexiest woman alive, and the pleasure he'd evoked in her body was beyond even her wildest fantasies. And the way he'd taken care of her… The way she'd felt when she was with him…

Working and living with Tristan had made her believe she'd found the other half of her soul. That she'd brought things to his life that had been lacking, and he'd done the same for her.

She put her head on her desk and realized that she wasn't going to be able to stay on here at the Sabina Group. There was no way she could sit in this office every day and pretend that she wasn't still in love with Tristan.

It was well after six and she was still working. She was scheduled to meet Tristan and his family and friends at Del Posto for dinner at eight-thirty. After calling Tristan a coward, she couldn't stand him up.

Her phone rang.

"Sabina Group, this is Sheri."

"Sheri, this is Palmer at the security desk. There is a Count Guillermo de Cuaron y Bautista de la Cruz here to see you."

"To see *me?*"

"Yes."

Why was Gui here? "Please send him up."

"I will."

She hung up the phone and pulled her mirror out of the bottom drawer of her desk, thinking she should fix her makeup, then realized she hadn't put any on this morning. She'd reverted to the old Sheri. She needed the comfort of her big comfy clothes and her plain appearance. There was a lot to be said for not being noticed.

"Ms. Donnelly, I'd like a word with you." Gui strode into her office like he owned it. But he stopped in his path and put his hands on his hips, cursing succinctly under his breath. She caught about every other word, since his Spanish accent was fairly heavy. "What the hell is going on with you and Tristan?"

"I think you should ask him that question. I'm taking care of some last-minute things here at the office. I think we're all meeting at the restaurant for dinner."

He shook his head. "I already talked to him, at the airport. And I came over here to find out what has happened between the two of you."

"Ask him again."

"I thought the problem was you."

She glanced up at Gui and realized there was a bit of truth in what he'd said. "The problem *is* me."

Gui shook his head. "How is it you?"

"I want things from him that he can't give me."

"Love?"

"How'd you know?"

"Because I know Tristan, and that's the one thing he thinks he cannot offer you."

There was something about Gui that made her want to pour out her soul. Something so understanding in those hazel eyes of his. "I think it might be me. I'm not the kind of woman who inspires that in any man."

"Don't say that, Sheri. Tristan wasn't always the man you see before you today."

"He wasn't?"

"He was badly hurt when Cecile died. He used to be the most gregarious of all of us. So filled with a big joy for loving. And then when Cecile was diagnosed with cancer…he thought they'd beat it at first. He put his entire life on hold to stay by her side."

Sheri ached to hear his words, but they mirrored what she already knew. Tristan had told her himself that he couldn't love anymore. That he'd had his once in a lifetime. It was just her bad luck that she had found *her* forever-love in him.

"I know all that. I thought I could love him enough for both of us. But that was silly, and now we're both moving on."

"I'm not sure that you haven't changed him, Sheri. He's a different man today than he was at Christos's wedding, and that's thanks to you."

"I doubt that. I'm not the type of woman who can change a man's life."

Gui sat down on the corner of her desk. "Yes, you are. Don't give up on him yet. Will you give him one more chance?"

She shook her head. She couldn't bear the pain of losing him again.

The phone rang, but it was after hours so she let it go to voice mail. "Why do you care?"

"Because Tristan is one of my dearest friends and you've made him happier in the last few weeks than I've seen him in years."

She was afraid to believe him. But at the same time, she knew Gui wouldn't lie to her. "I'm afraid to take another chance on him. I just made up my mind that he wasn't going to stay with me."

"You strike me as a fighter, Sheri. Someone who wouldn't let the chance of a lifetime slip away."

She looked up at Gui and realized that he was right. She was letting go of Tristan too easily. She loved the man, and that wasn't going to change. Shouldn't she keep fighting for him?

Sheri's absence was palpable to Tristan as the day drew on. Blanche and Rene had a lot of questions about her, and the more he talked with his siblings about her, the more he realized how much he cared for her.

When they got back to his place, he waited for Sheri to come and greet them but she must still be at the office, hiding from him. He felt the emptiness in a new way. Echoing around him.

Gui had been shocked by how he looked. When Tristan had mentioned that the engagement was definitely off, Gui had left in disgust to run an errand. And Tristan realized that his plan to make Sheri his fake fiancée hadn't been well thought out. He'd never considered how he'd feel when she left his life.

Blanche had nothing but good things to say about Sheri and Tristan found himself laughing at the stories she told about shopping with the woman he'd been trying to keep out of his heart for the last few weeks. As he pictured her in his mind, he realized he hadn't done a very good job of it.

He loved her. How could he not have realized

what he was feeling for her? The only excuse he had was that it was different than the sweet and gentle love he'd had for his Cecile. With Sheri the love was bigger than he was, passionate. And that's what had him running scared.

Dammit, she had been right when she'd called him a coward. He had been running from her, because he'd been afraid to risk being hurt again.

Realizing that, he knew he had to make things right for her. Had to find a way to win her back before she had to face his friends and family tomorrow night at the engagement gala. He wanted it to be a real celebration, otherwise what was the point?

He called the office, but Sheri's phone went to voice mail. He hung up without leaving a message. He had no idea when she was going to show up, or even where she was. But he did know she'd come to the restaurant for dinner. Because she always kept her word.

And that was another reason he loved her. She wasn't fickle or shallow. She couldn't tell a lie to him. Her love would never leave him, or let him feel betrayed.

He knew he needed to do something to show Sheri that he was serious about her and that he wasn't running away any longer. And he knew it would take more than the hour he had until he was supposed to start meeting his friends and family at Del Posto. He went and found his mother.

"Maman?"

"*Oui,* Tristan."

"I need your help."

"With?"

"I've hurt the woman I love and I need to make a big gesture to make it up to her, but we have reservations at a restaurant across town."

"How can I help, *mon fils?*"

"Be my hostess while I take care of a few details here. And when Sheri arrives, keep her there."

"Where will you be?"

"Taking care of details," he said, kissing his mother on the forehead.

"Okay, I'll do this. Are you sure about this girl? You always swore love was no longer in the cards for you."

"*Oui, maman.* I am more than sure. She's re-awakened a part of me I thought was dead."

His mother smiled at him and then hugged him tightly. "I'm so glad to hear it. A part of me has long wept for that deadness inside you."

After his family left for the restaurant, Tristan made several quick, demanding phone calls.

Knowing the kind of romantic person Sheri was, with her secret dreams of how love should be, he arranged for flowers to fill the apartment. He ordered the finest French champagne sent up from his wine cellar and then called his favorite jeweler for a necklace. When the flowers arrived, he decked out the balcony to resemble the one at his villa that night in Mykonos. Now he had every detail he could think of in place—except for Sheri.

His mobile rang. A quick glance at the caller ID window showed him it was Gui. "What's up, Gui?"

"Where are you?"

"My place. Why?"

"Because Sheri is at the restaurant turning heads, but she's asking where you are. You need to get down here."

"I'm on my way. Don't let her leave."

"I won't."

Tristan's driver had him across town in no time at all. He walked into the restaurant and stopped in his tracks. Sheri wasn't sitting quietly in a corner the way she had during many of the activities that week back on Mykonos. Instead, she was in the center of his family and friends, wearing a stylish dress and holding court. He couldn't move as his heart skipped a beat.

This was what he'd been afraid to let himself see. That Sheri was the other half of his soul and he needed her more than he'd ever expected to need any woman. If she left him… God, he couldn't even go there in hypothetical. He needed her.

How could he have thought he'd be able to survive without her in his life?

He walked up to her and all the words he'd rehearsed escaped him. He saw her flush as he looked at her. He wanted her and he was sure she knew the signs of his arousal well enough by now to tell that. But he wanted more than just her sexy little body. He also wanted the joy in her eyes, the witty, sassy mouth of hers. He wanted it all.

And he didn't want to tell her in front of the world. She deserved to hear about how he felt for her the first time in private. Where he could do a proper job of it.

"Tristan?"

"Hmm?"

"Are you okay?"

He shook his head. "I'm tired."

"Well, I'm sorry to hear that," she said.

"Don't you want to know why?"

She nibbled on her lower lip. "Okay, I'll ask. Why are you tired?"

"Because I've been running for too long."

"What have you been running from?"

"I've been running from you, *ma petite,* and that has to stop." He reached out and snagged her wrist. "Please excuse us," he said to his family.

"Not so fast. We want to hear more about this running you've been doing."

"Forget it, Rene. My private life is supposed to be private. Isn't that what you've been telling me?"

"Indeed," Rene said.

Christos and Ava stepped in between Rene and Tristan to say hello. They looked wonderful together, smiling and happy and…loving. Tristan clapped his hand on his friend's shoulder, thanking him for flying in and promising to see them the next day. Then he drew Sheri away from the crowd and toward the exit.

"Why are we leaving? You just arrived."

"I need to be alone with you."

Tristan didn't say much in the car ride from Del Posto to his apartment, but he held her hand the entire time, rubbing his thumb against her palm and bringing her hand to his mouth several times to kiss it.

She wondered if simply changing her attitude

had changed his, but she knew that couldn't be it. Something had happened to Tristan, too. He was acting so different. When they got to his apartment building, he held her hand all the way up in the elevator and then made her close her eyes when they got to the front door.

"Why?"

"Because I said so."

"And I'm going to do this why?" she asked, teasing him.

He lifted her off her feet and into his arms, kissing her hard. "Stop sassing me or I really will spank you."

She shook her head. "Tristan, what is going on with you?"

"I am in love."

Tears burned her eyes as those words came from his mouth. She didn't believe them. He'd been too adamant about not falling again. "Put me down."

"No."

"Tristan, I mean it."

"So do I."

He reached down, unlocked his front door and carried her over the threshold. He set her on her feet in the foyer. She was blinking, trying not to cry, but it wasn't working.

"I wanted to do this properly."

"Do what properly? You don't have to pretend to feel something for me you don't feel."

"I am not pretending, *ma petite.*"

She wasn't sure she believed him, but she knew he wouldn't lie to her. He never had.

"When did you realize you loved me?" she asked him.

"Today, when I was surrounded by my family. I did not realize how much you'd done with them. They were all telling me stories about you and I realized that no matter how hard I'd tried not to fall for you, I already had.

"I love you, Sheri. And it does scare me. Because as much as I thought that Cecile was my once-in-a-lifetime love, I have come to realize that love is also what I feel for you. I need you in my life."

She was afraid to believe him. "It's okay if you don't love me. I'm not going to walk away from you like I did last night. That was wrong—"

"You are not listening to me, *ma petite.* I love you. I am not going anywhere without you anymore. No running unless you are by my side."

She was still afraid to believe him but there was sincerity in his eyes that made her want to.

He must have read the hesitation on her face

because he leaned down and kissed her. And when he lifted his head he said, softly, "I am not going anywhere."

Those words she believed. No man had ever said them to her before. "Promise?"

"Yes, I do. What about you?"

"I'm not going anywhere, either. I'm staying by your side from now on."

"Why is that?"

"I love you, Tristan."

He smiled at her and lifted her off her feet. He carried her through his apartment out onto the balcony that offered a splendid view of the Manhattan skyline.

"You're already wearing my engagement ring, but I need to ask you again…Sheri Donnelly, my love, the woman who owns my heart, will you marry me?"

She looked up at him as he stood next to her on the balcony. Taking a deep breath, she leaned up and kissed him before pulling back. "Yes, Tristan, I will marry you."

He pulled her into his arms and made love to her, sealing the bond they'd just made with their bodies. And she knew she'd found the happiness she'd always thought would elude her. She and

Tristan had found something rare, the kind of love that touched few people's lives, and she felt blessed to have him as her own.

* * * * *

ONE MONTH WITH THE MAGNATE

BY
MICHELLE CELMER

Bestselling author **Michelle Celmer** lives in southeastern Michigan with her husband, their three children, two dogs and two cats. When she's not writing or busy being a mum, you can find her in the garden or curled up with a romance novel. And if you twist her arm really hard, you can usually persuade her into a day of power shopping.

Michelle loves to hear from readers. Visit her website, www.michellecelmer.com, or write her at PO Box 300, Clawson, MI 48017, USA.

To my editor Charles, who has been, and continues to
be, an amazing source of support and encouragement.
It has been a privilege, a joy and a lot of
fun working with you.

One

This was, without a doubt, the lowest Isabelle Winthrop-Betts had ever sunk.

Not even the sting of her father's open palm across her cheek had caused the humiliation she was feeling now thanks to Emilio Suarez, a man she once loved with all her heart and had planned to marry.

Her father had made sure that never happened. And Isabelle couldn't blame Emilio for the bitterness in his eyes as he sat behind his desk in his corner office at Western Oil headquarters, like a king on a throne addressing a local peasant.

Thanks to her husband, Leonard, that was really all she was now. She had gone from being one of the richest women in Texas, to a pauper. Homeless, penniless, widowed and about to be thrown in prison for fraud. And all because she had been too naive and trusting. Because when her husband had put documents in front of her, instead of reading them, she had blindly signed. How could she question the man who had rescued her from hell? Who had probably saved her life?

And the son of a bitch had up and died before he could exonerate her.

Thanks, Lenny.

"You have a lot of nerve asking me for help," Emilio said in the deep, caramel-smooth voice that strummed every one of her frayed nerve endings, but the animosity in his tone curdled her blood. Not that he wasn't justified in his anger, not after the way she'd broken his heart, but she'd had no choice. She didn't expect him to understand that, she just hoped he would take pity on her.

His charcoal gray eyes bore through her, and she fought not to wither under their scrutiny. "Why come to me? Why not go to your rich friends?"

Because his brother, Alejandro, was prosecuting her case. Besides, she had no friends. Not anymore. They had all invested with Lenny. Some had lost millions.

"You're the only one who can help me," she said.

"Why would I want to? Maybe I want to see you rot in prison."

She swallowed the hurt his words caused, that he hated her that much.

Well, he would be happy to learn that according to her lawyer, Clifton Stone, nothing would prevent that now. The evidence against her was overwhelming and her best bet was a plea bargain. And while the idea of spending even another minute in jail terrified her, she was prepared to take full responsibility for her actions and accept any punishment they considered appropriate. Unfortunately, Lenny had gotten her mother involved in his scams, too. After suffering years of physical and emotional abuse from her husband, Adriana Winthrop deserved some happiness. Not to spend the rest of her life in prison. Not for something that was Isabelle's fault.

"I don't care what happens to me," Isabelle told him. "I want my mother's name cleared. She had no part in any of Leonard's scams."

"Leonard's and *your* scams," he corrected.

She swallowed hard and nodded.

One dark brow rose. "So, you're admitting your guilt?"

If blind trust was a crime, she was definitely guilty. "It's my fault that I'm in this mess."

"This is not a good time for me."

She'd seen coverage on the news about the accident at the refinery. The explosion and the injured men. She'd tried to visit him last week, but the front of the Western Oil headquarters building had been crawling with media. She would have waited another week or two, but she was running out of time. It had to be now. "I know it's a bad time and I'm sorry. This couldn't wait."

Arms folded across his chest, he sat back in his chair and studied her. In a suit, with his closely cropped hair combed back, he barely resembled the boy she'd known from her adolescence. The one she had fallen head over heels in love with the instant she'd laid eyes on him, when she was twelve and he was fifteen. Although, it had taken him until college to notice her.

His mother had been their housekeeper and in her father's eyes, Emilio would never be good enough for his precious daughter. That hadn't stopped her from seeing Emilio in secret, fully aware of the price she would pay if they were caught. But they had been lucky—until her father learned of their plans to elope.

Not only had he punished her severely, he'd fired Emilio's mother. He accused her of stealing from them, knowing that no one else would hire her.

She wished her father could see them now. Emilio sitting there like the master of the universe and her begging for his help. He would be rolling in his grave.

See Daddy, he was good enough for me after all. Probably even better than I deserved.

Emilio never would have hurt her, never would have sacrificed her reputation out of greed. He was honest and trustworthy and loyal.

And right now, seriously pissed at her.

"So you're doing this for your mother?" he asked.

Isabelle nodded. "My lawyer said that with all the media attention, it's unlikely that your brother will be willing to deal. She'll serve some time."

"Maybe I'd like to see her rot in prison, too," he said.

She felt her hackles rise. Adriana Winthrop had never been anything but kind to him and his mother. She had done *nothing* to hurt them. She'd only been guilty of being married to an overbearing, abusive bastard. And even that wasn't entirely her fault. She had tried to leave and he'd made her live to regret it.

"Your appearance," he said. "Is it supposed to make me feel sorry for you?"

She resisted the urge to look down at the outdated blouse and ill-fitting slacks she had rummaged from the bag of clothes her mother had been donating to charity. Obviously he'd expected her to be wearing an outfit more suited to her previous station, but when her possessions had been seized, she kept nothing. For now, this was the best she could do.

"I don't feel sorry for you, Isabelle. It seems to me you're getting exactly what you deserve."

That was one thing they could agree on.

She could see that coming here had been a waste of time. He wasn't going to help her. He was too bitter.

Oh, well. It had been worth a try.

She rose from the chair, limp with defeat. Her voice trembled as she said, "Well, thank you for seeing me, Mr. Suarez."

"Sit down," he snapped.

"For what? You obviously have no intention of helping me."

"I never said I wouldn't help you."

Something in his eyes softened the slightest bit and hope welled up inside of her. She lowered herself into the chair.

"I'll talk to my brother on your mother's behalf, but I expect something in return."

She had expected as much, but the calculating look he wore sent a cold chill down her spine. "What?"

"You will agree to be my live-in housekeeper for thirty days. You'll cook for me, clean my house, do my laundry. Whatever I ask. At the end of the thirty days, if I'm satisfied with your performance, I'll talk to my brother."

In other words, he would make her work for him the way his mother had worked for her. Clever. Obviously he saw her plea for help as an opportunity to get revenge. What had happened to the sweet and kindhearted boy she used to know? The one who never would have been capable of dreaming up such a devious plan, much less have the gall to implement it. He had changed more than she could ever have guessed, and it stung to know that it was probably her fault. Had she hurt him so much when she left that he'd hardened his heart?

And what of his *offer?* The day her father died she had vowed never to let a man control her again. But this wasn't about her. She was doing this for her mother. She *owed* her. Besides, she had swallowed her pride so many times since the indictment, she was getting used to the bitter taste.

Despite what Emilio believed, she was no longer the

shy, timid girl of her youth. She was strong now. Anything he could dish out, she could take.

"How do I know I can trust you?" she asked. "How do I know that after the thirty days you won't change your mind?"

He leaned forward, eyes flaming with indignation as they locked on hers. "Because I have never been anything but honest with you, Isabelle."

Unlike her, his tone implied. He was right. Even though she'd had a valid reason for breaking her word, but that hardly seemed worth mentioning. Even if she told him the truth she doubted he would believe her. Or care.

He leaned back in his chair. "Take some time to think about it if you'd like."

She didn't need time. She didn't have any to spare. Less than six weeks from now she and her lawyer would meet with the prosecutor, and her lawyer warned her that it didn't look good. For her or her mother.

This wasn't going to be a pleasant thirty days, but at least she knew Emilio wouldn't physically harm her. He may have become cold and callous, but he had never been a violent man. He'd never made her feel anything but safe.

What if he changed? a little voice in her head taunted, but she ignored it. The decision had already been made.

She sat straight, squared her shoulders and told him, "I'll do it."

Isabelle Winthrop was a viper.

A lying, cheating, narcissistic viper.

Yet Emilio couldn't deny that despite the fifteen years that had passed, she was still the most physically beautiful woman he had ever laid eyes on.

But her soul was as black as tar.

She'd had him duped, all those years ago. He thought

she loved him. He had believed, despite the fact that she was a Winthrop and he was the son of a domestic servant, they would be married and live happily ever after. She told him she didn't care about the money or the status. She would be happy so long as they had each other. And he had fallen for it, right up until the minute he read the article in the paper announcing her marriage to finance guru Leonard Betts. A multi*billionaire*.

So much for her not caring about money and status. What other reason would she have to marry a man twenty-five years older?

When all was said and done, his relationship with Isabelle hadn't been a total loss. She had taught Emilio that women were not to be trusted, and he'd learned from her deceit never to put his heart on the line again.

That didn't mean he wasn't ready to dish out a little good old-fashioned revenge.

As for her being a criminal like her husband, he wasn't sure what to believe. According to the law, if she signed it, she was legally responsible. Now that Leonard was dead, someone had to pay.

Guilty or not, as far as Emilio was concerned, she was getting exactly what she deserved. But he was not prepared to be dragged down with her.

"There's just one condition," he told her.

She nervously tucked her pale blond hair behind her ears. Hair that he used to love running his fingers through. It was once shiny and soft and full of body, but now it looked dull and lifeless. "What condition?"

"No one can know about this." If it got out that he was helping her, it could complicate his chances for the CEO position at Western Oil. He was in competition with COO Jordan Everett and his brother, Nathan Everett, Chief Brand Officer. Both were friends and worthy opponents.

But Emilio deserved the position more. He'd earned it through more hard work than either of them could ever imagine with their Harvard educations that Daddy footed the bill for.

Maybe he was a fool to risk everything he'd worked so hard for, but Isabelle was offering an opportunity for revenge that he just couldn't pass up. After his father died, his mother worked her fingers to the bone trying to provide for Emilio and his three brothers. It was years after being fired by the Winthrops when she finally admitted to her children the verbal abuse she'd endured from Isabelle's father. Not to mention occasional improper sexual advances. But the pay was good, so she'd had no choice but to tolerate it. And after he had fired her, accused her of stealing from them, no respectable family would even think of hiring her.

Now Emilio's mother, his entire family, would finally be vindicated.

"Are you sure you don't want to brag to all of your friends?" Isabelle asked him.

"I'm the chief financial officer of this company. It wouldn't bode well for me or Western Oil if people knew I was in business with a woman indicted for financial fraud. If you tell a soul, not only is the deal off, but I will see that you *and* your mother rot in prison for a very long time."

"I can't just disappear for thirty days. My mother will want to know where I am."

"Then tell her you're staying with a friend until you get back on your feet."

"What about the authorities? I'm out on bond. They need to know where I'm staying. I could go back to jail."

"I'll take care of it," he said. He was sure he could work something out with his brother.

She looked wary, like she thought maybe it was a trick, but clearly she had no choice. She needn't have worried though. Unlike her, he honored his word.

"I won't tell anyone," she said.

"Fine." He slid a pad of paper and a pen across the desk to her. "Write down where you're currently staying and I'll have my driver come by to get you tonight."

She leaned forward to jot down the address. He assumed she would be staying with her mother, or in a high-class hotel, but what she wrote down was the name and address for a motel in one of the seedier parts of town. She really must have been in dire straits financially. Or she was pretending to be.

Several million dollars of the money they had stolen had never been recovered. For all he knew, she had it stashed somewhere. Of course, if she had been planning to run, wouldn't she have done it by now? Or was she waiting to cut a deal for her mother, then intending to skip town?

It was something to keep in mind.

"Be ready at seven," he told her. "Your thirty days will start tomorrow. Agreed?"

She nodded, chin held high. She wouldn't look so proud when he put her to work. Isabelle had never lifted a finger to do a thing for herself. He was sorry he wouldn't be home to witness what he was sure would be a domestic disaster.

The thought almost made him smile.

"Do you need a ride back to the hotel?" he asked.

She shook her head. "I borrowed my mother's car."

"That must be a change for you. Having to drive yourself places. It's a wonder you even remember how."

He could tell that she wanted to shoot back a snarky comment, but she kept her mouth shut and her eyes all but dared him to give it his best shot. She was tough, but she had no idea who she was dealing with. He wasn't the naive, trusting man he'd been before.

He stood and she did the same. He reached out to shake on the deal, and she slipped her finely boned hand into his—her breath caught when he enclosed it firmly, *possessively*. Though she tried to hide it, being close to him still did something to her. Which was exactly what he was counting on. Because bringing her into his home as a housekeeper was only a ruse to execute his true plan.

When they were together, Isabelle had insisted they wait until they were married to make love, so he had honored her wishes for a torturous year. Then she left him high and dry. Now it was time for some payback.

He would seduce Isabelle, make her want him, make her *beg* for it, then reject her.

By the time he was through with her, prison would seem like Club Med.

Two

"Is that who I think it was?"

Emilio looked up from his computer to find Adam Blair, the current CEO of Western Oil, standing in his office doorway. He should have known word of his *visitor* would get around fast. Her disguise—if that had been her intention with the ridiculous clothes, the straight, lifeless hair and absence of makeup—not to mention the fake name she had given the guards when she insisted on seeing him, obviously hadn't worked. When he saw her standing there in the lobby, her shoulders squared, head held high, looking too proud for her own good, he should have sent her away, but curiosity had gotten the best of him.

Emilio had warned Adam months ago, just before news of the Ponzi scheme became public, that he had a past connection to Isabelle. But he'd never expected her to turn up at his office. And he sure as hell hadn't considered that she would have the audacity to ask for his help. She was probably accustomed to getting exactly what she wanted.

"That was Isabelle Winthrop-Betts," he told Adam.

"What did she want?"

"My help. She wants her mother's name cleared, and she wants me to talk to my brother on her behalf."

"What about her own name?"

"She more or less admitted her guilt to me. She intends to take full responsibility for everything."

Adam's brows rose. "That's…surprising."

Emilio thought so, too. With a federal prosecutor for a sibling, he had heard of every scheme imaginable from every type of criminal. Freely admitting guilt wasn't usually one of them. Isabelle was clearly up to something. He just hadn't figured out what. He had considered that she and her mother were planning to take the unrecovered money and disappear, but why bother exonerating her first? Maybe he could gain her trust, encourage her to tell him her plans, then report her to the authorities.

"So, will you help her?" Adam asked.

"I told her I would talk to Alejandro." Which he still had to do, and he wasn't looking forward to it.

"Also surprising. The last time we talked about her, you seemed awfully bitter."

Not only was Adam a colleague, he was one of Emilio's closest friends. Still, he doubted Adam would even begin to understand his lust for revenge. He wasn't that kind of man. He'd never been betrayed the way Emilio had. Emilio would keep that part of his plan to himself. Besides, Adam would no doubt be opposed to anything that might bring more negative press to Western Oil.

What he didn't know wouldn't hurt him.

"Call me sentimental," Emilio said.

Adam laughed. "Sorry, but that's the last thing I would

ever call you. Sentimental isn't a word in your vocabulary, not unless it's regarding your mother. Just tell me you're not planning on doing something stupid."

There were many levels of stupid. Emilio was barely scratching the surface.

"You have nothing to be concerned about," he assured Adam. "You have my word."

"Good enough for me." Adam's cell buzzed, alerting him that he had a text. As he read it, he smiled. "Katy just got to the house. She's staying in El Paso for a few days, then we're driving back to Peckins together."

Katy was Adam's fiancée. She was also his former sister-in-law and five months pregnant with their first child. Or possibly Katy's dead sister's baby. They weren't sure.

"Have you two set a date yet?" Emilio asked.

"We're leaning toward a small ceremony at her parents' ranch between Christmas and New Year's. I'll let you know as soon as we decide. I'd just like to make it official before the baby is born." Adam looked at his watch. "Well, I have a few things to finish before I leave for the day."

"Send Katy my best."

Adam turned to leave, then paused and turned back. "You're sure you know what you're doing?"

Emilio didn't have to ask what he meant. Adam obviously suspected that there was more to the situation than Emilio was letting on. "I'm sure."

When he was gone, Emilio picked up the phone and dialed his brother's office.

"Hey, big brother," Alejandro answered when his secretary connected them. "Long time no see. The kids miss their favorite uncle."

Emilio hadn't seen his nephews, who were nine, six and two, nearly often enough lately. They were probably the closest thing he would ever have to kids of his own, so he tried to visit on a regular basis. "I know, I'm sorry. Things have been a little crazy here since the refinery accident."

"Any promising developments?"

"At this point, no. It's looking like it may have been sabotage. We're launching an internal investigation. But keep that between us."

"Of course. It's ironic that you called today because I was planning to call you. Alana had a doctor's appointment this morning. She's pregnant again."

Emilio laughed. "Congratulations! I thought you decided to stop at three."

"We did, but she really wanted to try for a girl. I keep telling her that with four boys in my family, we'd have better luck adopting, but she wanted to give it one more try."

Emilio couldn't imagine having one child now much less four. There had been a time when he wanted a family. He and Isabelle had talked about having at least two children. But that was a long time ago. "Are the boys excited?" he asked his brother.

"We haven't told them yet, but I think they'll be thrilled. Alex and Reggie anyway. Chris is a little young to grasp the concept."

"I don't suppose you've heard from Estefan," Emilio asked, referring to their younger brother. Due to drugs, gambling and various other addictions, they usually only heard from him when he needed money or a temporary place to crash. Their mother lived in fear that one day the phone would ring and it would be the coroner's office asking her to come down and identify his body.

"Not a word. I'm not sure if I should feel worried or relieved. I did get an email from Enrique, though. He's in Budapest."

Enrique was the youngest brother and the family nomad. He'd left for a summer backpacking trip through Europe after graduating from college. That was almost three years ago and he hadn't come home yet. Every now and then they would get a postcard or an email, or he would upload photos on the internet of his latest adventures. Occasionally he would pick up the phone and call. He kept promising he'd be home soon, but there was always some new place he wanted to visit. A new cause to devote his life to.

Emilio and Alejandro talked for several minutes about family and work, until Emilio knew he had to quit stalling and get to the point of his call. "I need a favor."

"Anything," Alejandro said.

"Isabelle Winthrop will be checking out of her motel this evening. As far as your office is concerned, she's still staying there."

There was a pause, then Alejandro muttered a curse. "What's going on, Emilio?"

"Not what you think." He told his brother about Isabelle's visit and his "agreement" with her. Leaving out his plan to seduce her, of course. Family man that Alejandro was, he would never understand. He'd never had his heart broken the way Emilio had. Alana had been his high school sweetheart. His first love. Other than a short break they had taken in college to explore other options— which lasted all of two weeks before they could no longer stand to be apart—they had been inseparable.

"Are you completely out of your mind?" Alejandro asked.

"I know what I'm doing."

"If Mama finds out what you're up to, she's going to kill you, then she's going to kill *me* for helping you!"

"I'm doing this for Mama, for *all* of us. For what Isabelle's father did to our family."

"And it has nothing to do with the fact that Isabelle broke your heart?"

A nerve in his jaw ticked. "You said yourself that she's guilty."

"On paper, yes."

"She all but admitted her guilt to me."

"Well, there've been developments in the case."

Emilio frowned. "What kind of developments?"

"You know I can't tell you that. I shouldn't be talking to you about this, period. And I sure as hell shouldn't be helping you. If someone in my office finds out what you're doing—"

"No one will find out."

"My point is, it won't just be your job on the line."

He hadn't wanted to pull out the big guns, but Alejandro was leaving him no choice. "If it weren't for me, little brother, you wouldn't be in that cushy position."

Though Alejandro had planned to wait until his career was established for marriage and kids, Alana had become pregnant with Alex during Alejandro's last year of law school. With a wife and baby to support, he couldn't afford to stay at the top-notch school he'd been attending without Emilio's financial help.

Emilio had never held that over him. Until now.

Alejandro cursed again and Emilio knew he had him. "I hope you know what you're doing."

"I do."

"I'll be honest though, and you did not hear this from me, but with a little more pressure from her lawyer, we would have agreed to a deal on her mother's charge. She would have likely come out of this with probation."

"Isabelle's lawyer told her you wouldn't deal."

"It's called playing hardball, big brother. And maybe her lawyer isn't giving her the best advice."

"What do you mean?"

"I'm not at liberty to say."

"Is he a hack or something?"

"Not at all. He was Betts's lawyer. Clifton Stone. A real shark. And he's representing her *pro bono*."

"Why?"

"She's broke. All assets were frozen when she and Betts were arrested, and everything they owned was auctioned off for restitution."

"Everything?"

"Yeah. It was weird that she didn't fight for anything. No clothes or jewelry. She just gave it all up."

"I thought there was several million unrecovered."

"If she's got money stashed somewhere, she's not touching it."

That could have simply meant that the minute her mother's name was cleared, she would disappear. Why pay for a top-notch defense when she wouldn't be sticking around to hear the verdict? The crappy motel and the outdated clothes could have all been another part of the ruse.

"So why is her lawyer giving her bad advice?"

"That's a good question."

One he obviously had no intention of answering. Not that it mattered to Emilio either way.

"Are you sure this is about revenge?" Alejandro asked.

"What else would it be?"

"All these years there hasn't been anyone special in your life. What if deep down you still have feelings for her? Maybe you still love her."

"Impossible." His heart had been broken beyond repair, and had since hardened into an empty shell. He had no love left to give.

* * *

Emilio had a beautiful house. But Isabelle wouldn't have expected any less. The sprawling stucco estate was located in one of El Paso's most prestigious communities. She knew this for a fact because, until she married Lenny, she used to live in the very same area. Her parents' home had been less than two blocks away. Though she was willing to bet from the facade that this was even larger and more lavish. It was exactly the sort of place Emilio used to talk about owning someday. He'd always set his sights high, and it looked as though he'd gotten everything he ever wanted.

She was happy for him, because he deserved it. Deep down she wished she could have been part of his life, wished she still could be, but it was too late now. Clearly the damage she had done was irreparable. Some people weren't meant to have it all, and a long time ago she had come to terms with the fact that she was one of those people.

Not that she was feeling sorry for herself. In fact, she considered herself very lucky. The fifteen years she had been married to Lenny, she'd had a pretty good life. She had never wanted for a thing. Except a man who loved and desired her, but Lenny had loved her in his own way. If nothing else, she had been safe.

Until the indictment, anyway.

But she would have years in prison to contemplate her mistakes and think about what might have been. All that mattered now was clearing her mother's name.

The limo stopped out front and the driver opened the door for her. The temperature had dipped into the low fifties with the setting sun and she shivered under her light sweater. She was going to have to think about getting herself some warmer clothes and a winter jacket.

It was dark out, but the house and grounds were well lit. Still, she felt uneasy as the driver pulled her bag from the back. He set it on the Spanish tile drive, then with a tip of his hat he climbed back into the limo. As he drove off, Isabelle took a deep breath, grabbed her bag and walked to the porch, a two-story high structure bracketed by a pair of massive white columns and showcased with etched glass double doors. Above the door was an enormous, round leaded window that she imagined let in amazing morning light.

Since Emilio knew what time she was arriving, she'd half expected him to be waiting there to greet her, but there was no sign of him so she walked up the steps and rang the bell. A minute passed, then another, but no one came to the door. She wondered if maybe the bell was broken, and knocked instead. Several more minutes passed, and she began to think he might not be home. Was he held up at the office? And what was she supposed to do? Sit there and wait?

She had a sudden sinking feeling. What if this was some sort of trick? Some sick revenge. What if he'd never planned to let her in? Hell, maybe this wasn't even his house.

No, he wouldn't do that. He may have been angry with her, he may have even hated her, but he could never be that cruel. When they were together he had been the kindest, gentlest man she had ever known.

She reached up to ring the bell one last time when behind her someone said, "I'm not home."

Her heart slammed against her rib cage and she spun around to find Emilio looking up at her from the driveway. He wore a nylon jacket and jogging pants, his forehead was dotted with perspiration and he was out of breath.

Still a jogger. Back in college, he'd been diligent about

keeping in shape. He'd even convinced her to go to the gym with him a few times, but to the annoyance of her friends, her naturally slim build never necessitated regular exercise.

He stepped up to the porch and stopped so close to her that she could practically feel the heat radiating off his body. He smelled of a tantalizing combination of aftershave, evening air and red-blooded man. She was torn between the desire to lean close and breathe him in, or run like hell. Instead she stood her ground, met his penetrating gaze. He'd always been tall, but now he seemed to tower over her with the same long, lean build as in his youth. The years had been good to him.

He looked at her luggage, then her. "Where's the rest?"

"This is all I brought."

One dark brow rose. A move so familiar, she felt a jab of nostalgia, a longing for the way things used to be. One he clearly did not share.

"You travel light," he said.

Pretty much everything she owned was in that one piece of luggage. A few of her mother's fashion rejects and the rest she'd purchased at the thrift store. When the feds had seized their home, she hadn't tried or even wanted to keep any of the possessions. She couldn't stand the thought of wearing clothes that she knew had been purchased with stolen money.

The clothes, the state of the art electronic equipment, the fine jewelry and priceless art had all been auctioned off, and other than her coffee/espresso machine, she didn't miss any of it.

Leaving the bag right where it was—she hadn't really expected him to carry it for her—Emilio turned and punched in a code on the pad beside the door. She heard a click as the lock disengaged, and as he opened the door the lights automatically switched on.

She picked up her bag and followed him inside, nearly gasping at the magnificence of the interior. The two-story foyer opened up into a grand front room with a curved, dual marble stairway. In the center hung an ornately fashioned wrought iron chandelier that matched the banister. The walls were painted a tasteful cream color, with boldly colored accents.

"It's lovely," she said.

"I'll show you to your quarters, then give you a tour. My housekeeper left a list of your daily duties and sample menus for you to follow."

"You didn't fire her, I hope."

He shot her a stern look. "Of course not. I gave her a month paid vacation."

That was generous of him. He could obviously afford it. She was thankful the woman had left instructions. What Isabelle knew about cooking and cleaning could be listed on an index card with lines to spare, but she was determined to learn. How hard could it be?

Emilio led her through an enormous kitchen with polished mahogany cabinets, marble countertops and top-of-the-line steel appliances, past a small bathroom and laundry room to the maid's quarters in the back.

So, this was where she would spend the next thirty days. It was barely large enough to hold a single bed, a small wood desk and padded folding chair, and a tall, narrow chest of drawers. The walls were white and completely bare but for the small crucifix hanging above the bed. It wasn't luxurious by any stretch of the imagination, but it was clean and safe, which was more than she could say for her motel. Checking out of that hellhole, knowing she would no longer wake in the middle of the night to the sound of roaches and rodents scratching in the walls, and God only knows what sort of illegal activity just outside her door, had in itself almost been worth a month of humiliation.

She set her bag on the faded blue bedspread. "Where is your housekeeper staying while I'm here?" she asked. She hoped not in the house. The idea of someone watching over her shoulder made her uneasy. This would be humiliating enough without an audience.

"She's not a live-in. I prefer my privacy."

"Yet, you're letting *me* stay," she said.

Up went the brow again. "I could move you into the pool house if you'd prefer. Although you may find the lack of heat less than hospitable."

She was going to have to curb the snippy comments. At this point it probably wouldn't take much for him to back out of their deal.

He nodded toward the chest. "You'll find your uniform in the top drawer."

Uniform? He never said anything about her wearing a uniform. For one horrifying instant she wondered if he would seize the opportunity to inflict even more humiliation by making her wear a revealing French maid's outfit. Or something even worse.

She pulled the drawer open, relieved to find a plain, drab gray, white collared dress. The same kind his mother wore when she worked for Isabelle's parents. She almost asked how he knew what size to get, but upon close inspection realized that the garment would be too big.

She slid the drawer closed and turned to face Emilio. He stood just inside the doorway, arms folded, expression dark—an overwhelming presence in the modest space. And he was blocking the door.

She felt a quick jab of alarm.

She was cornered. In a bedroom no less. What if his

intentions were less than noble? What if he'd brought her here so he could take what she'd denied him fifteen years ago?

Of course he wouldn't. Any man who would wait a year to be with a woman knew a thing or two about self-control. Besides, why would he want to have sex with someone he clearly hated? He wasn't that sort of man. At least, he never used to be.

He must have sensed her apprehension. That damned brow lifted again and he asked, with a look of amusement, "Do I frighten you, Izzie?"

Three

Izzie. Emilio was the only one who ever called her that. Hearing it again, after so many years, made Isabelle long to recapture the happiness of those days. The sense of hopefulness. The feeling that as long as they had each other, they could overcome any obstacles.

How wrong she had been. She'd discovered that there were some obstacles she would never overcome. At least, not until it was too late.

She squared her shoulders and told Emilio, "You don't scare me."

He stepped closer. "Are you sure? For a second there, I could swear you looked nervous."

She resisted the urge to take a step back. But not from fear. She just didn't appreciate him violating her personal space. She didn't like the way it made her feel. Out of control. Defenseless. His presence still did something to her after all this time. He would never know how hard it had been to tell him no back then, to wait. So many times she had come *this close* to giving in. If he had pushed a little harder, she probably would have. But he had been too much of a gentleman. A genuinely good guy. He had respected her.

Not anymore.

"I know you," she said. "You're harmless."

He moved even closer, so she had to crane her neck to look into his eyes. "Maybe I've changed."

Unlikely. And she refused to back down, to let him intimidate her.

She folded her arms and glared up at him, and after a few seconds more he backed away, then he turned and walked out. She assumed she was meant to follow him. A proper host would have given her time to unpack and freshen up. He might have offered her something to drink. But he wasn't her host. He was her employer. Or more appropriately, her warden. This was just a prison of a different kind. A prison of hurt and regret.

On the kitchen counter lay the duty list he'd mentioned. He handed it to her and when she saw that it was *eight* pages single-spaced she nearly swallowed her own tongue. Her shock must have shown, because that damned brow quirked up and Emilio asked, "Problem?"

She swallowed hard and shook her head. "None at all."

She flipped through it, seeing that it was efficiently organized by room and listed which chores should be performed on which day. Some things, like vacuuming the guest rooms and polishing the chrome in the corresponding bathrooms, were done on a weekly basis, alternating one of the five spare bedrooms every day. Other duties such as dusting the marble in the entryway and polishing the kitchen counters was a daily task. That didn't even include the cooking.

It was difficult to believe that one person could accomplish this much in one day. From the looks of it, she would be working from dawn to dusk without a break.

"I'm putting a few final touches on the menus, but you'll have them first thing tomorrow," Emilio said. "I'm assuming you can cook."

Not if it meant doing much more than heating a frozen dinner in the microwave or boiling water on a hot plate. "I'll manage."

"Of course you'll be responsible for all the shopping as well. You'll have a car at your disposal. And you're welcome to eat whatever you desire." He gave her a quick once-over, not bothering to hide his distaste. "Although from the looks of you, I'm guessing you don't eat much."

Eating required money and that was in short supply these days. She refused to sponge off her mother, whose financial situation was only slightly less grave, and no one was interested in hiring a thief six weeks from a twenty-to-life visit to the slammer. Besides, Isabelle had been such a nervous wreck lately, every time she tried to eat she would get a huge lump in her throat, through which food simply refused to pass.

She shrugged. "Like they say in Hollywood, there's no such thing as too thin."

"I see you still have the same irrational hang-ups about your body," he snapped back, his contempt so thick she could have choked on it. "I remember that you would only undress in the dark and hide under the covers when I turned the light on."

Her only hang-up had been with letting Emilio see the scars and bruises. He would have wanted an explanation, and she knew that if she'd told him the truth, something bad would happen. She'd done it to protect him and he was throwing it back in her face.

If this was a preview of what she should expect from the next thirty days, it would be a long month. But she could take it. And the less she said, the better.

The fact that she remained silent, that she didn't rise to her own defense, seemed to puzzle him. She waited for his next attack, but instead he gestured her out of the kitchen. "The living room is this way."

If he had more barbs to throw, he was saving them for another time.

She could hardly wait.

Though Emilio's hospitality left a lot to be desired, his home had all the comforts a person could possibly need. Six bedrooms and eight baths, a state of the art media room and a fitness/game room complete with autographed sports memorabilia. He had a penchant for Mexican pottery and an art collection so vast he could open a gallery. The house was furnished and decorated with a lively, southwestern flair.

It was as close to perfect as a home could be, the apotheosis of his ambitions, yet for some reason it seemed…empty. Perfect to the point of feeling almost unoccupied. Or maybe it simply lacked a woman's touch.

When they got to the master suite he stopped outside the door. "This room is off-limits. The same goes for my office downstairs."

Fine with her. That much less work as far as she was concerned. Besides, his bedroom was the last place she wanted to be spending any time.

He ended the tour there, and they walked back down to the kitchen. "Be sure you study that list, as I expect you to adhere to those exact specifications."

Her work would be exemplary. Now that she'd had a taste of how bitter he was, it was essential that she not give him a single reason to find fault with her performance. Too much was at stake. "If there's nothing more, I'll go to my room now," she said.

"No need to rush off." He peeled off his jacket and tossed it over the back of a kitchen chair. Underneath he wore a form-fitting muscle shirt that accentuated every plane of lean muscle in his chest and abs, and she was far from immune to the physical draw of an attractive man. Especially one she had never completely fallen out of love with. Meaning the less time she spent with him, the better.

He grabbed a bottled water from the fridge, but didn't offer her one. "It's early. Stick around for a while."

"I'm tired," she told him. "And I need to study that list."

"But we haven't had a chance to catch up." He propped himself against the counter, as though he was settling in for a friendly chat. "What have you been up to the past fifteen years? Besides defrauding the better part of Texas high society."

She bit the inside of her cheek.

"You know what I find ironic? I'll bet if your parents had to guess who they thought was more likely to go to federal prison, you or me, they would have chosen the son of Cuban immigrants over their precious daughter."

Apparently his idea of catching up would consist of thinly veiled insults and jabs at her character. *Swell.*

"No opinion?" he asked, clearly hoping she would retaliate, but she refused to be baited. Others had said much worse and she'd managed to ignore them, too. Reporters and law officials, although the worst of it had come from people who had supposedly been her friends. But she wouldn't begrudge a single one of them their very strong opinions. Even if the only thing she was truly guilty of was stupidity.

"It's just as well," Emilio said. "I have work to catch up on."

Struggling to keep her face devoid of emotion so he wouldn't see how relieved she was, she grabbed the list and walked to her quarters, ultra-aware of his gaze boring into her back. Once inside she closed the door and leaned against it. She hadn't been lying, she was truly exhausted. She couldn't recall the last time she'd had a decent night's sleep.

She gazed longingly at the bed, but it was still early, and she had to at least make an effort to familiarize herself with her duties before she succumbed to exhaustion.

She hung her sweater on the back of the folding chair and sat down, setting the list in front of her on the desk.

According to the housekeeper's schedule, Emilio's car picked him up at seven-thirty sharp, so Isabelle had to be up no later than six-thirty to fix his coffee and make his breakfast. If she was in bed by ten, she would get a solid eight and a half hours' sleep. About double what she'd been getting at the motel if she counted all the times she was jolted awake by strange noises. The idea of feeling safe and secure while she slept was an enticing one, as was the anticipation of eating something other than ramen noodles for breakfast, lunch and dinner.

If she could manage to avoid Emilio, staying here might not be so bad after all.

Usually Emilio slept like a baby, but knowing he wasn't alone in the house had him tossing and turning most of the night.

It had been odd, after so many years apart, to see Isabelle standing on his front porch waiting for him. After she married Betts, Emilio had intended never to cross paths with her again. He'd declined invitations to functions that he knew she would be attending and chose his friends and acquaintances with the utmost care.

He had done everything in his power to avoid her, yet here she was, sleeping in his servants' quarters. Maybe the pool house would have been a better alternative.

He stared through the dark at the ceiling, recalling their exchange of words earlier. Isabelle had changed. She used to be so subdued and timid. She would have recoiled from his angry words and cowered in the face of his resentment, and she never would have dished out any caustic comments of her own. A life of crime must have hardened her.

But what had Alejandro said? She was guilty on paper, but there had been new developments. Could she be innocent?

That didn't change what she had done to him, and what her father had done to Emilio's family. She could have implored him to keep his mother on as an employee, or to at least give her a positive recommendation. She hadn't even tried.

In a way, he wished he had never met her. But according to her, it was destiny. She used to say she knew from the first moment she laid eyes on him that they were meant to be with one another, that fate had drawn them together. Although technically he had known her for years before he'd ever really noticed her. His mother drove them to school in the mornings, he and his brothers to public school and Izzie to the private girls' school down the road, and other than an occasional "hi," she barely spoke to him. To him, she had never been more than the daughter of his mother's employer, a girl too conceited to give him the time of day. Only later had she admitted that she'd had such a crush on him that she'd been too tongue-tied to speak.

During his junior year of high school he'd gotten his own car and rarely saw her after that. Then, when he was in college, she had shown up out of the blue at the house he'd rented on campus for the summer session. She had just graduated from high school and planned to attend classes there in the fall. She asked if he would show her around campus.

Though it seemed an odd request considering they had barely ever spoken, he felt obligated, since her parents paid his mother's salary. They spent the afternoon together, walking and chatting, and in those few hours he began to see a side of her that he hadn't known existed. She was intelligent and witty, but with a childlike innocence he found compelling. He realized that what he had once mistaken for conceit and entitlement was really shyness and self-doubt. He found that he could open up to her, that despite their vast social differences, she understood him. He liked her, and there was no doubt she had romantic feelings toward him, but she was young and naive and he knew her parents would never approve of their daughter dating the son of the hired help. He decided that they could be friends, but nothing more.

Then she kissed him.

He had walked her back to her car and they were saying goodbye. Without warning she threw her arms around his neck and pressed her lips to his. He was stunned—and aroused—and though he knew he should stop her, the scent of her skin and the taste of her lips were irresistible. They stood there in the dark kissing for a long time, until she said she had to get home. But by then it was too late. He was hooked.

He spent every minute he wasn't at work or in class that summer with her, and when they were apart it was torture. They were only dating two weeks when he told her he loved her, and after a month he knew he wanted to marry her, but he waited until their six month anniversary to ask her formally.

They figured that if they both saved money until the

end of the school year they would have enough to get a small place together, then they would elope. He warned her it would be tight for a while, maybe even years, until he established his career. She swore it didn't matter as long as they were together.

But in the end it *had* mattered.

Emilio let out an exasperated sigh and looked at the clock. Two-thirty. If he lay here rehashing his mistakes he was never going to get to sleep. These were issues he'd resolved a long time ago. Or so he'd thought.

Maybe bringing Isabelle into his home had been a bad idea. Was revenge really worth a month of sleepless nights? He just had to remind himself how well he would sleep when his family was vindicated.

Emilio eventually drifted off to sleep, then roused again at four-fifteen wide-awake. After an unsuccessful half hour of trying to fall back to sleep, he got out of bed and went down to his office. He worked for a while, then spent an hour in the fitness room before going upstairs to get ready for work. He came back down at seven, expecting his coffee and breakfast to be waiting for him, but the kitchen was dark.

He shook his head, disappointed, but not surprised. His new housekeeper was not off to a good start. Her first day on the job could very well be her last.

He walked back to her quarters and raised his hand to knock, then noticed the door wasn't latched. With his foot he gave it a gentle shove and it creaked open. He expected to find Isabelle curled up in bed. Instead she sat slumped over at the desk, head resting on her arms, sound asleep. She was still wearing the clothes from last night, and on the desk, under her arms, lay the list of her duties. Her bag sat open but unpacked on the bed, and the covers hadn't been disturbed.

She must have dozed off shortly after going to her room, and she must have been pretty exhausted to sleep in such an awkward position all night.

He sighed and shook his head. At least one of them had gotten a good night's rest.

A part of him wanted to be angry with her, wanted to send her packing for neglecting her duties, but he had the feeling this had been an unintentional oversight. He would give her the benefit of the doubt. Just this once. But he wouldn't deny himself the pleasure of giving her a hard time about it.

Four

"Isabelle!"

Isabelle shot up with such force she nearly flung the chair over, blinking furiously, trying to get her bearings. She saw Emilio standing in the doorway and her eyes went wide. "Wh-what time is it?"

"Three minutes after seven." He folded his arms, kept his mouth in a grim line. "Were you expecting breakfast in bed?"

Her skin paled. "I was going to set the alarm on my phone. I must have fallen asleep before I had the chance."

"And you consider that a valid excuse for neglecting your duties?"

"No, you're right. I screwed up." She squared her shoulders and rose stiffly from the chair. "I'll pack my things and be out of here before you leave from work."

For a second he thought she was playing the sympathy

card, but she wore a look of resigned hopelessness that said she seriously expected him to terminate their agreement.

He probably should have, but if he let her go now he would be denying himself the pleasure of breaking her. Lucky for her, he was feeling generous this morning. "If you leave, who will make my coffee?"

She gazed up at him with hope in her eyes. "Does that mean you're giving me a second chance?"

"Don't let it happen again. Next time I won't be so forgiving."

"I won't, I promise." She looked over at the dresser. "My uniform—"

"Coffee first."

"What about breakfast?"

"No time. I only have twenty-five minutes until the company car is here to pick me up."

"Sorry." She edged past him through the door and scurried to the kitchen.

He went to his office to put the necessary paperwork in his briefcase, and when he walked back into the kitchen several minutes later the coffee was brewed. Isabelle wasn't there, so he grabbed a travel mug and filled it himself. He took a sip, surprised to realize that it was actually good. A little stronger than his housekeeper, Mrs. Medina, usually made it, but he liked it.

Isabelle emerged from her room a minute later wearing her uniform. He looked her up and down and frowned. The oversize garment hung on her, accentuating her skeletal physique. "It's too big."

She shrugged. "It's okay."

It was an old uniform a former employee had left so he hadn't really expected it to fit. "You'll need a new one."

"It's only for thirty days. It's fine."

"It is not *fine*. It looks terrible. Tell me what size you wear and I'll have a new one sent to the house."

She chewed her lip, avoiding his gaze.

"Are you going to tell me, or should I guess?"

"I'm not exactly sure. I've lost weight recently."

"So tell me your weight and height and they can send over the appropriate size."

"I'm five foot four."

"And…?"

She looked at the floor.

"Your weight, Isabelle?"

She shrugged.

"You don't know how much you weigh?"

"I don't own a scale."

He sighed. Why did she have to make everything so difficult?

"Fitness room," he said, gesturing to the doorway. "I have a scale in there."

She reluctantly followed him and was even less enthusiastic about getting on the digital scale. As she stepped on she averted her eyes.

The number that popped up was nothing short of disturbing. "Considering your height, you have to be at least fifteen or twenty pounds underweight."

Isabelle glanced at the display, and if her grimace was any indication, she was equally unsettled by the number. Not the reaction he would have expected from someone with a "there's no such thing as too thin" dictum.

"Am I correct in assuming this weight loss wasn't intentional?" he asked.

She nodded.

It hadn't occurred to him before, but what if there was something wrong with her? "Are you ill?"

She stepped down off the scale. "It's been a stressful couple of months."

"That's no excuse to neglect your health. While you're here I expect you to eat three meals a day, and I intend to make you climb on that scale daily until you've gained at least fifteen pounds."

Her eyes rounded with surprise.

"Is that a problem?" he asked.

For an instant she looked as though she would argue, then she pulled her lip between her teeth and shook her head.

"Good." He looked at his watch. "I have to go. I'll be home at six-thirty. I expect dinner to be ready no later than seven."

"Yes, sir."

There was a note of ambivalence in her tone, but he let it slide. The subject of her weight was clearly a touchy one. A fact he planned to exploit. And he had the distinct feeling there was more to the story than she would admit. Just one more piece to this puzzle of a woman who he thought he knew, but wasn't at all what he had expected.

Though Isabelle wasn't sure what her father had paid Emilio's mother, she was positive it wasn't close to enough.

She never imagined taking care of a house could be so exhausting. The dusting alone had taken nearly three hours, and she'd spent another two and a half on the windows and mirrors on the first floor. Both tasks had required more bending and stretching than any yoga class she'd ever attended, and she'd climbed the stairs so many times her legs felt limp.

Worse than the physical exhaustion was how inept she was at using the most basic of household appliances. It had taken her ten minutes to find the "on" switch on the vacuum, and one frayed corner on the upstairs runner to learn that the carpet setting didn't work well for fringed rugs. They got sucked up into the spinny thing inside and ripped off. She just hoped that Emilio didn't notice. She would have to figure out some way to pay to get it fixed. And soon.

Probably her most puzzling dilemma was the cupboard full of solutions, waxes and paraphernalia she was supposed to use in her duties. Never had she imagined there were so many different types of cleaning products. She spent an hour reading the labels, trying to determine which suited her various tasks, which put her even further behind in her duties.

Her new uniforms arrived at three-thirty by messenger. Emilio had ordered four in two different sizes, probably to accommodate the weight he was expecting her to gain. The smallest size fit perfectly and was far less unflattering than the oversize version. In fact, it fit better and looked nicer than most of the street clothes she currently owned. Too bad it didn't contain magic powers that made her at least a little less inept at her duties.

When she heard Emilio come through the front door at six-thirty, she hadn't even started on the upstairs guest room yet. She steeled herself for his latest round of insults and jabs and as he stepped into the kitchen, travel cup in one hand, his briefcase in the other, her heart sailed up into her throat. He looked exhausted and rumpled in a sexy way.

He set his cup in the sink. Though she was probably inviting trouble, she asked, "How was work?"

"Long, and unproductive," he said, loosening his tie. "How was your day?"

A civilized response? Whoa. She hadn't expected that. "It was...good."

"I see you haven't burned the house down. That's promising."

So much for being civil.

"I'm going to go change," he said. "I trust dinner will be ready on time."

"Of course." At least she hoped so. It had taken her a bit longer to assemble the chicken dish than she'd anticipated, so to save cooking time, she'd raised the oven heat by one hundred degrees.

He gave her a dismissive nod, then left the room. She heard the heavy thud of his footsteps as he climbed the stairs. With any luck he wouldn't look down.

A minute passed, and she began to think that she was safe, then he thundered from the upstairs hallway, "Isabelle!"

Shoot.

It was still possible it wasn't the rug he was upset about. Maybe he'd checked the guest room and saw that she hadn't cleaned it yet. She walked to the stairs, climbing them slowly, her hopes plummeting when she reached the top and saw him standing with his arms folded, lips thinned, looking at the corner of the runner.

"Is there something you need to tell me?" he asked.

It figured that he would ignore all the things she had done right and focus in on the one thing she had done wrong. "The vacuum ate your rug."

"It *ate* it?"

"I had it on the wrong setting. I take full responsibility." As if it could somehow *not* be her fault.

"Why didn't you mention this when I asked how your day went?"

"I forgot?"

One dark brow rose. "Is that a question?"

She took a deep breath and blew it out. "Okay, I was hoping you wouldn't notice."

"I notice *everything*."

Apparently. "I'll pay for the damage."

"How?"

Good question. "I'll figure something out."

She expected him to push the issue, but he didn't.

"Is there anything else you've neglected to mention?"

Nothing she hadn't managed to fix, unless she counted the plastic container she'd melted in the microwave, but he would never notice that.

She shook her head.

Emilio studied her, as if he were sizing her up, and she felt herself withering under his scrutiny.

"That's better," he said.

She blinked. "Better?"

"The uniform. It actually fits."

Did he just compliment her? Albeit in a backhanded, slightly rude way. But it was a start.

"You ate today?" he asked.

"Twice." For breakfast she'd made herself fried eggs swimming in butter with rye toast slathered in jam and for lunch she'd heated a can of clam chowder. It had been heavenly.

He looked down at the rug again. "This will have to be rebound."

"I'll take care of it first thing tomorrow."

"Let me know how much it will be and I'll write a check."

"I'll pay you back a soon as I can." She wondered what the hourly wage was to make license plates.

"Yes, you will." He turned and walked into his bedroom, shutting the door.

Isabelle blew out a relieved breath. That hadn't gone

nearly as bad as she'd expected. With any hope, dinner would be a smashing success and he would be so pleased he would forget all about the rug.

Though she had the sneaking suspicion that if it was the most amazing meal he'd ever tasted, he would complain on principle.

Dinner was a culinary catastrophe.

She served him overcooked, leathery chicken in lumpy white sauce with a side of scorched rice pilaf and a bowl of wilted salad swimming in dressing. He wouldn't feed it to his dog—if he had one. But what had Emilio expected from someone who had probably never cooked a meal in her entire life?

Isabelle hadn't stuck around to witness the aftermath. She'd fixed his plate, then vanished. He'd come downstairs to find it sitting on the dining room table accompanied by a highball glass *full* of scotch. Maybe she thought that if she got him good and toasted, he wouldn't notice the disastrous meal.

He carried his plate to the kitchen and dumped the contents in the trash, then fixed himself a peanut butter and jelly sandwich and ate standing at the kitchen sink. Which he noted was a disaster area. Considering all the dirty pots and pans and dishes, it looked as though she'd prepared a ten course meal. He hoped she planned to come out of hiding and clean it up.

As he was walking to his office, drink in hand, he heard the hum of the vacuum upstairs. Why the hell was she cleaning at seven-thirty in the evening?

He climbed the stairs and followed the sound to the first guest bedroom. Her back was to him as she vacuumed around the queen-size bed. He leaned in the doorway and watched her. The new uniform was a major improvement, but she still looked painfully thin. She had always been finely boned and willowy, but now she looked downright scrawny.

But still beautiful. He used to love watching her, even if she was doing nothing more than sitting on his bed doing her class work. He never got tired of looking at her. Even now she possessed a poise and grace that was almost hypnotizing.

She turned to do the opposite side of the bed and when she saw him standing there she jolted with alarm. She hit the Off switch.

"Surprised to see me?" he asked.

She looked exhausted. "Did you need something?"

"I just thought you'd like to know that it didn't work."

She frowned. "What didn't work?"

"Your attempt to poison me."

He could see that he'd hurt her feelings, but she lifted her chin in defiance and said, "Well, you can't blame a girl for trying. Besides, now that I think about it, smothering you in your sleep will be so much more fun."

He nearly cracked a smile. "Is that why you're trying to incapacitate me with excessive amounts of scotch?"

She shrugged. "It's always easier when they don't fight back."

She'd always had a wry sense of humor. He just hadn't expected her to exercise it. Unless she wasn't joking. It might not be a bad idea to lock his bedroom door. Just in case.

"Why are you up here cleaning?" he asked.

She looked at him funny, as though she thought it was a trick question. "Because that's what you brought me here to do?"

"What I mean is, shouldn't you be finished for the day?"

"Maybe I should be, but I'm not."

It probably wasn't helping that he'd instructed Mrs. Medina to toss in a few extra tasks on top of her regular duties, though he hadn't anticipated it taking Isabelle quite this long. He'd just wanted to keep her busy during the day. Apparently it had worked. A little *too* well.

"I have work to do and the noise is distracting," he told her.

She had this look, like she wanted to say something snotty or sarcastic, but she restrained herself. "I'll try to keep the noise down."

"See that you do. And I hope you're planning to clean the kitchen. It's a mess."

He could tell she was exasperated but struggling to suppress it. "It's on my list."

He wondered what it would take to make her explode. How far he would have to push. In all the time they were together, he'd never once seen her lose her temper. Whenever they came close to having a disagreement she would just…shut down. He'd always wondered what it would be like to get her good and riled up.

It was an intriguing idea, but tonight he just didn't have the energy.

He turned to leave and she said, "Emilio?"

He looked back.

"I'm really sorry about dinner."

This was his chance to twist the knife, to put her in her place, but she looked so damned humble he didn't have the heart. She really was trying, holding up her end of the bargain. And he…well, hell, he was obviously going soft or something. He'd lost his killer instinct.

"Maybe tomorrow you could try something a little less complicated," he said.

"I will."

As he walked away the vacuum switched back on.

Despite a few screwups, her first day had been less of a disaster than he'd anticipated.

Emilio settled at his desk and booted his computer, and after a few minutes the vacuum went silent. About forty-five minutes later he heard her banging around in the kitchen. That continued for a good hour, then there was silence.

At eleven he shut down his computer, turned off the lights in his office and walked to the kitchen. It was back to its previous, clean state, and his travel cup was washed and sitting beside the coffeemaker. He dumped what was left of his drink down the drain, set his glass in the sink and was about to head upstairs when he noticed she'd left the laundry room light on. He walked back to switch it off and saw that Isabelle's door was open a crack and the desk lamp was on.

Maybe he should remind her to set her alarm, so he didn't have to get breakfast in the coffee shop at work again tomorrow.

He knocked lightly on her door. When she didn't answer, he eased it open. Isabelle was lying face down, spread-eagle on her bed, still dressed in her uniform, sound asleep. She hadn't even taken off her shoes. She must have dropped down and gone out like a light. At least this time she'd made it to the bed. And on the bright side, she seemed in no condition to be smothering him in his sleep.

The hem of her uniform had pulled up, giving him a nice view of the backs of her thighs. They were smooth and creamy and he couldn't help but imagine how it would feel to touch her. To lay a hand on her thigh and slide it upward, under her dress.

The sudden flash of heat in his blood, the intense pull of arousal in his groin, caught him off guard.

Despite all that had happened, he still desired her.

Maybe his body remembered what his brain had struggled to suppress. How good they had been together.

Though they had never made love, they had touched each other intimately, given each other pleasure. Isabelle hadn't done much more than kiss a boy before they began dating. She had been the most inexperienced eighteen-year-old he'd ever met, but eager to learn, and more than willing to experiment, so long as they didn't go all the way. He had respected her decision to wait until marriage to make love and admired her principles, so he hadn't pushed. Besides, it hadn't stopped them from finding other ways to satisfy their sexual urges.

One thing he never understood though was why she had been so shy about letting him see her body. Despite what he had told her yesterday, he'd never believed it had anything to do with vanity. Quite the opposite. For reasons he'd never been able to understand, she'd had a dismally low opinion of herself.

After she left him, he began to wonder if it had all been an act to manipulate him. Maybe she hadn't been so innocent after all. To this day he wasn't sure, and he would probably never know the truth. He was long past caring either way.

He shut off the light and stepped out of her room, closing the door behind him. The lack of sleep was catching up to him. He was exhausted. What he needed was a good night's rest.

Everything would be clearer in the morning.

Five

Isabelle hated lying. Especially to her mother, but in this case she didn't have much choice. There was no way she could admit the truth.

They sat at the small kitchen table in her mother's apartment, having tea. Isabelle had been avoiding her calls for three days now, since she moved into Emilio's house, but in her mother's last message her voice had been laced with concern.

"I went by the motel but they told me you checked out. Where are you, Isabelle?"

Isabelle had no choice but to stop by her mother's apartment on her way home from the grocery store Thursday morning. Besides, she'd picked up a few things for her.

"So, your new job is a live-in position?" her mother asked.

"Room and board," Isabelle told her. "And she lets me use her car for running errands."

"What a perfect position for you." She rubbed Isabelle's arm affectionately. "You've always loved helping people."

"She still gets around well for her age, but her memory isn't great. Her kids are afraid she'll leave the stove on and burn the house down. Plus she can't drive anymore. She needs me to take her to doctor appointments."

"Well, I think it's wonderful that you're moving on with your life. I know the last few months have been difficult for you."

"They haven't been easy for you, either." And all because of Isabelle's stupidity. Not that her mother ever blamed her. She'd been duped by Lenny, too, and held him one hundred percent responsible.

"It's really not so bad. I've made a few new friends in the building and I like my job at the boutique."

Though her mother would never admit it, it had to be humiliating selling designer fashions to women she used to socialize with. But considering she had never worked a day in her life, not to mention the indictment, she had been lucky to find a job at all. Even if her salary was barely enough to get by on. It pained Isabelle that her mother had to leave the luxury of her condo to live in this dumpy little apartment. She'd endured so much pain and heartache in her life, she deserved better than this.

"This woman you work for…what did you say her name is?" her mother asked.

She hadn't. That was one part of the lie she'd forgotten about. "Mrs. Smith," she said, cringing at her lack of originality. "Mary Smith."

Why hadn't she gone with something really unique, like Jane Doe?

"Where does Mrs. Smith live?"

"Not too far from our old house."

Her brow crinkled. "Hmm, the name isn't familiar. I thought I knew everyone in that area."

"She's a very nice woman. I think you would like her."

"I'd like to meet her. Maybe I'll come by for a visit."

Crap. Wouldn't she be shocked to learn that Mrs. Smith was actually Mr. Suarez.

"I'll talk to her children and see if it's okay," Isabelle told her. She would just have to stall for the next month.

"Have you been keeping up with the news about Western Oil?" her mother asked, and Isabelle's heart stalled. Did she suspect something? Why would she bring Emilio up out of the blue like that?

"Not really," she lied. "I don't watch television."

"They showed a clip of Emilio and his partners at a press conference on the news the other day. He looks good. He's obviously done well for himself."

"I guess he has."

"Maybe you should…talk to him."

"Why?"

"I thought that maybe he would talk to his brother on your behalf."

"He wouldn't. And it wouldn't matter if he did. I'm going to prison. Nothing is going to stop that now."

"You don't know that."

"Yes, I do."

She shook her head. "Lenny would never let that happen. He may have been a thief, but he loved you."

"Lenny is dead." Even if he had intended to absolve her of guilt, he couldn't do it from the grave. It was too late.

"Something will come up. Some new evidence. Everything will be okay."

She looked so sad. Isabelle wished she could tell her

mother the truth, so at least she wouldn't have to worry about her own freedom. But she'd promised Emilio.

Isabelle glanced at her watch. "I really have to get back to work."

"Of course. Thank you for the groceries. You didn't have to do that."

"My living expenses are practically nonexistent now, and as you said, I like helping people."

She walked Isabelle to the door.

"That's a nice car," she said, gesturing to the black Saab parked in the lot.

It was, and it stuck out like a sore thumb amidst the vehicles beside it. "I'll drop by again as soon as I can."

Her mother hugged her hard and said, "I'm very proud of you, sweetheart."

The weight of Isabelle's guilt was suffocating. But she hugged her back and said, "Thanks, Mom."

Her mother waved as she drove away, and Isabelle felt a deep sense of sadness. Hardly a week passed when they didn't speak on the phone, or drop by for visits. They were all the other had anymore. What would her mother do when Isabelle went to prison? She would be all alone. And she was fooling herself if she really believed Isabelle could avoid prison. It was inevitable. Even if Emilio wanted to help her—which he obviously didn't—there was nothing he could do. According to her lawyer, the evidence against her was overwhelming.

Isabelle couldn't worry herself with that right now. If she did the dread and the fear would overwhelm her. She had a household to run. Which was going more smoothly than she had anticipated. Her latest attempts in the kitchen must not have been too awful, either, because Emilio hadn't accused her of trying to poison him since Monday, though he'd found fault with practically everything else she did.

Okay, maybe not *everything*. But when it came to his home, he was a perfectionist. Everything had its place, and God help her if she moved something, or put it away in the wrong spot. Yesterday she'd set the milk on the refrigerator shelf instead of the door and he'd blown a gasket. And yeah, a couple of times she had moved things deliberately, just for the satisfaction of annoying him. He did make it awfully easy.

Other than a few minor snafus, the housekeeping itself was getting much easier. She had settled into a routine, and some of her chores were taking half the time they had when she started. Yesterday she'd even had time to sit down with a cup of tea, put her feet up and read the paper for twenty minutes.

In fact, it was becoming almost *too* easy. And she couldn't help but wonder if the other shoe was about to drop.

Emilio stood by the window in Adam's office, listening to his colleagues discuss the accident at the refinery. OSHA had released its official report and Western Oil was being cited for negligence. According to the investigation, the explosion was triggered by a faulty gauge. Which everyone in the room knew was impossible.

That section had just come back online after several days of mandatory safety checks and equipment upgrades. It had been inspected and reinspected. It wasn't negligence, or an accident. Someone *wanted* that equipment to fail.

The question was why?

"This is ridiculous," Jordan said, slapping the report down on Adam's desk. "Those are good men. They would never let something like this happen."

"Someone is responsible," Nathan said from his seat opposite Adam's desk, which earned him a sharp look from his brother.

Somber, Adam said, "I know you trust and respect every man there, Jordan, but I think we have to come to terms with the fact that it was sabotage."

Thankfully the explosion had occurred while that section was in maintenance mode, and less than half the men who usually worked that shift were on the line. Only a dozen were hurt. But one injured man was too many as far as Emilio was concerned. Between lawsuits and OSHA fines, financially they would take a hit. Even worse was the mark on their good name. Until now they'd had a flawless safety record. Cassandra Benson, Western Oil's public relations director, had been working feverishly to put a positive spin on the situation. But their direct competitor, Birch Energy, owned by Walter Birch, had already taken advantage of the situation. Within days of the incident they released a flood of television ads, and though they didn't directly target Western Oil, the implication was clear— Birch was safe and valued their employees. Western Oil was a death trap.

Western Oil was firing back with ads boasting their innovative techniques and new alternative, environmentally friendly practices.

"I don't suppose you'll tell me how the investigation is going," Jordan said.

Adam and Nathan exchanged a look. When they agreed to launch a private investigation, it was decided that Jordan wouldn't be involved. As Chief Operations Officer he was the one closest to the workers in the refinery. They trusted him, so he needed a certain degree of deniability. A fact Jordan was clearly not happy about.

They had promised to keep him in the loop, but

privately Adam had confided in Emilio that he worried Jordan wouldn't be impartial. That he might ignore key evidence out of loyalty to the workers.

Jordan would be downright furious to know that two of the new men hired to take the place of injured workers were in reality undercover investigators. But the real thorn in Jordan's side was that Nathan was placed in charge of the investigation. That, on top of the competition for the CEO position, had thrust their occasional sibling rivalry into overdrive. Which didn't bode well for either of them. And though Emilio considered both men his friends, there had been tension since Adam announced his intention to retire.

"All I can say is that it's going slowly," Nathan told Jordan. "How is morale?"

"Tom Butler, my foreman, says the men are nervous. They know the line was thoroughly checked before the accident. Rumor is someone in the refinery is to blame for the explosion. They're not sure who to trust."

"A little suspicion could work to our advantage," Nathan said. "If the men are paying attention to one another, another act of sabotage won't be so easy."

Jordan glared at his older sibling. "Yeah, genius. Or the men will be so busy watching their coworkers they won't be paying attention to their own duties and it could cause an accident. A real one this time."

Emilio stifled a smile. Normally Jordan was the most even-tempered of the four, but this situation was turning him into a bona fide hothead.

"Does anyone have anything *constructive* to add?" Adam asked, looking over at Emilio.

"Yeah, Emilio," Jordan said. "You've been awfully quiet. What's your take on this?"

Emilio turned from the window. "You feel betrayed,

Jordan. I get that. But we *will* get to the bottom of this. It's just going to take some time."

After several more minutes of heated debate between Nathan and Jordan that ultimately got them nowhere, Adam ended the meeting and Emilio headed out for the day. He let himself in the house at six-thirty, expecting to find Izzie in the kitchen making what he hoped would be an edible meal. She'd taken his advice to heart and was trying out simpler recipes. The last two nights, dinner hadn't been gourmet by any stretch of the imagination. To call it appetizing had been an even wider stretch, but he'd choked it down.

Tonight he found two pots boiling over on the stove— one with spaghetti sauce and the other noodles—and a cutting board with partially chopped vegetables on the counter. Izzie was nowhere to be found. Perhaps she didn't grasp the concept that food could not cook itself. It required supervision.

Grumbling to himself, he jerked the burner knobs into the Off position, noting the sauce splattered all over the stove. Shedding his suit jacket, he checked her room and the laundry room, but she wasn't there, either. Then he heard a sound from upstairs and headed up.

As soon as he reached the top and saw that his bedroom door was open, his hackles rose. She knew damned well his room was off-limits.

He charged toward the door, just as she emerged. Her eyes flew open wide when she saw him. He started to ask her what the hell she thought she was doing, when he noticed the blood-soaked paper towel she was holding on her left hand.

"I'm sorry," she said. "I didn't mean to invade your privacy. I was looking for a first-aid kit. I thought it might be in your bathroom."

"What happened?"

"I slipped with the knife. It's not a big deal. I just need a bandage."

A cut that bled enough to soak through a paper towel would require more than a bandage. He reached for her hand. "Let me see."

She pulled out of his reach. "I told you, it's not a big deal. It's a small cut."

"Then it won't hurt to let me look at it." Before she could move away again, he grabbed her arm.

He lifted away the paper towels and blood oozed from a wound in the fleshy part between the second and third knuckle of her index finger. He wiped it away to get a better look. The cut may have been small, but it was deep.

So much for a relaxing night at home. He sighed and said, "Get your jacket. I'll drive you to the E.R."

She jerked her hand free. "No! I just need a bandage."

"A bandage is not going to stop the bleeding. You need stitches."

"I'll butterfly it."

"Even if that did work, you still should see a doctor. You could get an infection."

She shook her head. "I'll wash it out and use antibiotic ointment. It'll be fine."

He didn't get why she was making such a big deal about this. "This is ridiculous. I'm taking you to the hospital."

"*No,* you're not."

"Izzie, for God sakes, you need to see a doctor."

"I can't."

"*Why?*"

"Because I have no way to pay for it, okay? I don't have health insurance and I don't have money."

The rush of color to her cheeks, the way she lowered her eyes, said that admitting it to him mortified her.

He assumed she had money stashed somewhere for emergencies, but maybe that wasn't the case. Was she really that destitute?

"Since it was a work-related accident, I'll pay for it," he said.

"I'm not asking for a handout."

"You didn't ask, I offered. You hurt yourself in my home. I consider it my responsibility."

She shook her head. "No."

"Isabelle—"

"I am not going to the doctor. I just need a first-aid kit."

"Obstinado," he muttered, shaking his head. The woman completely baffled him. Why wouldn't she just accept his help? She'd had no problem sponging off her rich husband for all those years. Emilio would have expected her to jump at his offer. Had she suddenly grown a conscience? A sense of pride?

Well, he wasn't going to sit and argue while she bled all over the place. He finally threw up his hands in defeat. "Fine! But I'm wrapping it for you."

For a second he thought she might argue about that too, but she seemed to sense that his patience was wearing thin. "Fine," she replied, then grumbled under her breath, "and you call *me* stubborn."

Six

Isabelle followed Emilio through his bedroom to the bathroom and waited while he grabbed the first-aid kit from the cabinet under the sink. He pulled out the necessary supplies, then gestured her over to the sink and turned on the cold water.

"This is probably going to hurt," he told her, but as he took her hand and placed it under the flow, she didn't even flinch. He gently soaped up the area around the cut with his thumb to clean it, then grabbed a bottle of hydrogen peroxide. Holding her hand over the sink, he poured it on the wound. As it foamed up, her only reaction was a soft intake of breath, even though he knew it had to sting like hell.

He grabbed a clean towel from the cabinet and gently blotted her hand dry. It was starting to clot, so there was hope that a butterfly would be enough to stop any further bleeding if he wrapped it firmly enough. Although he still thought stitches were warranted. Without them it could leave a nasty scar.

He sat on the edge of the counter and pulled her closer, so she was standing between his knees. She didn't fight him, but it was obvious, by the tension in her stance as he spread ointment on the cut, that she was uncomfortable being close to him.

"Something wrong?" he asked, glancing up at her. "You seem…tense."

She avoided his gaze. "I'm fine."

If she were fine, why the nervous waver in her voice? "Maybe you don't like being so close to me." He lifted his eyes to hers, running his thumb across her wrist. The slight widening of her eyes, when she was trying hard not to react, made him smile. "Or maybe you do."

"I definitely don't."

Her wildly beating heart and the blush of her cheeks said otherwise. There was a physical reaction for him, as well. A pull of desire deep inside of him. Despite everything she had done, she was still a beautiful, desirable woman. And he was a man who hadn't been with a woman in several months. He just hadn't had the time for all the baggage that went along with it.

"Are you almost finished?" Isabelle asked.

"Almost." Emilio took his time, applying the butterfly then smoothing a second, larger bandage over the top to hold it in place.

"That should do it," he said, but when she tried to pull her hand free, he held on. "How about a kiss, to make it feel better?"

Her eyes widened slightly and she gave another tug. "That's really not necessary."

"I think it is." And perhaps she did, too, because she didn't try to pull away as he lifted her hand to his mouth and pressed his lips to her palm. He felt her shiver, felt her skin go hot. He kissed her palm again, then the inside of her wrist, breathing warm air against her skin. "You like that."

"Not at all."

"Your body says otherwise."

"Well, obviously it's confused."

That made him smile. "You still want me. Admit it."

"You're delusional," she said, but there was a hitch in her voice, a quiver that belied her arousal. She was hot for him.

This was going to be too easy.

Izzie gently pulled from his grasp. "I have to finish dinner."

She turned, but before she could walk away he slipped his arms around her waist and pulled her close to him. She gasped as her back pressed against his chest, her behind tucked snugly against his groin. When she felt the ridge of his erection, she froze.

He leaned close, whispered in her ear, "What's your hurry, Isabelle?"

All she had to do was tell him to stop and he would have without question, but she didn't. She stood there, unmoving, as if she were unsure of what to do. He knew in that instant she was as good as his. But not until she was begging for it. He wanted total submission. The same unconditional and unwavering devotion he had shown her fifteen years ago.

He nuzzled her neck and her head tipped to the side. He couldn't see her face, but he sensed that her eyes were closed.

"You smell delicious, Isabelle." He caught her earlobe between his teeth and she sucked in a breath. "Good enough to eat."

"We can't do this," she said, her voice uneven, her breathing shallow.

He brushed his lips against her neck. "Are you asking me to stop?"

She didn't answer.

He slid his hands up, over her rib cage, using his thumbs to caress the undersides of her breasts. They were as full and supple as they had been fifteen years ago. He wanted to unbutton her dress and slip his hands inside, touch her bare skin. Taste her.

But all in good time.

"My bed is just a few steps away," he whispered in her ear, wondering just how far she was willing to let this go. He didn't have to wait long to find out.

"Stop."

He dropped his hands and she whirled away from him, her eyes wide. "Why did you do that? You don't even like me."

A grin curled his mouth. "Because you wanted me to."

"I most certainly did not."

"We both know that isn't true, Isabelle." He pushed off the edge of the counter and rose to his feet. He could see that she wanted to run but she stood her ground. "You like it when I touch you. I know what makes you feel good."

"I'm not stupid. You don't really want me."

"I would say that all evidence points to the contrary."

Her gaze darted to his crotch, then quickly away. "I have to go finish dinner."

"Don't bother. I had a late lunch. Save the sauce for later."

"Fine."

"But that doesn't mean you should skip dinner. I want to see another pound on the scale in the morning." She had only gained two so far this week, though she swore she'd been eating three meals a day. "And take something for your hand. It's going to hurt like hell."

"I will," she said, but his concern clearly confused her.

And it was a sensation she would be experiencing a lot from now on, he thought with a smile.

Isabelle headed downstairs on unsteady legs, willing her heart to slow its frantic pace, her hands to stop trembling.

What the *hell* had she been thinking? Why had she let Emilio touch her that way? Why had she let him touch her at all? She had been perfectly capable of bandaging her own finger. She should have insisted he let her do it herself. But she foolishly believed he was doing it because he cared about her, cared that she was hurt.

When would she learn?

He didn't care about her. Not at all. He was just trying to confuse her. This was just some twisted plot for revenge.

And could she blame him? Didn't she deserve anything he could dish out? Put in his position, after the way she'd hurt him, would she have done things any differently?

She'd brought this on herself. That's what her father used to tell her, how he justified his actions. She'd spent years convincing herself that it wasn't her fault, that he was the one with the problem. What if she was wrong? What if she really had deserved it back then, and she was getting exactly what she deserved now? Maybe this was her penance for betraying Emilio.

She heard him come downstairs and braced herself for another confrontation, but he went straight to his office and shut the door.

Limp with relief, she cleaned up the mess from the unfinished meal then fixed herself a sandwich with the leftover roast beef from the night before, but she only managed to choke down a bite or two. She covered what was left with plastic wrap and put it in the fridge—if there was one thing she had learned lately, it was to not waste food—then locked herself in her room. It was still early, but she was exhausted so she changed into her pajamas and curled up in bed. Her finger had begun to throb, but it didn't come close to the ache in her heart. Maybe coming here had been a mistake. In fifteen years she hadn't figured out how to stop loving Emilio.

Maybe she never would.

"How's the finger?" Emilio asked Isabelle the next evening as he ate his spaghetti. He usually sat in the dining room, but tonight he'd insisted on sitting at the kitchen table. If that wasn't awkward enough, he kept *watching* her.

At least he hadn't complained about dinner, despite the fact that the noodles were slightly overdone and the garlic bread was a little singed around the edges. He seemed to recognize that she was trying. Or maybe he thought if he complained she might make good on her threat and smother him in his sleep.

"It's fine," she said. It still throbbed, but the ibuprofen tablets she'd been gobbling like candy all day had at least taken the sharp edge off the pain.

"We'll need to redress it."

We? As if she would let him anywhere near her after last night.

"I'll do it later," she said.

He got up to carry his plate to the sink, where she just happened to be standing, loading the dishwasher. She couldn't move away without looking like she was running from him, and she didn't want him to know he was making her nervous. He already held most of the cards in this game he'd started. And she had little doubt that it was a game.

The key was not letting him know that he was getting to her, that she even cared what he thought.

He put his plate and fork in the dishwasher. "I should check it for signs of infection."

He reached for her arm but she moved out of his grasp. "I can do it myself."

"Suit yourself," he said, wearing a cocky grin as he turned to wash his hands.

Ugh! The man was insufferable. Yet the desire to lean into him, to wrap her arms around him and breathe in his scent, to lay her cheek against his back and listen to the steady thump of his heart beating, was as strong now as it had been all those years ago. She'd spent more than half her life fantasizing about him, wishing with all her heart that they could be together, and for one perfect year he had been hers.

But she had made her choice, one that up until a few days ago, she'd learned to accept. Now her doubts had begun to resurface and she found herself rehashing the same old *what ifs*. What if she had been stronger? What if she stood up to her father instead of caving to his threats?

What if she'd at least had the courage to tell Emilio goodbye?

She had tried. She went to see him, to tell him that she had decided to marry Lenny. She knew he would never understand why, and probably never forgive her, but she owed him an explanation. Even if she could never tell him the truth.

But the instant she'd seen his face, how happy he was to see her, she'd lost her nerve and, because she couldn't bear to see him hurting, she pretended everything was okay. She hadn't stopped him when he started kissing her, when he took her hand and led her to his room. And because she couldn't bear going the rest of her life never knowing what it would be like to make love to him, she'd had every intention of giving herself to him that night.

Emilio had been the one to put on the brakes, to say not yet. He had been concerned that she would regret giving in so close to their wedding day. She hadn't had the heart, or the courage, to tell him that day would never come.

Would things have been different if she had at least told him she was leaving? For all she knew, they might have been worse. He might have talked her into telling him the truth, and that would have been a disaster.

She never expected him to forgive her—she hadn't even forgiven herself yet—but she had hoped that he would have moved on by now. It broke her heart to know how deeply she had hurt him. That after all this time he was *still* hurting. If he wasn't why would he be so hell-bent on hurting her back?

Maybe she should give him what he wanted, allow him his vengeance if that was what it would take to reconcile the past. Maybe she owed it to him—and to herself. Maybe then she could stop feeling so guilty.

After last night she could only assume he planned to use sex to get his revenge. If she slept with him, would he feel vindicated? And was she prepared to compromise her principles by having sex with a man who clearly hated her? Or did the fact that she still loved him make it okay?

Before she could consider the consequences of her actions, she stuck her hand out.

"Here," she said. "Maybe you should check it. Just in case."

He looked at her hand, then lifted his eyes to her face. There was a hint of amusement in their smoky depths. "I'm sure you can manage on your own."

Huh?

He dried his hands, then walked out of the kitchen.

She followed him. "What do you want from me, Emilio?"

He stopped just outside his office door and turned to her. "Want?"

He knew exactly what she meant. "I know I hurt you, and I'm *sorry*. Just tell me what you want me to do and I'll do it."

His stormy gaze leveled on her and suddenly she felt naked. How did he manage to do that with just a look? How did he make her feel so stripped bare?

He took a step toward her and her heart went crazy in her chest. She tried to be brave, to stand her ground, but as he moved closer, she found herself taking one step back, then another, until she hit the wall. Maybe offering herself up as the sacrificial lamb hadn't been such a hot idea, after all. Maybe she should have worked up to this just a little slower instead of jumping right into the deep end of the pool. But it was too late now.

In the past he had always been so sweet and tender, so patient with her. Now he wore a look that said he was about to eat her alive. It both terrified and thrilled her, because despite the years that had passed, deep down she still felt like the same naive, inexperienced girl. Way out of her league, yet eager to learn. And in all these years the gap seemed to widen exponentially.

Emilio braced a hand on one side of her head, leaning in, the faint whisper of his scent filling her senses—familiar, but different somehow. If she were braver she would have touched him. She *wanted* to. Instead she stood frozen, waiting for him to make the first move, wondering how far he would take this, and if she would let him. If she *should*.

Emilio dipped his head and nuzzled her cheek, his breath warm against her skin, then his lips brushed the column of her throat and Isabelle's knees went weak.

Thank goodness she had the wall to hold her steady. One kiss and she was toast. And it wasn't even a *real* kiss.

His other hand settled on the curve of her waist, the heat of his palm scorching her skin through the fabric of her uniform. She wanted to reach up and tunnel her fingers through the softness of his hair, slide her arms around his neck, pull him down and press her mouth to his. The anticipation of his lips touching hers had her trembling from the inside out.

He nipped the lobe of her ear, slid his hand upward and as his thumb grazed the underside of her breast she had to fight not to moan. Her nipples tingled and hardened. Breath quickened. She wanted to take his hand and guide it over her breast, but she kept her own hands fisted at her sides, afraid that any move she made might be the wrong one.

His lips brushed the side of her neck, her chin. This was so wrong, but she couldn't pull away. Couldn't stop him. She didn't *want* him to stop.

His lips brushed her cheek, the corner of her mouth, then finally her lips. So sweet and tender, and when his tongue skimmed hers she went limp with desire. In that instant she stopped caring that he was using her, that he didn't even like her, that to him this was just some stupid game of revenge. She didn't even care that he would probably take her fragile heart and rip it all to pieces. She was going to take what she wanted, what she needed, what she'd spent the last fifteen years *aching* for.

One minute her arms were at her sides and the next they were around his neck, fingers tunneling through his hair, and something inside Emilio seemed to snap. He shoved her backward and she gasped as he crushed her against the wall with the weight of his body. The kiss went from sweet and tender to deep and punishing so fast it stole her breath.

He cupped her behind, arched against her, and she could feel the hard length of his erection against her stomach. If not for the skirt of her dress, she would have wound her legs around his hips and ground into him. She wanted him to take her right there, in the hallway.

But as abruptly as it had begun, it was over. Emilio let go of her and backed away, leaving her stunned and confused and aching for more.

"Good night, Isabelle," he said, his voice so icy and devoid of emotion that she went cold all over. He stepped into his office and shut the door behind him and she heard the lock click into place. She had to fight not to hurl herself at it, to keep from pounding with her fists and demand he finish what he started.

She had never been so aroused, or so humiliated, in her life. She wasn't sure what sort of game he was playing, but as she sank back against the wall, struggling to make sense of what had just happened, she had the sinking feeling that it was far from over.

Damn.

Emilio closed and locked his office door and leaned against it, fighting to catch his breath, to make sense of what had just happened.

What had gone wrong?

Things had been progressing as planned. He had been in complete control. He'd had Isabelle right where he wanted her. Then everything went to hell. Their lips touched and his head started to spin, then she wrapped her arms around his neck, rubbed against him and he'd just…*lost* it.

He'd been seconds from ripping open that god-awful uniform and putting his hands on her. He had been this-close to shoving up the skirt of her dress, ripping off her panties and taking her right there in the hallway, up against the wall. He wanted her as much now as he had fifteen years ago. And putting on the brakes, denying himself the pleasure of everything she offered, had been just as damned hard.

That hadn't been part of the plan.

On the bright side, making Isabelle bend to his will, making her beg for it, was clearly not going to be a problem.

He crossed the room to the wet bar and splashed cold water on his face. This had just been a fluke. A knee-jerk reaction to the last vestiges of a long dormant sexual attraction. It was physical and nothing more. So from now on, losing control wasn't going to be an issue.

Seven

Isabelle stood at the stove fixing breakfast the next morning, reliving the nightmarish events of last night. How could she have been so stupid? So naive?

Just tell me what you want and I'll do it.

Well, she'd gotten her answer. He hadn't come right out and said it, but the implications of his actions had been crystal clear. He wanted to make her want him, get her all hot and bothered, then reject her. Simple yet effective.

Very effective.

As much as she hated it, as miserable and small as he'd made her feel, didn't she deserve this? Hadn't she more or less done the same thing to him fifteen years ago? Could she really fault him for wanting revenge?

She had gotten herself into this mess, she'd asked for his help, now she had to live with the consequences. She could try to resist him, try to pretend she didn't melt when he touched her, but she had always been a terrible liar. And honestly, she didn't have the energy to fight him.

The worst, most humiliating part was knowing that if she told him no, if she asked him to stop, he would. He would never force himself on her. He'd made that clear the other night. The problem was, she didn't *want* to tell him no.

Unlike Emilio, she couldn't switch it off and on. Her only defense was to avoid him as often as possible. And when she couldn't? Well, she would try her hardest to not make a total fool of herself again. She would try to be strong.

She would hold up her end of the bargain, and hopefully everyone would get exactly what they wanted. She just wished she didn't feel so darned edgy and out of sorts, and she knew he was going to sense it the second he saw her.

According to Mrs. Medina's "list," Emilio didn't leave for work until nine-thirty on Saturdays, so Isabelle didn't have to see him until nine when he came down for breakfast. If she timed it just right, she could feed him right when he walked into the kitchen, then hide until his ride got there.

Of course he chose that morning to come down fifteen minutes early. She was at the stove, trying not to incinerate a pan of hash brown potatoes, when he walked into the room.

"Good morning," he said, the rumble of his voice tweaking her already frayed nerves.

She took a deep breath and told herself, *You can do this.* Pasting on what she hoped was a nothing-you-do-can-hurt-me face, she turned...and whatever she had been about to say died the minute she laid eyes on him.

He wasn't wearing a suit. Or a tie. Or a shirt. Or even shoes. All he wore was a pair of black silk pajama bottoms slung low on his hips. That was it. His hair was mussed from sleep and dark stubble shadowed his jaw.

Oh boy.

Most men declined with age. They developed excess flab or a paunch or even unattractive back hair, but not Emilio. His chest was lean and well-defined, his shoulders and back smooth and tanned and he had a set of six-pack abs to die for. He was everything he had been fifteen years ago, only better.

A lot better.

Terrific.

She realized she was staring and averted her eyes. Was it her fault she hadn't seen a mostly naked man in a really long time? At least, not one who looked as good as he did.

Lenny had had the paunch, and the flab, and the back hair. Not that their relationship had ever been about sex.

Ever the dutiful housekeeper, she said, "Sit down, I'll get you coffee." Mostly she just wanted to keep him out of her half of the kitchen.

He took a seat on one of the stools at the island. She grabbed a mug from the cupboard, filled it and set it in front of him.

"Thanks."

Their eyes met and his flashed with some unidentifiable emotion. Amusement maybe? She couldn't be sure, and frankly she didn't want to know.

Make breakfast, run and hide.

She busied herself with cutting up the vegetables that would go in the omelet she planned to make, taking great care not to slice or sever any appendages. Although it was tough to keep her eyes on what she was doing when Emilio was directly in her line of vision, barely an arm's reach away, looking hotter than the Texas sun.

And he was *watching* her.

She would gather everything up and move across to the opposite counter, where her back would be to him instead, but she doubted his probing stare would be any less irritating. She diced the green onions, his gaze boring into her as he casually sipped his coffee.

"Don't you have to get ready for work?" she asked.

"You trying to get rid of me, Isabelle?"

Well, *duh*. "Just curious."

"I'm working from home today."

She suppressed a groan. Fantastic. An entire day with Emilio in the house. With any luck, he would lock himself in his office and wouldn't emerge until dinnertime. But somehow she doubted she would be so lucky. She also doubted it was a coincidence that he chose this particular day to work at home. She was sure that every move he made was calculated.

She chopped the red peppers, trying to ignore the weight of his steely gray stare.

"I want you to clean my bedroom today," he said, reaching across to the cutting board to snatch a cube of pepper.

Of course he did. "I thought it was off-limits."

"It is. Until I say it isn't."

She stopped chopping and shot him a glance.

He shrugged. "My house, my rules."

Another calculated move on his part. He was just full of surprises today. He was manipulating her and he was good at it. He knew she had absolutely no recourse.

He sipped his coffee, watching her slice the mini bella mushrooms. But he wasn't just watching. He was *studying* her. She failed to understand what was so riveting about seeing someone chop food. Which meant he was just doing it to make her uncomfortable, and it was working.

When she couldn't take it any longer, she said in her most patient tone, "Would you please stop that?"

"Stop what?"

"Watching me. It's making me nervous."

"I'm just curious to see what you're going to cut this time. The way you hold that knife, my money is on the tip of your thumb. Although I'm sure if we keep it on ice, there's a good chance they can reattach it."

She stopped cutting and glared at him.

He grinned, and for a second he looked just like the Emilio from fifteen years ago. He used to smile all the time back then. A sexy, slightly lopsided grin that never failed to make her go all gooey inside. And still did.

She preferred him when he was cranky and brooding. She had a defense for that. When he did things like smile and tease her, it was too easy to forget that it was all an act. That he was only doing it to manipulate her.

Although she hoped someday he would show her a smile that he actually meant.

"Despite what you think, I'm not totally inept," she said.

"No?"

"No."

"So the pan on the stove is supposed to be smoking like that?"

At first she thought he was just saying it to irritate her, then she remembered that she'd been frying potatoes. She spun around and saw that there actually was black smoke billowing from the pan.

"Damn it!" She darted to the stove, twisted off the flame, grabbed the handle and jerked the pan off the burner. But she jerked too hard and oil sloshed over the side. She tried to jump out of the way, but she wasn't fast enough and molten hot oil splashed down the skirt of her dress, soaking through the fabric to the top of her thigh.

She gasped at the quick and sharp sting. She barely had time to process what had happened, to react, when she felt Emilio's hands on her waist.

He lifted her off her feet and deposited her on the edge of the counter next to the sink. And he wasn't smiling anymore. "Did you burn yourself?"

"A—a little, I think."

He eased the skirt of her uniform up her thighs. So far up that she was sure he could see the crotch of her bargain bin panties, but protesting seemed silly at this point since he obviously wasn't doing it to get fresh with her. And she knew there was something seriously wrong with her when all she could think was *thank God I shaved my legs this morning.*

The middle of her right thigh had a splotchy red spot the size of a saucer and it burned like the devil.

Emilio grabbed a dish towel from the counter and soaked it with cool water, then he wrung it out and laid it against her burn. She sucked in a breath as the cold cloth hit her hot skin.

"Are you okay?" he asked, his eyes dark with concern. "Do you feel light-headed or dizzy?"

She shook her head. What she felt was mortified.

Not totally inept, huh?

She couldn't even manage fried potatoes without causing a disaster. Although, this was partially his fault. If he'd worn a damn shirt, and if he hadn't been *looking* at her, she wouldn't have been so distracted.

Emilio got a fresh towel from the drawer and made an ice pack large enough to cover the burn, while she sat there feeling like a complete idiot.

"I guess I was wrong," she said.

He lifted the towel to inspect her leg and it immediately began to sting. "About what?"

"I am inept."

"It was an accident."

Huh?

He wasn't going to rub this in her face, try to make her feel like an even bigger idiot? He wasn't going to make fun of her and call her incompetent?

Was this another trick?

"It's red, but it doesn't look like it's blistering. I think your uniform absorbed most of the heat." He laid the ice pack very gently on the burned area. The sting immediately subsided. He looked up at her. "Better?"

She nodded. With her sitting on the counter they were almost eye to eye and, for the first time that morning, she really *saw* him.

Though he looked pretty much the same as he had fifteen years ago, there were subtle signs of age. The hint of crow's-feet branded the corners of his eyes, and there were a few flecks of gray in the stubble on his chin. The line of his jaw seemed less rigid than it used to be, and the lines in his forehead had deepened.

He looked tired. Maybe what had happened at the refinery, compounded by his deal with her, was stressing him out. Maybe he hadn't been sleeping well.

Despite it all, to her he was the same Emilio. At least, her heart thought so. That was probably why it was hurting so much.

But if Emilio really hated her, would it matter that she'd hurt herself? Would he have been so quick to jump in and take care of her? Would he be standing here now holding the ice pack on her leg when she could just as easily do it herself?

He may have been hardened by life, but maybe the sweet, tender man she had fallen in love with was still in there somewhere. Maybe he would be willing to forgive her someday. Or maybe she was fooling herself.

Maybe you should tell him the truth.

At this point it would be a relief to have it all out in the open. But even if she tried, she doubted he would believe her.

"You're watching me," he said, and she realized that he'd caught her red-handed. Oh well, after last night he had to know she still had feelings for him. That she still longed for his touch.

She averted her eyes anyway. "Sorry."

"Did you know that you cursed? When you saw the pan was smoking."

Had she? It was all a bit of a blur. "I don't recall."

"You said 'damn it.' I've never heard you swear before."

She shrugged. "Maybe I didn't have anything to swear about back then."

It wasn't true. She'd had plenty to swear about. But she had been so terrified of slipping up in front of her father, it was safer to not swear at all. He expected her to be the proper Texas debutant. His perfect princess. Though she somehow always managed to fall short.

She still didn't swear very often. Old habits, she supposed. But sometimes a cuss or two would slip out.

He lifted the ice pack and looked at her leg again. "It's not blistered, so it's not that bad of a burn. How does it feel?"

"A little worse than a sunburn."

"Some aloe and a couple of ibuprofen should take care of the pain." He set the pack back on her leg. "Hold this while I go get it."

She was about to tell him that she could do it herself, but she sort of liked being pampered. He would go back to hating her soon, and lusting for revenge. She figured she might as well enjoy it while she could.

Isabelle heard his footsteps going up the stairs, then coming back down and he reappeared with a bottle of aloe and a couple of pain tablets. He got a glass down from the cupboard and filled it with water from the dispenser on the fridge. He gave her that and the tablets and she dutifully swallowed them. She assumed he would hand over the bottle of aloe so she could go in her room and apply it herself. Instead he squirted a glob in his palm and dropped the ice pack into the sink.

There was nothing overtly sexual about his actions as he spread the aloe across her burn, but her body couldn't make the distinction. She felt every touch like a lover's caress. And she wanted him. So badly.

So much for trying to resist him. He wasn't even trying to seduce her and she wanted to climb all over him.

"Why are you being so nice to me?" she asked.

He braced his hands on the edge of the counter on either side of her thighs and looked up at her. "Truthfully, Izzie, I don't know."

It was the probably the most honest thing he had said to her, and before she could even think about what she was doing, she reached up and touched his cheek. It was warm and rough.

His eyes turned stormy.

She knew this was a bad idea, that she was setting herself up to be hurt, but she couldn't stop. She wanted to touch him. She didn't care that it was all an illusion. It felt real to her, and wasn't that all that mattered? And who knows, maybe this time he wouldn't push her away.

She stroked his rough cheek, ran her thumb across his full lower lip. He breathed in deep and closed his eyes. He was holding back, gripping the edge of the countertop so hard his knuckles were white.

She knew she was playing with fire and she didn't care. This time she *wanted* to get burned.

Eight

Isabelle leaned forward and pressed a kiss to Emilio's cheek. The unique scent of his skin, the rasp of his beard stubble, was familiar and comfortable and exciting all at once. Which was probably why her heart was beating so hard and her hands were trembling. The idea that he might push her away now was terrifying, but she wanted this more than she'd ever wanted anything in her life.

She kissed the corner of his mouth, then his lips and he lost it. He wrapped his hands around her hips and tugged her to the edge of the countertop, kissing her hard. Her breasts crushed against his chest, legs went around his waist. This would be no slow, sensual tease like last night.

She had always fantasized about their first time being sweet and tender, and preferably in a bed. There would be candles and champagne and soft music playing. Now none of that seemed to matter. She wanted him with a desperation she'd never felt before. She wanted him to rip off her panties and take her right there in the kitchen, before he changed his mind.

She tunneled her fingers through his hair, fed off his mouth, his stubble rough against her chin. He slid his hands up her sides to her breasts, cupping them in his palms, capturing the tips between his fingers and pinching. She gasped and tightened her legs around him, praying silently, *Please don't stop.*

He tugged at the top button on her uniform, and when it didn't immediately come loose he ripped it open instead. The dress was ruined, anyway, so what difference did it make? And it thrilled her to know that he couldn't wait to get his hands on her.

He peeled the dress off her shoulders and down her arms, pinning them to her sides, ravaging her with kisses and bites—her shoulders and her throat and the tops of her breasts. Then he yanked down one of her bra cups, took her nipple into his mouth, sucking hard, and she almost died it felt so good.

Please, *please* don't stop.

She felt his hand on her thigh, held her breath as it moved slowly upward, the tips of his fingers brushing against the crotch of her panties…

And the doorbell rang.

Emilio cursed. She groaned. Not now, not when they were *so* close.

"Ignore it," she said.

He cursed again, dropping his head to her shoulder, breathing hard. "I can't. A courier from work is dropping off documents. I need them." He glanced at the clock on the oven display. "Although he wasn't supposed to be here until *noon.*"

This was so not fair.

He backed away and she had no choice but to drop her legs from around his waist.

This was *so* not fair.

"You're going to have to get it," he said.

"Me?" Her uniform was in shambles. Ripped and stained and rumpled.

"Consider the alternative," he said, gesturing to the tent in the front of his pajama pants.

Good point.

He lifted her off the counter and set her on her feet. She wrestled her dress back up over her shoulders and tugged the skirt down over her thighs as she hurried to the door. With the button gone she would have to hold her uniform together, or give the delivery guy a special tip for his trouble.

She started to turn and Emilio caught her by the arm.

"Don't think for a second that I'm finished with you."

Oh boy. The heat in his eyes, the sizzle in his voice made her heart skip a beat. Was he going to finish what he started this time? No, what *she* had started.

The idea of what was to come made her knees weak.

The doorbell rang again and he set her loose. "Go."

She dashed through the house to the foyer, catching a glimpse of herself in the full-length mirror by the door. She cringed at her rumpled appearance, convinced that the delivery person would know immediately that she and Emilio had been fooling around. Well, so what if he did? As long as he didn't recognize her, who cared?

Holding the collar of her dress closed, she yanked the door open, expecting the person on the other side to be wearing a delivery uniform. But the man standing on Emilio's porch was dressed in faded jeans, cowboy boots and a trendy black leather jacket. His dark hair was shoulder length and slicked back from his face, and there was something vaguely familiar about him.

He blatantly took in Isabelle's wrinkled and stained uniform, the razor burn on her chin and throat, her mussed hair. One brow tipped up in a move that was eerily familiar, and he asked with blatant amusement, "Rough morning, huh?"

Emilio cursed silently when he recognized the voice of the man on the other side of the door. After three months without so much as a phone call, why did his brother have to pick now to show his face again?

Talk about a mood killer.

He just hoped like hell that Estefan didn't recognize Isabelle, or this could get ugly.

Emilio rounded the corner to the foyer and pushed his way past Isabelle, who didn't seem to know what to say.

"I've got this," he said, and noted with amusement that as she stepped back from the door, she shot a worried glance at his crotch.

"I'll go change," she said, heading for the kitchen.

"Hey, bro," Estefan said, oozing charm. "Long time no see."

He looked good, and though he didn't appear to be under the influence, he was a master at hiding his addictions. Estefan was a handsome, charming guy, which was why people caved to his requests after he let them down time and time again. But not Emilio. He'd learned his lesson.

"What do you want, Estefan?"

"You're not going to invite me inside?"

With Isabelle there? Not a chance. If he had the slightest clue what Emilio was doing, he would exploit the situation to his own benefit.

"I don't even know where you've been for the past three months. Mama has been worried sick about you."

"Not in jail, if that's what you're thinking."

No, because if he'd been arrested, Alejandro would have heard about it. But there were worse things than incarceration.

"I know you probably won't believe this, but I'm clean and sober. I have been for months."

He was right, Emilio didn't believe it. Not for a second. And even if he was, on the rare occasions he'd actually stuck with a rehab program long enough to get clean, it hadn't taken him long to fall back into his old habits.

"What do you want, Estefan?"

"Do I need a reason to see my big brother?"

Maybe not, but he always had one. Usually he needed money, or a place to crash. Occasionally both. He'd even asked to borrow Emilio's car a couple of times, because his own cars had a habit of being repossessed or totaled in accidents that were never Estefan's fault.

He wanted something. He always did.

"Unless you tell me why you're here, I'm closing the door."

The smile slipped from Estefan's face when he realized charm wasn't going to work this time. "I just want to talk to you."

"We have nothing to talk about."

"Come on, Emilio. I'm your baby brother."

"Tell me where you've been."

"Los Angeles, mostly. I was working on a business deal."

A shady one, he was sure. Most of Estefan's "business" deals involved stolen property or drugs, or any number of scams. The fact that he was a small-time criminal with a federal prosecutor for a brother was the only thing that had kept him from doing hard time.

"You're really not going to let me in?" he asked, looking wounded.

"I think I already made that clear."

"You know, I never took you for the type to do the hired help. But I also never expected to see Isabelle Winthrop working for you. Unless the maid's uniform is just some kinky game you play."

Emilio cursed under his breath.

"Did you think I wouldn't recognize her?"

He had hoped, but he should have known better.

"I don't suppose Mama knows what you're doing."

He recognized a threat when he heard one. He held the door open. "Five minutes."

With an arrogant smile, Estefan strolled in.

"Wait here," Emilio said, then walked to the kitchen. Isabelle had changed into a clean uniform and was straightening up the mess from breakfast. She'd fixed her hair and the beard burns had begun to fade.

He should have waited until he shaved to kiss her, but then, he hadn't been expecting her to make the first move. And he hadn't meant to reciprocate. So much for regaining his control. If Estefan hadn't shown up, Emilio had no doubt they would be in his bed right now. Which would have been a huge mistake.

This wasn't working out at all as he'd planned. He wasn't sure if it was his fault, or hers. All he knew was that it had to stop.

She tensed when he entered the room, looking past him to the doorway. He turned to see that his brother had followed him. Figures. Why would he expect Estefan to do anything he asked?

"It's okay," Emilio told Isabelle. "We're going to my

office to talk. I just wanted to tell you to forget about breakfast."

She nodded, then squared her shoulders and met Estefan's gaze. "Mr. Suarez."

"Ms. Winthrop," he said, the words dripping with disdain. "Shouldn't you be in prison?"

The old Isabelle would have withered from his challenge, but this Isabelle held her head high. "Five more weeks. Thanks for asking. Can I offer you something to drink?"

"He's not staying," Emilio said, gesturing Estefan to follow him. "Let's get this over with."

When they were in his office with the door closed, Estefan said, "Isabelle Winthrop, huh? I had no idea you were that hard up."

"Not that it's any of your business, but I'm not sleeping with her." Not yet, anyway. And he was beginning to think making her work as his housekeeper might have to be the extent of his revenge. There were consequences to getting close to her that he had never anticipated.

"So, what is she doing here?"

"She works for me."

"Why would you hire someone like her? After what her family did to our mother. After what she did to you."

"That's my business."

A slow smile crossed his face. "Ah, I get it. Make her work for you, the way our mother worked for her. Nice."

"I'm glad you approve."

"What does she get out of it?"

"She wants Alejandro to cut a deal for her mother, so she won't go to prison."

"So, Alejandro knows what you're doing?"

Emilio took a seat behind his desk, to keep the balance

of power clear. "Let's talk about you, Estefan. What do *you* want?"

"You assume I'm here because I want something from you?"

Emilio shot him a look, putting a chink in the arrogant facade. Estefan crossed the room to look out the window. He didn't even have the guts to look Emilio in the face. "I want you to hear me out before you say anything."

Emilio folded his arms across his chest. *Here we go.*

"There are these people, and I owe them money."

Emilio opened his mouth to say he wouldn't give him a penny, but Estefan raised a hand to stop him. "I'm not asking you for a handout. That's not why I'm here. I have the money to pay them. It's just not accessible at the moment."

"Why?"

"Someone is holding it for me."

"Who?"

"A business associate. He has to liquidate a few assets to pay me, and that's going to take several days. But these men are impatient. I just need a place to hang out until I get the funds. Somewhere they won't find me. It would only be for a few days. Thanksgiving at the latest."

Which was *five* days away. Emilio didn't want his brother around for five minutes, much less the better part of a week.

"Suppose they come looking for you here?" Emilio asked.

"Even if they did, this place is a fortress." He crossed the room, braced his hands on Emilio's desk, a desperation in his eyes that he didn't often let show. "You have to help me, Emilio. I've been trying so hard to set my life straight. After I pay this debt I'm in the clear. I have a friend in rodeo promotions who is willing to give me a job. I could start over, do things right this time."

He wanted to believe his brother, but he'd heard the same story too many times before.

Estefan must have sensed that Emilio was about to say no because he added, "I could go to Mama, and you know she would let me stay, but these are not the kind of people you want anywhere near your mother. There's no telling what they might do."

Leaving Emilio no choice but to let him stay. And Estefan knew it. Emilio should have guessed he would resort to emotional blackmail to get his way. He also suspected that if he refused, it was likely everyone would find out that Isabelle was in his home.

He rose from his chair. "Five days. If you haven't settled your debt by then, you're on your own."

Estefan embraced him. "Thank you, Emilio."

"Just so we're clear, while you're staying in my house there will be no drinking or drugs."

"I don't do that anymore. I'm clean."

"And you won't tell anyone that Isabelle is here."

"Not a soul. You have my word."

"And you will *not* give her a hard time."

Estefan raised a brow.

"My house, my rules."

He shrugged. "Whatever you say."

"I'll have Isabelle get a room ready for you."

"I have a few things to take care of. But I'll be back later tonight. Probably late."

"I'll be in bed by midnight, so if you're not back by then, you're in the pool house for the night."

"If you give me the alarm code—"

Emilio shot him a *not-in-this-lifetime* look.

He shrugged again. "I'll be back by midnight, then."

Estefan left and Emilio went to find Isabelle. She was kneeling on the kitchen floor, cleaning up the oil that spilled by the stove. Only then did he remember that she'd burned her leg, and wondered if it still hurt.

Maybe he should have considered that before he put the moves on her. Of course, he hadn't started it this time, had he? Seducing her had been the last thing on his mind.

Okay, maybe not the *last* thing…

She saw him standing there and shot to her feet. "I'm so sorry. If I had known it was him at the door—"

"I told you to answer it, Isabelle. It's not your fault."

"He won't tell anyone, will he?"

"He promised not to. He's going to be staying here for a few days. Possibly until Thanksgiving."

"Oh."

"It won't change anything. Except maybe you'll be feeding one more person."

"There are always leftovers, anyway."

"What he said to you, it was uncalled for. It won't happen again. I told him that he's not allowed to give you a hard time."

"Because you're the only one allowed to make disparaging comments?"

Something like that. Although now when he thought about saying something rude, it just made him feel like a jerk. He kept thinking about what Alejandro said, about the new developments. That she might be innocent. And even if she was involved somehow, was he so beyond reproach that he felt he had the right to judge her?

That didn't change what she had done to him, and what her father did to his family. For that she was getting exactly what she deserved.

"I'm sorry I ruined breakfast," she said. "I guess hash browns are a little out of my league."

Or maybe it was the result of him distracting her. He never would have done it if he had known she would get hurt. "So you'll make easier things from now on."

"I don't think frying potatoes would be considered complicated. I think I'm just hopeless when it comes to cooking. But thanks for taking care of me. It's been a really long time since someone has done something nice for me. Someone besides my mom, anyway."

"Your husband didn't do nice things for you?" He didn't mean to ask the question. He didn't give a flying fig what her husband did or didn't do. It just sort of popped out.

"Lenny took very good care of me," she said, an undercurrent of bitterness in her voice. "I didn't want for a single thing when I was married to him."

But she wasn't happy, her tone said.

Well, she had made her own bed. Emilio would have given her anything, *done* anything to make her happy. But that hadn't been enough for her.

Her loss.

She pulled off her gloves, wincing a bit when it jostled her bandaged finger.

"It still hurts?" he asked, and she shrugged. "Any signs of infection?"

"It's fine."

That was her standard answer. It could be black with gangrene and she would probably say it was fine. "When was the last time you changed the dressing?"

"Last night…I think."

From the condition of the bandage he would guess it was closer to the night before last. Clearly she wasn't taking care of it. He didn't want to be responsible if it got infected.

He held out his hand. "Let's see it."

She didn't even bother arguing, she just held her hand out to him. He peeled the bandage off. The cut itself had closed, but the area around it was inflamed. There's no way she could not have known it was infected. "Damn, Isabelle, are you *trying* to lose a finger?"

"I've been busy."

"Too busy to take care of yourself?" He dropped her hand. "You still have the antibiotic ointment?"

She nodded.

"Use it. I want you to put a fresh dressing on it three times a day until the infection is cleared up."

"I will. I promise."

"I need you to get one of the guest rooms ready. Preferably the one farthest from mine. Estefan will be back later tonight."

"So, he's not here?"

"He just left."

She was watching him expectantly. He wasn't sure why, but then he remembered what he'd told her when the doorbell rang, that he wasn't finished with her.

"About what happened earlier. I think it would be best if we keep things professional from now on."

"Oh," she said, her eyes filled with confusion. And rejection. He shouldn't have felt like a heel, but he did. Isn't this what he'd wanted? To get her all worked up, then reject her? Well, the plan had worked brilliantly. Even better than he'd anticipated. What he hadn't counted on was how much he would want her, too.

"Well, I had better get the room ready," she said. She paused, as though she was waiting for him to say something, and when he didn't, she walked away, leaving him feeling like the world's biggest jerk.

The last few weeks had been stressful to say the least. He would be relieved when Isabelle was gone, and the investigation at the refinery came to a close, and he was securely in the position of CEO. Life would be perfect.

So why did he have the sneaking suspicion it wouldn't be so simple?

Nine

So much for hoping Emilio might forgive her, that he still wanted her. He wanted to keep their relationship *professional*. And they had come so close this afternoon. If it hadn't been for Estefan showing up…

Oh, well. Easy come, easy go.

Clearly he didn't want Estefan knowing he was involved with someone like her. It was bad enough she was living in his house. And could she blame him for feeling that way? Aside from the fact that her father had ruined their mother's reputation, Isabelle was a criminal.

Alleged criminal, she reminded herself.

Unfortunately, now Emilio seemed to be shutting her out completely. He hadn't come out of his office all day, or said more than a word or two to her. No insults or wry observations. He'd even eaten his dinner at his desk. Just when she'd gotten used to him sitting in the kitchen making fun of her.

Isabelle loaded the last of the dinner dishes in the dishwasher and set it to run. It was only eight and all her work for the day was finished, but the idea of sitting around feeling sorry for herself on a Saturday night was depressing beyond words. Maybe it was time she paid her mom another visit. They could watch a movie or play a game of Scrabble. She could use a little cheering up, and she knew that no matter what, her mother was there for her.

If Emilio would let her go. The only way she could get there, short of making her mother come get her, or taking a cab, was to use his car. She could lie and say she was going grocery shopping, but when she came home empty-handed he would definitely be suspicious. And would he really buy her going shopping on a Saturday night? Besides, she didn't like lying.

She could just sneak out without telling him, and deal with the consequences when she got back.

Yeah, that was probably the way to go.

She changed out of her uniform, grabbed her purse and sweater and when she walked back into the kitchen for the car keys Emilio was there, getting an apple from the fridge. He looked surprised to see her in her street clothes.

Well, shoot. So much for sneaking out.

"Going somewhere?" he asked.

"I finished all my work so I thought I would go see my mother. I won't be late."

"Did Estefan get back yet?"

"Not yet."

"You're taking the Saab?"

She nodded, bracing for an argument.

"Well, then, drive safe."

Drive safe? That was *it?* Wasn't he going to give her a hard time about going out? Or say something about her taking his car for personal use? Instead he walked out of the kitchen and a few seconds later she heard his office door close.

Puzzled, she headed out to the garage, wondering what had gotten into him. Not that she liked it when he acted like an overbearing jerk. But this was just too weird.

The drive to her mother's apartment was only fifteen minutes. Her car was in the lot, and the light was on in her living room. Isabelle parked and walked to the door. She heard laughter from inside and figured that her mother was watching television. She knocked, and a few seconds later the door opened.

"Isabelle!" her mom said, clearly surprised to see her. "What are you doing here?"

"Mrs. Smith didn't need me for the night and I was bored. I thought we could watch a movie or something."

Normally her mother would invite her right in, but she stood blocking the doorway. She looked nervous. "Oh, well…now isn't a good time."

Isabelle frowned. "Is something wrong?"

"No, nothing." She glanced over her shoulder. "It's just…I have company."

Company? Though Isabelle hadn't noticed at first, her mother looked awfully well put together for a quiet night at home. Her hair was swept up and she wore a skirt and blouse that Isabelle had never seen before. She looked beautiful. But for whom?

"Adriana, who is it?" a voice asked. A *male* voice.

Her mother had a *man* over?

As far as Isabelle knew, she hadn't dated anyone since her husband died three years ago. She had serious trust issues. And who wouldn't after thirty-five years with a bastard like Isabelle's father?

But was he a boyfriend? A casual acquaintance?

Her mother blushed, and she stepped back from the door. "Come in."

Isabelle stepped into the apartment and knew immediately that this was no "friendly" social call. There were lit candles on the coffee table and an open bottle of wine with two glasses. The good crystal, Isabelle noted.

"Isabelle, this is Ben McPherson. Ben, this is my daughter."

Isabelle wasn't sure what she expected, but it sure wasn't the man who stood to greet her.

"Isabelle!" he said, reaching out to shake her hand, pumping it enthusiastically. "Good to finally meet you!"

He was big and boisterous with longish salt-and-pepper hair, dressed in jeans and a Hawaiian shirt. He looked like an ex-hippie, with a big question mark on the *ex,* and seemed to exude happiness and good nature from every pore. He was also the polar opposite of Isabelle's father.

And though she had known him a total of five seconds, Isabelle couldn't help but like him.

"Ben owns the coffee shop next to the boutique where I work," her mother said.

"Would you like to join us?" Ben asked. "We were just getting ready to pop in a movie."

The fact that she almost accepted his offer was a testament to how low her life had sunk. The last thing her mother needed was Isabelle crashing her dates. Being the third wheel was even worse than being alone.

"Maybe some other time."

"Are you sure you can't stay for a quick glass of wine?"

"Not while I'm driving. But it was very nice meeting you, Ben."

"You, too, Isabelle."

"I'll walk you to your car," her mother said, and she told Ben, "I'll be right back."

Isabelle followed her mother out the door, shutting it behind them.

"Are you upset?" her mother asked, looking worried.

"About what?"

"That I have a man friend."

"Of course not! Why would I be upset? I want you to be happy. Ben seems very nice."

A shy smile tilted her lips. "He is. I get coffee in his shop before work. He's asked me out half a dozen times, and I finally said yes."

"So you like him?"

"He still makes me a little nervous, but he's such a nice man. He knows all about the indictment, but he doesn't care."

"He sounds like a keeper." She nudged her mom and asked, "Is he a good kisser?"

"Isabelle!" she said, looking scandalized. "I haven't kissed anyone but your father since I was sixteen. To be honest, the idea is a little scary."

They got to the car and Isabelle turned to face her. "Are you physically attracted to him?"

She smiled shyly and nodded. "I think I just need to take things slow."

"And he understands that?"

"We've talked. About your father, and the way things used to be. He's such a good listener."

"How many times have you seen him?"

"This is our third date."

She'd seen him *three* times and hadn't said anything? Isabelle thought they told each other everything.

And who was she to talk when she'd told her mother she worked for the fictional Mrs. Smith?

"You're upset," her mother said, looking crestfallen.

"No, just a little surprised."

"I wanted to tell you, I was just…embarrassed, I guess. If that makes any sense. I keep thinking that he's going to figure out that I'm not such a great catch, and every date we go on will be our last."

She could thank Isabelle's dad for that. He'd put those ideas into her head.

"He's lucky to have you and I'm sure he knows it."

"He does seem to like me. He's already talking about what we'll do next weekend."

"Well, then, I'd better let you get back inside." She gave her mother a hug. "Have fun, but not *too* much fun. Although after three dates, I would seriously consider letting him kiss you."

Her mother smiled. "I will."

"I'll see you Thursday, then. Is there anything you need me to bring?"

"Oh, I was thinking…well, the thing is, my oven here isn't very reliable, and…actually, Ben invited me to Thanksgiving dinner with him and a few of his friends. I thought you could come along."

That would be beyond awkward, especially when his friends found out who she was. But she could see that her mother really wanted to go, and she wouldn't out of guilt if Isabelle didn't come up with a viable excuse.

"Mrs. Smith's family asked me to have dinner with them," she lied. "They've been so kind to me, the truth is I felt bad telling them no. So if you want to eat with Ben and his friends, that's fine."

"Are you sure? We always spend Thanksgiving together."

Not after this year, unless her mother wanted to eat at the women's correctional facility. It was good that she was making new friends, getting on with her life. To fill the void when Isabelle was gone.

She forced a smile. "I'm sure."

She gave her one last hug, then got in the car. Her mother waved as she drove off. It seemed as if she was finally getting on with her life. Isabelle wanted her to be happy, so why did she feel like dropping her head on the steering wheel and sobbing?

Probably because, for a long, long time, Isabelle and her mom had no one but each other. They were a team.

Her mother had someone else now. And who did Isabelle have? Pretty much no one.

But she was not going to feel sorry for herself, damn it. What would be the point of creating new relationships now anyway, when in five weeks she would be going to prison?

She didn't feel like going back to Emilio's yet, so instead she drove around for a while. When she reached the edge of town, she was tempted to just keep going. To drive far from here, away from her life. A place where no one knew her and she could start over.

But running away never solved anything.

It was nearly eleven when she steered the car back to Emilio's house. She parked in the garage next to his black Ferrari and headed inside, dropping her purse and sweater in her room before she walked out to the kitchen to make herself a cup of tea. She put the kettle on to boil and fished around the cupboard above the coffeemaker on her tiptoes for a box of tea bags.

"Need help?"

She felt someone lean in beside her. She looked up, expecting to find Emilio, but it was Estefan standing there.

She jerked away, feeling...violated. He was charming, and attractive—although not even close to as good-looking as Emilio—but something about him always gave her the creeps. Even when they were younger, when his mother would drive them to school, Isabelle didn't like the way he would look at her. Even though he was a few years younger, he made her nervous.

He still did. She had to dig extra deep to maintain her show-no-fear attitude.

Estefan flashed her an oily smile and held out the box of tea bags. She took it from him. "Thank you."

"No problem." He leaned against the counter and folded his arms. *Watching* her.

"Did Emilio show you to your room?" she asked, mainly because she didn't know what else to say.

"Yep. It's great place, isn't it?" He looked around the kitchen. "My brother did pretty well for himself."

"He has."

"Probably makes you regret screwing him over."

So much for Estefan not giving her a hard time. She should have anticipated this.

"It looks like you've got a pretty sweet deal going here," Estefan said.

She wondered how much Emilio had told him. From the tone of their conversation at the front door—yes, she'd eavesdropped for a minute or two—Emilio hadn't been happy to see his brother. Would he confide in someone he didn't trust? And what difference did it make?

"You get to live in his house, drive his cars, eat his food. It begs the question, what is he getting in return?"

Housekeeping and cooking. But clearly that wasn't what he meant. He seemed certain there was more to it than that. Why didn't he just come right out and call her a whore?

The kettle started to boil so she walked around the island to the stove to fix her tea. Emilio had belittled and insulted her, but that had been different somehow. Less... sinister and vindictive. She just hoped that if she didn't give him the satisfaction of a reaction, Estefan would get bored and leave her alone.

No such luck.

He stepped up behind her. So close she could almost feel his body heat. The cloying scent of his aftershave turned her stomach.

"My brother is too much of a nice guy to realize he's being used."

She had the feeling that the only one using Emilio was Estefan, but she kept her mouth shut. And as much as she would like to tell Emilio how Estefan was treating her, she would never put herself in the middle of their relationship. She would only be around a few weeks. Emilio and Estefan would be brothers for life.

She turned to walk back to her room, but Estefan was blocking her way. "Excuse me."

"You didn't say *please*."

She met his steely gaze with one of her own, and after several seconds he let her through. She forced herself to walk slowly to her room. The door didn't have a lock, so she shoved the folding chair under the doorknob—just in case. She didn't really think Estefan would get physical with her, especially with his brother in the house. But better safe than sorry.

Life at Emilio's hadn't exactly been a picnic, but it hadn't been terrible, either, and she'd always felt safe. She had the feeling that with Estefan around, those days were over.

Ten

Though he wouldn't have believed it possible, Emilio was starting to think maybe his brother really had changed this time. Good to his word, he hadn't asked Emilio for a penny. Not even gas money. He'd spent no late nights out partying and, as far as Emilio could tell, had remained sober for the three days he'd been staying there. The animosity that had been a constant thread in their relationship for as many years as Emilio could remember was gradually dissolving.

When they were growing up, Estefan had always been jealous of Emilio, coveting whatever he had. The cool after-school jobs, the stellar grades and college scholarships. He just hadn't wanted the hard work that afforded Emilio those luxuries. But now it seemed that Estefan finally got it; he'd figured out what he needed to do, and he was making a valiant effort to change.

At least, Emilio hoped so.

Though things at Western Oil were still in upheaval, and

he had work he could be doing, Emilio had spent the last couple of evenings in the media room watching ESPN with his brother. He felt as if, for the first time in their lives, he and Estefan were bonding. Acting like real brothers. Besides, spending time with him was helping Emilio keep his mind off Isabelle.

Since he told her that he wanted to keep things professional, he hadn't been able to stop thinking about her. The way she tasted when he kissed her, the softness of her skin, the feel of her body pressed against his. She was as responsive to his touch, as hot for him now, as she had been all those years ago. And now that he knew he couldn't have her, he craved her that much more. This time it had nothing to do with revenge or retribution. He just plain wanted her, and he could tell by the way she looked at him, the loneliness and longing in her eyes, that she wanted him, too. And so, apparently, could Estefan.

"She wants you, bro," Estefan said Tuesday evening after dinner, while they were watching a game Emilio had recorded over the weekend.

"Our relationship is professional," he told his brother.

"Why? You could tap that, then kick her to the curb. It would be the ultimate revenge. Use her the way she used you."

Which was exactly what Emilio had planned to do, but for some reason now, it just seemed…sleazy. Maybe he was ready to let go of the past. Maybe all this time he'd just been brooding. He wasn't the only man to ever get his heart broken. Maybe it was time he stopped making excuses, stopped attaching ulterior motives to her decision and face facts. She left him because she'd fallen in love with someone else, and it was time he stopped feeling sorry for himself and got on with his life.

"Honestly, Estefan, I think she's getting what she has

coming to her. She's widowed, broke and a month away from spending the rest of her life in prison. She's about as low as she can possibly sink, yet she's handling it with grace and dignity."

"If I didn't know better, I might think you actually *like* her."

That was part of the problem. Emilio wasn't sure how he felt about her. He didn't hate her, not anymore. But he couldn't see them ever being best pals. Or even close friends. As the saying went, fool me once, shame on you…

Once she was in prison, he doubted he would ever see her again. It wasn't as if he would be going to visit her, or sending care packages.

If she actually went to prison, that is. The new lead his brother had mentioned could prove her innocence. And if it did? Then what?

Then, nothing. Innocent or guilty, sexually compatible or not, there was nothing she could say or do that would make up for the past. Not for him, and not for his family. Even if he wanted to be with her, his family would never accept it. Especially his mother. And they came first, simple as that.

Estefan yawned and stretched. "I have an early start in the morning. I think I'll turn in."

Emilio switched off the television. "Me, too."

"By the way," Estefan said, "I talked to my business associate today. He hit a snag and it's looking like I won't get that money until a few days after Thanksgiving. I know I said I would be out of here—"

"It's okay," Emilio heard himself say. "You can stay a few extra days."

"You're sure?"

"I'm sure."

"Thanks, bro."

They said good-night and Emilio walked to the kitchen to pour himself a glass of juice to take up to bed with him. By the light of the range hood he got a glass down from the cupboard and the orange juice from the fridge. He emptied the carton, but when he tried to put it in the trash under the sink, the bag was full.

He sighed. Mrs. Medina had specifically instructed Izzie to take the kitchen trash out nightly. He couldn't help but wonder if she'd forgotten on purpose, just to annoy him. If that was the case, he was annoyed.

He considered calling her out to change it, on principle, but it was after eleven and she was usually in bed by now. Instead he pulled the bag out, tied it and put a fresh one in. He carried the full bag to the trash can in the garage, noting on his way the dim sliver of light under Isabelle's door. Her lamp was on. Either she was still awake, or she'd fallen asleep with the light on again.

He dropped the bag in the can, glancing over at the Saab. Was that a *scratch* on the bumper?

He walked over to look, and on closer inspection saw that it was just something stuck to the paint. He rubbed it clean, made a mental note to tell Isabelle to take it to the car wash the next time she was out, then headed back inside. He expected to find the kitchen empty, but Isabelle was standing in front of the open refrigerator door. She was wearing a well worn plaid flannel robe and her hair was wet.

"Midnight snack?" he asked.

She let out a startled squeak and spun around, slamming the door shut. "You scared me half to death!"

He opened his mouth to say something sarcastic when his eyes were drawn to the front of her robe and whatever he'd been about to say melted somewhere into the recesses of his brain. The robe gaped open at the collar, revealing the uppermost swell of her bare left breast. Not a huge deal normally, but in his present state of craving her, he was transfixed.

Look away, he told himself, but his eyes felt glued. All he could think about was what it felt like to cup it in his palm, her soft whimpers as he took her in his mouth and how many years he had wondered what it would be like to make love to her.

Where was his self-control?

Isabelle followed his gaze down to the front of her robe. He expected her to pull the sides together, maybe get embarrassed.

She didn't. She lifted her eyes back to his and just stood there, daring him to make a move.

Nope, not gonna do it.

Then she completely stunned him by tugging the tie loose and letting the robe fall open. It was dark, but he could see that she wasn't wearing anything underneath.

Damn.

You are not going to touch her, he told himself. But Isabelle clearly had other ideas. She walked over to him, took his hand and placed it on her breast.

Damn.

He could have pulled away, could have told her no. He *should* have. Unfortunately his hand seemed to develop a mind of its own. It cupped her breast, his thumb brushing back and forth over her nipple. Isabelle's eyes went dark with arousal.

She reached up and unfastened his belt.

If he was planning to stop her, now would be a good time, but as she undid the clasp on his slacks, he just stood there. She tugged the zipper down, slipped her hand inside…

He sucked in a breath as her hand closed around his

erection, and for the life of him he couldn't recall why he thought this was a bad idea. In fact, it seemed like a damned good idea, and if he was going to be totally honest with himself, it had been an inevitability.

But not here. Not with Estefan in the house. His bedroom wouldn't be a great idea, either.

"Your room," he said, so she took his hand and led him there.

The desk lamp was on, and he half expected her to shut it off, the way she used to. Not only did she leave the light on, but the minute the door was closed, she dropped her robe. Standing there naked, in the soft light… *Damn.* He'd never seen anything so beautiful, and he'd only had to wait fifteen years.

"You have to promise me you won't stop this time," she said, unfastening the buttons on his shirt.

Why stop? If they didn't do this now, it would just happen later. A day, or a week. But it would happen.

He took his wallet from his back pocket, pulled out a condom and handed it to her. "I promise."

Isabelle smiled and pushed his shirt off his shoulders. "You'll never know how many times I thought of you over the years."

Did you think of me when you were with him? He wanted to ask, but what if he didn't like the answer?

She pushed his pants and boxers down and he stepped out of them. "Do you know what I miss more than anything?" she said.

"What do you miss?"

"Lying in bed with you, under the covers, wrapped around each other, kissing and touching. Sometimes we were so close it was like we were one person. Do you remember?"

He did, and he missed it, too, more then she could

imagine. There had been a lot of women since Izzie, some who had lasted weeks, and a few who hung around for months, but he never felt that connection. He'd never developed the closeness with them that he'd felt with her.

She pulled back the covers on the bed and lay down. Emilio slipped in next to her, but when she tried to pull the covers up over them, he stopped her. "No covers this time. I want to look at you."

She reached up to touch his face and he realized that her hands were shaking. Could she possibly be nervous? This woman who, a few minutes ago, seemed to know exactly what she wanted and wasn't the least bit afraid to go after it?

He put his hand over hers, pressing it to his cheek. "You're trembling."

"I've just been waiting for this for a really long time."

"Are you sure you want to do this?"

"Emilio, I have never been more sure of anything in my life." She wound her arms around his neck and pulled him down, wrapped herself around him, kissed him. It was like…coming home. Everything about her was familiar. The feel of her body, the scent of her skin, her soft, breathy whimpers as he touched her.

He felt as if he was twenty-one again, lying in his bed in his rental house on campus, with their entire lives ahead of them. He remembered exactly what to do to make her writhe in ecstasy. Slow and sweet, the way he knew she liked it. He brought her to the edge of bliss and back again, building the anticipation, until she couldn't take it anymore.

"Make love to me, Emilio." She dug her fingers through his hair, kissed him hard. "I can't wait any longer."

He grabbed the condom and she watched with lust-glazed eyes as he rolled it on. The second he was finished she pulled him back down, wrapping her legs around his waist.

He centered himself over her, anticipating the blissful wet heat of that first thrust, but he was barely inside when he met with resistance. She must have been tense from the anticipation of finally making love. He couldn't deny he was a bit anxious himself. He put some weight into it and the barrier gave way. Isabelle gasped, digging her nails into his shoulders and she was *tight*. Tighter than any wife of fifteen years should be.

He eased back, looking down where their bodies were joined, stunned by what he saw. Exactly what he would have expected…if he'd just made love to a virgin.

No way. "Isabelle?"

It was obvious by her expression that she had been hoping he wouldn't figure it out. How was this even possible?

"Don't stop," she pleaded, pulling at his shoulders, trying to get him closer.

Hell no, he wasn't going to stop, but if he had known he could have at least been more gentle.

"I'm going to take it slow," he told her. Which in theory was a great plan, but as she adjusted to the feel of him inside her, she relaxed. Then "slow" didn't seem to be enough for her. She began to writhe beneath him, meeting his downward slide with a thrust of her hips. He was so lost in the feel of her body, the clench of her muscles squeezing him into euphoria, that he was running on pure instinct. When she moaned and bucked against him, her body fisting around him as she climaxed, it did him in. His only clear thought as he groaned out his release was *perfect*. But as he slowly drifted back to earth, reality hit him square between the eyes.

He and Isabelle had finally made love, after all these years, and he was her first. Exactly as it was meant to be.

So why did he feel so damned…guilty?

"You know, I must have imagined what that would be like about a thousand times over the past fifteen years," she said. "But the real thing is way better than the fantasy."

Emilio tipped her face up to his. "Izzie, why didn't you tell me?"

She didn't have to ask what he meant. She lowered her eyes. "I was embarrassed."

"Why?"

"You don't run across many thirty-four-year-old virgins."

"How is this even possible? You're young and beautiful and sexy. Your husband never wanted to…?"

"Can we not talk about it?" She was closing down, shutting him out, but he wanted answers, damn it.

"I want to know how you can be married to a man for fifteen years and never have sex with him."

She sat up and pulled the covers over her. "It's complicated."

"I'm a reasonably intelligent man, Izzie. Try me."

"We…we didn't have that kind of relationship."

"What kind of relationship did you have?"

She drew her knees up and hugged them. "I really don't want to talk about this."

"Did you love him?"

She bit her lip and looked away.

"Isabelle?"

After a long pause she said, "I…respected him."

"Is that your way of saying you were just in it for the money?"

She didn't deny it. She didn't say anything at all.

If she loved Betts, Emilio would understand her leaving

him. It sucked, but he could accept it. Knowing it was only about the money, seeing the truth on her face, knowing that she'd really been that shallow, disturbed him on too many levels to count.

"This was a mistake," he said. He pushed himself up from the bed and grabbed his pants.

"Emilio—"

"No. This never should have happened. I don't know what the hell I was thinking."

She was quiet for several seconds, and he waited to see what she would do. Would she apologize and beg him to stay? Tell him she made a horrible mistake? And would it matter if she did?

"You're right," she finally said, avoiding his gaze. "It was a mistake."

She was agreeing with him, and she was right, so why did he feel like putting his fist through the wall?

He tugged his pants on.

"So, what now?" she asked.

"Meaning what?"

"Are you going to back out on our deal?"

He grabbed his shirt from off the floor. "No, Isabelle, I won't. I keep my word. But I would really appreciate if you would stay out of my way. And I'll stay out of yours."

He was pretty sure he saw tears in her eyes as he jerked the door open and walked out. And just when he thought this night couldn't get any worse, his brother was sitting in the kitchen eating a sandwich and caught him red-handed.

Damn it.

When he saw Emilio his eyes widened, then a wry smile curled his mouth.

Emilio glared at him. "Don't say a word."

Estefan shrugged. "None of my business, bro."

Emilio wished Estefan had walked into the kitchen

before Isabelle started her stripping routine, then none of this would have happened.

But one thing he knew for damned sure, it was not going to happen again.

Eleven

This was for the best.

At least, that was what Isabelle had been trying to tell herself all day. She would rather have Emilio hate her, than fall in love and endure losing her again. That wouldn't be fair. Not to either of them. She was tired of feeling guilty for hurting him. She just wanted it to be over. For good.

She should have left things alone, should never have opened her robe, offered herself to him, but she'd figured for him it was just sex. She never imagined he might still have feelings for her, but he must have, or it wouldn't have matter if she loved Lenny or not.

She ran the vacuum across the carpet in the guest room, cringing at the memory of his stunned expression when he realized she was a virgin. She didn't know he would be able to tell. A testament to how naive and inexperienced she was. But as first times go, she was guessing it had been way above average. Everything she had ever hoped, and she couldn't regret it. She loved Emilio. She'd wanted him to be her first. As far as she was concerned, it was meant to be.

Except for the part where he stormed off mad.

When he'd asked her about Lenny, she had almost told him the truth. It had been sitting there on the tip of her tongue. Now she was relieved she hadn't. It was better that he thought the worst of her.

She turned to do the opposite side of the room, jolting with alarm when she realized Estefan was leaning in the bedroom doorway watching her.

His mere presence in the house put her on edge, but when he watched her—and he did that a lot—it gave her the creeps. When she dusted the living room he would park himself on the couch with a magazine, or if she was fixing dinner he would come in for a snack and sit at one of the island stools. Occasionally he would assault her with verbal barbs, which she generally ignored. But most of the time he just stared at her.

It was beyond unsettling.

Estefan raised the beer he was holding to his lips and took a swallow. Isabelle had distinctly heard him tell Emilio that he was clean and sober, yet the second he rolled out of bed every day, which was usually noon or later, he went straight to the fridge for a cold one.

The breakfast of champions.

It wasn't her place to tattle on Estefan, and even if she told Emilio what he was doing, she doubted he would believe her. It was also the reason she didn't tell him that she'd caught Estefan in his office going through his desk. He claimed he'd been looking for a pen, when she knew for a fact he'd been trying to get into the locked file drawer.

He was definitely up to something.

She turned off the vacuum. She knew she should keep

her mouth shut, but she couldn't help herself. "Would you care for some pretzels to go with that?"

"Funny." His greasy smile made her skin crawl. "Where are the keys for the Ferrari?"

"Why?"

"I need to borrow it."

"I have no idea. Why don't you call Emilio and ask him?"

"I don't want to bother him."

No, he knew his brother would say no, so it was easier to take it without his permission.

"I guess I'll have to take the Saab instead."

"Why don't you take your bike?"

"No gas. Unless you want to loan me twenty bucks. I'm good for it."

She glared at him. Even if she had twenty bucks she wouldn't give it to him. He shouldn't even be driving. He would be endangering not only himself, but everyone else on the road.

He shrugged. "The Saab it is, then."

It wasn't as if she could stop him. Short of calling the police and reporting him, she had no recourse. And in her experience, the police never really helped anyway.

Besides, she had enough to worry about in her own life without sticking her nose into Estefan's business.

"So, this arrangement not working out the way you planned it?" Estefan asked.

She wondered what Emilio had told him, if anything.

"Still a virgin at thirty-four." He shook his head. "Let me guess, was your husband impotent, or did you just freeze him out?"

The humiliation she felt was matched only by her anger at Emilio for telling Estefan her private business. She knew he was mad, but this was uncalled for. Was that his way of getting back at her?

Estefan flashed her that greasy smile again. "If you needed someone to take care of business, all you had to do was ask. I'm twice the man my brother is."

The thought of Estefan coming anywhere near her was nauseating. "Not if you were the last man on earth."

His expression darkened. "We'll see about that," he said, then walked away.

She wasn't sure what he meant by that, but the possibilities made her feel uneasy. He wouldn't have the nerve to try something, would he?

Tomorrow was Thanksgiving and he was supposed to be leaving. She would just have to watch her back until then.

Emilio's Thanksgiving was not going well so far.

He stood in his closet, fresh out of a shower, holding up the shirt Isabelle had just ironed for him, noting the scorch mark on the left sleeve. "This is a three hundred dollar silk shirt, Isabelle."

"I'm sorry," she said, yet she didn't really look sorry.

"I just wanted it lightly pressed. Not burned to a crisp."

"I didn't realize the iron was set so hot. I'll replace it."

"After you pay me back for the rug? And the casserole dish you broke. And the load of whites that you dyed pink. Not to mention the grocery bill that has mysteriously risen by almost twelve percent since you've been here."

"Maybe I could stay an extra week or two and work off what I owe you."

Terrific idea. But she would inevitably break something else and wind up owing him even more. Besides, he didn't want her in his house any longer than necessary. If there was any way he could get his housekeeper back today and let Isabelle go on time served, he would, but he'd promised her a month off.

He balled the shirt up and tossed it in the trash can in the corner. "It would probably be in everyone's best interest if you avoided using the iron."

She nodded.

He turned to grab a different shirt and a pair of slacks. He was about to drop his towel, when he noticed she was still standing there.

He raised a brow. "You want to watch me get dressed?"

"I wasn't sure if you were finished."

"Finished what?"

"Yelling at me."

"I wasn't *yelling*."

"Okay, disciplining me."

"If I were disciplining you, it would have involved some sort of punishment." Not that he couldn't think of a few. Putting her over his knee was one that came to mind. She could use a sound spanking. But he'd promised himself he was going to stop thinking of her in a sexual way and view her as an employee. Tough when he couldn't seem to stop picturing her naked and writhing beneath him.

"How about…chastising?" she said. "Dressing-down?"

"Exaggerate much? I was *talking* to you."

"If you say so."

Why the sudden attitude? If anyone had the right to be pissed, it was him.

"Is there anything else you need?" she asked.

"Could you tell my brother to be ready in twenty minutes?"

She saluted him and walked out.

He'd like to know what had gotten her panties in such a twist. Maybe she just didn't like the fact that he'd called her out on her marriage being a total sham. That he'd more or less made her admit she married Betts for his money. In which case she was getting exactly what she deserved.

He got dressed, slipped on his cashmere jacket and grabbed his wallet. Estefan was waiting for him in the kitchen. He wore jeans and a button-down shirt that was inappropriately open for a family holiday gathering, and the thick gold chain was downright tacky, but Emilio kept his mouth shut. Estefan was trying. He'd been on his best behavior all week.

Almost *too* good.

"Ready to go?"

"I'll bet you want to let me drive," Estefan said.

Reformed or not, he was not getting behind the wheel of a car that cost Emilio close to half a million dollars. "I'll bet I don't."

Estefan grumbled as they walked out to the garage. Emilio was about to climb in the driver's seat of the Ferrari when he glanced over at the Saab. "Son of a—"

"What's the matter?" Estefan asked.

The rear quarter panel was buckled. For a second he considered that someone had hit it while it was parked, but then he looked closer and noticed the fleck of yellow paint embedded in the black. Not car paint. More like what they used on parking barriers.

He shook his head. "Damn it!"

"Bro, go easy on her. I'm gonna bet she's used to having a driver. It's a wonder she even remembers how to drive."

He walked to the door, yanked it open and yelled, "Isabelle!"

She emerged from her room, looking exasperated. "What did I do this time?"

"Like you don't already know." He gestured her into the garage.

She stepped out. "What?"

"The *car*."

She looked at the Saab. "What about it?

Why was she playing dumb? She knew what she did. "The other side."

She walked around, and as soon as she saw the damage her mouth fell open. "What happened?"

"Are you telling me you don't recall running into something?"

She looked from Emilio, to Estefan, then back to the car. She didn't even have the courtesy to look embarrassed for lying to him. She squared her shoulders and said, "Put it on my tab."

That was it? That was all she had to say? "You might have mentioned this."

"Why? So you could make bad driver jokes about me?"

"What the hell has gotten into you, Isabelle?"

She shrugged. "I guess I'm finally showing my true colors. Living up to your expectations. You should be happy."

She turned and walked back into the house, slamming the door behind her.

"Nice girl," Estefan said.

No, this wasn't like her at all. "Get in the car."

When they were on the road Estefan said, "Dude, she's not worth it."

He knew that, in his head. Logically, they had no future together. The trick was getting the message to his heart. The protective shell he'd built around it was beginning to crumble. He was starting to feel exposed and vulnerable, and he didn't like it.

"Make her leave," Estefan said.

"I can't do that. I gave her my word." Besides, he didn't think she had anywhere else to go.

"Dude, you don't owe her anything."

He'd promised to help her, and in his world, that still meant something. Estefan hadn't kept a promise in his entire life.

They drove the rest of the way to Alejandro's house in silence.

When they stepped through the door, the kids tackled them in the foyer, getting sticky fingerprints all over Emilio's cashmere jacket and slacks, but he didn't care.

"Kids! Give your uncles a break," Alejandro scolded, but he knew they didn't mind.

Chris, the baby, was clinging to Emilio's leg, so he hoisted him up high over his head until he squealed with delight, then gave him a big hug. Reggie, the six-year-old, tugged frantically on his jacket.

"Hey, Uncle Em! Guess what! I'm going to be big brother again!"

"Your dad told me. That's great."

"Jeez, dude," Estefan said with a laugh. "*Four* kids."

Alejandro grinned and shrugged. "Alana wanted to try for a girl. After all these years I still can't tell her no."

"I think she should make a boy," Reggie said. "I don't want a sister."

Emilio laughed and ruffled the boy's hair. "I think she'll get what she gets."

"Hey, Uncle Em, guess who's here!" Alex, the nine-year-old said, hopping excitedly.

"Alex." Alejandro shot his oldest a warning look. "It's supposed to be a surprise."

"Who's here?" Emilio asked him, and from behind him he heard someone say, "Hey, big brother."

He spun around to see his youngest brother, Enrique, standing in the kitchen doorway. He laughed and said, "What the hell are you doing here? I thought you were halfway around the world."

"Mama talked me into it and Alejandro bought my ticket." He hugged Emilio, then Estefan.

"You look great," Estefan told him. "But I'll bet Mama's not very happy about the long hair and goatee."

"She's not," their mama said from the kitchen doorway, hands on her hips, apron tied around her slim waist. She was a youthful fifty-eight, considering the hard life she'd lived. First growing up in the slums of Cuba, then losing her husband so young and raising four boys alone.

"He does look a little scruffy," Alana teased, joining them in the foyer.

"But I finally have all my boys together," their mama said. "And that's all that matters."

Emilio gave his sister-in-law a hug and kiss. "Congratulations, sis."

She grinned. "I'm crazy, right? In this family I'm probably more likely to give birth to conjoined twins than a girl."

Emilio shrugged. "It could happen."

"Why are we all standing around in the foyer?" Alejandro said. "Why don't we move this party to the kitchen?"

For a day that had begun so lousy, it turned out to be the best Thanksgiving in years. The food was fantastic and it was great to have the whole family together again. The best part was that his mama was so excited to have Enrique home, it took her several hours to get around to nagging Emilio about settling down.

"It's not right, you living alone in that big house," she said, as they all sat in the living room, having after dinner drinks. Except Estefan, who was on the floor wrestling with the nephews. He'd been on his best behavior all day.

"I like living alone," Emilio told her. "And if I ever feel the need to have kids, I can just borrow Alejandro's."

"You need to fill it with niños of your own," she said sternly.

"Why don't you nag Enrique about getting married?" Emilio said.

She rubbed her youngest son's arm affectionately. "He's still a baby."

Emilio laughed. "So what does that make me? An old man?"

"You are pretty damn old," Enrique said, which got him plenty of laughs.

Chris climbed into Emilio's lap and hugged him, staring up at him with big brown eyes. And Emilio was thinking that maybe having a kid or two wouldn't be so bad, just as Chris threw up all down the front of his shirt.

"Oh, sweetie!" Alana charged over, sweeping him up off Emilio's lap. "Emilio, I'm so sorry!"

"It's okay," Emilio said, using the tissues his brother handed him to clean himself up.

"Honey, take your brother up and get him a clean shirt. You're the same size, right?"

"I'm sure I have something that will work," Alejandro said, and Emilio followed him upstairs to his bedroom.

Alejandro handed him a clean shirt and said, "While I've got you here, there's something I wanted to ask you."

He peeled off his dirty shirt and gave it to his brother. "What's up?"

"How much do you know about Isabelle's father?"

He was having such a good day, he didn't want to ruin it by thinking about Isabelle and her family. "I'm not sure what you mean. Other than the fact that he was a bastard, not too much I guess."

"Did you know he had a serious gambling problem?"

"So he was an even bigger bastard than we thought. So what?"

"He'd also had charges filed against him."

"For what?"

"Domestic abuse."

Emilio frowned. "Are you sure?"

"Positive. And he must have had friends in high places because I had to dig deep."

Emilio shrugged into the shirt and buttoned it. It was slightly large, but at least it didn't smell like puke. "So he was an even *bigger* bastard."

"There's something else." His grim expression said Emilio probably wasn't going to like this. "There were also allegations of child abuse."

Emilio's pulse skipped. Had Izzie been abused? "Allegations? Was there ever any proof?"

"He was never charged. I just thought you would want to know."

"Can you dig deeper?"

"I could, if it were relevant to my case."

"Are you suggesting I should investigate this further?"

Alejandro shrugged. "That would be a conflict of interest. Although I can say that if it were me, I would try to get a hold of medical records."

"Could this exonerate her?"

"I'm not at liberty to say."

"Damn it, Alejandro."

He sighed. "Probably not, but it might be relevant in her defense."

"I thought she was taking a plea."

"She is, on the advice of counsel, and I think we've already established that she may not be getting the best advice."

So in other words, Alejandro wanted him to dig deeper. He couldn't deny that the idea she might have been mistreated was an unsettling one. He could just ask her, but if she hadn't told him by now, what were the odds she would admit it? And if she had been, wouldn't he have noticed? Or maybe it was something that happened when she was younger.

"I'll look into it."

"Let me know what you find."

He followed his brother back downstairs, but he'd lost his holiday spirit. He felt…unsettled. And not just about the possible abuse. It seemed as though quite a few things lately weren't…adding up. Like why her husband kept her in the lap of luxury and expected nothing in return, and Isabelle's sudden change of personality to Miss Snarky.

"You ready to go?" he asked Estefan an hour later.

"I think I'm going to crash here tonight. Get some quality time with the nephews."

He glanced over at Alejandro, who nodded.

His mama protested him leaving so early, so he used exhaustion from work as an excuse. Everyone knew things had been hectic since the explosion.

He said his goodbyes and headed home. When he pulled into the garage just before nine, he was surprised to find the Saab there. He figured Isabelle would have taken it to her mother's. Or maybe she thought he wouldn't want her driving it now.

He crouched down to look at the dent. He didn't doubt that it was caused by backing into something. She probably wasn't paying attention to where she was going. If she had just fessed up when it happened, it wouldn't have been a big deal. Although it wasn't like her to lie. Every time she screwed up, she owned up to it, and she had looked genuinely surprised when he pointed it out.

Curious, he walked around to the driver's side and got in. He stuck the key in and booted the navigation system, going through the history until he found what he was looking for.

Damn it. What the hell had she been thinking?

Shaking his head, he got out and let himself in the house. There was an empty wine bottle on the counter by the sink. Cheap stuff that Isabelle must have picked up at the grocery store.

He checked the dishwasher and found a dirty plate, fork, cup and pan inside. She hadn't gone to her mother's. She'd spent the holiday alone.

Twelve

Isabelle wasn't in her bedroom, so Emilio went looking for her. He found her asleep in the media room, curled up in a chair in her pajamas, another bottle of wine on the table beside her, this one three quarters empty, and beside it the case for the DVD *Steel Magnolias*. The movie whose credits were currently rolling up the screen. There was a tissue box in her lap and a dozen or so balled up on the seat and floor.

Far as he could tell, she'd spent her Thanksgiving watching chick movies, crying and drinking herself into a stupor with cheap wine.

"Isabelle." He jostled her shoulder. "Isabelle, wake up."

Her eyes fluttered open, fuzzy from sleep, and probably intoxication. "You're home."

"I'm home."

She smiled, closed her eyes and promptly fell back to sleep.

He sighed. Short of dumping a bucket of cold water over her head—which he couldn't deny was awfully tempting— he didn't think she would be waking up any time soon. He just wished she would have told him she was spending Thanksgiving alone.

And he would have…what? Invited her to his brother's? Stayed home with her and ignored his family? He wouldn't have done anything different, other than feel guilty all day.

He picked her up out of the chair and hoisted her into his arms. Her eyes fluttered open and her arms went around his neck. "Where are we going?" she asked in a sleepy voice.

"I'm taking you to bed."

"Oh, okay." Her eyes drifted closed again and her head dropped on his shoulder. He started to walk in the direction of her quarters, but the thought of leaving her in there, alone, isolated from the rest of the house in that uncomfortable little bed…he just couldn't do it.

He carried her upstairs instead, to the spare bedroom beside his room. He pulled the covers back and laid her down, unhooking her arms from around his neck. It was dark, but he could see that her eyes were open.

"Where am I?"

"The guest room. I thought you would be more comfortable here."

"I had too much to drink."

"I know."

She curled up on her side, hugging the pillow. "I don't usually drink, but I didn't think it would be so hard."

"What?"

"Being alone today."

Damn. "Why didn't you go to your mother's?"

"She wanted to be with Ben and his friends."

He had no idea who Ben was. Maybe a friend or boyfriend. "You couldn't go with her?"

"She needs to meet people, make new friends, so it won't be as bad when I'm gone."

By gone he assumed she meant in prison. So she'd spent the day alone for her mother's sake. Not the actions of a spoiled, selfish woman.

He thought about the news his brother had sprung on him tonight and wondered if it could be true, if Isabelle had been abused as a child.

He sat on the edge of the bed. "Isabelle, why didn't you tell me the truth about the car?"

"I told you why."

"What I mean is, why didn't you tell me that it wasn't you who caused the damage?"

She blinked. "Of course I did."

More lies. "I looked in the navigation history. Unless you spent the afternoon at a strip joint downtown, it was Estefan who took the car." He touched her cheek. "Why would you take the fall for him?"

Looking guilty, she shrugged. "You're brothers. I didn't want to get between you."

"You're right, we are brothers. So I know exactly what he's capable of." He brushed her hair back, tucked it behind her ear. "Is there anything else? Anything I should know?"

She gnawed her lip.

"Isabelle?"

"He's been drinking."

Emilio cursed. "How much?"

"As soon as he gets up, pretty much until you get home." She took his hand. "I'm sorry, Emilio."

"I'm disappointed, but not surprised. I've been through this too many times with him before."

"But it sucks when people let you down."

She would know.

"I have a confession to make," she said.

"About Estefan?"

She shook her head. "I ruined your shirt on purpose."

Oddly enough, his first reaction was to laugh. "Why?"

"I was mad at you. For telling Estefan that I was a virgin."

What? "I never told him that. I never told him anything about us, other than it was none of his business."

"So how did he know? He made a remark about it yesterday."

"He was in the kitchen when I walked out of your room. Maybe he heard us talking?"

"All the way from the kitchen? We weren't talking *that* loud."

She was right. He would have had to be listening at the door.

She must have reached the same conclusion, because she made a face and said, "Ew."

"He's staying at Alejandro's tonight, and tomorrow he's out of here."

"No offense, but he's always given me the creeps. Even when he was a kid. I didn't like the way he stared at me."

Then she probably wouldn't want to know that Estefan used to have a crush on her. Apparently he thought that someday they would be together, because he had been furious when he found out that Emilio was dating her. He accused Emilio of stealing her from him.

"Emilio?" she said, squeezing his hand.

"Huh?"

"I didn't marry Lenny for his money. That isn't why I left you. You can think whatever horrible things about me that you want, but don't think that. Okay?"

"I don't think you're horrible. I wanted to, but you're making it really hard not to like you."

"Don't. I don't want you to like me."

"Why?"

"Because I'm going to prison and I don't want to hurt you again. It's better if you just keep hating me."

"Do you hate me?"

"No. I *love* you," she said, like that should have been perfectly obvious. "I always have. But we can't be together. It's not fair."

He didn't even know what to say to that. How could he have ever thought she was selfish? The truth is, she hadn't changed at all. She was still the sweet girl he'd been in love with fifteen years ago. And if her leaving him really had nothing to do with Betts's money, why did she do it?

He knew if he asked her, she wouldn't tell him. He could only hope that the medical records would be the final piece to the puzzle. But there was still one thing he'd been wondering about.

"How was it your mother wound up indicted?"

"After my father died, she knew virtually nothing about finances. She didn't even know what she and my father were worth, and it was a lot less than she expected. He was heavily in debt, and nothing was in my mother's name. After the debts were paid, there wasn't much left. Lenny said he could set up a division of the company in her name. He would do the work and she would reap the benefits, only it didn't turn out that way. She's in trouble because of me."

"I fail to see how that's your fault."

"I encouraged her to sign. I trusted Lenny."

"Does she blame you?"

"Of course not. If she knew I was planning to take a plea in exchange for her freedom, she would have a fit. But my lawyer said that was the only way. She's been through enough."

Izzie's mother had always been kind to him and his brothers, and his mother never had a negative thing to say about her. If she wasn't involved, he didn't want to see her go to jail, either, but if Isabelle was innocent she shouldn't be serving herself up as the sacrificial lamb. She should be trying to fight this.

"I'm sleepy," she said, yawning.

After all that wine, who wouldn't be? "And you're probably going to have one hell of a hangover in the morning."

"Probably."

"Scoot over," he said.

"Why?"

He unbuttoned his shirt. "So I can lie down."

"But—"

"Just go to sleep." The one thing they had never done was spend the night together. He figured it was about time.

And drunk or not, he'd be damned if he was going to let her spend the rest of her Thanksgiving alone.

Isabelle woke sometime in the night with her head in a vise, in a strange room, curled up against Emilio's bare chest.

Huh?

Then she remembered that he had carried her to bed, and the conversation they'd had. Though that part was a little fuzzy. She was pretty sure the gist of it was that Emilio wasn't mad at her anymore. Which was the exact opposite of what she had wanted.

She considered getting up and going to her own bed, but she must have fallen asleep before she got the chance. The next time she woke, Emilio was gone, and someone was inside her skull with a jackhammer.

She crawled out of bed and stumbled downstairs to the kitchen. Emilio was sitting at the island dressed for work, eating a bowl of cereal. When he heard her walk in he turned. And winced.

She must have looked as bad as she felt.

"Good morning," he said.

Not. "Shoot me and put me out of my misery."

"How about some coffee and ibuprofen instead?"

Honestly, death sounded better, but she took the tablets he brought to her and choked down a few sips of coffee.

"Why are you up so early?" he asked.

"I'm supposed to be up. It's a work day."

"Not for you it isn't." He took her coffee cup and put it in the sink, then he took her by the shoulders and steered her toward the stairs. "Back to bed."

"But the house—"

"It can wait a day."

He walked her upstairs to the guest room and tucked her back into bed. "Get some sleep, and don't get up until you're feeling better. Promise?"

"Promise."

He kissed her forehead before he left.

She must have conked right out, because when she woke again, sunshine streamed in through the break in the curtains, and when she sat up she felt almost human. She looked over at the clock on the dresser and was stunned to find it was almost noon. After a cup of coffee and a slice of toast and a few more ibuprofen, she was feeling almost like her old self, so she showered, dressed in her uniform and got to work. She wouldn't have time to do all her chores, but she could make a decent dent in them.

She was polishing the marble in the foyer when Estefan came in, looking about as bad as she felt this morning.

"Rough night?" she asked.

He smirked and walked straight to the kitchen. She heard the fridge open and the rattle of a beer bottle as he pulled it out. Figures. The best thing for a hangover was more alcohol, right?

She went back to polishing, but after several minutes she got an eerie feeling and knew he was watching her.

"Is there something you needed?" she asked.

"Have you got eyes in the back of your head or something?"

She turned to him. "Are you here for your things?"

His eyes narrowed. "Why?"

She just assumed Emilio would have called him by now. Guess not.

His eyes narrowed. "What did you tell Emilio?"

She squared her shoulders. "Nothing he didn't already know."

"You told him about the car?"

"I didn't have to. He looked up the history on the GPS. He knows it was you driving."

He cursed under his breath and mumbled, "It's okay. I can fix this."

She knew she should keep her mouth shut, but she couldn't help herself. "He knows about the drinking, too, and the fact that you were listening outside my bedroom door the other night."

He cut his eyes to her, and with a look that was pure venom, tipped his half-finished beer and dumped it onto her newly polished floor.

Nice. Very mature.

He walked up the stairs to his room. Hopefully to pack.

Isabelle cleaned up the beer with paper towels then repolished the floor. She cleaned all the main floor bathrooms next, buffing the chrome fixtures and polishing the marble countertops.

When she was finished she found Estefan in the living room, booted feet up on the glass top coffee table, drinking Don Julio Real Tequila straight from the bottle.

"You're enjoying this, aren't you?" he asked. "That I have to go, and you get to stay. That once again you mean more to him than his own brother."

Once again? What was that supposed to mean?

"You're leaving him no choice, Estefan."

"What the hell do you know? Emilio and I, we're family," he said, pounding his fist to his chest. "He's supposed to stand behind me. This is all your fault."

She knew his type. Everything was always someone else's fault. He never took responsibility for his own actions.

He took another swig from the bottle. "I loved you, you know. I would have done anything to have you. Then Emilio stole you from me."

Stole her?

So in his mind they had been embroiled in some creepy love triangle? Well, that wasn't reality. Even if there had been no Emilio, she never would have been attracted to Estefan.

He shoved himself up from the couch, wavering a second before he caught his balance. "I'm tired of coming in second place. Maybe I should take what's rightfully mine."

Meaning what?

He started to walk toward her with a certain look, and every instinct she had said *run*.

First thing when he got to work, Emilio called the firm Western Oil had hired to investigate the explosion and explained what he needed.

"Medical records are privileged," the investigator told him.

"So you're saying you can't get them?"

"I can, but you can't use the information in court."

"I don't plan to."

"Give me the name."

"Isabelle Winthrop."

There was a pause. "The one indicted for fraud?"

"That's the one." There was another pause, and he heard the sound of typing. "How long will this take?"

"Hold on." There was more typing, then he said, "Let me make a call. I'll get back to you in a couple of hours."

The time passed with no word and Emilio began to get impatient. He ate lunch at his desk, then forced himself to get some work done. By three o'clock, he was past impatient and bordering on pissed. He was reaching for the phone to call the firm back when his secretary buzzed him.

"Mr. Blair would like to see you in his office."

"Tell him I'll be there in a few minutes."

"He said right now."

He blew out a breath. "Fine."

When he got there Adam's secretary was on the phone, but she waved him in.

Adam stood at the window behind his desk, his back to the door.

"You wanted to see me, boss?"

He didn't turn. "Close the door and sit down."

He shut the door and took a seat, even though he preferred to stand, wondering what he could have done to earn such a cool reception. "Something wrong, Adam?"

"You may not know this, but due to the sensitive nature of the information we receive from the investigators in regard to the refinery accident, the mail room has implicit instruction to send any correspondence directly to my office."

Oh hell.

"So," he said, turning and grabbing a thick manila envelope from his desk, "When this arrived with your name on it, it came to me."

Emilio could clearly see that the seal on top had been broken. "You opened it?"

"Yeah, I opened it. Because for all I know you were responsible for the explosion, and you were trying to reroute key information away from the investigation."

The accusation stung, but put in Adam's place, he might have thought the same thing. He never should have used the same agency. He had just assumed they would call him, at which point he would have told them to send the files to his house.

"You want to explain to me why you need medical records for Isabelle Winthrop?"

"Not really."

Adam sighed.

"It's personal."

"How personal?"

"I just…needed to know something."

He handed Emilio the file. "You needed to know if someone was using her as their own personal punching bag?"

Emilio's stomach bottomed out. He hoped that was an exaggeration.

He pulled the file out of the envelope. It was thorough. Everything was there, from the time she was born until her annual physical the previous year. He flipped slowly through the pages, realizing immediately that Adam was not exaggerating, and what he read made him physically ill.

It seemed to start when she was three years old with a dislocated shoulder. Not a common injury for a docile young girl. From there it escalated to several incidences of concussions and cracked ribs, and a head injury so severe it fractured her skull and put her in the hospital for a week. He would venture to guess that there were probably many other injuries that had gone untreated, or tended by a personal physician who was paid handsomely to keep his mouth shut.

He scraped a hand through his hair. Why hadn't anyone connected the dots? Why hadn't someone *helped* her?

What disturbed him the most, what had him on the verge of losing his breakfast, was the hospital record from fifteen years ago. That weekend had been engraved in his memory since he opened the morning paper and saw the feature announcing Isabelle and Betts's wedding. Four days earlier Isabelle had been treated for a concussion and bruised ribs from a "fall" on campus. Emilio had seen her just two days later and he hadn't had a damned clue.

In the year they had been together what else hadn't he seen?

Then he had a thought that had bile rising in his throat. He was pretty sure that last concussion and the bruised ribs were his fault.

"Son of a bitch."

"Emilio," Adam said. "What's going on?"

Emilio had forgotten Adam was standing there.

"My brother thinks she might be innocent." In fact, he was ninety-nine point nine percent sure she was. "She's... she's been staying with me the last couple of weeks."

Adam swore and shook his head. "You said you wouldn't do anything stupid."

"If she's innocent, she needs my help. That's more clear now than ever."

"Just because someone knocked her around, it doesn't mean she's not a criminal."

"If you knew her like I do, you would know she isn't capable of stealing anything."

"Sounds like your mind is already made up."

It was. And he was going to help her. He had to.

"Emilio, if it gets out to the press what you're doing—"

"It's not going to."

"And if it does? Is she worth decimating your career? Your reputation?"

He was stunned to realize that the answer to that question was yes. Because it would only be temporary, then everyone would know she didn't do it. He would spend his last penny to get to the truth if that's what it took.

"If the press gets hold of this, I'll take full responsibility. As far as I'm concerned, Western Oil is free to hang me out to dry."

"Wow. You must really care about this woman."

"I do." But what really mattered was that fifteen years ago he'd failed her. In the worst possible way. He refused to make that mistake again.

Thirteen

Emilio left work early, and when he opened the front door he heard shouting and banging.

What the hell?

He dropped his briefcase by the door, followed the sound and found Estefan outside his office. The door was closed and Estefan was pounding with his fist shouting, "Let me in, you bitch!"

"What the hell is going on?"

Estefan swung around to face him. He was breathing hard, his eyes wild with fury. "Look what she did to me!"

Deep gouges branded his right cheek. Nail marks.

"*Isabelle* did that? What happened?"

"Nothing. She just attacked me."

That didn't sound like her at all. She'd never had a violent bone in her body. "Move out of the way," he said. "I'll talk to her."

He reluctantly stepped back.

"Wait in the living room."

"But—"

"In the living room."

"Fine," he grumbled.

Emilio waited until his brother was gone, then knocked softly. "Isabelle, it's Emilio. Let me in."

There was a pause, then he heard the lock turn. He opened the door and stepped into the room, and Isabelle launched herself into his arms. She clung to him, trembling from the inside out.

"Let me look at you. Are you okay?" He held her at arm's length. Her uniform was ripped open at the collar and she had what looked liked finger impressions on her upper arms.

He didn't have to ask her what happened. It was obvious. "Son of a bitch."

"He said he was going to take what was rightfully his," she said, her voice trembling. "He was drinking again."

Son of a bitch.

"I kind of accidentally told him that you were going to make him leave. He was really mad."

"I'm going to go talk to him. I want you to go upstairs, in my bedroom, shut the door and wait for me there. Understand?"

She nodded.

If this got out of hand he wanted her somewhere safe. He watched as she dashed up the stairs, waited until he heard the bedroom door close, then walked to the living room, where his brother was pacing by the couch. "What the hell did you do, Estefan?"

Outraged, his brother said, "What did *I* do? Look at my face!"

"You forced yourself on her."

"Is that what she told you? She's a liar. Man, she *wanted* it. She's been coming on to me for days. She's a whore."

Teeth gritted, Emilio crossed the room and gave his brother a shove. Estefan staggered backward, grabbing the couch to stop his fall. He righted himself, then listed to one side, before he caught his balance.

He *was* drunk.

"What's the matter with you, Emilio?"

"What's the matter with *me?* You tried to *rape* her!"

Estefan actually laughed. "If you wanted to keep her all to yourself you should have said so."

Emilio swung, connecting solidly with Estefan's jaw. Estefan jerked back and landed on the floor.

"Emilio, what the hell!"

It took every ounce of control Emilio possessed not to beat the hell out of his brother. "You've crossed the line. Get your stuff and get out."

"You would choose that lying bitch over your own flesh and blood?"

"Isabelle has more integrity in the tip of her finger than you've ever had in your entire miserable excuse for a life."

His expression went from one of outrage to pure venom. This was the Estefan that Emilio knew. The one he had hoped he'd seen the last of. "I'll make you regret this."

Regret? He was already full of it. He thought about what might have happened if he hadn't come home early and he felt ill. What if Estefan had gotten into his office? "The only thing I regret is thinking that this time you might have changed."

"She's using you. Just like she did before."

"You know nothing, Estefan."

"I know her daddy wasn't very happy when I told him about your so-called engagement."

"You told him?"

"You should be thanking me. You were too good for her."

"You stupid son of a bitch. You have no clue what you did."

"I saved your ass, that's what I did."

He'd never wanted to hurt someone as much as he wanted to hurt Estefan right now. Instead he took a deep, calming breath and said, "Pack your things, and get out. As far as I'm concerned, we are no longer brothers."

While his brother packed, Emilio stood watch by the door and called him a cab. Estefan was too drunk to drive himself anywhere. Emilio didn't care what happened to him, but he didn't want him hurting someone else.

Estefan protested when Emilio snatched his keys away.

"Call me and tell me where you are, and I'll have your bike delivered to you."

He slurred out a few more threats, then staggered to the cab. Emilio watched it drive away, then he grabbed his case and headed up to his bedroom. Isabelle was sitting on the edge of his bed. She shot to her feet when he stepped in the room.

"He's gone," Emilio said. "And he isn't coming back."

She breathed a sigh of relief.

Emilio dropped his case on the floor by the bed, pulled her into his arms and held her. "I am so sorry. If I even suspected he would pull something like this I never would have let him stay here. And I sure as hell wouldn't have left you alone with him."

"I guess it was a case of unrequited love," she said, her voice still a little wobbly. "Who knew?"

He had, but he never imagined Estefan was capable of rape. He had been raised to respect women. They all had. There was obviously something wrong in Estefan's head.

"When I think what might have happened if I hadn't come home early…" He squeezed her tighter.

"He's going to tell people that I'm staying here, isn't he?"

"You can count on it." Definitely the family. With any luck he wasn't smart enough to go to the press, or they wouldn't listen.

She looked crestfallen. "If I leave today, right now, maybe it won't be so bad. You can deny I was here at all. And I will, too. No one has to know."

She was nearly raped, and she was worried about *him*. It was sickening how he had misjudged her, how he thought she could have anything to do with her husband's crimes. "You're not going anywhere, Izzie."

"But—"

"I don't care if anyone knows you're here."

"Why?"

"Because you're innocent."

"How do you know that?"

He shrugged. "Because I do."

She didn't seem to know what to say.

"There's something we need to talk about, something I need to know."

She frowned, as though she knew she wasn't going to like what was coming next.

"What did your father do when he found out we were eloping?"

"What makes you think he knew?"

"Because Estefan told him."

She sucked in a quiet breath.

"He did it to get back at me. He said he did it to help me, but I know he was just jealous."

"I always wondered how my father found out."

"Is that why he did it?"

"Did what?"

He opened his briefcase, pulled out the file and handed it to her. She started to read the top page and the color leeched from her face. She sank to the edge of the bed.

He sat beside her. "The concussion, the bruised ribs. He did that because of me, didn't he?"

She flipped through the pages, then looked up at him, eyes wide. "Where did you get this?"

"Why didn't you tell me, Izzie? Why didn't you tell me what he did to you?"

She shrugged, setting the file on the bed beside her. "Because that's not the way it works."

"I could have helped you."

She shook her head. "No one could help us."

Us? "Your mother, too?"

"My father was a very angry man. But if there's any justice in this world, I can rest easy knowing he's rotting in hell for what he did to us."

He could barely wrap his head around it. How could he have been so blind? Why didn't he see?

"I know you don't like to talk about it, but I have to know. Why did you do it? Why did you leave me for Betts?"

"It was the only way to keep her safe."

"Your mother?"

She nodded.

"Tell me what happened."

She bit her lip, wringing her hands in her lap.

He took her hand in his and held it. "Please, Isabelle."

"My father found out about us and *punished* me. When he was finished, he told me that if I ever saw you again he was going to disown me. I would be completely cut off. I was so sick of it, I told him I didn't care. I said I didn't want his money, and I didn't care if I ever saw him again.

I said I was going to marry you, and my mother was going to come live with us and nothing he could do would stop me." She took a deep, unsteady breath. "And he said...he said that if I married you, something terrible would happen to my mother. He said she would have an 'accident.'" She looked up at him. "My father did not make idle threats, and the look in his eyes...I knew he would kill her just to spite me. And to prove his point he punished her, too, and it was even worse than what he did to me. She couldn't get out of bed for a week."

Sick bastard. If Isabelle had a concussion and bruised ribs, he couldn't even imagine what he must have put her mother through.

Emilio felt sick to his stomach, sick all the way to his soul. "Did he force you to marry Betts?"

"Not exactly. Usually he was good about hiding the marks, but this time he didn't even try. My parents had been friends with Lenny for years. Long story short, he happened to stop by and saw the condition we were in. He was horrified. He'd suspected that my father was abusive, but he had no idea how bad it was. He wanted to call the police, but my mom begged him not to."

"Why? They could have helped you."

"Because she tried that before. My father was a very powerful man. The charges had a way of disappearing."

Alejandro had said as much.

"Lenny figured if he couldn't help my mother, he could at least get me out of there. He knew my father would agree to a marriage."

"A marriage between his nineteen-year-old daughter and a man in his forties?"

"My father saw it as a business opportunity. He had debts, and Lenny promised to make them go away."

The gambling Alejandro had mentioned. Just when

Emilio didn't think he could feel more disgust, her father sank to a whole new level of vile. "He *sold* you."

She shrugged. "More or less."

"So what was the going rate for a nineteen-year-old virgin?"

She lowered her eyes. "Lenny wouldn't tell me. Hundreds of thousands. Maybe millions. Who knows."

"If you had told me then, I would have taken you away. You and your mother. I would have killed your father if that's what it took to keep you both safe. I would kill him now if he wasn't already dead."

"And that's exactly why I couldn't tell you. If you only knew how many times she tried to leave. But he always found us and brought us back. He would have hurt you if you had tried to help. Look what he did to your mother just to spite me. At least Lenny had been able to take me away from it. And you were safe and free to live your life."

It was hard to fathom that Izzie's husband, a man that Emilio had despised for so many years, had really saved her life.

Only to turn around and ruin it again, he reminded himself.

"The sad fact is, I never should have come to see you that day on campus," Izzie said. "I should have known he would never let it happen, not if there wasn't something in it for him."

"I've never said this about another human being, but I'm glad your father is dead."

Her smile was a sad one. "No more than my mother and I."

"I'm sorry I've been such a jerk."

She shrugged. "I hurt you."

"That doesn't make it right."

She reached up, stroked his cheek. "Emilio, not a day

has gone by when I didn't miss you, and wished it were you I had married. It's going to sound silly, but I never stopped loving you. I still haven't."

A sudden surge of emotion caught him completely by surprise. He slipped his arms around her and pulled her against him, pressed his face against the softness of her hair. He wanted to hold her close and never let go, yet he couldn't help thinking he didn't deserve her love. He'd failed her, and all because he couldn't see past his own wounded pride. He should have trusted her. When he read in the papers that she was marrying Betts, he should have known something was wrong, that she would never willingly betray him.

He had promised to take care of her, to protect her and he'd let her down when she needed him most.

"Isabelle—"

She put her fingers over his lips to shush him. "No more talking."

She slid her arms around his neck and kissed him. And kept kissing him, until the past ceased to matter. All he cared about was being close to her. They would start over today, this very minute, and things would be different this time. He would take care of her and protect her. The way it should have been fifteen years ago.

Though there was no rush, Isabelle seemed in a hurry to get them both naked. She shoved his jacket off his shoulders, then undid the buttons on his shirt and pushed that off, too. Then she unbuttoned her dress and pulled it up over her head. Her bra was next to go, until all that was left was her panties.

She took those off, then pulled back the covers and stretched out on the bed, summoning him with a smile and a crooked finger.

"I like that you're not shy anymore," he said rising to take off his pants.

"There are no bruises or marks to hide now."

He hadn't even considered that. "Is that why you never let me see you undressed?"

"I wanted to, but I knew there would be questions."

"Isabelle."

"No more talking about the past. Let's concentrate on today. On right now. Make love to me, and nothing else will matter."

That was by far the best idea she'd had all day.

Fourteen

Emilio stripped out of his clothes and climbed into bed with Isabelle. Since Tuesday she hadn't stopped thinking about making love to him again. Only this time she wasn't nervous. This time she had nothing to hide. He knew her secrets. She could relax and be herself. Until the weight of everything she had hidden from him was finally gone, she hadn't realized what a heavy load she'd carried. And when Emilio took her in his arms and kissed her, she knew he was back to being the man he used to be. Sweet and tender and thoughtful.

Ironically that wasn't what she wanted now. She was eager to experiment. She wanted it to be crazy and exciting. There were hundreds of different ways to make love and she wanted to try as many as she could before she had to go. She wanted it to be fun.

"Emilio, I'm not going to break."

He gazed down at her, brow furrowed. "I just don't

want to hurt you again. And after what happened to you today…if you want to wait, we can take a few days."

They had so little time left, she didn't want to waste any of it. And she didn't want him to feel as if he had to treat her with kid gloves. "First of all, if you're referring to Tuesday night, you did not hurt me."

Up went the brow.

"Okay, maybe it hurt a little, but only for a minute. And it wasn't a bad hurt, if that makes sense. And after that it was…*amazing*. And as far as what happened today, yeah it scared the hell out of me, but that has nothing to do with us. I know you would never hurt me."

"But I did." He stroked her hair back from her face, touched her cheek. "I've been a total jerk the last couple weeks, and you've done absolutely nothing to deserve it."

"Except the rug, and the casserole dish, and the pink laundry. And of course the scorched shirt."

"That doesn't count. I put you in a position to fail so I could throw it back in your face."

"And I've forgiven you."

He sighed and rolled onto his back. "Maybe that's part of the problem. Maybe I feel like I don't deserve your forgiveness."

She sat up beside him. "In that case, you have to forgive *yourself*. You've got to let it go. Trust me on this one. If I hadn't made peace with my father, and Lenny, I would probably be in a padded room by now."

"How? How do you let it go?"

She shrugged. "You just do."

"I'm just so…*mad*."

"At yourself?"

"At myself, and at your father. For what he did to you, and everything he stole from us. Everything that we could have been. If it wasn't for him, we would be married, we would probably have kids." He pushed himself up on his elbows. "I'm pissed at Estefan for ratting us out, and Alejandro for prosecuting you when I'm pretty sure he knows damn well that you're innocent. I'm pissed at every person who suspected your father was abusive and did nothing about it. I feel like I'm mad at the whole damned world!"

"So let it out."

"I can't."

"Yes, you can." She reached over and pinched his left nipple. Hard.

"Hey!" He batted her hand away, looking stunned, as if he couldn't believe she would do something like that. Sweet, nonconfrontational Isabelle. "What was that for?"

He was going to have to accept that she had changed. "Did it hurt?"

"Yeah, it hurt."

"Good." She did the same thing to the right side.

"Ow! Stop that!"

She pinched the fleshy skin under his bicep next and he jerked away.

"Izzie, stop it."

She climbed into his lap, straddling his thighs. "Make me."

She moved to pinch him again and his hand shot out to manacle her wrist, and when she tried to use her other hand, he grabbed that wrist, too. She struggled to yank free, but he held on tighter, almost to the point of pain. But that was good, that was what she wanted. She didn't want him to look at her as some frail flower he needed to protect. She wanted him to know how tough she was.

Since her hands were restrained, she leaned in and bit him instead, on his left shoulder. Not hard enough to break the skin, but enough to cause pain.

He jerked away. "Isabelle! What's gotten into you?"

"Are you pissed?"

"Yes, I'm pissed!"

"Good." She leaned in to do it again, but he'd apparently had enough. Finally. He pulled her down on top of him then rolled her onto her back, pinning her wrists over her head.

She'd never thought of herself as the type who would be into anything even remotely kinky, but she was so hot for him, she was afraid she might spontaneously combust. Emilio settled between her thighs, holding her to the mattress with the weight of his body, and it was clear that he liked it, too. A lot.

She hooked her legs around his, arching against him. He groaned and his eyes went dark, breath rasped out. So she did it again, bucking against him.

"Izzie." His voice held a warning, stop or else, but she *wanted* the "or else."

Lifting her head, she scraped her teeth across his nipple. She would keep biting and pinching and bucking until he gave her what she wanted. Only this time he turned the tables on her. He dipped his head and took her nipple in his mouth, sucked hard.

She cried out, pushing against his hands, digging her nails into her palms. *"Yesss."*

"You *like* this," he said.

His eyes said that he'd finally figured it out. He knew what she wanted.

It was about damned time.

She knew Emilio liked to be composed at all times, but she wanted him to lose control, to do something crazy.

He kissed her, like he never had before. A hard, punishing kiss. He started to work his way down, to her neck and her shoulders, kissing and nipping. Then he slipped lower still, letting go of her wrists so he could press her thighs wide. She thought they would make love right away, but clearly he had other ideas.

She held her breath in anticipation, gasping as he took her in his mouth. Oral sex had been a regular routine for them, and it was always good, but never like this. He was *devouring* her. She clawed her nails through his hair, so close to losing it…then he thrust a finger inside of her, then another, then a third, slow and deep, and pleasure seized her like a wild animal.

Emilio rose up and settled between her thighs, thrusting hard inside of her, and the orgasm that had begun to ebb slowly away suddenly picked up momentum again, only this time from somewhere deep inside. Somewhere she'd never felt before. Maybe her soul. It erupted into a sensation so beautiful and perfect, so exactly what she ever hoped it could be, tears welled in her eyes. And she was so utterly lost in her own pleasure she didn't realize he had come, too, until he flopped onto his back beside her.

"Wow," he said, breathing hard.

"So, are you still mad?"

He laughed—a genuine honest to goodness laugh. A sound she hadn't heard out of him in a very long time. "Not at all. In fact, I can't recall the last time I was so relaxed."

She smiled and curled up against his side. "Good."

"I didn't hurt you?"

"Are you kidding? That was *perfect.*" And it must have been really good for him, too, because he was still mostly hard. Then she realized something that made her heart drop. "Emilio, you didn't use a condom."

"I know."

She shot up in bed. "You *know?* You did it *deliberately?*"

He didn't even have the decency to look remorseful.

"Not exactly. I realized the minute I was inside of you, but I didn't think you would appreciate me stopping to roll one on."

"Did it occur to you that I could get pregnant?"

"Of course."

"What did you think? That me being pregnant with his brother's baby will stop Alejandro from putting me in prison? They put pregnant women in prison all the time. Are you prepared to raise a baby alone? To be a single dad for the next twenty-to-life? Maybe if I get out early on good behavior I'll see him graduate high school."

"You're not going to prison."

She groaned and dropped her head in her hands. The man was impossible.

"Do you think you could be pregnant?" he asked.

"My period is due soon, so I'd say it's unlikely."

He actually looked disappointed. How had he gone from hating her one day, to wanting to have babies with her the next? This was crazy. Even if she didn't go to prison his family would never accept her.

"Can I ask you a question?" he said.

"Sure."

"Since you've told me everything else, would you explain how you never slept with Lenny? Because I really don't get it. I can't go five minutes without wanting to rip your clothes off."

"He had a heart condition and he was impotent. Ultimately he did screw me, just not in the bedroom."

"After your father died you could have divorced him."

"There didn't seem to be much point. There was only one other man I wanted." She touched his arm. "And I knew he would never take me back, never forgive me."

"I guess you were wrong."

"It would probably be better if you hadn't."

"You're *not* going to prison."

"Yes, I am. Nothing is going to stop that now."

"I just got you back, Izzie. I'm not letting you go again."

But he was going to have to. He couldn't keep her out of prison by sheer will. He was going to have to accept that they were living on borrowed time.

"Things are going to change around here," he said.

"What things?"

"First off, I'm calling my housekeeper back."

"You can't do that. You gave her the month off. It's not fair."

"So I'll hire a temp."

"But I like doing it."

He raised a brow at her.

"I do. And it gives me something to do. A way to pass the time, since I doubt all those charities I used to volunteer for would be interested in my services any longer."

"Are you sure?"

"Positive."

"Okay, but you're not allowed to wear the uniform anymore. And I'm buying you some decent clothes."

"There's no point."

"There sure as hell is. The ones you have are awful."

"And I'll only need them for another few weeks. Getting anything new would be a waste of money."

She could tell he wanted to argue, but he probably figured there was no point. She was not going to budge on this one. Besides, the last thing she wanted was for him to spend money on her. She didn't deserve it.

"You're obviously not staying in the maid's quarters any longer. You're moving in here with me. If you want to."

"Of course I do." It was probably a bad idea. The closer they got, the harder it would be when she had to go, but she had the feeling nothing would prevent that now. They might as well spend all the time they could together.

"You have a say in this, too," he said. "Is there anything you'd like to add? Anything you want?"

There were so many things she wanted. She wanted to marry him, and have babies with him. She wanted to do everything they had talked about before. It's all she had ever wanted. But why dwell on a future that wasn't meant to be?

The phone rang, so she grabbed the cordless off the bedside table and handed it to him. He looked at the display and cursed under his breath. "Well, that didn't take long."

He sat up and hit the talk button. "Hello, Mama."

Isabelle winced. Estefan hadn't wasted any time running to his mother, had he?

He listened for a minute, then said, "Yes, it's true."

She could hear his mother talking. Not what she was saying, but her tone came through perfectly. She was upset.

"I know he was drunk. Are you really surprised?"

More talking from his mother's end, then Emilio interrupted her. "Why don't I come over there right now so we can talk about this?"

She must have agreed, because then he said, "I'll be over as soon as I can."

He hung up and set the phone back on the table. "I guess you got the gist of that."

"Yeah."

"I shouldn't be too long."

"Take your time." He wasn't the only one who needed to talk to their mother. "I was thinking maybe I could go talk to my mother, too. I'd hate for her to hear it from someone besides me."

"I think that's a good idea. I'll pick up Chinese food on my way home."

"Sounds good." Although after dealing with their parents, she wondered if either of them would have much of an appetite.

Fifteen

Emilio parked in the driveway of his mother's condo. The year he'd made his first million he'd bought it for her. He'd wanted to get her something bigger and in a more affluent part of the city, but she had wanted to live here, in what was a primarily Hispanic neighborhood. Not that this place was what anyone would consider shabby. It had been brand-new when he bought it, and he made sure it had every upgrade they offered, and a few he requested special. After sacrificing so much for Emilio and his brothers, she deserved the best of everything.

He walked to the front door and let himself inside. "Mama?"

"In the kitchen," she called back.

He wasn't surprised to find her at the counter, apron on, adding ingredients to a mixing bowl. She always baked when she was upset or angry.

"What are you making?"

"Churros, with extra cinnamon, just the way you like them." She gestured to the kitchen table. "Sit down, I'll get you something to drink."

She pulled a pitcher of iced tea from the fridge and poured him a glass. He would have preferred something stronger, but she never kept alcohol of any kind in the house.

Handing it to him, she went back to the bowl, mixing the contents with a wooden spoon. "I guess you saw your brother's face."

"I saw it."

"He said she attacked him. For no good reason."

"Attempted rape is a pretty good reason."

She cut her eyes to him. "Emilio! Your brother would never do that. He was raised to respect women."

Emphatically as she denied it, something in her eyes said she was afraid it might be true.

"If you had seen Isabelle, the ripped uniform and the bruises on her arms… She was terrified."

She muttered something in Spanish and crossed herself.

"He needs help, Mama."

"I know. He told me that bad people are after him. He asked to stay here. I told him no."

"Good. We can't keep trying to save him. We have to let him hit rock bottom. He has to want to help himself."

"You told him you're no longer brothers. You didn't mean it."

"I did mean it. He hurt the woman I love."

"How can you love her after what she did to you? She left you for that rich man. She only cared about money. That's the only reason she's back now."

"She came to me because she wanted help for her mother, not herself. And she didn't marry Betts for his money. The only reason she left me for him is because her father threatened to hurt her mother."

He waited for the shock, but there was none, confirming what he already suspected. "You knew about the abuse, didn't you? You knew that Isabelle's father was hurting them. You *had* to."

She didn't answer him.

"Mama."

"Of course I knew," she said softly. "The things that man did to them." She closed her eyes and shook her head, as if she were trying to block the mental image. "It made me sick. And poor Mrs. Winthrop. Sometimes he beat her so badly, she would be in bed for days. And Isabelle, she always stayed right by her mother's side. I never speak ill of the dead, but that man did the world a favor when he died."

"You should have told me. I could have helped her."

She shook her head. "No. He would have hurt you, too. I was always afraid that something bad would happen if he found out about you and Isabelle."

"Well, he found out." He almost told her that Estefan was the one who ratted him out, but he didn't want to hurt her any more than necessary.

"You had the potential to go so far, Emilio. I was relieved when she left you."

"Even though you knew how much I loved her?"

"I figured you would get over her eventually."

"But I didn't. As bitter as I was, I never stopped loving her."

Was that guilt in her eyes? "What difference does it make now? Alejandro said she's going to prison."

"Not if I can help it."

She set the spoon down and pushed the bowl aside. "She stole money."

"No, she didn't. She's innocent."

"You know that for a fact?"

"I know it in my heart. In every fiber of my being. She's not a thief."

"Even if that's true, everyone thinks she's guilty."

He shrugged. "I don't care what everyone thinks."

"Emilio—"

"Mama, do you remember what you told me when I asked you why you never remarried? You said Papa was your one true love, and there could be no one else. I finally understand what you meant. I was lucky enough to get Izzie back. I can't lose her again."

"Even if it means ruining everything you've worked so hard for?"

"That's not going to happen. First thing Monday, I'm hiring a new attorney."

"People will find out."

"They probably will."

"And I could argue with you until I'm blue in the face and it won't do any good, will it?"

He shook his head.

She drew in a deep breath, then blew it out. "Then I will pray for you, Emilio. For you and Isabelle."

"Thank you, Mama." At this point, he would take all the help he could get.

Isabelle called her mother Friday, but she was out with Ben. They went to dinner with friends, then they left Saturday morning for an overnight trip to Phoenix to see an old college buddy of Ben's. Isabelle didn't get a chance to talk to her until Monday morning. She took the news much better than Isabelle expected. In fact, she suspected all along that Isabelle had been "bending" the truth.

"Sweetheart," she said, fixing them each a cup of tea

in her tiny kitchenette. "You know I can always tell when you're lying. And, *Mrs. Smith?*"

Isabelle couldn't help but smile. "Not very creative, huh?"

"I thought it was awfully coincidental that you were working in the same neighborhood where Emilio lived. Then I mentioned him and you got very nervous."

"And people think I'm capable of stealing millions of dollars." She sighed. "Not only am I a terrible liar, but I don't even know how to balance a checkbook."

Her mother walked over with their tea and sat down at the table.

"I'm sorry I lied to you, but I promised Emilio I wouldn't tell anyone I was staying there. It was part of our deal."

"Emilio is going to help you, right?"

"He's going to talk to his brother on your behalf. You won't be serving any time."

"But what about you?"

They had been through this so many times. "There isn't anything he can do. You know what Lenny's lawyer said. The evidence against me is indisputable."

"There has to be something Emilio can do. Can't he talk to his brother? Make some sort of deal?"

She was just as bad as Emilio, refusing to accept reality. She wished they would both stop being so stubborn. But she didn't want her mother to worry so she said, "I'll ask him, okay?"

Her mother looked relieved.

"So, tell me about this weekend trip. Did you have fun?"

She lit up like a firefly. "We had a *wonderful* time. Ben has the nicest friends. The only thing that was a little unexpected was that they put us in a bedroom together."

Her brows rose. "Oh really?"

"Nothing happened," she said, then her cheeks turned

red and she added, "Well, nothing much. But he is a very nice kisser."

"Only nice?"

Her smile was shy, with a touch of mischief. "Okay, better than nice."

They talked about her trip with Ben and what they had planned for the coming weekend. He clearly adored her mother, and the feeling was mutual. Isabelle was so happy she had found someone who appreciated her, and made her feel good about herself. At the same time she was a little sad that she wouldn't be around to see their relationship grow. Of course, they could always write letters, and her mother could visit.

Maybe she was a little jealous, too, that she had finally found her heart's desire, and it had to end in only a few weeks. They wouldn't even get to spend Christmas together.

She drove back to Emilio's fighting the urge to feel sorry for herself. When she pulled in the driveway there was an unfamiliar car parked there. A silver Lexus. She considered pulling back out. What if it was someone who shouldn't know she was staying there? But hadn't Emilio said he didn't care who knew?

She pulled the Saab in the garage and let herself in the house. Emilio met her at the door. "There you are. I was about send out a search party."

"I went to see my mother."

"Is everything okay? She wasn't angry?"

"Not at all."

"I need to get you a cell phone, so I can reach you when you're out."

For less than a month? What was the point? "Is there something wrong?"

"Nothing. In fact, I have some good news. Come in the living room, there's someone I want you to meet."

There was a man sitting on the couch, a slew of papers on the table in front of him. When they entered the room, he stood.

"Isabelle, this is David Morrison."

He was around Emilio's age, very attractive and dressed in a sharp, tailored suit. "Ms. Winthrop," he said, shaking her hand. "It's a pleasure to meet you."

"You, too," she said, shooting Emilio a questioning look.

"David is a defense attorney. One of the best. He's going to be taking over your case."

"What?"

"We're firing Clifton Stone."

"But…why?"

"Because he's giving you bad advice," Mr. Morrison said. "I've been going over your case. The evidence against you is flimsy at best. We'll take this to trial if necessary, but honestly, I don't think it will come down to that."

"I was using Lenny's lawyer because he was representing me pro bono. I can't afford a lawyer."

"It's taken care of," Emilio said.

She shook her head. "I can't let you do this."

"The retainer is paid. Nonrefundable. It's done."

"But I can't go to trial. The only way my mother will avoid prison is if I plead out." She turned to her "new" attorney. "Mr. Morrison—"

"Please, call me David."

"David, I really appreciate you coming to see me, but I can't do this."

"Ms. Winthrop, do you want to spend the next twenty years in prison?"

Was this a trick question? Did anyone *want* to go to prison? "Of course not."

"If you stick with your current attorney, that's what will happen. I've seen lawyers reprimanded and in some cases disbarred for giving such blatantly negligent counsel. Either he's completely incompetent, or he has some sort of agenda."

Agenda? How could he possibly benefit from her going to prison? "What about my mother? What happens to her?"

"Alejandro already told me they wouldn't ask for more than probation," Emilio said.

"When did he say that?"

He hesitated, then said, "The day you came to see me in my office."

So all this time she'd been working for him for no reason? She should be furious, but the truth was, it was a million times better here than at that dumpy motel. And if she hadn't come here, Emilio would have gone the rest of his life hating her. Maybe now they even had some sort of future together. Marriage and family, just like they had planned. Hope welled up with such intensity she had to fight it back down. She was afraid to believe it was real.

"You really think you could keep me and my mother out of prison?" she asked David.

"Worst case you may end up with probation. It would go a long way if the last few million of the missing money were to surface."

"If I knew where it was I would have handed it over months ago. I gave them everything else."

"I'm going to do some digging and see what turns up. In the meantime, I need you to sign a notice of change of counsel to make it official."

She signed the document, but only after thoroughly reading it—she had learned her lesson with Lenny—then David packed up his things and left.

"I told you I wouldn't let you go to prison," Emilio said,

sounding smug, fixing himself a sandwich before he went back to work.

"I still don't like that you're paying for it. What if someone finds out?"

"I've already said a dozen times—"

"You don't care who finds out. I know. But I do. Until I know for sure that I'm not going to prison, I don't want anyone to know. Even if that means waiting through a trial."

"I suppose that means we'll have to wait to get married."

Married? She opened her mouth to speak, but nothing came out. She knew he wanted to be with her, but this was the first time he had actually mentioned marriage.

"I was hoping we could start a family right away," he said, putting the turkey and the mayo back in the fridge. "If we haven't already, that is. But we've waited this long. I guess a few more months won't kill me. Just so long as you know that I love you, and no matter what happens, I'm not letting you go again."

He loved her, and wanted to marry her, and have a family with her. She threw her arms around him and hugged him tight. This was more than she ever could have hoped for. "I love you, too, Emilio."

"This is all going to work out," he told her, and she was actually starting to believe it.

"So, do you have to go back to work?" she asked, sliding her hands under his jacket and up his chest.

He grinned down at her. "That depends what you have in mind."

Though they had spent the better part of the weekend making love in bed—and on the bedroom floor and in the shower, and even on the dining room table—she could never get enough of him. "We haven't done it in the kitchen yet."

He lifted her up and set her on the counter, sliding her skirt up her thighs. "Well, that's an oversight we need to take care of immediately."

Sixteen

Isabelle never imagined things could be so wonderful. She and Emilio were going to get married and have a family—even though he hadn't officially asked her yet—and she and her mother weren't going to prison. Her life was as close to perfect as it could be, yet she had this gut feeling that the other shoe was about to drop. That things were a little *too* perfect.

Emilio wasn't helping matters.

He called her from work Thursday morning to warn her that a package would be arriving. But it wasn't one package. It was a couple dozen, all filled with clothes and shoes from department stores and boutiques all over town. It was an entire wardrobe, and it was exactly what she would have picked for herself.

Her first instinct was tell him to send it back, but now that she wasn't going to prison she did need new clothes.

"How did you know what I would like?" she asked Emilio when she called to thank him.

"I had help."

"What kind of help?"

"A personal shopper, so to speak. I swore her to secrecy."

Her? Who would know her exact taste, that Emilio knew to contact? There was really only one person. "My *mother?*"

"I knew you wouldn't get the clothes yourself, and who better to know what you like?"

"I talked to her this morning and she didn't say a word."

"She wanted it to be a surprise. If there's anything that you don't like just put it aside and I'll have it returned."

"It's all perfect."

"There should be something coming later this afternoon, too. A few things I picked out."

Isabelle called her mother to thank her, but she wasn't home so she left a message. After that she waited, very impatiently, until the package with Emilio's purchases arrived later that afternoon. She carried it into the living room where she had been sorting and folding all the other things.

Sitting on the couch, she ripped it open. It was lingerie. The first two items she pulled out were soft silk gowns in pink and white. When she saw what was underneath the gowns she actually blushed. Sexy items of silk and lace that were scandalously revealing. She'd never owned anything so provocative. There had never been any point.

She called Emilio immediately to thank him.

"I wasn't sure if they would be a little too racy," he said.

"No, I love them!"

"You'll have to try them on for me later."

"I might just be wearing one when you walk in the door," she said, and could practically feel his sexy smile right through the phone line.

"In that case I may just have to come home early."

After they hung up Isabelle was gathering all her new clothes to take upstairs when the doorbell rang again.

More new clothes?

She walked to the foyer and pulled the door open, expecting another delivery man, but when she saw who was standing there her heart plummeted. "Mrs. Suarez."

"May I come in?" Emilio's mother asked.

"Of course," she said, stepping aside so she could come inside. "Emilio isn't here."

"I came to talk to you."

The last time she had seen Mrs. Suarez, Isabelle's father had been accusing her of stealing from them. And after threatening to have her arrested, and her younger children taken away by Social Services, he'd fired her.

The phone started to ring. "Let me grab that really fast," Isabelle said, dashing to the living room where she'd left the cordless phone, answering with a breathless, "Hello?"

It was her mother. "Hi honey, I just got your message. I'm so glad you like the clothes. Wasn't that a sweet thing for Emilio to do?"

"Yes, it was. Mom, can I call you back?"

"Is everything okay?"

"Everything is fine." She glanced over and realized Mrs. Suarez had followed her. She was looking at the piles of clothes strewn over the furniture, specifically the lingerie, and she did not look happy.

Oh, hell.

"I'll call you soon." She disconnected and turned to Mrs. Suarez. "Sorry about that."

"How is your mother?"

"Really good." She gestured to the one chair that wasn't piled with clothes. "Please, sit down. Can I get you something to drink?"

His mother sat. "No, thank you."

Isabelle moved some of the clothes from the end of the couch and sat down.

"It looks like you've been shopping." With her son's money her look said. Talk about awkward.

"Actually, Emilio had my mother pick them out and they were delivered a little while ago."

"He's a very generous man." Her tone suggested that generosity was wasted on someone like Isabelle. Or maybe Isabelle was being paranoid. Put in his mother's position, she might not trust her, either.

There was an awkward pause, and Isabelle blurted out, "I'm so sorry for what happened with Estefan."

She looked puzzled. "Why are *you* sorry? Emilio said Estefan forced himself on you. You had every right to defend yourself. I see the bruises are fading."

Isabelle glanced down at her arms. The marks Estefan had left there had faded to a greenish-yellow. "I still feel bad for scratching him."

"Estefan is part of the reason I'm here. I wanted to apologize on his behalf. I felt it was my duty as his mother."

"Is he okay?"

"I don't know. He disappeared again. It could be months before I see him." Isabelle must have looked guilty because Mrs. Suarez added, "This is not your fault."

Logically she knew that, but she felt responsible.

"I also wanted to talk to you about Emilio."

She'd assumed as much.

"He says you're innocent."

"I have a new attorney. He says he thinks I'll be acquitted, or let off with probation."

"And Emilio is paying for this new lawyer?"

"I didn't want him to, but he insisted. And if he hadn't, I would have spent the next twenty years in prison."

"Emilio has done you many favors. Now I want you to do him a favor."

"Of course. Anything."

"Leave."

Leave? She didn't know what to say.

"Only until you are found innocent." Her eyes pleaded with Isabelle. "My son has worked so hard to get where he is, and because he loves you, he would risk throwing it all away. If you love him, you won't allow that to happen."

"And if I'm not acquitted? If I wind up with probation?"

Mrs. Suarez didn't say anything, but it was written all over her face. She wanted Isabelle to leave him for good. And her reasoning was totally logical.

The CFO of a company like Western Oil couldn't be married to a woman out on probation for financial fraud. They would have no choice but to fire him, and he would never find another job like it. At least, not one that would pay him even a fraction of what he was worth. Not to mention that he would lose all his friends.

Because of her, he would be a pariah.

He said he loved her and didn't care what people thought, but with his life in shambles he might feel differently. He would begin to resent her, and they would be right back to where they were before, only this time he would hate her not for leaving, but for staying. She couldn't do that to him.

Just once she had wanted something for herself, she

had wanted to be happy. For the first time in her life she wanted to do something selfish.

But Mrs. Suarez was right. It was time for her to go.

"I had an interesting talk with Cassandra," Adam said from Emilio's office doorway.

He glanced up from his computer screen. He had just a few things he needed to finish up before he went home for the night. "Is there another public relations nightmare on the horizon?"

"You tell me."

"Meaning what?"

He stepped into his office and shut the door. "Cassandra got a call from a reporter asking if it was true that there was a connection between Isabelle Winthrop-Betts and the CFO of Western Oil."

He sighed. *Here we go.*

"What did she tell them?"

"That she knows of no association, then she came and asked me about it. So I'm asking you, what's the status of her case? Someone is digging, and I get the feeling something big is about to break."

"I hired a new attorney. He wants to take it to trial. He thinks he can get an acquittal."

"But it will take some time."

"Probably."

Adam shook his head.

"If you have something to say, just say it, Adam."

"If she goes to trial and the story breaks about the two of you… Emilio, the damage will be done. You'll never make CEO. The board would never allow it. I can't guarantee they won't vote to terminate you immediately."

"Let me ask you something. Suppose Katy was accused

of a crime, and you knew she was innocent. Would you stand behind her, even if it meant making sacrifices?"

Adam took a deep breath and blew it out. "Yes, of course I would."

"Then why is everyone so surprised that I'm standing behind Isabelle? Do I want to be CEO? Do I think I'm the best man for the job? You're damn right I do. But what kind of CEO, what kind of *man* would I be if didn't stand up for the things I believe in? If I abandoned Isabelle when she needs me most?"

"You're right," Adam said. "I admire what you're doing, and I'll back you as long as I can."

"I know you will. And when it comes to the point that you can't help me, don't lose a night's sleep over it. This is my choice."

His secretary buzzed him. "I'm sorry to interrupt, Mr. Suarez, but your brother is on line one. He says it's important."

"Which brother?"

"Alejandro."

"Go ahead and take it," Adam said. "We'll talk later."

Adam left, and Emilio hit the button for line one. "Hey, Alejandro, what's up?"

"Hey, big brother, I was wondering if you're going to be home this evening."

"This was so important you would interrupt a meeting with my boss?"

"Actually, it is. I need to talk to you. In person."

"What time?"

"The earlier the better. Alana doesn't like it when I come home too late."

Emilio thought about Isabelle's promise to model the new lingerie. If he met with Alejandro early, then he and Isabelle would have the rest of the evening.

"Why don't you meet me at my house in an hour?"

"Sounds good. Will Isabelle be there?"

"Of course. Is that a problem?"

"No, I'll see you in an hour."

Seventeen

As his driver took him home, Emilio got to thinking about what Alejandro could possibly need to discuss that was so urgent. It couldn't have anything to do with Isabelle's case, because he wasn't allowed to question her without her lawyer present.

His driver dropped him at the front door and Emilio let himself inside—and nearly tripped over the suitcases sitting there. "What the hell?"

Isabelle appeared at the top of the stairs, and she was clearly surprised to see him. She was dressed in what he was guessing were her new clothes. She looked young and hip and classy. So different from the scrawny, desperate woman who had come to see him in his office.

"You're home early," she said, her tone suggesting that wasn't a good thing.

"Yeah, I'm home." He set his briefcase on the floor next to the open door. "What the hell is going on?"

She walked down the stairs, met him in foyer. "I was going to leave you a note."

"You're going somewhere?"

"I'm moving out."

"Why?"

"Because I have to. I can't let you risk your career for me."

"Isabelle—"

"I'm not talking forever. As soon as I'm acquitted we can be together again. But until then, we can't see each other. Not at all. If your career was ruined because of me, your family would never forgive me, and I would never forgive myself."

"And what if you aren't acquitted? David said you might possibly get probation."

She bit her lip, and he could guess the answer.

"I'm not losing you again, Isabelle."

"Hopefully you won't have to. I'm going to fight it Emilio. I will do anything I have to for an acquittal. But if I don't get it…I'm not sure how, but I'll pay you back for the lawyer's fee."

"I don't give a damn about the lawyer's fees. And I'm not letting you do this."

"You don't have a choice."

He could see by her expression that she meant it. She was really leaving, whether he liked it or not. His heart started to race and suddenly he couldn't pull in enough air. The thought of losing her again filled him with a sense of panic that seemed to well up from the center of his being.

This could not be happening. Not again.

"Knock, knock," someone said, and they both turned to see Alejandro standing on the porch at the open door. He stepped inside, saw the suitcases and asked Isabelle, "Going somewhere?"

"Nowhere out of your jurisdiction, if that's what you're worried about. I'm going to stay at my mother's for a while."

"No, she isn't," Emilio said.

She cut her eyes to him. "*Yes,* I am."

"Can I ask why?" Alejandro said.

"She's worried that her being here is going to damage my career, despite the fact that I keep telling her I don't give a *damn* about my career."

"I think you both need to listen to what I have to say."

"If has to do with my case, I can't talk to you without my lawyer present," Isabelle said.

"Trust me, you're going to want to hear this."

"I won't answer any questions."

"You won't have to." He handed her a white 6x9 envelope Emilio hadn't even noticed he was holding. "Open it."

She did and dropped the contents into her hand, looking confused. "My passport?"

"I don't get it," Emilio said. "Are you suggesting she should leave the country?"

Alejandro laughed. "I thought she might like it back, now that all the charges against her have been formally dropped."

Emilio was certain he misheard him. "Say again?"

"All the charges against Isabelle have been dropped."

Emilio looked over at Isabelle and realized she was practically hyperventilating.

"And my mother?" she asked.

"Your mother, too."

"You're serious?" she said. "This isn't just some twisted joke?"

"It's no joke."

She pressed her hand over her heart and tears welled in her eyes. She turned to Emilio. "Oh, my God, it's over."

He held out his arms and she walked into them, hugging him hard, saying, "I can't believe it's really over."

"What the hell happened?" Emilio asked his brother.

Isabelle turned in his arms and said, "Yeah, what the hell happened?"

Alejandro grinned. "You want the full story, or the condensed version?"

"Maybe we should go for the condensed version," she said. "Since you'll have to explain it all to me again when my head stops spinning."

"It was your husband's lawyer, Clifton Stone. He had the missing money."

"Stone?" Isabelle said, looking genuinely shocked. "I had no idea he was involved. I never even considered it."

"Is that why he wanted her to take a plea?" Emilio asked. "To take the attention off himself?"

"Yeah. Dumb move on his part. It's what made us suspicious in the first place, but we knew he wouldn't cooperate. We had to flush him out. We figured if we were patient he would do something stupid."

"So you knew all along that she was innocent?" Emilio asked.

"If I thought she was guilty do you think I would have dropped you all those bread crumbs, Emilio? I wanted you to get curious, to take matters into your own hands. And it worked. When you hired the new defense attorney, Stone panicked. He was going to run, and he led us right to the money."

"And he told you I wasn't involved?" Isabelle asked.

"He must have been paranoid about being caught because he saved every piece of correspondence between himself and your husband. Phone calls, emails, texts, you name it. He offered them up in exchange for a plea. He said they would exonerate you and your mother."

"And they did?" Emilio asked.

"Oh yeah. They were full of interesting information. If Betts hadn't died, I'm sure Stone would have flipped on him to save his own neck."

"So that's it?" Isabelle asked. "It's done?"

"The case is officially closed."

Emilio shook his brother's hand. "Thank you, Alejandro."

"Yes, thank you," Isabelle said.

"Well, I'm going to get out of here. I get the feeling you two have a lot to talk about." He started out the door, then stopped and turned back. "How about dinner at my place this weekend? Just the four of us. And the kids, of course."

That was an olive branch if Emilio had ever seen one.

"I'd like that," Isabelle said.

"Great. I'll have Alana call you and you can figure out a time." He shot his brother one last grin then left, shutting the door behind him.

Isabelle turned to Emilio and wrapped her arms around him. "I still can't believe it's really over. It feels like a dream."

"Does this mean you'll stay now?"

She looked up at him. "Only if you want me to."

He laughed. "You think? I had only reduced myself to *begging*."

She smiled up at him. "Then yes, I'll stay."

"We need to celebrate. We should open some champagne."

"Definitely."

"Or we could go out and celebrate."

She rose up on her toes to kiss him. "I think I'd rather

stay in tonight. I seem to recall a promise to model some lingerie."

A smile spread across his face. "I think I like the sound of that. But there's something I need to do first. Something I should have done a long time ago."

"What?"

He had hoped to do this in a more romantic setting, but he couldn't imagine a better time than now. "Isabelle, I never thought we would get a second chance together, and I don't want to spend another day without knowing that you'll be mine forever." He dropped down on one knee and took her hand. "Would you marry me?"

Tears welled in her eyes. "Of course I'll marry you."

He rose and pulled the ring box from his jacket pocket. "This is for you."

She opened it, and her look of surprise, followed by genuine confusion, was understandable.

"At this point you're wondering why a man of my means would give you a 1/4 carat diamond ring of questionable quality."

She was too polite to say he was right, but he could see it in her face.

"When I asked you to marry me before, I couldn't afford a ring, and you couldn't wear one anyway, because your father would find out. We decided that we would look for one together the day before we eloped. Remember?"

"I remember."

"Well, I couldn't wait. I saved up for months and bought this for you."

"And you kept it all this time?"

He shrugged. "I just couldn't let it go. I guess maybe deep down I hoped we'd get a second chance. I know it's small, and if you don't want to wear it I completely understand. I thought you might want to turn it into a necklace, or—"

"No." She took the ring from him, tears rolling down her cheeks, and slipped it on her finger. "You could offer me the Hope Diamond and it would never come close to meaning as much to me as this does."

"Are you sure?"

"Absolutely. I'll wear it forever."

He touched her cheek. "I love you, Isabelle."

"I love you so much." She rose up on her toes and kissed him, then she touched his face, as if she couldn't believe it was real. "Is this really happening?"

"Why do you sound so surprised?"

"Because I always thought I wasn't supposed to be this happy, that it just wasn't in the cards for me. That for some reason I didn't deserve it. And suddenly I've got everything I ever hoped for. I keep thinking it has to be a dream."

"It's very real, and you do deserve it." And he planned to spend the rest of his life proving it to her.

* * * * *

WHAT THE
MILLIONAIRE WANTS...

BY
METSY HINGLE

Metsy Hingle is an award-winning, bestselling author of series and single-title romantic suspense novels. Metsy is known for creating powerful and passionate stories, and her own life reads like a romance novel—from her early years in a New Orleans orphanage and foster care, to her long, happy marriage to her husband, Jim, and the rearing of their four children. She recently traded in her business suits and fast-paced life in the hotel and public-relations arena to pursue writing full-time. Metsy loves hearing from readers. For a free bookmark, write to Metsy at PO Box 3224, Covington, LA 70433, USA or visit her website at www.metsyhingle.com.

For the City of New Orleans and its people
who continue to inspire me

One

"I am not for sale, Mr. Hawke."

Jackson Hawke bit back a smile as he stared at the woman across the desk. "I'm not trying to buy you, Ms. Spencer. I'm merely offering to employ you."

"I already have a job," she informed him with the cool disdain of a true Southern belle. "I'm the general manager of the Contessa Hotel."

He had to give her points for moxie, Jack thought. He had expected any number of reactions to the news that he had acquired the defaulted bank loan on the small New Orleans hotel. He had made a career of taking over financially troubled companies, revamping them and turning the once-failing operations into profit centers. In each case, his presence was seldom welcome. More often than not his arrival was met with trepidation or anger, and in some cases both. He had expected no less from the owners of the Contessa Hotel. What he hadn't anticipated was defiance. And *defiant* was the only way to describe the woman seated across from him. Unfortunately for Ms. Laura Jordan Spencer, her defiance didn't change the fact that he now owned her family's hotel. "True. But given the circumstances, your position here could prove to be temporary," he countered.

"There is nothing temporary about my position here, Mr. Hawke," she advised him, a hint of temper coloring her voice. "My great grandfather built this hotel nearly a hundred years ago and it's been owned by the Jordan family ever since. I'm sorry if you were led to believe that we would consider selling the property. But I can assure you, the Contessa is *not* for sale."

"I have a receipt for fifteen million dollars that says otherwise," he told her.

"Which I'm sure the bank will refund you once I've straightened out this…this misunderstanding."

He leaned forward, met her gaze. "Take another look at those documents, Ms. Spencer," he said, motioning toward the packet of legal papers he'd presented her, which outlined his acquisition of the hotel via her mother's defaulted bank loan. "There *is* no misunderstanding. Hawke Industries now owns this hotel."

Anger flared in her green eyes. "I don't care what those papers say. I'm telling you there's been a mistake," she insisted and punched the button on the intercom. "Penny, try Mr. Benton at the bank again."

"You're wasting your time," he told her. He already

knew from his meeting with the bank chairman the previous afternoon that the man had left town that morning.

"The only one wasting my time, Mr. Hawke, is you," she fired back.

While she waited for her assistant to place the call, Jack used the opportunity to study her more closely. He noted the almond-shaped eyes, the stubborn chin, the smooth skin and lush mouth. She wasn't classically beautiful or slap-you-in-the-face sexy. But there was something about her, a sensuality that simmered beneath the all-business exterior. Judging by the quelling look she shot him, his appraisal hadn't gone unnoticed. Nor had it been appreciated.

At the buzz of the intercom, she grabbed the phone. "Yes. I see," she said. "Thank you, Penny."

"Still not available, I take it," he remarked when she hung up the phone.

"He and his family have left for the Thanksgiving holiday. His office is trying to reach him. When they do, I'll get this mess straightened out."

"Talking with Benton isn't going to change the facts, Ms. Spencer. Your mother pledged this hotel as collateral on a loan and Hawke Industries purchased that note, along with several others, from the bank. Since your mother defaulted on that loan, the Contessa Hotel now belongs to Hawke Industries."

"I'm telling you, you're wrong," she insisted. "There is no way my mother would have ever pledged the Contessa."

Tiring of her refusal to accept the obvious, Jack snatched the stack of legal documents, pulled out the collateral mortgage note signed by her mother and slapped it in front of her. "Look at it," he commanded. "That's a promissory note signed by your mother, pledging her stock in the Contessa as guarantee on the loan. Are you going to deny that's her signature?"

Something flickered in her eyes as she stared at the damning document. For the first time since he'd arrived and introduced himself to her as the hotel's new owner, the lady looked uncertain. Just as quickly it was gone and the defiance was back. "I don't care what that says. Even if my mother had wanted to use the hotel as collateral for a loan, she couldn't have."

"And why is that?"

"Because my sister and I each own ten percent of the hotel's stock. And neither of us would ever consent to her using the hotel."

"She wouldn't have needed your consent—not to pledge her own stock. Which is exactly what she did," he pointed out.

"My mother would never do such a thing. Not without telling me first."

There was something in her voice, a hint of uncertainty. There was also a flicker of fear in her eyes. It was that fear that stirred something inside him. "Didn't you say your mother was out of the country on business?"

She nodded. "She and her husband are opening a night-club in France."

"Well, maybe she meant to tell you, but just never got around to it," he offered, surprising himself with this sudden surge of empathy. He frowned. Emotion was something he never allowed to enter into his business dealings. It was his own cardinal rule. In the dozens of takeovers he'd engineered, no amount of tears, pleas or offers of sexual favors had deterred him from his course.

"She *has* been busy getting ready for the grand opening."

But he could tell from the lack of conviction in Laura's voice that she didn't believe that telling her about the loan had slipped her mother's mind any more than he did. He had learned firsthand that when it came to money and sex—blood was no thicker than water. Apparently, Deirdre Jordan Spencer Vincenzo Spencer Baxter Arnaud had sold her daughter's legacy and hadn't bothered to inform her of what she'd done.

"At any rate, if, and I'm not saying that she did, but if my mother did pledge her shares of the Contessa as collateral on a loan, I'm sure she didn't understand exactly what that entailed," she told him.

Her stubborn denial sobered him. Shaking off his uncharacteristic spurt of compassion, Jack reminded himself that this was business. Sentiment had no place in business. He didn't intend to let a pretty face, a great pair of legs and a mountain of attitude deter him from his plan. "Or perhaps your mother understood exactly what pledging the hotel as collateral meant."

She stiffened. "Just what is it you're implying, Mr. Hawke?"

"I'm not implying anything, Ms. Spencer. I'm simply pointing out that if your mother had wanted to sell the hotel, but knew you would be opposed to it, using it as collateral on a loan and then defaulting on that loan would be a means of accomplishing her goal."

"How dare you!"

"Why don't we skip the outrage, Ms. Spencer. You strike me as a smart woman. Don't tell me it hasn't crossed your mind. Your mother isn't interested in this place. Why else would she have dumped it in your lap and left the country?

Not that I blame her. The hotel was barely breaking even when your grandfather was alive. Since his death, it's been losing money steadily."

She narrowed her eyes suspiciously. "I won't waste my breath asking where you got your information." Temper laced her voice causing the trace of a Southern accent she bore to be more pronounced. "But apparently your source doesn't have all the facts. If he or she did, they would have informed you that the hotel has shown a steady improvement over the past four months. Whatever difficulties the Contessa may have had in the past, they're over. The hotel is doing just fine now."

"Showing a slim profit on last month's financial statement is a long way from being fine."

"I—"

Jack held up his hand. "I'm aware of what you've done since you took over the management six months ago. But you and I both know that this hotel is in need of major upgrades. I intend to see that it not only survives, but that it dominates the small luxury hotel market in this area." He paused, then pressed his point home, saying, "Since you own ten percent of the hotel's stock and are familiar with its operations, I'm willing to allow you to be a part of those plans. Or not. It's your choice. Either way, I'm prepared to make you and your sister both a fair offer for your stock."

"I'm not interested in selling my stock. And neither is my sister."

"Don't be too hasty, Ms. Spencer. After all, you haven't heard my offer yet. And neither has your sister."

"I don't need to hear it. I don't—"

"I'll give you and your sister each two million dollars for your stock. And—"

"I'm not interested."

"Please, do allow me to finish," he said pointedly and noted the angry color flooding her cheeks. "In addition, I'm willing to offer you a management contract with the Contessa at a substantial increase in salary. A salary, which, I might add, is far greater than the one you earned when you were working for the Stratton Hotel group or the Windsor," he added, mentioning the two hotels where his research revealed she had held positions previously.

She hiked up her chin a notch. "Perhaps you should have your hearing checked, Mr. Hawke. As I've already told you, I'm not for sale and neither is the Contessa."

But before he could point out that he already owned the majority of the hotel's stock, there was a tap at the door. "I'm sorry to interrupt, Laura," the perky brunette assistant who had ushered him into the office earlier said from the doorway.

"It's okay, Penny. What is it?"

"You're needed downstairs." She looked over at him, then back at her boss. "You know, for that meeting you scheduled with the kitchen staff."

"Thank you, Penny. Tell them I'm on my way."

Jack didn't miss the look that passed between the two women before her assistant retreated. He suspected it wasn't a meeting that required Laura Spencer's immediate presence. More than likely it was another crisis, one of the many that had plagued the hotel in recent years. As beautiful as the Contessa was and the potential profit she would generate for Hawke Industries, age had taken its toll on the structure. The hotel would continue to deteriorate unless it underwent the necessary maintenance and upgrades it so sorely needed. He intended to see that the hotel was returned to its former glory and became profitable—with or without Laura Spencer's cooperation.

She stood. "As you heard, I'm late for a meeting, Mr. Hawke. So this discussion is over."

It wasn't often that he found himself so clearly dismissed and certainly not by someone who was in no position to call the shots. A part of him was annoyed. While another part of him couldn't help but admire her spirit. Standing, Jack adjusted his gray suit coat. "I suggest you call your attorneys, Ms. Spencer, and have them review the documents I gave you."

"I intend to."

"Once you've confirmed that Hawke Industries is now the majority stockholder of the Contessa Hotel, I want to meet with you to discuss the hotel's operations. Preferably, tomorrow morning."

"I won't be available tomorrow morning," she informed him.

"Then the afternoon. Two o'clock okay with you?"

"I'll be tied up then, too."

Jack stared at her. Once again, he was surprised by her defiance. His name alone had struck fear in the hearts of many a hardened CEO. Apparently, that wasn't the case with Laura Spencer. He liked the fact that she wasn't afraid of him. And he wasn't averse to the rest of the package, either, he admitted. Under different circumstances he might have entertained the idea of something more personal with her. While he didn't consider himself to have a specific type, he enjoyed the company of intelligent, attractive women. He knew from her education and work history that Laura Spencer was smart. With her big eyes, soft skin and hair that was some shade between red and brown, she certainly was attractive. The perfect package really—except for her connection to the hotel deal. It was that connection that was the problem. Regardless of how attractive he found her on a personal level, he had no intention of letting it get in the way of business. Reminding himself of the business at hand, he said, "Tomorrow evening then. We can discuss my plans for the hotel over dinner."

"I already have plans," she told him.

The intercom buzzed. "Laura, they *really* need you for that meeting."

"I'm on my way," she said. "I have to go."

"I don't suppose there's any point in suggesting another day or time because you'll be tied up then, too," he stated, knowing full well what she was doing. If she agreed to a meeting with him, then she would, in effect, be admitting that everything he had told her was true. Her family no longer owned the Contessa Hotel.

"How perceptive of you, Mr. Hawke. As a matter of fact, my entire week is full and I won't have a moment to spare."

"Then I suggest you make time, Ms. Spencer. Because like it or not, you are going to have to deal with me." And without waiting for her to respond, Jack turned and exited the office.

As she left the hotel's kitchen, Laura pressed her fingers to her temple. The splitting headache that had started with the arrival of Jackson Hawke earlier was quickly working its way toward a migraine. Nodding to various hotel employees, she made her way across the lobby to the elevators. At least her temperamental chef's latest emergency—table salt being substituted for kosher salt—had been fixed relatively easily. She'd simply borrowed some kosher salt from a neighboring restaurant so Chef André could finish his masterpiece. Then she had dispatched one of the busboys to the supply house to swap the incorrectly delivered salt. While the celebrity chef she had hired away from a major restaurant caused her a few hassles, the income he generated by keeping the hotel's dining room filled far outweighed the headaches, she reminded herself. Besides, at the moment dealing with a temperamental chef was the least of her worries. Her real worry was Jackson Hawke. Just the thought of him made the pounding in her head increase.

Laura stepped into the elevator and pressed the button for the executive floor. If only the *real* emergency that Jackson Hawke had dropped in her lap could be solved as easily. Of course, she could always hope that the man was wrong—that her mother hadn't pledged her hotel stock and that Hawke hadn't actually bought her note. Laura called up an image of him in her mind's eye. She thought about the way he'd trained those blue eyes on her, the confidence in his expression, the hard line of his jaw. She sighed. Sure, she could hope he was wrong, Laura told herself. But Jackson Hawke hadn't struck her as a man who was often wrong about anything.

Stepping out of the elevator, she headed down the corridor toward the block of offices. When she entered the reception area and discovered her assistant on the phone, she retrieved her messages and began to flip through them.

Penny placed her hand over the receiver and mouthed, "Everything okay?"

Laura nodded and motioned for Penny to join her when she was finished with the call. Once inside her own office, Laura snagged a bottle of water from the mini-fridge and walked over to her desk. She opened the side drawer and reached for the bottle of aspirin. After shaking out two tablets, she washed them down with water and then sat in her chair. But five minutes later, Laura could feel the aura starting around the edges of her eyes and she knew the aspirin wasn't going to cut it this time. She was going to need the pills her doctor had prescribed for the migraines. She hated taking the meds, she admitted. While they knocked out her migraine, they also zapped her energy and made her feel fuzzy for the rest of the day. And today of all days, she needed a clear head and all the energy she could muster.

Shifting her gaze to the credenza, Laura glanced at the framed photo of her with her various half siblings and step-siblings at her mother's most recent wedding. She looked at the smiling green-eyed blonde beside her—her half sister, Chloe. At twenty-two, Chloe was four years her junior and the product of her mother's fourth marriage to soap opera star Jeffrey Baxter. An actress living on the West Coast, her sister was into healthy eating and treating the body's ailments with alternatives other than drugs.

Deciding it was worth a shot to try one of Chloe's methods before resorting to the pills, Laura began the deep-breathing techniques that her sister had shown her. And because she couldn't bring herself to chant the mantra aloud without feeling like an idiot, she repeated the words silently.

I can feel my heartbeat slowing. I can feel the blood flowing down my arms, to my fingertips. My fingers are growing warmer. I can feel the tension leaving my body. I am relaxed. I am calm.

Continuing the silent chant, she closed her eyes. But the minute she did so, an image of Jackson Hawke filled her mind. She remembered in vivid detail the cut of the charcoal-gray suit he wore, how the blue in his tie was the exact shade of his eyes. Even seated, he had looked tall and forbidding as he'd told her that he now owned the Contessa. And just thinking of Hawke made her head pound even harder.

"So much for natural healing," she muttered and opened her eyes. Still reluctant to take anything stronger than aspirin, Laura lowered her gaze to the bottom drawer of her desk.

Don't do it.

Ignoring the voice in her head, Laura pulled open the drawer and stared at her stash of candy. She had banished the forbidden sweets from her sight two weeks ago in her effort to cut her sugar intake and take off the five pounds she'd been carrying on her hips since Halloween. Biting her lower lip, she recalled the promise she had made to herself only three days ago. No more junk food. That meant no cookies. No candy. No ice cream. No milk-chocolate bars with the gooey caramel inside.

Don't do it, Laura.

Torn, Laura stared at the tempting treats. Her mouth watered. Still she hesitated. She'd promised herself, no sweets unless it was an emergency. Didn't Jackson Hawke and a monster headache constitute an emergency? Of course they did, she reasoned. Snatching up the bite-sized chocolate-and-caramel bar, she ripped off the wrapper, bit into the decadent treat and moaned.

"Uh-oh."

Laura opened her eyes and spied Penny standing in the doorway. She popped the remainder of the forbidden chocolate into her mouth and swallowed. Calories or not, she felt better already, Laura decided.

After taking a seat in the chair across from her desk, Penny glanced at the candy wrapper and said, "Since Chef André didn't walk out like he keeps threatening to do, I'm guessing that guy Hawke is the reason you deep-sixed the new diet. Who is he, Laura? And what did he want?"

Laura gave her assistant a quick rundown of the situation and the stunned look on the other woman's face mirrored her own feelings when Jackson Hawke had dropped the bombshell on her an hour earlier. But now that some of the shock had started to wear off, she knew she had to figure out a plan to stop Hawke. "I know this is a shock, Penny. It was to me, too. But I need you to keep quiet about this—at least until I can find out exactly what our position is. If word were to get out, it could cause a panic among the staff and I can't afford that. It's been difficult enough getting workers since Hurricane Katrina," she said, referring to the storm that had nearly destroyed New Orleans in 2005. Not only had the city lost more than half of its population, but the destruction had claimed entire neighborhoods and depleted the workforce. "And any buzz in the marketplace about management changes could set off a run of cancellations, not to mention that we'd probably lose out on any contracts."

"I won't breathe a word," Penny assured her. She paused, worry clouding her brown eyes. "But what if what this guy Hawke says is true? What if he really does own the hotel? Do I need to start looking for another job?"

"Hawke didn't strike me as a stupid man. Regardless of what happens, he'll need someone who knows about the day-to-day operations of the hotel, where and who to go to for the emergencies that pop up. And that person is you. I don't think you need to worry about your job, Penny."

But her assistant's concern made her realize that if Hawke did take over the hotel, Laura would need to do everything she could to ensure the job security of her employees. It was what her grandfather would have done, what he would have wanted her to do. If only her grandfather were here now, she thought.

"What about you? If Hawke is telling the truth, what will you do?"

"I don't know," Laura told her honestly. She thought about her childhood, of moving to new places each time her mother married and started a new life. But come summer, she had always returned to New Orleans, to her grandfather, to the Contessa. Even when she'd gone away to college and then had gone to work for other hotels out of state, she had known that the Contessa was still there, waiting for the day when she would return home for good. Only now when she had finally come back, her grandfather was gone. And Jackson Hawke was here, trying to take the Contessa from her. She wouldn't let him.

She couldn't. She looked at her assistant. "But I can tell you what I'm not going to do and that's roll over and play dead. Try Benton's office again, then get my attorney, my mother and my sister on the phone for me."

If Jackson Hawke wanted her hotel, then he was darn well going to have to fight her for it.

Two

So far, she'd struck out. Sighing, Laura put down her pen and stretched her arms above her head. She still hadn't spoken with her attorney or her sister. And her conversation with Benton had not gone well at all. She still couldn't believe her mother had actually used the Contessa as collateral on a loan and not told her. Benton hadn't given her much in the way of details. Instead he'd referred her to her mother. Unfortunately, the time difference and distance between New Orleans and France had made reaching her mother difficult. Glancing at the clock, she calculated the time overseas and concluded it was now after two o'clock in the morning in France. Aware of her mother's love of the night life, Laura tried the number again.

"Oui," her mother answered on the fourth ring, her voice breathless.

"Mother, it's Laura."

"Laurie, darling," she replied, genuine pleasure in her voice. "Philippe, it's Laurie calling from America."

She could hear Philippe shout out a greeting from the background and Laura made the obligatory hello to her mother to give to him. "Mother? Mother?" Laura pressed when her mother began to converse with Philippe in French.

"I'm sorry, darling. Philippe wanted me to tell you how well things are going here with the new club and to see when you can come for a visit. He's eager to show it off to you and Chloe." Without waiting for her to answer, her mother went on, "Do you think you girls could come? Why, it's been nearly a year since I've seen you, Laurie. And it would be so lovely to have my babies here for a visit. We could…"

Laura closed her eyes a moment as her mother rambled. She didn't bother trying to explain to her that at twenty-six and twenty-two, she and Chloe could hardly be considered babies. Finally, she said, "Mother, please. This is important. I need to know if you used your stock in the Contessa as collateral for a bank loan."

For a long moment, her mother was silent. Then she said, "It was just as a formality. A guarantee, until I paid back the loan."

Telling herself not to panic, that not even her mother could have spent all that money so quickly, she asked, "How much of the money do you have left?"

At her mother's silence, the knot that had formed in her stomach when Jackson Hawke had walked into her office tightened. Just when she thought her mother wasn't going to respond, she said, "I don't have any of it left."

Laura felt as though the wind had been knocked out of

her. There was nothing left? All of the money was gone? Suddenly a roaring started in her ears. Her stomach pitched. Feeling as though she were going to be sick, Laura leaned forward and put her head between her knees.

"Laurie? Laurie, are you still there?"

When the initial wave of nausea had passed, Laura straightened and leaned back in the chair. Lifting the phone receiver she still held in her hand to her ear, she managed to say, "I'm here."

"Darling, you sound…strange. Are you okay?"

No, she wasn't okay, Laura wanted to scream. Her foolish, reckless mother had placed the Contessa at risk. And because she had, Jackson Hawke might very well be able to take the hotel away from them, away from her. "You're sure it's all gone? There's nothing left?"

"I'm sure."

"What did you do with all that money?" Laura demanded.

Her mother explained how she had invested six million dollars into the nightclub that Philippe had been so keen to open in France. "I used some of it to pay for repairs to the hotel that the insurance didn't cover after the hurricane and the rest of it went to pay the back taxes on the hotel."

Laura knew the hotel had been underinsured at the time of the hurricane and, as a result, not all of the repairs had been fully covered. But the taxes? "The taxes couldn't possibly have been that much," Laura argued. "Since the hurricane, the assessment values have decreased, not increased."

"The taxes were from before the hurricane…from when your grandfather was still alive and running the hotel."

Laura frowned. That didn't make any sense, she thought and told her mother so. "Granddad always paid the Contessa's bills—even if it meant using his own money to do it. He would have made sure the taxes were paid."

"Apparently, he didn't. Or he couldn't. Evidently, the hotel wasn't doing well for quite some time before your grandfather became ill and he got behind on some of the bills. The tax assessor came to see me not long after the funeral and told me the taxes were three years in arrears, plus there were penalties. He was going to put a lien on the hotel. So I went to the bank and borrowed the money to pay them off."

Once again, Laura felt as though she'd had the wind kicked out of her. She'd known the hotel had gone through a rough patch and that her grandfather had hired a marketing firm to help him. But she hadn't realized things had been that bad. "Why didn't Granddad tell me? I would have come home and helped him with the hotel."

"That's probably why he didn't tell you, because he knew you would have come rushing home. And that wouldn't have been good for your career."

But Laura suspected her grandfather hadn't told her because he hadn't believed she was capable of running the Contessa. A sharp sting went through her as she recalled her grandfather dismissing the idea of her working at the Contessa after she'd graduated from college. He'd insisted she was too green to run a property like the Contessa and had told her to take the job she'd been offered by Stratton Hotels. Lost in thought, Laura didn't realize her mother had spoken until she heard her name said sharply. "I'm sorry. What did you say?"

"I said, how did you find out I pledged my stock to the bank for the loan?"

"Because the bank sold your note, Mother."

"Yes, I know. To some company with a bird's name."

"Hawke Industries," Laura supplied and she certainly didn't consider the man for whom the company was named to be some tame, feathered creature. Rather he was a predator—just like his name implied.

"That's right. I remember getting a notice from them, telling me they owned the note for my loan now."

"They own more than the note, Mother. You defaulted on the loan and now Jackson Hawke owns eighty percent of the stock in the Contessa."

Jackson Hawke sat in the penthouse suite of the Contessa Hotel late that evening and waited for the e-mail on Laura Spencer to arrive on his computer. Following his meeting with her, he had had the investigative firm he used compile a complete background check on her. He'd asked for everything—from her favorite flavor of ice cream right down to her shoe size. He frowned as he recalled his assistant's remark that it sounded personal. It wasn't, Jack told himself. It was business. Strictly business. And he intended to keep it that way.

As he waited for the file, Jack took a sip of his wine and considered, once again, his earlier encounter with Laura Spencer. While he had anticipated her objections and could even understand her denial at losing the hotel, he hadn't expected to find her outright defiance so stimulating. If he were honest, Jack admitted, the woman intrigued him. And it had been a very long time since anything or anyone had truly intrigued him.

A beep indicated the new e-mail and Jack clicked onto

the file document and began reading the investigator's preliminary report. Much of the information he was familiar with already, having attained the data during his initial investigation of the Contessa and its principals. But he skimmed through the basics on Laura Spencer again anyway—noting the names of her parents, the schools she had attended, the places she had lived, her employment history. As he perused the information in the file, he paused at the newspaper and magazine clippings Fitzpatrick Investigations had included with the report.

He studied a color photo that had appeared in a soap-opera magazine more than twenty years ago of a young Laura on the steps of a church following her mother's wedding to an actor. Another photo showed a six-year-old Laura standing with her grandfather in front of the Contessa Hotel as the older man shook hands with the city's mayor. Even then, there was no mistaking the stubborn tilt of Laura's chin, the pride in her eyes, the promise of quiet beauty in her features. More clippings followed. Laura graduating as valedictorian from a high school in Boston. Laura in her freshman year at college in New Orleans. Laura making her society debut as a maid in one carnival ball and reigning as queen in another. Laura named as an assistant manager at the Stratton West Hotel in California. He paused at a more recent clipping of an elegantly dressed and smiling Laura on the arm of a man wearing a tuxedo. Jack clenched his jaw as he recognized her escort—Matt Peterson. Just the sight of his stepbrother's face sent anger coursing through him. And along with the anger came the painful memories, the old hurt. Jack read the caption beneath the picture.

Ms. Laura Spencer and Mr. Matthew Peterson at the Literacy Gala hosted by Mr. and Mrs. Edward Peterson.

How had he missed this? And just how serious was Laura's relationship with Peterson? he wondered. After dashing off an e-mail to Fitzpatrick Investigations, demanding answers, he considered how Peterson's involvement with Laura might impact his deal. While his stepbrother didn't have the money to bail Laura out, Peterson's old man and stepmother did. And there was nothing the pair wouldn't do for their golden-boy son.

Bitterness rose like bile in his throat as Jack thought of Peterson's stepmother—his own mother—who had left her family for her husband's business partner and best friend. Whether Laura was seriously involved with Matthew Peterson didn't matter, Jack told himself. All that mattered was the deal. If his stepbrother tried to play knight in shining armor for Laura, it would only make the deal that much sweeter when Jack foreclosed on the hotel and crushed Matthew in the process.

Irritated, but not sure why, Jack shut off his computer. Deciding he needed to stretch his legs and clear his head, he pocketed his room key and exited the hotel suite.

Twenty-five minutes later, he returned to the hotel, carrying a paper bag filled with a large cup of coffee and a chocolate éclair that he'd picked up at a hole-in-the-wall coffee shop located a few blocks from the hotel. While the crisp November air had refreshed him and tempered his restlessness, it had also awakened his appetite. One foot inside the tiny shop and he'd opted for the sugar-laden pastry.

"Evening, Mr. Hawke. I see you found the place I told you about," the doorman remarked as he approached the hotel.

"I sure did, Alphonse. Bernice said for you to come by and have a slice of apple pie and a cup of coffee after your shift," Jack said, relaying the message the waitress had asked him to pass on to her sweetheart.

Alphonse grinned, showing a mouthful of even white teeth. "That little girl makes the finest apple pie in all of New Orleans," he boasted. "You be sure to try some before you head home."

"I'll do that," Jack promised as he entered the hotel, his gaze sweeping over the lobby. He noted the magnificent chandelier, the marble floors, the artwork and massive urn of fresh flowers that spoke volumes about the hotel's quality. As nice and lucrative as the newer chain hotels were, they couldn't duplicate the old-world elegance and sense of history found in a place like the Contessa.

Despite the toll time and the lack of funds had taken on the hotel, the Contessa still exuded an air of luxury and privilege to those who walked through her doors. It was on the promise of that luxury and privilege appealing to the discriminating traveler, as well as the movie community that had adopted the city, that he had banked fifteen million dollars. It was a good investment, one based on numbers, not sentiment, Jack told himself as he pressed the button for the elevator.

After pushing the button again, he waited for one of the hotel's two elevators to arrive. Two minutes turned into three, then four. When he hit the button a third time, he took another look at the large dial above the elevator banks that indicated the cars' positions. He noted that one of the elevators remained on the eighth floor while the other was making a very slow descent from the twelfth floor. When it, too, stopped at the eighth floor, he frowned. Walking over to the front desk, he read the clerk's name tag and said, "Charlene, I think there's a problem with the elevators. They seem to be stuck on the eighth floor."

"I'm sorry for the inconvenience, sir. We've been having a little trouble with the elevators lately. I'll notify maintenance right away and have them check it out. I'm sure they will be operational in a moment," she advised him and picked up the phone to report the problem.

Making a mental note to add servicing and refurbishing the elevators to his list of immediate hotel improvements needed, Jack headed for the stairs. When he reached the sixth floor where the executive offices were, he paused before opening the door. He told himself he was simply going to check the status of the elevators and find out if they were moving again. But when he reached the elevator bank, he angled his gaze down the hall toward the management offices, where the lights were still burning.

A check of his watch told him it was after ten o'clock— long past quitting time, even for the hotel's general manager. But as he approached the suite of offices, he didn't have to wonder who'd be working so late.

Jack looked to his left toward Laura's office. The door was slightly ajar and he could hear music—a hauntingly beautiful piece that was one of his own favorites. Obviously, he and Laura shared similar tastes in music.

Pausing in the doorway, he saw that Laura was seated behind the mahogany desk, her head tipped back against the massive black leather chair and her eyes closed. He used the moment to study her. The hair that he had classified as a color somewhere between red and brown that morning was a deep, rich red in the lamplight. Her skin was fair and had a smooth, creamy glow. Jack could just make out the faint dusting of freckles across Laura's nose. His gaze dipped to her mouth. Her lips were bare—no splash of bright color, no slick of gloss—which made her far more attractive in his book. She'd shed the red suit jacket she'd worn earlier to reveal a long, smooth neck and more creamy skin. The white silk blouse gently skimmed her shoulders and draped breasts that were neither large nor small, but just the right size to fill a man's hands.

As though sensing his presence, she opened her eyes. For the space of a heartbeat, she didn't move. She simply stared at him. Then suddenly she straightened and reached for the stereo remote. The music died midnote.

"You didn't have to turn it off. That CD is a favorite of mine," he told her and stepped into the room.

Ignoring his comment, Laura's voice was cool as she said, "If you're looking for your room, Mr. Hawke, it's on the top floor."

"Thank you for pointing that out, Ms. Spencer," he said. So she had discovered he was a guest in her hotel. He'd known that she would. A good general manager made a point of reviewing the hotel's guest list. She had apparently reviewed hers and found his name on it, which, judging from her expression, had not pleased her. He walked over to her desk and set down the bag with his coffee and éclair.

"The business office is closed."

"And yet you're still here," he pointed out. "I didn't realize being the hotel GM meant working day *and* night. I'm surprised your boyfriend doesn't object to the long hours."

"Was there something you wanted, Mr. Hawke?"

He paused a moment, considered the loaded question and the woman. Evidently from the way she narrowed her eyes, Laura realized what he was considering had nothing to do with business. Deciding it was best not to go there, he finally said, "Actually, I was taking the stairs up to my room when—"

"Why were you using the stairs?"

"Because the elevators aren't working."

When she grabbed for the phone, he reached across the desk and caught her wrist. Gently removing the telephone receiver from her hand, he replaced it on the cradle. "The front desk has already alerted maintenance."

Laura pulled her wrist free. "I'm sorry you were inconvenienced," she told him. "I'm sure maintenance will have the problem fixed shortly. In the meantime, if you need to get to your room, you can use the service elevator. I'll show you where it is."

"That's okay. I'm in no hurry. I'll just wait for the elevator," Jack told her. Deciding to take advantage of the fact that he had her one-on-one, he sat down in the chair in front of her desk. "But since I'm here and you don't appear to have any pressing meetings scheduled at the moment, maybe now would be a good time for us to talk about the hotel. I'm assuming you've spoken with the bank and confirmed my ownership position of the hotel."

"Actually, I haven't confirmed anything other than the fact that you purchased my mother's note. And until I speak with my attorney and find out what your legal claim is on the property, I see no reason for us to have any discussion about the hotel."

"All right. We won't discuss the hotel. But I would like

to drink my coffee before it gets cold. That is, if you don't mind," he added even as he removed the large foam cup from the paper bag. He took out the chocolate éclair that was wrapped in a thin white pastry sheet. Looking over at her, he noted that her eyes were trained on the treat. "Maybe you'd like to join me? I bought the large-size coffee."

"No, thank you," she said.

"Some of the éclair, then?"

"No, thanks," she told him, but Jack didn't miss the way she looked at the pastry.

Ignoring her protest, he divided the éclair in two and placed half of the chocolate pudding-filled confection on one of the napkins, then set it in front of her. When she simply stared at it, he said, "Go ahead."

"I'm not hungry," she told him.

"What's hunger have to do with it?" he asked and bit into his half. He didn't bother to hide his enjoyment. The rich pudding inside the chocolate-iced pastry shell was delicious. "Alphonse was right. Bernice does make the best éclairs."

"This came from Bernice's Kitchen?"

He nodded, took another bite, swallowed. "I was looking for a cup of coffee and wasn't exactly dressed for the dining room," he said, indicating the casual slacks, sweater and bomber jacket he wore. "Alphonse recommend Bernice's."

"Bernice is a genius when it comes to baking." The wariness in her expression faded, giving way to a look of anticipation as she dragged her fingertip through the chocolate pudding spilling from the torn pastry. "I tried to hire her as a pastry chef for the Contessa, but she turned me down flat. Said she didn't think it was a good idea for her and Alphonse to be working at the same place, that it might take some of the mystery out of their relationship."

Jack arched his brow. "I got the impression they were in a...um...long-term relationship."

"They've been dating for fifteen years, engaged for the last four. They don't want to rush things," she told him, the hint of a smile curving her lips.

"After fifteen years, I'd say there's little chance of that happening."

"It seems to work for them," she said and brought her finger to her mouth.

There was something inherently sensual about the sight of Laura licking her finger, Jack thought. He found himself wondering what she would look like while making love. Would those green eyes darken with need and heat? Would her lips part, her breathing quicken? Would that smooth, cool skin feel as soft as it looked?

The direction of his thoughts annoyed him, but it didn't surprise him, he admitted. He was a healthy male who enjoyed the opposite sex and the pleasures to be found in a woman's body. But when it came to women and sex, he had no delusions. Plain and simple, he believed in lust, not love. And right now he was experiencing a serious case of lust for Laura Spencer.

She scooped another finger full of pudding and as though sensing his gaze, Laura looked up. Her body went still. Her eyes locked with his as awareness sizzled like electrical currents between them.

Jack watched as Laura's lips parted and when he heard the slight hitch in her breath, he felt another stab of lust. The pudding on her fingertip fell with a splat onto the napkin on her desk. But her eyes remained locked with his. Not bothering to think about what he was doing or how it might impact his business, Jack pushed back his chair and started toward her. He had just reached the side of her desk when he heard the tap at the door.

A disapproving male voice came from the doorway asking, "Am I interrupting something?"

Three

For a moment, Laura couldn't breathe. The air seemed to have backed up in her lungs as Jackson Hawke stood at the side of her desk looking at her as though he wanted to swallow her whole. And heaven help her, for a moment, she had almost wanted him to.

"Laura?"

Shaking off the moment of insanity that had gripped her, Laura yanked her attention to the doorway where her attorney, Daniel Duquette, stood looking both concerned and curious. "Daniel," she said, her voice sounding more breathless than she would have liked. She cleared her throat. "What are you doing here?"

Daniel strode from the doorway into the office, slanted a glance at Hawke before shifting his focus back to her. "I've been tied up in depositions in Baton Rouge all day and just got back. When I picked up my messages, there was one saying that you needed to see me, that it was urgent. The front desk said you were still here, so I decided to stop by on my way home. Is everything okay?"

Everything was far from okay, Laura thought. But now was not the time to go into all that was wrong—not with Jackson Hawke standing there, measuring Daniel with his eyes and on the heels of whatever madness had stricken her. Because it certainly had been sheer madness that had caused her to react to Hawke as she had. The man was her enemy, she reminded herself. "Not exactly. And I do need to talk with you," she said, hoping Hawke would take the hint.

"I think that's supposed to be my cue to leave," Hawke said drily before he shifted his gaze from her to Daniel. "I don't believe we've met. I'm Jackson Hawke," he said and extended his hand.

Daniel shook his hand. "Daniel Duquette," he replied, his brow creasing. "You wouldn't happen to be the same Jackson Hawke with Hawke Industries who engineered the takeover of the Wilhelm family's company last year, would you?"

"Guilty as charged."

As she witnessed the exchange, Laura had a vague recollection of the small chain of family-owned inns that had been bought out by a corporation. She'd heard that the sale hadn't been a friendly one, that the two brothers who'd owned the properties that had been in their family for years had been split on whether or not to sell. There had been a great rift in the family because of it and because of the sale. The man behind that had been Jackson Hawke?

"So what brings you to New Orleans, Mr. Hawke?"

"Business."

"Thanks for sharing the éclair," Laura said, eager to get rid of Hawke and talk to Daniel about the mess her mother had gotten them into.

Hawke held her gaze for several moments. "You're quite welcome."

"Good night, Mr. Hawke."

He dipped his head in acknowledgment, but Laura didn't miss the gleam in his blue eyes that told her he hadn't forgotten what had almost happened between them. "I'll call your assistant in the morning about scheduling that meeting. Duquette," he said with a passing glance, and without waiting for a reply he strode out of the room.

The door had barely closed when Daniel asked, "What was that all about? And what's Jackson Hawke doing here?"

Laura sat down in her chair and released a breath she hadn't even realized she'd been holding. "He's the reason I called you. My mother pledged her stock in the Contessa as collateral for a bank loan and defaulted on the loan. Hawke bought her note and now he's trying to take over the Contessa."

Daniel let out a whistle. "Damn."

"My sentiments exactly," she said. "I spoke with the bank chairman briefly by phone and he wasn't much help. I'm going to meet with him after the Thanksgiving holidays. I know it's late, but could you take a look at these documents and tell me if there's anything I can do to stop Hawke from taking over the hotel?"

"Sure. Let's see what you've got." Daniel removed a pair of glasses from his coat pocket, slipped them on and began to read through the sheaf of papers she'd handed him. "I assume your mother received notices from both the bank and Hawke telling her she was in default of the loan," he said as he flipped through the pages.

"She remembers receiving something about the payments being late. She meant to contact them and explain she needed an extension, but because of the time difference and the new club opening, she never got around to making the call." Laura cringed inwardly as she heard herself repeating her mother's excuse. It was typical Deirdre behavior, she thought. When confronted with a problem, more often than not, her mother would go into her Scarlett O'Hara mode and plan on dealing with the matter another day. Only she never did deal with the problem. It either took care of itself or it got worse. But this time her mother's irresponsibility had proven disastrous.

Finally, he removed his glasses and looked up. "It looks legit. Unless your mother can come up with fifteen million dollars in the next thirty days to repay the loan, Hawke Industries can claim the stock she pledged as collateral and take over the hotel. I'm sorry, Laura."

So was she. But she refused to give up and play dead. Already, a plan was forming in her mind. "In other words, if I can come up with the fifteen million dollars and pay off the loan before the thirty days are up, then Hawke can't take the hotel. Right?"

"Right. But where are you going to get fifteen million dollars?"

"I don't know," she told him honestly. "But I'm not going to just hand over the Contessa to Jackson Hawke without at least trying to save her."

* * *

He had given her enough time, Jack decided. It hadn't been easy, but he had made himself wait three days—until after Thanksgiving had passed. Since his mother had walked out on him and his father all those years ago, holidays had been just like any other day as far as he'd been concerned. On those few occasions when his father had attempted to make Thanksgiving or Christmas some warm, fuzzy family event, it had invariably ended with Samuel Hawke pining for the woman who'd run out on them both, then drowning his heartache in a bottle of whiskey. Once his father had died, Jack had been able to stop pretending that holidays were some special family affair.

But something told him that that was just what they were for Laura Spencer—special, warm and fuzzy family affairs. He couldn't help wondering how she had spent her Thanksgiving. He knew her mother was in France and that her father lived on the East Coast. He also knew she had a slew of step and half siblings scattered across the country. Evidently, she hadn't traveled to see any of them since she was already at the hotel on the Friday morning following the big turkey day.

Or had she canceled her plans because of him? It was a strong possibility that she had, he conceded. Pushing aside a twinge of guilt that he might have caused her to spend Thanksgiving alone, Jack assured himself that Laura would make up for it at Christmas. She'd probably fly to France and spend it with her mother, he reasoned. Unless, of course, she was planning to spend Christmas with his stepbrother, Matt.

Jack considered that a moment, recalled one of the few

times he had visited his mother, her new husband and stepson. The visit had been at Christmas and the entire scene had been something out of a Norman Rockwell painting—only it was a picture in which Jack hadn't belonged. Laura would belong though. He frowned at the image of Laura with Matt and his family gathered around a Christmas tree, opening gifts, drinking eggnog. According to Fitzpatrick Investigations, she and his stepbrother had been seeing each other for more than a year and it was rumored they'd been seriously involved when she had moved back to New Orleans.

Jack frowned. He knew Matt Peterson. The man thought far too highly of himself to restrict himself to any one female. A leopard didn't change its spots and neither would his stepbrother. Laura might think that she was the only woman in Peterson's life, but Jack would bet his vintage Corvette that there were several someone elses. But if Peterson had devoted a year to Laura as the report indicated, his stepbrother had done so for a reason. More than likely that reason had something to do with the senatorial race Peterson was rumored to be considering. Jack considered that angle for a moment. Laura was pretty, smart, well educated and poised. While her parents might be maritally challenged, her family tree was a good one and Laura herself was scandal-free. She would definitely be an asset on a senatorial candidate's arm and help him to get votes. Her return to New Orleans would have put a kink in Peterson's plans, but Jack doubted the man had abandoned his goal. He might have shelved it for a while, but Peterson didn't like losing any more than Jack did. It had been one of the few things they'd had in common. According to

Fitzpatrick's report, the pair had supposedly remained "close" friends despite her move. Just how close were they? he wondered. How many times had Matt tasted her mouth, touched that soft-looking skin, felt her body beneath his?

Envy sliced through him like a scalpel, swift and sharp. Annoyed by the stab of jealousy, Jack reminded himself that his stepbrother had nothing that he wanted. All Jack wanted was to get down to business. Determined to do just that, he entered the executive offices of the hotel. "Is she in?" he asked the receptionist, his voice sharper than he'd intended.

"Yes, but—"

Ignoring her attempts to waylay him, he marched into Laura's office. "Good morning," he said as he approached her desk.

"It was."

Dismissing the barb, Jack met her gaze. Her eyes were the same clear green as the waters in St. Thomas, he decided, and damned but he couldn't help wondering what it would take to make those eyes turn dark and smoky for him. Irritated with himself and her, Jack decided there was no point in dancing around his reason for being there. His voice was cold, brusque, as he said, "I assume you've had an opportunity to speak with your attorney by now."

"I have."

He put down his briefcase and withdrew the management contract he had prepared for Laura, along with the purchase agreement for her stock. He also pulled out the letter of resignation he'd had drawn up in the event it was needed. While the transition would be simpler for him if she stayed on at the hotel, he was prepared for her to quit and to buy out her stock. "Then you know that my purchase of your mother's note is legal."

"Legal, maybe. But certainly not ethical."

Refusing to debate her, he continued, "Then you also know that by defaulting on the loan, she forfeited the stock that she pledged as collateral on the loan. Which means Hawke Industries now owns the controlling interest in the Contessa."

He paused, waited for her to respond. But Laura remained silent. Her demeanor remained unchanged.

Keeping his voice level, he said, "My plan is to turn the Contessa into a five-star property again and recapture the market share it's lost. As I've already told you, I would prefer that you stay on at the hotel as the general manager. But if you choose not to stay, then I'm prepared to accept your resignation and purchase your stock." He slid both agreements and the resignation letter across the desk so that they rested in front of her. "It's your call, Ms. Spencer. Are you going to stay? Or are you leaving?"

Laura didn't even look at the documents he had placed before her. Instead, she met his gaze. There was something hard and determined in her eyes as she said, "I'm not going anywhere, Mr. Hawke."

The news surprised him. After their previous conversations, he had been sure she would turn him down flat. The fact that she hadn't both pleased and concerned him. He was pleased because it would be good for business to have her stay on. It concerned him because he had the hots for her, he admitted. And she was more than likely sleeping with his stepbrother, he reminded himself. The thought of Laura with the golden boy his mother had chosen as her son over him chafed at Jack, made him feel raw. He couldn't help wondering how Peterson would feel to come out on the losing end for once. Irritated with himself for allowing his thoughts to stray from the business at hand, he tapped the documents on the desk. "In that case, I'll need you to sign a new management contract with Hawke Industries. It's pretty straightforward, with all the standard clauses and the increase in salary I mentioned earlier."

"I'm sure the contract is fine."

He nodded. "Still, you may want to have your attorney look it over anyway."

"That won't be necessary."

"It's your call," he told her.

"Yes, it is."

Jack wasn't sure why, but her agreeable demeanor seemed off. "There's also a purchase agreement for your stock, if you should change your mind about selling it. My previous offer of—"

"I won't change my mind."

Something was off, Jack told himself again. Instinct, some unexplained ability that told him if a venture would be a hit or a flop, kicked in now. The woman was up to something. He felt it in his gut, felt it in his bones. "Why do I get the feeling that you're just itching to throw those contracts in my face?"

She picked up the contracts, fingered them. Looking directly at him, she smiled and said, "Because I am."

There was a confidence in her smile, a spark in her green eyes that he found intriguing. Intriguing and sexy as hell. "I admire your honesty. But you might want to think twice before you do that."

"Why? Because it would be an unwise career move on my part?" she asked.

"Something like that."

"You'd probably be right—if you were my boss and had the authority to fire me," she began. Obviously too edgy to sit, she stood and paced behind her desk. She paused, turned and looked at him. "But you don't."

"The last time I checked, owning eighty percent of the stock in a company constitutes the controlling interest, which does make me your boss and gives me the authority to pretty much do whatever I damn well please."

"That would be true—if you owned the stock. But you don't own it. At least not yet," she informed him triumphantly.

"Is that so?"

"Yes, that's so. You see, that note that you so cleverly got the bank to sell you gives me thirty days to cure the default on my mother's loan. Once I do that, my mother keeps her stock in the Contessa and your deal, Mr. Hawke, is null and void."

So that was her plan. Jack would have laughed were it not for the fact that this stunt of hers would cost him both time and money with delays. He didn't intend to allow her to cost him either—not without a price. "You think you can go out and find fifteen million dollars like that?" he asked with a snap of his fingers.

"I didn't say it would be easy."

"Try next to impossible."

"Nothing's impossible," she fired back at him.

"Trying to block my purchase of this hotel is," he assured her. Standing, he walked around to her side of the desk, a deliberate move on his part to intimidate her.

Instead he found himself far too aware of her, of the way the office light caught the copper in her hair, the way her black silk blouse curved over her breasts, the way the scent she wore reminded him of exotic islands and sex. Desire hit him like a one-two punch. He wanted her. Maybe part of him wanted her because she belonged to his stepbrother. But another part of him wanted her because he sensed a fire in her and he wanted to be the one to ignite it.

"Why? Because you're so rich and powerful?"

"Yes." Leaning closer, he lowered his voice and said, "And because I never lose."

"There's a first time for everything."

Jack didn't bother to hide his amusement. "And you think that you'll be the one to beat me?"

"I don't think I can beat you, Hawke. I *know* I can."

"You sound pretty sure of yourself."

"I am," she insisted.

Before he could quell the impulse, he countered, "Sure enough to wager on the outcome?"

"You mean a bet?"

"That's right. You say you can stop me from taking over the hotel. I say you can't. Are you willing to put your money where your mouth is?"

"I am, if you are," she told him.

"Oh, I am. I most definitely am."

She was insane to have dared the man the way she had, Laura admitted. But blast him, he had been so smug, so sure of himself. The fact that he had been standing so close to her hadn't helped, either. She had hoped those moments of heightened awareness between them in her office a few nights ago had been a fluke, that stress and thoughts of spending the Thanksgiving holiday without any of her family had caused her sexual chemistry radar to go askew. But if it had, then her radar still wasn't working because she'd felt those same ripples of awareness when he'd entered the room, that same quickening of her pulse each time he drew closer.

"So what are the stakes?"

"The stakes?" she repeated, doing her best to shake off his effect on her nervous system.

"Yes. You know, the prize that you're going to fork over to me when you lose our bet and I foreclose on the Contessa."

Laura sobered at his cocky remark. Taking a step back, she said, "You mean the prize that *you're* going to fork over to me when I beat you at your own game."

His lips twitched. "So what are the stakes?"

"Dinner," she suggested. "The loser pays for a seven-course meal at the restaurant of the winner's choice."

"Dinner?" he scoffed. "That's your idea of a bet?"

"What do you expect me to offer? My car? My condo?" she tossed back at him, and suddenly felt queasy at the thought of losing either.

"I don't have any use for a three-year-old BMW and you don't have enough equity in your condo to make it worth my trouble."

Anger bulldozed right over any misgivings she'd had about challenging the man as she realized he had had her investigated. Temper driving her, she put her hands on her hips and looked him square in the eyes. "And just what are you going to give up when you lose and *I* win?"

"I have a Jaguar that you'd look good in," he said with

a smile that lit up his eyes and made his face go from handsome to dangerously sexy.

"Far be it from me to take away your little toy and force you to be driven around in a limo."

"And I'd hate to have to see you hoof it to work in those high heels or be forced to sleep on the couch in your office," he countered.

He didn't think she could do it, Laura realized. He honestly didn't believe she could outmaneuver him and save the hotel. She could see it in those blue eyes, sense it in the way his muscles had tightened when she'd challenged him. She could feel it in the way he was watching her now—like a hawk with a helpless mouse in his sights. The realization that he thought she'd already lost only fed her temper. And it was her temper that had the words falling off her tongue as she declared, "Believe me, I won't be the one hoofing it to work or sleeping on a couch, Hawke."

"You won't have to. After all, it really wouldn't be fair of me to foreclose on your hotel, then take your car and home, too."

Suspecting that he was trying to bait her, Laura kept a rein on her temper, determined not to let it get her into any more hot water. With a nonchalance she was far from feeling, she said, "Well, since you ruled out dinner, I guess the bet's off."

"Not necessarily," he said.

"We can't agree on the stakes," she pointed out.

He stared at her for a long moment, long enough for Laura to see his enjoyment in sparring with her turn to something else, something hot, something sexual. "I have another idea on what the stakes could be," he said finally. "But I've got a feeling you're not going to like it."

Laura knew at once what those stakes were. She'd seen it in his eyes the very first time he had looked at her, felt it the other night when he had almost kissed her. He wanted to have sex with her. That he would even suggest such a thing infuriated her. It also made her stomach tighten, her skin heat. "You're right. I don't like it. And despite what you might think, going to bed with you just isn't my idea of a prize."

He laughed. "That's a pretty big assumption you've made."

Laura could feel the color rush to her cheeks and cursed her fair skin. Refusing to back down, she said, "All right. So what *did* you have in mind?"

"Never mind my idea," he said, his amusement fading. He inched a step closer. That dark and hungry look was back in his eyes, in his voice, as he said, "While it's not what I had in mind initially, I like your idea better. A lot better."

"The bet was a stupid idea in the first place. Let's just forget the whole thing," she told him, hating the fact that just having him move closer made her heart start racing again.

"Why? Don't think you can pull it off after all?"

Pride had her spine stiffening and the words firing from her lips. "I know I can pull it off."

"Then the bet stands. When I win, you spend the night in my bed."

Laura's pulse scattered. "And what do I get when I win?" she demanded, wishing she had never started this thing, wishing she could figure a way to get out of it without losing face…or something more.

"Your mother's promissory note—free and clear—and you get to keep or return the money you borrowed."

Laura blinked. "You can't be serious. That would mean you'd lose the fifteen million dollars you paid for the note."

"I won't lose," he assured her.

His words set her competitive juices stirring once again. She so wanted to wipe that smug look off his face. "Like I said, there's a first time for everything."

He grinned. "If you're right, then you have nothing to worry about. But if you're wrong and you can't come up with the money in time, then I foreclose on the hotel and I get you—in my bed for an entire night."

It was crazy. No, it was beyond crazy, she thought. It was insane. *He* was insane. Because only a madman would make such a bet. "Not that I'm complaining, mind you. But don't you think the stakes are a bit lopsided? At least for you. I mean, it hardly seems fair that I stand to have a fifteen-million-dollar loan wiped out whereas all you stand to gain is a night of sex."

He ran his eyes down the length of her in a way that made her skin feel as though he had touched her. "I'm satisfied with the stakes."

"I should think a man with your ego could satisfy his sexual needs for a lot less money," she tossed back, annoyed by her reaction to him.

"Oh, but I'd much prefer to have those needs satisfied by *you,* Ms. Spencer," he said, his voice dropping to a seductive whisper that sent a shiver along her nerve endings. "So, do we have a deal?"

For a moment, Laura said nothing. She was every bit as crazy as he was to even consider such an outrageous thing, she reasoned. The man was a corporate shark. Every article and interview she had been able to dig up on him all proclaimed his genius as a businessman. He hadn't lied. He seldom lost. When it came to doing business—or in the

Contessa's case, engineering a hostile takeover—Jackson Hawke would be a lethal opponent. And regardless of how good she was at her job, she'd be lying to herself if she thought that finding the money she needed to cure the defaulted loan would be easy. At best it was a long shot. But if she could pull it off, somehow raise enough money in time, she would win the bet, get the Contessa and be able to pay back the loans. "You're really serious? You'd risk fifteen million dollars against a night…a night of sex?"

"A night of sex with *you*," he amended. "And, yes, I'd risk it."

Still, she hesitated. She'd be a fool not to accept the deal he was offering her. And if she lost?

"Of course, if you're ready to concede that you can't come up with the money and dispense with the thirty days so I can foreclose, we can call off the bet."

Laura yanked up her chin. "I'll do no such thing. You've got yourself a bet. And if I were you, Hawke, I'd get ready to lose fifteen million dollars."

He smiled, a knowing smile that made the air in her lungs grow shallow. "And if I were you, Spencer, I'd get ready to spend a night in my bed—without the benefit of sleep."

Four

Jack stood on the corner outside the restaurant where he'd gone for dinner and waited for the light to change. Still restless despite the long walk, he hit the speed dial for Fitzpatrick Investigations. When it went to voice mail, he grimaced. "It's Hawke. I need you to get me whatever you can find on Matthew Peterson, both personal and business. And I need it ASAP. Send whatever you find to my e-mail address."

Hitting the off button, he considered calling his assistant at home, then opted against it. Unless it was an emergency, Dotty would not be at all happy to have him calling her at home on a Sunday night. As she'd told him often enough, weekends were for family.

Instead, he holstered his cell phone and when the light changed, he headed back down Saint Charles Avenue in the direction of the hotel. The air was cool, but not cold like

New York. Not that you could tell by the way the people were dressed with their gloves and heavy coats, he thought. And given the number of red-and-green scarves he'd seen, people were already into the Christmas frenzy. December was still a few days away, but the storefronts and restaurants were already trimmed in lights. Christmas trees filled several windows and wreaths hung from doors. Even the lobby of the Contessa sported pots of red and white poinsettias and a huge tree.

Jack frowned as he thought of how all the Christmas craziness was going to impact him getting business done. He hated the distraction the holidays caused almost as much as he hated weekends. And he really hated weekends, Jack admitted. Nobody wanted to work on weekends and unless you were in the retail or service end of business, nobody did. That meant there were no stock deals to be done, no bank transactions to be made, no business brokering to negotiate and no attorneys or board of directors available to draw up contracts and vote on his deals. He hated that. He hated wasting time and he hated waiting for the hours to tick by until Monday morning rolled around and he could get back to work.

Sidestepping a couple with a baby stroller, Jack continued toward the hotel. Despite what his assistant claimed, he was not a workaholic who needed a wife. He had all the female company he wanted. As for work, it was mastering the game that drove him. That and the need to win. And having Laura in his bed was a bet he was looking forward to winning. He was thinking about all the delectable ways he intended to enjoy Laura when he neared the hotel and spied her standing under the porte cochere with her back to him and a cell phone at her ear. As he drew closer, he caught the tail end of her conversation.

"No. It's just that I was hoping we could go tonight to see the Celebration in the Oaks together."

He knew from the doorman that the Celebration in the Oaks was some big Christmas thing at the park. Was she talking to Peterson? he wondered. Was he in town? Was Peterson the reason he hadn't seen Laura at the hotel all weekend? Jack clenched his jaw as he thought about Laura spending the past two days with his stepbrother. He had never liked Matt Peterson. Even when their fathers had been partners and friends, the two of them had never gotten along. Two years older than him, Peterson had been a manipulative bully who had gotten his kicks by getting Jack into trouble. Later, when his mother had run off with Peterson's father, Matt had delighted in taunting him, calling him and his father losers.

"Yes. Of course I understand. Business should come first."

For a moment, Jack heard his mother's voice in his head, admonishing him for eavesdropping when he'd overheard her making plans to meet his father's partner. He didn't care if it was wrong or rude, he decided, and dismissed the memory. He remained where he was, several feet away from Laura, but close enough to listen to what she was saying. Although he made a show of studying the firs that had been draped with white lights near the hotel's entrance, his focus remained on Laura and her conversation.

"I know. It's just that it's been a while since I've seen you and I was looking forward to us spending some time together."

The disappointment in her voice had envy curling in his

gut. The fact that he was fairly sure it was his stepbrother she was pining over made the uncharacteristic jealousy he was experiencing all the more difficult to swallow. It also made him angry—with her and with himself—and all the more determined to wipe every memory of Peterson from her mind when he claimed her as his prize. The admission sent a stab of guilt through him. Just as quickly, he dismissed it. He was not using Laura to exact revenge on Peterson, he told himself. The chemistry had been there between them even before he'd known she was involved with his stepbrother. The fact that he would be taking her from Peterson when he bedded her would simply be an unexpected bonus.

"No. Don't worry about picking me up. I'm just going to take a taxi home and call it an early night." She paused. "You, too."

After she flipped the phone closed, she turned around and stopped cold when she saw him. "Hawke, what are you doing out here?"

"I was on my way into the hotel when I thought I recognized you standing over here. I wasn't sure it was actually you at first since this is the first time I've seen you in jeans—which, by the way, look great on you," he added. It was the truth. Those long legs of hers were made for skirts, but they looked every bit as sexy in the snug-fitting jeans.

"Thanks."

"You're welcome." Judging by her body language, Jack could see that he was making her nervous and he wasn't sure if that pleased him or not. He wanted her nervous with anticipation about being in his bed, not nervous because she was afraid of him. "I haven't seen you around the hotel the past couple of days and was beginning to think you were avoiding me."

"I decided to take the weekend off and catch up on some personal stuff."

Personal stuff like hooking up with his stepbrother? he wondered and felt that envy burning his gut again. "Have you told your boyfriend about our little bet yet?"

"I haven't told *anyone* about our bet," she informed him.

"Why not? Afraid he won't like the idea of you sleeping with me?"

"*I* don't like the idea that there's even the remote possibility that I might have to sleep with you. So I'd just as soon no one else know that I agreed to something so stupid."

Irritated by her response and his need to prove her a liar, Jack inched a step closer. He wanted to haul her up against him, kiss her senseless until she was begging him to make love to her. And because his own need was so great and he feared he wouldn't stop with a kiss, he did neither. Instead, he reached out and drew the back of his fingers gently down her cheek. His gaze never left her face and he watched her eyes widen, darken at his touch. Then slowly, very slowly, he rubbed his thumb along her bottom lip. Her lips parted. He heard her gasp, felt the warmth of her breath against his fingertips. He was reconsidering kissing her after all when Laura stepped back.

"I need to go," she said and started to leave.

"Laura, wait," he called as he followed her toward the hotel's entrance.

He wasn't sure if it was because he'd called her by her name or if she heard the regret in his voice, but she stopped, turned. Before he could apologize for coming on like a Neanderthal, she held up her hand and said, "No, you wait. I don't know if you're trying to intimidate me or seduce me, but it isn't going to work because I'm not going to sleep with you. At least, not unless I have to."

"Fair enough."

"I—" Evidently surprised by his answer, she fell silent, leaving the rest of what she'd planned to say unfinished. "Then I guess there's nothing more to say except goodnight. So if you'll excuse me, I think I'll go grab a taxi and head for home."

"What about the Celebration in the Oaks?" Jack asked as he fell into step beside her. When she slanted a glance his way, he explained, "I couldn't help overhearing. Sounded like your boyfriend canceled on you."

He waited for her to confirm or deny his statement. She did neither. Not until they stopped at the end of the line for the taxi stand did she say, "Something came up. I'll just go another time."

The disappointment in her voice was also in her expression. And, once again, Jack found himself irritated by the notion of her with Peterson. A burning need to wipe his stepbrother's memory from her mind and replace it with his spread through him. "Alphonse said this Celebration in the Oaks is some kind of Christmas-lights display in the park. He said that it's worth seeing."

"It is," she assured him as a gust of wind blew down the street. Pulling up the collar of her denim jacket, she brushed the hair away from her eyes. "The gates open at dark every night from now until the end of the year. You should go see it while you're here."

"You still here, Ms. Spencer?" Alphonse said as she reached the front of the taxi line. "Evening, Mr. Hawke."

"Alphonse," Jack said.

"I thought you were over at City Park looking at the pretty Christmas lights with your—"

"Something came up and we had to cancel," she told him. "But I'm going to need a taxi to get home."

"No problem," he said and whistled for the next cab to come forward. "Sorry you didn't get to go see the Oaks, ma'am. I know how much you loved going to see them with your grandfather."

"Thanks, Alphonse. But I'll just go see them another time."

The taxi arrived and Alphonse opened the door. But before Laura got in, Jack caught her arm and said, "Why wait? Why not go now? With me."

Laura still wasn't sure what had possessed her to agree to accompany Jack to view the Celebration in the Oaks. Granted, her moods had been all over the place for nearly a week now—ever since Jackson Hawke had walked into her office and pulled the rug from beneath her high heels. Her emotions had run the gamut—from anger to despair and fear, from hatred to outrage and lust—and every one of those emotions had been ignited by Hawke. But of all of them, it was her attraction to the man that worried her the most. When she'd found herself wanting him to kiss her, she'd realized just how dangerously close she'd come to making a monumental mistake.

The man was her enemy, she reminded herself. He was a thief out to steal her legacy. And whether she won or lost the foolhardy bet they'd made, she'd be an idiot to risk losing her heart to the man. Yet, when he'd asked her to come with him to the Celebration in the Oaks, there had been something in his eyes, a loneliness, that had touched something deep inside her. She'd remembered the staff telling her that he'd ordered room service and spent Thanksgiving Day alone in his room. It made her realize how fortunate she'd been because she'd never spent any holiday alone. It was one of the advantages, she supposed, of her parents' multiple marriages. There was always family somewhere and she was always welcome. Last year had been one of the few times she hadn't celebrated Thanksgiving with her own family, opting instead to join Matt and his family.

She thought of Matt, realized she hadn't called him back as she had promised. And while she had used her sister, Chloe's, visit as an excuse for cutting the conversation short, the truth was she hadn't wanted to go another round with Matt. While she cared deeply for him, she didn't love him—at least it wasn't the kind of love that her grandparents had shared, the kind of love that she wanted. And despite his claim, she didn't believe that Matt really loved her that way, either. If he did, he would have understood why the Contessa meant so much to her. He didn't. Nor did he understand why she'd left California and returned home to try to salvage the hotel. He certainly wouldn't understand her desperation now to save it from falling into the hands of Jackson Hawke.

Shifting her glance, she took advantage of the dimly lit backseat and studied Hawke. In the jeans and bomber jacket, he seemed far less forbidding, she thought. With his black hair mussed from the wind and the beginnings of a five-o'clock shadow darkening his jaw, he was, surprisingly, even more handsome. But even dressed casually, there was an air of alertness, a fearlessness and determination that exuded power. There was also something inherently sensual about him that told her this was a man of passion, a man of strong appetites. The fact that he'd made it clear he wanted to indulge those appetites with her should have appalled her. And it did. But it also ignited a longing inside her that had desire curling in her belly whenever she was near him.

Embarrassed by the admission, Laura stared out of the taxi window and warned herself what a mistake it would be if she were ever to let Hawke know just how tempting she found him. Her silent warning was still ringing in her head when the taxi swerved to avoid a pothole and sent her body careening sideways, nearly into Hawke's lap. Pressing her hands against his chest to right herself, Laura looked up and made the mistake of glancing into his eyes. The heat simmering in them set off a tingling sensation inside her. Suddenly aware that his arms were cradling her, she straightened and scooted back to her side of the seat. "Sorry," she murmured.

"No problem," he told her, the husky timbre in his voice only adding to the charged atmosphere.

"Sorry about the rough ride, folks," the driver said, his eyes meeting theirs in the rearview mirror. "These here streets took a real beating in Katrina, and being under water for all those weeks didn't help."

"We understand," Hawke told him, but his gaze remained fixed on her.

"The streets weren't in the best of shape even before the

storm and now they're a whole lot worse," she commented, trying to diffuse the moment. As though to prove her point, the car hit another rut that had her body bumping against his again. He made no comment as she returned to her side of the taxi and this time, she held on to the hand grip above the door.

"She's right," the taxi driver commented, apparently oblivious to the tension. "A lot of the streets are still a mess. But the people are starting to come back. And mark my words, New Orleans is gonna be just fine. It's just gonna take more time than most folks thought."

While the driver answered a call from his dispatcher, Jack said, "He's right about it taking longer for the city to recover. I imagine leaving a hotel like the Stratton West to take over operation of the Contessa wasn't an easy decision."

"It was for me," she said, grateful that he was focused on business and not on her.

"Really? Most people in your position wouldn't have given up a big paycheck with a growing operation so easily."

"I'm not most people," she informed him.

"No, you're not. Maybe that's why you intrigue me, Laura Spencer."

Unsure how to respond, Laura chose to remain silent and spent the final minutes of the drive looking out the window, trying to ignore the man seated beside her. Eager to escape the intimacy of the darkened car, she was already unbuckling her seat belt as the taxi pulled up to the entrance of the park.

"This is as far as I can take you, folks," the driver informed them as he parked the car. "No driving tours allowed anymore, not since Katrina."

After paying the taxi driver, Jack joined her in line.

"Since you paid for the taxi, I'll take care of the entry fees."

But before she could even open her wallet, he handed the admission clerk a crisp fifty-dollar bill. "I've got it," he said. "You can buy us coffee later."

Too eager to see the display to argue with him, Laura said nothing. Once they had their hands stamped, they walked into the park and she entered a virtual wonderland of lights. She tried to take in everything at once—the towering oak trees dripping with white lights that looked like stars, the Christmas trees and storybook characters fashioned from lights, the delight on the faces of the children as they spied Santa Claus.

"Is it like you remembered it?"

Laura glanced to her side and realized Jack was watching her. "Yes. And no. A lot of it's the same, but it's different, too. There used to be more trees, more lights," she explained as the two of them began to walk through the park. "There was a road over there where cars could drive through and see all the lights. On the really cold or rainy nights, that's what a lot of people did. There were also horse-drawn carriages you could take the tour in. When Chloe and I were younger, we used to sing 'Jingle Bells' and pretend we were riding in a one-horse open sleigh."

"A sleigh, huh?"

She didn't have to look at him. She could hear the smile in his voice. Laughing, she shrugged. "What can I say? We're snow-deprived Southerners."

He laughed.

The sound surprised her. It was the first time she'd

actually heard him laugh. Unable to resist, she sneaked a peek up at him. He was smiling, and not just that slight twitch at the corners of his mouth, but an honest-to-goodness smile that revealed perfect teeth and radiated in his eyes. For the first time since she'd met him, Jackson Hawke actually looked happy, she thought. And she wasn't sure why, but knowing that she was responsible made her feel warm inside.

"Is that a train I hear?" he asked.

"Yes," Laura told him, suddenly enjoying herself. "There's a miniature train ride that goes through the park and there's this huge elevated train exhibit that has these tiny replicas of the streetcars and historic buildings and landmarks around New Orleans. It's like a mini-version of the city. Come on, I'll show it to you."

Laura showed him the train exhibit. She showed him Storyland. She showed him the vintage rides in the Carousel Gardens, sadly pointing out that several were no longer working because of the damage they'd sustained in the storm. She showed him the gallery of Christmas trees decorated with handmade ornaments made by local schoolchildren that lined the walkways of the Carousel Gardens. Finally, she showed him her favorite part of the exhibit—the antique wooden carousel. "It's more than a hundred years old," she told him and explained how the severity of the storm and the exposure to water had left the carousel inoperable. "I know it doesn't look all that great now because the paint is faded and chipped and so much of the gilding still needs to be redone, but you should have seen it before the storm. It was beautiful."

"I'm sure it was. It's amazing it even survived the storm."

"It's a miracle. I just hope they'll be able to get the funds they need to restore it. Since the park doesn't get any state or federal funding, the only money for repairs has to come from donations and admissions. With the population half of what it was pre-Katrina, there's less money." She sighed. "It would be such a shame if other little girls and boys never got to ride on it like I did."

"Boys, don't run," a harried-looking and very pregnant woman called out to the twin boys wearing green jackets and matching hats who were streaking toward them. "Please, would you catch them for me?"

"Whoa," Jack said, reaching out and corralling them. "Hey, buddies, what do you say we wait for your mom?"

"You're big," one of the boys said. "Are you a Saints football player?" he asked, referring to the city's beloved team.

"Afraid not. But you guys are so fast, I bet you could play for them when you get big."

"I'm so sorry," the woman said as she reached them. She smoothed a hand over her stomach. "Their little sister makes keeping up with them harder than it used to be."

"Not a problem," Jack told her. "We were just chatting about football. I think you've got yourself two running backs in the making here."

The woman laughed and ruffled their heads. "Their daddy would love that. In fact, he's home watching Sunday-night football right now. I must have been out of my mind to not make him come with me."

"We're going to see *The Cajun Night Before Christmas* exhibit," one of the boys said.

"Are you now?" Jack replied.

Both boys nodded. "It's supposed to be just like the book. If you want to see it, you just need to follow this road."

"Over there?" he asked, pointing in the direction they'd indicated.

"Yeah."

Still hunkered down beside the boys, Jack lowered his voice and said, "You know, I could have sworn I saw one of Santa's elves hiding up in one of those trees over there."

Both boys' eyes grew wide as they looked toward the trees. "Really?"

Jack nodded. "I figure they must be here, checking out the boys and girls and reporting to Santa which ones are extra good. You boys might want to walk with your mom so they can tell Santa how good you two are."

"Come on, Mom. You'd better hold our hands and take it slow."

"Yeah, you shouldn't run. You might trip or something," the other twin added.

"Thanks," the woman mouthed as she and her sons headed in the direction of the trees with the elves.

"That was really sweet of you. I'm sure their mother was very grateful," Laura told him, touched by his actions.

"Hey, I was telling the truth. I think I did see an elf in those trees," he said, smiling once again.

"Which tree?"

"That one right over there," he said and, grabbing her by the hand, he brought her several yards back from the road and pointed up to a huge oak. "That one. I saw a pair of little green eyes peeking out of those branches."

Laura peered up at the branches in question. "I don't see anything," she told him and when she turned to look at him, the smile dissolved on her lips. He was still holding her hand and he was watching her with an intensity, with a longing, that stole her breath.

She didn't know how it happened. She didn't know if he took another step toward her or if she moved toward him. Then his mouth was on hers. The kiss was gentle, slow, just a simple brushing of lips against lips. Then she felt the tip of his tongue. Sighing, she opened her mouth to him. Heat exploded inside her and just when her senses hit overload, he was easing back, ending the kiss. Still dazed and wondering why he had stopped, she heard the voices. A family was approaching on the path near them.

"I didn't think you would want an audience," he said simply.

He was right. She wouldn't and it embarrassed her that she had been so engrossed in the kiss that she hadn't heard them. "Thanks."

"Don't thank me. For a moment there, I considered not stopping," he told her as he brushed his thumb along her jaw.

Confused and shaken by his effect on her, Laura stepped back and in doing so pulled her hand free. She walked back over to the carousel to take another look at it before leaving.

Jack followed and stopped beside her. "So tell me about the carousel."

"What do you want to know?"

"About the history of it. How long it's been here. How old you were the first time you came to see it."

Laura filled him in on the history, or as much of it as she knew. She told him how it had been her grandfather who had first brought her to see it. "I was four at the time," she told him. "My mom was married to Jeffrey Baxter, the soap star, then, and we were living in California. She had just had Chloe and was finding a four-year-old and a newborn a lot to handle. So she sent me down here to visit my grandfather. I was feeling a little homesick, so he took me to see the Christmas lights in the oaks to distract me. And the minute I saw the carousel, I fell in love with it."

"Which one was your horse?" he asked.

Laura looked over at him, surprised at his perceptiveness. "The palomino over there, with the red saddle," she said, pointing out the horse she had always ridden. "I named him Pegasus."

"The flying horse, huh?" he remarked because it was one of the horses crafted with its legs in flight.

"Yes," she said and laughed at herself. "I really did think he could fly. In fact, I had myself convinced that the carousel was enchanted and that when everyone left for the night all the horses and animals would come to life."

"Ever test your theory?"

"Yes," she admitted proudly and smiled at the memory. "When I was six, I snuck away from my grandfather just before closing time and went and hid in the carousel house."

"What happened?"

"None of the carousel animals came to life, but everyone else did. My grandfather and the security guards and staff were looking for me. My grandfather thought I'd been kidnapped and everyone was upset. I got in a lot of trouble with my granddad and wasn't allowed to have any desserts or treats for an entire week after that."

He let out a whistle. "No desserts for a week? That must have been really tough," he said, but from the grin on his face, it was clear he didn't think it had been tough at all.

"Trust me, it was torture," she assured him with a laugh. "I'd have sooner given up my favorite doll than give up dessert for a week."

"Have a sweet tooth, do you?" he teased.

"I was six," she pointed out. Then recalling how his appearance had caused her to hit her candy stash, she amended her answer by saying, "I've gotten better." But the memory of *why* she'd hit the candy stash in the first place brought reality crashing back. The man she had been sharing such tender moments with was Jackson Hawke. Her enemy. The man who was trying to foreclose on her hotel. The man with whom she'd made the crazy bet and agreed to sleep with if she lost. "It's getting late. I'd better see about getting a taxi and heading home."

"What about the rest of the exhibit?" he asked.

"I think we've seen everything."

"What about that new one—that Cajun story one."

"*The Cajun Night Before Christmas*. It's an animated children's story by a local author and artist. I wouldn't have thought you'd be interested," she said honestly. In fact, she wouldn't have thought he'd be interested in any of the exhibits, but he'd seemed to genuinely enjoy himself. And if she were honest, she had enjoyed sharing them with him.

"I wouldn't have thought I'd be interested, either, but I am."

The man confused her. He was a mass of contradictions. Just when she had him pegged as a rich and arrogant man who would wager a fifteen-million-dollar note against a night with her in his bed, he spendt an evening looking at Christmas lights with her and listening to stories about her childhood. On the one hand, she despised the businessman who threatened to take away a part of her heritage. On the other hand, she liked the kind man who had been so gentle with the little boys and considerate of their mother. She liked the man who had laughed with her, the man who had made her first visit to the carousel since her grandfather's death a happy one.

"Laura?"

The sound of him calling her by her first name snapped her out of her reverie. "Yes?"

"You zoned out there for a minute. Either that or I shocked you into silence. Which is it?"

"Both," she admitted.

"So what do you say? Do you want to see that other exhibit with me?"

Laura hesitated. Spending more time with this man wasn't a good idea, she told herself. She was beginning to like him, feel drawn to him. The last thing she could afford was to lose her focus when the Contessa was at stake. "I think I'll pass. But you go on ahead."

"Maybe another time, then," he said. "I'll head back to the hotel."

But when the taxi arrived, Jack insisted on sharing it with her. He also insisted the driver take her home first. Once they reached her place and she'd tucked her share of the cab fare into his hand, she said, "Good night."

He touched her arm. "Laura?"

She paused, turned to face him. "Yes?"

"Thanks for tonight. I'll see you in the morning."

And in the morning, he would be her enemy again, she reminded herself as she quickly exited the taxi and raced up the steps to her house.

Five

Seated in the dining room of the Contessa Hotel, Jack kept his eyes trained on the doorway and awaited the arrival of Chloe Baxter. Fitzpatrick had managed to locate Laura's half sister—in New Orleans, where she had been since Thanksgiving weekend. Funny how Laura had failed to mention the fact that her sister was visiting. But then, she had studiously avoided him since that night they'd gone to see the Christmas lights in the park. On those occasions when their paths had crossed, she had been all business. It was as though the woman he had laughed with and kissed in the park had never even existed.

Only he hadn't been able to stop thinking about that woman. It was difficult for him to look at her and not remember how sweet she had tasted, how good she had felt in his arms. Even more difficult was wondering if his stepbrother was the personal business she'd left town for two days ago. Jack closed his fist around the glass of Scotch as he considered that possibility. According to the detective, there had been no record of Peterson booking a flight in or out of New Orleans last weekend. But knowing Peterson's tastes and ability to manipulate, he could just as easily have gotten someone to fly him in on a private plane. Maybe one of his rich college buddies or someone in the moneyed crowd his father was so tight with. Or maybe even one of the corporate idiots that Peterson had conned into backing his political run.

Or maybe he'd been wrong and Peterson had never been in town after all. Had Laura gone to see him? It certainly would explain her sudden leave on personal business. According to Fitzpatrick Investigations, she had booked a flight to San Francisco with a stop in L.A., and there were no hotel reservations anywhere in her name. But then, why would she need a hotel room if she was sleeping with his stepbrother?

A white-hot anger seethed inside him at the image of Laura with Peterson. He tossed back a swallow of Scotch, but it did nothing to soothe the gnawing in his gut. If she was with his stepbrother, it wouldn't be for much longer, he assured himself. He knew through his sources in the financial arena that her attempt to secure a personal loan from the bank by pledging her own stock as collateral had been turned down. With only twenty days left on the thirty-day proviso, she was running out of options quickly. Once the designated time to cure the default was up, the hotel—or at least eighty percent of its stock and the controlling interest in it—would belong to him.

And so would Laura.

He would win their bet. And once he had her in his bed, he would wipe any trace of his stepbrother from her body, from her mind, from her soul.

Jack frowned. He was competitive. No one did what he did for a living without possessing a strong competitive streak. The truth was he enjoyed a challenge, thrived on taking risks. The higher the stakes, the more exciting he found the game. And he'd be lying to himself if the thought of taking Laura from Peterson didn't appeal to him on a very personal level. It did.

But it was more than that, Jack admitted. Even before he'd known about her connection to his stepbrother, she had set his competitive juices flowing and his hormones into a state of lust. Just remembering how she'd looked that night in the Carousel Gardens with her cheeks flushed, her eyes filled with desire and her body taut sent adrenaline pumping through his system. She'd been like some wild creature and every male hormone in his body demanded that he capture and possess her.

Disturbed by the admission, Jack shoved the images from his mind. Laura had been right. Making that bet with her had been crazy. *He* had been crazy. To offer the note he'd paid fifteen million dollars for against a night with her in his bed had been insane. It didn't matter that she stood little chance of winning the bet. The fact that he had even agreed to the terms had been flat-out reckless. Worse, it had been the act of a man making a decision guided by his hormones instead of by sound business sense.

So why did you do it, Hawke?

Because he wanted her. And he fully intended to have her.

"Would you like another Scotch, Mr. Hawke?"

Jack glanced down at his empty glass, then up at the waitress who stood at his table. Dressed in a crisp black-and-white uniform and wearing a name tag with Tina written on it, she gave him a friendly smile. Reasoning that he had no farther to travel than the elevator to his room, he said, "Sure."

"I'll be right back," she told him and wove her way through the busy restaurant toward the kitchen.

Shaking off his disturbing thoughts about Laura, Jack glanced around the restaurant. There was a nice crowd, he noted. Laura's decision to open the dining room on week-nights to draw from the local business clientele leaving work had been a smart move. So had extending the dinner hours on the weekends. Both were moves he would have implemented himself. Some well-placed advertisements and a few local TV and radio spots to capitalize on the popular chef's affiliation with the Contessa would fill the remaining tables. He made a mental note to discuss a series of print and TV ads with Laura. Of course, that was assuming she agreed to stay on as general manager when she lost the bet.

The bet.

Had Laura been thinking about those stakes as much as he had? he wondered. That kiss they had shared had given him a glimpse of what it would be like between them. Even now he wondered how the night might have ended had he not played the gentleman and ended it when he had.

"Here you go," the waitress said as she placed the Scotch in front of him.

"Thanks." Jack started to take a sip, then decided against it. Instead, he picked up the knife on the place setting before him. Made of quality stainless steel, he noted as he traced the blade with his fingertip. It was also sharp enough to cut his finger if he wasn't careful. A lot like Laura, he thought—attractive, of excellent quality and dangerous if a man wasn't careful.

He was always careful, Jack reminded himself. Putting aside the knife, he checked his watch. Thirty minutes late. Evidently, punctuality wasn't one of Chloe Baxter's virtues, he decided. He was just beginning to wonder if the woman would be a no-show when he spied the striking blonde in the doorway. At first, he wouldn't have pegged her for Laura's sister. On second glance though, he noted the shape of her eyes and the long legs were very much like Laura's. She was a real head-turner, Jack thought as the hostess led her toward his table. Judging by the number of appreciative male looks cast her way, he wasn't the only one who thought so. He stood as she approached. "Ms. Baxter," he said and extended his hand. "I'm Jackson Hawke."

She shook his hand firmly. "Mr. Hawke," she said in a voice that had a smoky tone to it.

Once she was seated, he asked, "Would you care for something to drink?"

She looked up at the waitress, smiled. "I'd love a glass of merlot."

Jack ordered a bottle from a select vintage and once the waitress was gone, he said, "I appreciate your agreeing to meet with me."

Amusement lit her hazel eyes. "We both know that I came here in exchange for your promise that you'd schedule a meeting with Meredith Grant to discuss her company, Connections."

"Yes. And I have to say, your request surprised me. As an actress, I would have thought you would have traded for an introduction for yourself to a producer or casting director. After all, I do know several. But instead, you asked for something for a former stepsister. Why is that?"

"Meredith's my sister. Just because our parents divorced doesn't mean she and I stop being sisters. And contrary to what most people think, not all actresses are self-centered divas. Meredith has been trying for months to get an appointment with you and your office keeps turning her down." She sat back in her seat, crossed her legs and met his gaze. "When you called and asked me to meet with you, I saw an opportunity to get her that appointment and took it."

Jack nodded. "I appreciate your candor, Ms. Baxter."

"Then I hope you'll appreciate that I intend to have you book that meeting with Meredith before I leave here today."

"I'll book the meeting—just as long as both you and Ms. Grant understand that I'm not interested in a matchmaking service."

"Connections does more than matchmaking," she told him. "It connects people for business reasons, too. That's what Meredith wants to meet with you about."

"Very well, Ms. Baxter. I'll keep my promise and book the meeting with Ms. Grant," he assured her. "In exchange, you promised to listen to my offer and hear about my plans for the hotel with an open mind. Agreed?"

"Agreed," she replied. "And the name's Chloe."

"Very well, Chloe. And my name's Jack."

"All right, Jack. I'm listening."

She listened while he told her about his reasons for wanting to buy the hotel. She listened as he explained the difficulties of competing in the hotel market in the post-Katrina city. She listened as he told her about his plans to restore the Contessa and make it a viable, revenue-producing property.

"If you're able to do what you say, it seems the smart thing for me to do would be to hold on to my stock because it'll be worth a lot more down the road."

"That's true. But that's at least a year or two away," he said as he leaned back in his chair. "Accepting my two million dollars now would mean you wouldn't have to take another waitress job and you could study full-time at the L.A. Theater Institute."

She lifted her eyebrow. "I suppose I shouldn't be surprised you did your homework on me. Laura said you were smart."

"Did she now? What else did your sister say about me?"

She smiled. "I think she mentioned something about your being an arrogant Neanderthal who—"

Laughing, he held up his hand. "I think I get the picture."

"I thought you would," she said with a twinkle in her eye. "Although I'm not sure the Neanderthal fits. I expected you to be bigger…and ugly."

He laughed.

So did she.

And they were both laughing when an unsmiling Laura walked into the dining room. Damn, but she looked good, Jack thought. No suit today, he noted. She was dressed in an ivory sweater with a red ribbon bow shooting across the shoulder and a skinny-fitting skirt of lipstick-red that gave him an enticing view of those killer legs. Her mouth was painted that same shade of red and Jack found himself itching to taste it.

"See something you like, Jack?"

Jack shot a look over at Chloe and, given the amused expression on her face and tone in her voice, his appraisal of her sister hadn't gone unnoticed. As Laura approached their table, Jack stood. "How was your…vacation? It was a vacation, wasn't it? Your assistant said you were off on personal business."

"My trip was fine," Laura said drily, her attention focused on her younger sister. "Hello, Chloe."

"Hi, sis. You're back early. I thought your flight wasn't due in until after nine tonight," Chloe said.

"I was able to get an earlier flight. I thought you had a date tonight," Laura said, accusation in her voice.

"I do—but not until later. So I decided to take Jack up on his dinner offer."

He knew very little about siblings, particularly siblings who loved one another. His only experience had been the hurtful experiences and bitterness that permeated his relationship with Matt Peterson. Whatever was going on between Laura and Chloe was different—and whatever it was, it was generating a lot of tension. In an effort to diffuse some of that tension, he said, "We were just about to order coffee and dessert. Would you like to join us?"

"No, thanks. I've got some paperwork to catch up on. Besides, I wouldn't want to interrupt you while you're trying to charm my sister into selling you her stock."

Chloe waved her hand in dismissal. "Lighten up, Laura. As charming as he is, Jack already knows that I have no intention of selling him my stock. Don't you, Jack?"

He did know it. But judging by the look of relief on Laura's face, she hadn't been quite so sure. "Yes, I know you're not going to sell," he said. "But it doesn't mean I haven't enjoyed our time together or that I'll stop trying to convince you." He looked over at Laura. "Either of you."

"And as I've already told you, you're wasting your time," Laura said.

Annoyed by her dismissal and wondering whether or not a rendezvous with his stepbrother, Matt, was the reason, Jack said, "Speaking of wasting time, before you take off on another trip, you might want to remember that there are only twenty days left before one of us has to pay up on that bet. I'm counting on that someone being you."

Back in her office, Laura tried to focus on the letters awaiting her signature and block out all thoughts of Jackson Hawke. The man was infuriating. She'd wanted to wipe that cocky smile off his face. And at the same time, she'd wanted to jump his bones. Just remembering the way he had looked at her—as if he'd wanted to swallow her whole—made her pulse stutter, her body hot.

"All right," Chloe said, marching into Laura's office and slamming the door behind her. "What's going on between you and Jack? And what's this about a bet?"

Laura didn't bother to look up from her paperwork. "I thought you had a date."

"Forget about my date. I want some answers."

Laura sighed. "Nothing's going on and the bet doesn't concern you."

"It sure didn't look like nothing to me. You two were generating enough heat between you to keep this hotel warm for the entire winter. And when Jack mentioned that bet, you turned as red as that skirt you're wearing before you stormed out of the dining room."

"You're wrong."

Chloe planted her hands on the desk, got in her face. "Laura, this is me you're talking to. I may not know anything about running a hotel, but I do know about sexual chemistry. And believe me, there was definitely some serious sexual chemistry cooking between you two."

Her sister was right, Laura admitted to herself. There was sexual chemistry between them. And for her there was something more, something she hadn't wanted. She had hoped that kiss in the park had just been a fluke, that these feelings she was starting to have for Jack weren't real and would disappear with the light of day and with some distance. But they hadn't disappeared. If anything, they were getting stronger. In fact, he was the reason she had come home early from California. She had actually missed him, had even wondered if she had misjudged him. She had gone so far as to hope that maybe she wasn't the only one who had felt there was something more than desire happening between them. Only when she'd seen him with Chloe, believing he was trying to buy her sister's stock, she'd realized she had been kidding herself. Sure, Jackson Hawke might want to have sex with her, but what he really wanted was the Contessa. His reminder that in twenty days he intended to take the Contessa from her only served to bring home that fact.

"Since I turned down two million dollars for my stock because this place means so much to you, I think I deserve some answers," Chloe pointed out. "Tell me what's going on and why you're so upset."

Laura told her sister everything. She told her about the bet she had made with Jack in the heat of the moment. She told her about the evening they had spent together at the park viewing the Christmas lights. She told her about the kiss and the feelings it had stirred inside her.

"It sounds to me like you might be falling for the guy," Chloe responded. "There's nothing wrong with that. You said you and Matt weren't exclusive anymore. And you can bet the wannabe-congressman isn't spending his nights alone. Or did he manage to convince you to change your mind about that when you were out in California?"

"Matt didn't convince me to change my mind about anything because I didn't see him. I went to see Papa Vincenzo and his family because I canceled on them at Thanksgiving," she said, referring to one of their former stepfathers.

"Then I don't see where you hooking up with Jack should be a problem."

"It's a problem because I'm not into one-night stands or casual sex. And that's what it would be with a man like Hawke."

"You don't know that," Chloe argued.

No, she didn't know it for a fact. But she had a pretty good idea that Hawke was not a man who was into long-term relationships or commitments. She was. "But I do know that the man's a shark. He's a corporate raider. Half the companies he buys, he dismantles and sells them off in pieces for a profit. And now he's intent on doing that to our hotel."

"Not according to him," her sister told her. "Besides, if you ask me, Mr. Jackson Hawke seemed a lot more interested in winning that bet and you than he is in foreclosing on the hotel."

"Yes, he is. Isn't he?" He did seem intent on the bet, Laura realized, and found herself wondering why. While she didn't doubt for a second that he wanted her, there had been moments when she'd caught him looking at her, with something more than desire in his eyes. There had been anger and determination and something else all mixed in with his wanting her. What she didn't understand was why. "Don't you find that odd? That he's more focused on the bet than the hotel?"

"What I think, dear sister, is you think too much." Walking around to the other side of Laura's desk, Chloe opened the drawer and stole a bag of chocolate-covered nuts from her stash. When Laura attempted to take them back, Chloe quickly moved out of her reach. "You know what else I think?" she asked as she ripped open the bag and popped several of the candies into her mouth.

"No. But I imagine you're going to tell me."

"I think Jackson Hawke's got a case of the hots for you. And I think you've got the hots for him. So I say quit analyzing it to death and enjoy it."

"And I say you're going to be late for your date," Laura said, wanting to end the discussion.

"All right, I'm going. But seriously, Laura, there are a lot worse things that could happen than to find yourself waking up in Hawke's bed."

There were a lot worse things that could happen than her ending up in Jackson Hawke's bed, Laura conceded. One worse thing that came to her mind was losing the

Contessa Hotel. Not wanting to think about that possibility or about Jack, she fortified herself with a chocolate peanut-butter cup, then tackled the mountain of reports and correspondence that had accumulated in her absence.

After she'd finished going through the budget reports and projections, she reached for the folder of incoming mail. A quick glance revealed several solicitations, bills and subscriptions. Then she spied an unopened envelope from the Jardine Law Firm. Her stomach pitched. It was the same firm that had handled the foreclosure paperwork for Hawke. Ripping open the envelope, she pulled out the document.

Quickly, she skimmed the legal jargon and zeroed in on the name *Hawke Industries*.

In accordance with Hawke Industries' purchase of the above-referenced note, Hawke Industries and/or its appointed representative are hereby granted access to said hotel property in order to perform the due diligence afforded Hawke Industries as purchaser of said note. Hawke Industries and/or its appointed representative will not be afforded the right to take any actions or implement any changes in the hotel, its management, personnel or operations until such time that the thirty-day grace period on the loan has expired and the shares of stock in the hotel are transferred to Hawke Industries. Also in accordance with the purchase of the above-referenced note, Hawke Industries and/or its appointed representative will be provided suitable office work space to perform said due-diligence process connected with the sale.

Laura didn't bother reading any further. He couldn't do this. He couldn't just waltz in and take over before the thirty days were up. And if he'd been planning to do this, why hadn't he told her? With temper blazing and the attorney's letter crumpled in her fist, she headed for the penthouse suite. The ride up the slow-moving elevator only added to her mood. By the time she exited the car, she was nearly trembling with anger and frustration. Marching over to the ornate door of the penthouse, she punched the doorbell to the suite. She counted to ten and when Jack didn't answer, she pounded on the door with her fist.

No answer.

She beat on the door again. "Hawke, open this door now." When he still failed to respond, Laura didn't hesitate. Reaching into her skirt pocket, she pulled out the master key card she always carried that allowed management access to all rooms in the hotel for emergency purposes. She zipped it into the lock. The green light kicked on, unlocking the door.

"Hawke, get out here," she demanded from the entrance.

Nothing.

"Hawke," she yelled as she tried to find him in the living and dining room areas. Ignoring the laptop computer and mounds of files, she began searching the rest of the suite. The first two bedrooms were empty. Growing angrier by the second, she pushed open the door to the master suite. Still no Hawke. She spied the door to the bathroom ajar, heard the buzz of an electric razor. Intent on confronting him, Laura made a beeline for the bathroom. She shoved the door open and sent it banging sharply against the wall. And there Jack stood in front of the sink, naked from the waist up, with a towel anchored around his hips and a razor buzzing in his hand.

Surprise flickered across his features for a moment as he shut off the razor. "Hello, Laura. Was there something you wanted?" he asked, an edge in his voice.

At the sharp tone, Laura jerked her gaze from his bare chest to his face and remembered that she was the one with reason to be angry—not him. But before she could tell him so, he was moving toward her.

"Let me guess. Your trip didn't turn out quite the way you'd planned and your friend didn't come through with the money like you thought he would."

"What are you talking about?" she replied, confused.

But he didn't seem to hear her. "Isn't that why you're here, Laura? Because you know you can't beat me, so you've come to pay off on our bet?"

"In your dreams."

"Actually, I've had quite a few dreams about having you in my bed, Laura. Especially after that night in the park. What about you? You have any dreams about what it'll be like between us?"

"*Nightmares* is more like it," she lied, vowing he'd never know that she had wondered what it would be like to make love with him. Even now she wasn't immune to him and was having a devil of a time ignoring the way the sprinkling of dark hair made a vee down his chest to his sexy abs before it disappeared beneath the towel hitched around his hips. Suddenly realizing what she was doing, Laura yanked her gaze back to his face. His mouth looked hard. His expression closed. But his eyes, his eyes were dark and hungry as they watched her watch him.

"If you're not here for sex, then why did you break into my room?"

"I didn't break in. I used the pass key," she informed him, holding up the card that she still held in her hand.

"Which is a violation of a guest's privacy and illegal."

"It's not illegal if you enter with cause," she defended, knowing that was a stretch.

He moved toward her, causing the towel to shift precariously. "And just what would that cause be, Laura?" he asked, his voice dangerously soft.

"This," she said, shoving the attorney's letter at him.

He barely gave the letter a glance. "How does notification that I'll be starting the due diligence on the hotel qualify as cause for illegal entry to my room?"

"Because I came to tell you that there isn't going to be any due diligence because there isn't going to be a foreclosure."

"Why? Did the friend you spent the past couple of days with lend you the money to stop me?"

"No. At least not yet." The truth was Papa Vincenzo hadn't given her an answer yet on lending her a portion of the money because he and his wife needed to meet with their accountants first. But even if they did give her a loan, it would only be for a fraction of the money she needed.

From the scowl on his face, her answer hadn't pleased him. "Pardon me," he said and she stepped to the side while he stretched out his left arm to the towel rack behind her. But instead of taking the towel and moving away, he continued to hold on to it, effectively caging her between him and the counter.

There was that look in his eyes again, that mingling of anger and desire, she noted. Laura's heart pounded as he leaned closer. Suddenly she was aware of how tall he was, just how wide those shoulders were. He smelled like soap and outdoors, she thought. Lifting her gaze, she stared at his face and noticed for the first time that his eyes were a blue so deep they were almost black. His hair was still damp and mussed from his shower, and she had this crazy urge to brush it away from his forehead. She noted the stubble along his chin that he hadn't had a chance to shave. She looked at his mouth, recalled how those lips had felt on hers that night in the park and all she could think was she wanted to kiss him again.

As though he could read her thoughts, Jack lowered his head until his mouth was only inches from hers. He waited a fraction of a second, no more. Yet it seemed like an eternity during which she could feel her pulse race, could feel her heart beat frantically like the wings of a hummingbird. And just when she thought surely she would explode, his mouth was on hers—hot, hungry, demanding. Somewhere Laura heard a moan. But she wasn't sure if it came from her or from Jack.

Then she couldn't think at all as Jack continued to kiss her. When she touched her tongue to his, Jack gentled the kiss. He kissed her slowly, deeply, thoroughly. Her head spun. Her stomach quivered. Every nerve in her body seemed to have come alive at the touch of his lips.

And she wanted more.

The papers she held in her hand fell to the floor, freeing her fingers to explore his face. She could feel the whiskers where she had interrupted his shave. She could smell the mixture of soap and a woodsy scent. She sieved her fingers through his damp hair and kissed him back.

One kiss strung into another and then another, each feeding that ache inside her, each one demanding more. Of their own volition, her hands slid down to his shoulders, to his chest, along the dusting of dark hair. When her fingers moved lower and unknotted the towel at his waist, Jack sucked in his breath. This time when she heard a groan, Laura knew it was Jack's. He devoured her with his mouth.

So caught up in the feel of him and the heat of his mouth, it took her a moment before she realized that Jack had stopped kissing her. When she opened her eyes and saw the hunger in his blue eyes, her heart began to race all over again.

"One of us is wearing too many clothes," he whispered in a voice that sent another wave of desire pumping through her. He drew the backs of his fingers slowly, gently, along the line of her breast.

Her nipples puckered. Her breath lodged in her throat and she closed her eyes, overwhelmed by the sensations. Even through her sweater and bra, she could feel the heat of his touch and another wave of desire pulsed through her. Opening her eyes, she looked at him, witnessed the strength of his arousal. The sight of him had heat pooling in her belly, between her thighs.

She took a step back and heard the papers crunch beneath her heel. Laura looked down, saw the letter from the attorney that had driven her to his suite in anger.

Suddenly sanity came crashing back. What was she doing? What had she been thinking? Hadn't she just told Chloe earlier that the man was a shark, that he was out to steal their hotel and score a one-night stand? She couldn't let him do either. Not and look at herself in the mirror in the morning. "This was a mistake. I never should have come here."

And without waiting for him to respond, Laura turned and ran from the bathroom and out of the suite.

Six

"I agreed to allow you to start the due diligence, didn't I?" Laura argued as she stood across the desk from Jack the next morning.

"Yes, you did. And I appreciate your cooperation," he told her, not bothering to point out that she really hadn't had much choice. She'd been on the defensive since his arrival that morning.

As he listened to her excuses for not providing him with the office he'd requested, he noted that she had taken great care to keep the subject on business. She'd made no mention of her visit to his suite the previous night or what had happened between them. He thought about that initial kiss, the anger that had driven him to possess her, the need to wipe Peterson from her mind and body until all she wanted was him. Only when she had kissed him back, she had tasted sweet and hot, just as she had that night in the park. Then all he could think about was quenching the thirst inside him with her. He had thought she'd felt the same way—until she had bolted from his suite.

Why had she bolted? It was a question he'd asked himself long after she had gone. And the answer he kept coming back to was Peterson. If she had been with his step-brother as he suspected, Peterson wouldn't have told her about their connection since he'd never claimed Jack as part of his family. Instead he would have warned her to stay away from him, that he was ruthless, the son of a loser and not to be trusted. The last thing Laura would want would be for her lover to find out that she had slept with his sworn enemy. And Peterson would find out he'd bedded Laura, Jack vowed. He would make sure of it. Then he would see how his stepbrother felt to be the one who came out the loser. As for Laura, he wouldn't hurt her, he promised himself. He'd simply let the sexual chemistry run its course and when it was over, they would both move on with their lives. No, the only one who would be hurt would be Peterson—and the blow would be more to his ego than anything else.

"…and all things considered, I don't think it's in the best interest of the hotel," Laura continued, laying out her reasons for not wanting him there and omitting the primary one; that they had been within minutes of tumbling into bed.

Despite her all-business attitude, the sexual tension was still there—like the proverbial pink elephant in the middle of a room that no one admitted to seeing. He could see it though. It was there in the way she avoided eye contact with him, in the way she seemed unable to remain still, in the way she tensed each time he came within a few feet of her. And from the shadows under her eyes, he suspected he wasn't the only one who'd had trouble sleeping last night. Not even a cold shower had been able to stop him from thinking about her, from wanting her. He still wanted her. Fortunately, he knew how to control that wanting and not allow it to control him and interfere with his business.

Unlike his father.

An image flashed through Jack's mind of his father sitting alone in the dark with a drink in his hand. His father had made the mistake of letting sentiment override his business sense and look what it had cost him. Samuel Hawke had lost not only his wife and company when Nicole had taken off with his business partner, but he'd also lost his will to live. He had learned from his father's mistakes, Jack reminded himself. He had no intention of letting that happen to him—regardless of how tempting he found Laura Spencer. Bedding Laura and shoving it in his stepbrother's face would be a fringe benefit, one that he would enjoy. But he wouldn't put it or her before business. No, business would always come first. That was why he'd decided to get the due diligence on a fast track, so that when the thirty-day proviso was up, he'd be ready to close the deal and set his plans for the hotel in motion. Whether those plans included Laura or not would be up to her.

"...so if you'll just give me a list of what reports and information you need to perform the due diligence, I'll see that they're sent to your suite."

Tuning back in to what Laura was saying, Jack caught only the tail end of her remark. But it was enough for him to know that she was still balking at giving him a work space in the corporate offices. "Maybe you didn't hear me the first time," Jack said, his voice firm. "I have no intention of working from my suite. I need an office, preferably one on this floor where the data is more accessible. It's all spelled out there in the letter from my attorney," he said, referring to the document he had returned to her. He walked around the desk and picked up the letter. Holding it up, he pointed to the appropriate clause. "According to those terms, the Contessa Hotel and its representative, that's you, will provide Hawke Industries and/or its representative, which is me, adequate office space to perform the due-diligence portion of the contract."

Laura snatched the letter from him, crumpled it in her fist. "I know what it says. I can read. But I can't give you what I don't have. There is no office available," she argued. "So you're just going to have to suck it up and work out of your suite like you've been doing."

"Wrong. I have no intention of spending my time coming down here to access data or having you send the information upstairs to me," he told her. "Even you have to agree that would be a waste of valuable time for both of us."

"I do agree. But I don't see where you have any choice. There is no office available."

"Then I suggest you make one available," Jack insisted.

"And just how am I supposed to do that?" she snapped.

"You're a smart woman. Figure something out. After all, you're the one who insisted we play by the rules, remember?" he pointed out, referring to the thirty-day grace period in the contract that she'd insisted on exercising. "The rules say I get an office."

"Anyone ever tell you what a jerk you are?"

"Repeatedly," he said.

She sat down in her chair, shoved the hair back from her face. After letting out a breath, she looked up at him again and said, "All right. Since I want as few people as possible to know why you're here, you can have my office."

"Where are you going to work?"

"What difference does it make? You're getting your office."

"It makes a difference because you're the hotel's general manager, at least for the time being, and I need you to run this place. After the foreclosure if you don't want to stay on, I'll bring someone else in to take over. But until then, your contract says that you're the GM. So I repeat, where are you going to work?"

She looked mad enough to chew nails, Jack thought. "I'll just work out of one of the suites—the way I wanted you to do."

He didn't want to displace the woman, he admitted. She also had a point about not wanting to ignite the rumor mill about the hotel's new ownership—at least not until he had finished his assessments and was ready to take the appropriate action. In the post-Katrina climate, staffing remained a problem citywide and he didn't want to lose valuable employees needlessly. "That won't work. You need to be here."

"Well, I don't see where I have a lot of choices. As you pointed out, I have to provide you with an office. Since there's none available, someone has to give up theirs and it's not going to be one of my staff. Your being here to supposedly conduct an evaluation of the hotel's operations for marketing purposes is going to raise enough questions. So the only option is for you to take my office."

"Then we'll share the office."

She blinked, evidently stunned by the suggestion. "You've got to be kidding."

"I seldom kid," he told her. Shoving aside a pile of folders, Jack sat on the edge of her desk. He didn't miss the sudden tension in her body at his close proximity. Nor did he miss the awareness that crept into her eyes. He'd seen it last night when she'd realized he was wearing nothing more than a towel. He'd watched desire cloud her anger. And watching her had fed his own hunger for her. The memory set off a sharp jab of need as he recalled how she'd tasted, how her hands had felt on his skin.

"The idea is ridiculous," she told him and averted her gaze.

Annoyed with himself and with her, Jack shut off the memories and stood. Determined to focus on business, he picked up the amethyst paperweight from her desk, tested its weight in his palm. "What's ridiculous is for either one of us to work out of a suite when this office is more than big enough for the two of us. And since a lot of the information I'll need will have to come from you, it makes sense for us to both work out of here."

"That may sound good in theory, but—"

"Would you rather have me in an office where someone might overhear me on the phone and learn something they shouldn't? If I'm working from here, neither one of us has still to worry about that happening." He paused, gave her a moment to digest the idea.

"I guess it could work," she conceded, reluctance in her voice. "But…"

"But what, Laura?" he countered, irritated by her refusal to look at him. "What's the real reason you don't want me here?"

Finally, she looked at him and the coolness was back in her green eyes. "Besides the fact that you're trying to steal my family's hotel, I don't want you here because I don't trust you."

Her words hit him like fists. Angry, he walked over to her and said, "Is it really me you don't trust, Laura? Or is it yourself? Could it be you're worried that if we're alone together we'll finish what we started last night?"

"That monster-size ego of yours is showing again, Hawke."

"My ego has nothing to do with it. You and I both know that you wanted me every bit as much as I wanted you last night. And the only reason you didn't wake up in my bed this morning is because you got cold feet."

She pushed away from the desk and stood, taking a step back and putting distance between them. "I didn't get cold feet. I came to my senses. Last night I was tired after my trip and I was upset and wasn't thinking clearly. What happened was a mistake."

Her mention of her trip to California, coupled with her denial, angered him even more. "Is that what it was?" he asked as he moved closer, crowding her personal space. "When you had your hot little hands all over my body and my tongue was in your mouth, that was a mistake?"

"Yes," she insisted. "And it's one I have no intention of repeating."

"Then tell me, sweet Laura. Just how do you intend to pay off on our bet when you lose? Because you are going to lose. And when you do, I intend to collect."

* * *

"I can't tell you how much I appreciate this and I promise I'll pay you back just as soon as I can arrange refinancing of the hotel," Laura told her former stepfather, who had just called to inform her he'd wired five hundred thousand dollars to her account.

"You just pay me back when you can and come for another visit soon," Vincent Vincenzo told her. "Be sure to say hello to your mother for me. *Ciao.*"

"*Ciao.*" Laura hung up the phone and leaned back in her chair. A range of emotions rushed through her. Relief. Gratitude. Love. Regardless of all the chaos her parents brought into her life with their merry-go-round of marriages, she had definitely been the lucky one because she had ended up with a wonderful extended family.

Grateful to have the office to herself for a change, Laura retrieved the plan she'd devised to come up with the money to pay off her mother's note. She added the loan from her stepfather to the list and studied the totals. Thanks to Chloe signing over her stock to her, she'd used it and her own stock as collateral on a four-million-dollar loan from another bank. Of course, the interest rate was outrageous. But she'd been desperate and had agreed to the terms. She'd netted another two hundred fifty thousand by cashing in her stocks, IRAs and savings account. Her accountant had warned her that the tax penalties would be a killer, but a big tax bill was the least of her worries at the moment. With the one hundred fifty grand she'd gotten from her own father and the one hundred grand from Chloe's dad, she had managed to come up with five million dollars. Now all she needed was for her mother to be successful in refinancing the nightclub for at least ten million dollars and she would have the fifteen million she needed to cure the defaulted loan.

Then the hotel and its stock would be returned to her family and Jackson Hawke would be out of her office, out of her hotel and out of her life. So why did the prospect of never seeing Jack again leave her feeling more unsettled than pleased? Not sure she wanted to examine the reasons too closely, Laura returned her finance plan to her drawer and dove into the weekly reports. She was still going through the reports when Jack entered the office.

In the nearly two weeks that they had shared an office, he had done nothing to be overly intrusive. His phone conversations were brief. His questions minimal. His interruptions few. He had made no further references to their bet. Nor had he attempted to kiss her again. Yet she had been keenly aware of his presence. The tension between them had been like a live wire dangling in a storm, leaving her on edge, waiting for the sparks to ignite. And each time she looked across the room and found his eyes on her, the desire she saw in them made her blood heat.

It simply made no sense. While she was no prude, sex wasn't something she took lightly. She'd only slept with two men in her life—her first love and Matt Peterson. In each case, she'd known the man for nearly a year and had strong feelings for him before she'd shared his bed. She'd known Jack for less than a month and the feelings he aroused in her were certainly not feelings of love. Yet, there was no denying her physical attraction to him. The admission worried her as much as it annoyed her.

"Isn't there someone else who can generate a copy of the report?"

Laura looked up at the sound of Jack's voice and glanced over to the table where he had been working. He'd shed the dark suit coat and silk tie he'd worn that morning, she noted. The crisp white shirt was open at the collar. The gold cuff links at his wrists caught the light as he put down his pen. Sitting back in his chair, he shoved a hand through his hair, and Laura couldn't help remembering sliding her own fingers through his damp hair that night in his hotel suite.

"All right, then. Just leave a message for him to call me when he gets in," Jack said and hung up the phone.

"Is there a problem?" she asked.

"I'm missing the copy of the marketing projections for the first quarter of next year and the guy who handles it took off this afternoon to go to see his daughter in a school Christmas pageant."

She smiled. "Jerry's daughter is in kindergarten and she's an angel in the pageant. I told him he could have the afternoon off," she told him. "But I should have a copy of the report you can use."

A few minutes later, after she'd located the report and handed it to him, he said, "Thanks."

"No problem." Curious, she asked, "So how is the due diligence coming? Have you been able to get everything you needed?"

"It's going pretty well. And yes, so far I've been able to get or access all the data I've asked for."

"How much longer do you think it'll take before you finish?"

His lips twitched. "What's the matter? Tired of sharing your office or just anxious to get rid of me?"

"Both."

He chuckled. "At least you're honest."

"You asked."

This time he actually laughed aloud. And Laura realized it was the first time she had heard him laugh since that night in the park. She couldn't help thinking that despite his fortune and power, Jack didn't seem to have a lot of laughter in his life. Or people, she realized. While he had lots of employees, she could never recall him mentioning any family or close friends.

"You're right. I did ask. And in answer to your question, it should only take me another week, maybe less to finish." He sat back, stretched his arms behind his head and looked up at her. "How about you? Any problems with the employees buying the story about me doing a marketing analysis?"

"Not really. Some people are curious and there have been a few questions," she advised him. Most of those questions had come from the accounting department, which she had expected since the info that Jack had requested was much more expansive than the data needed for marketing purposes. "But they seemed satisfied with the explanation I had Penny give them. And it hasn't been a secret that I'm trying to increase the hotel's revenues. They think that you're part of that plan."

"I guess I am, in a manner of speaking, if things go down as I plan."

"But not if they go as I've planned."

"True," he said with a smile. "Other than for the obvious reason that your family owned this hotel, why a career in hotel management?"

The question surprised her. It was the first time in nearly two weeks that he'd spoken to her about anything that didn't relate to the hotel's operation. "The truth is, I knew from the time I was a little girl that I wanted to be a hotelier. More specifically, I wanted to run this hotel." For the next fifteen minutes she told him about how enamored she had been by her grandfather's stories about the people who had stayed in the hotel, how he had taught her that each person was like a guest in their home. She told him how for nearly a hundred years the lives and loves of countless people had played out within the walls of the Contessa, that the hotel stood as a witness to history. "Did you know that an Austrian duke once stayed here?"

"A duke, huh?"

"Yes. It was in the early 1930s when my great-grandfather was running the hotel. Anyway, the duke and his consort were here for the Mardi Gras festivities. In particular, they were special guests attending the meeting of the courts of Rex and Comus on Mardi Gras night," she explained, telling him about the momentous occasion that had, for nearly a century, signaled the final events of the holiday. "They supposedly chose to stay at the Contessa because of it's old-world charm."

"That must have been quite a coup for your great-grandfather."

"It was. In fact, there's a photograph of him and my grandfather with the duke and duchess hanging over there." She stood and walked over to the wall in question where the photo from the bygone era was displayed.

"I assume the serious little boy is your grandfather," he said from behind her.

"Yes, and the man wearing the costume and mask is my great-grandfather, Robert Spencer," she said, and was surprised to turn and find Jack standing so close to her. Disarmed by his nearness, Laura returned her attention to the photograph and adjusted it.

"Is that your grandfather, too?" he asked, indicating another shot of a young man in a doorman's uniform, smiling and holding the door for guests. After assuring him the young man was indeed her grandfather, he said, "He certainly looks like he's enjoying his job."

"He did. My grandfather loved this place. Instead of having bedtime stories read to me as a child, I got stories about movie stars and royals and even bank robbers who had stayed here. I knew that I wanted to have my own stories to tell my children and grandchildren someday," she said wistfully and traced her fingers over the photo before turning. "What about you? What did you want to be when you grew up?"

"Rich."

Surprised, she thought he was kidding and said, "What happened to wanting to be a fireman or a cowboy?"

"They don't make enough money."

Again surprised by his response, she asked, "And just how old were you when you reached that conclusion?"

"Six."

He said it so matter-of-factly, she realized he was serious. She couldn't help wondering what had happened to him at six that would have had him set such a serious goal. So she asked, "What was so important about being rich?"

"Because when you're rich, people like you better. They want to be around you. They're nice to you because they know you have money and can buy them things, can take them places," he said.

"Having people hang out with you just for your money doesn't sound all that great to me. It certainly isn't the kind of friends that I would want."

"Maybe not," he said, a sardonic note in his voice. "But it sure beats people treating you like a loser because you don't have money or ditching you for somebody else who does."

Judging by the hard look in his eyes, Laura was sure Jack was speaking from personal experience. And the realization made her feel sad for him. "What they say is true, Jack. Money isn't everything."

"Sure it is. Money is power. And power is all that really matters."

"So is that why you do what you do? Buy companies like the Contessa for the power?"

"That's a big part of it," he conceded. "But there's also the challenge of turning a company around and making it profitable."

"So that you can make more money," she added drily.

"Yes."

"But where's the joy in that? Where's the passion?"

"The joy is in being able to make it happen. As for the passion, I find all the passion I need with the woman who's in my bed. You're the woman I would have found that passion with if you hadn't run out on me." He edged a step closer, cupped the back of her head with his hand.

"Jack," she said, her voice suddenly dry. Despite her attempts to resist him, Laura could feel her pulse start to stutter.

"You can still be that woman, Laura," he told her as he brushed his mouth against hers. "I want you."

She pressed her hands against his chest, unsure if she

intended to push him away or draw him closer. He slid his hand down her back, drew her to him, and the feel of his arousal sent waves of heat through her.

"All you have to do is say yes and we can go to my suite now. Then I'll show you what real passion is."

She was tempted. Oh, she was tempted, Laura admitted as he kissed her jaw, moved to her neck. The nip of his teeth to her sensitive flesh sent a shiver of need through her body.

"Laura." Penny buzzed through on the intercom. "I have Matt Peterson on line one for you."

It took Laura a moment before she registered the sudden stiffening of Jack's body or the way the hand that had been caressing her was now curled into a fist in her jacket. But that momentary cease in the assault to her senses was enough for Laura to catch her breath and realize where she was, what she was doing and who she was doing it with. The realization that Penny or anyone could have walked in on them was like a sobering blast of cold air. She eased back from him and his hands fell away. "I really need to take this call," she said.

"Right," he told her, his voice cool, his expression shuttered. And before she could say another word, his back was to her. After shoving his laptop into its case, he snapped it shut, then grabbed his jacket and started for the door. "When you make up your mind, you know where to find me."

Seven

"Hello, Matt," Laura said as she stared at the door through which Jack had exited so abruptly.

"Hi, beautiful. How are you?"

"Fine," she said absently, her thoughts still on Jack and his swift change of mood. "How about you?"

"Much better now that I've finally reached you."

At his sweet declaration, Laura shoved thoughts of Hawke from her mind and thought about Matt. An image of his face filled her mind's eye. Tall, blond and brown-eyed, Matt Peterson had Brad Pitt good looks and a double dose of charisma. A partner in a major law firm in L.A., he was smart, civic-minded and a man of action. He was sexy, exciting and fun to be with. In short, he was everything she thought she wanted in a man. And even though she cared deeply for him, she didn't love him—not with the deep-rooted passion she'd seen her parents find with their partners, but mostly not with the unshakable love that her grandparents had shared for one another.

"You're a hard woman to reach, babe. Have you been getting my messages?"

"Yes, I got them. And I'm sorry for not calling you back. It's just that I've been swamped and haven't had a moment to spare." It wasn't entirely true, she admitted silently. While the problems at the hotel and Hawke had eaten up most of her time, she hadn't called Matt back because she simply hadn't wanted to go another round with him about her returning to California.

"Sounds to me like you need a vacation. Why don't you take a break and come out here this weekend for a visit? It's been too long since I've seen you, Laura. I miss you."

"I can't, Matt. I've got too much going on here right now."

"Is there a problem?" he asked. "You sound…on edge."

His remark reminded Laura how perceptive Matt could be. For a moment, she considered telling him about the problem with Hawke, her mother's note and the impending foreclosure on the hotel. He was an attorney and businessman from an affluent family and could probably help her secure the funding she needed. But something told her the price he'd expect in return for his help would be too high. Matt wanted a socialite wife like his mother, a woman to adorn his arm, host his parties and be devoted to him and his interests. While some women would be happy in that role, she knew that she wouldn't. Even if that weren't the case, she would still be reluctant to tell him about Hawke. The thing with Hawke had turned personal and she didn't trust that Matt wouldn't sense the truth. It didn't matter that

Matt had dated others since her departure and done so with her blessing. Matt was far too competitive to view her interest in Hawke as anything other than a threat to him. If he knew how close she had come to sleeping with Hawke, he'd see it as a challenge to his manhood. And the last thing she wanted was to deal with Matt's ego.

"Laura, is everything all right?"

"Yes. I'm just tired," she told him, which was the truth—if only part of it.

"I told you going down there and trying to salvage that old place was a mistake. You're wearing yourself out. You should have stayed here in California."

"I didn't want to stay in California," she reminded him. "And I really don't want to argue with you about this again."

"I'm sorry, babe. I just hate the thought of you pushing yourself so hard. I worry about you."

"I know," she said with a sigh because she knew that he did care about her. And for the first time, she wondered if maybe she should have just ended things as she'd wanted to do six months ago instead of allowing Matt to convince her that they could still remain a part of each other's lives. If her move had done nothing else, it had confirmed her realization that she didn't want a future with Matt as anything more than a friend. Of course, this crazy attraction to Hawke certainly proved that she could never love Matt.

"Listen, I know you're too busy to come back now. But Christmas is only a couple of weeks away. What do you say you come spend Christmas here in L.A., then we'll drive up to see my parents at their place in Big Bear and do some skiing. I know they'd love to see you."

"It all sounds wonderful, Matt. But I can't," she told

him, realizing it wouldn't be fair for her to end things with him over the phone. "Chloe's staying with me for a few weeks and I don't want to leave her alone at Christmas."

"All right," he said, an edge in his voice. "Then I guess I'll just have to settle for seeing you after Christmas. In fact, see if you can get into L.A. by the twenty-eighth. One of my backers for the senatorial race is throwing a big party then to introduce me to some of his friends. And my parents are hosting their big New Year's Eve party, so there'll be lots of press coverage."

"I'm afraid I won't be able to make it then, either," she told him. "I promised Papa Vincenzo that I'd come see him and Maria and the boys before the New Year."

"Dammit, Laura. I get your feeling you need to be with Chloe for Christmas. Even if she is just your half sister, there's blood there," he said. "But what I don't get is you blowing off spending New Year's with me for those...those people?"

Angry now, Laura said, "Those people happen to be my family."

"Give me a break. Just because the guy was married to your mother for a little while doesn't make them your family. For crying out loud, the man's your ex-stepfather and his kids are your ex-stepbrothers. There's no blood tie there. Those people are nothing to you."

"That's where you're wrong, Matt. Those people are everything to me." And without waiting for him to reply, she hung up the phone.

Stepping inside of his suite at the hotel, Jack dumped his laptop case and coat on the chair near the door, then tossed his key card onto the table. He wanted to punch something. No, he amended, he wanted to punch *someone*.

Matt Peterson.

Anger ripped through him as he recalled Laura all hot and sweet and soft in his arms only to turn away from him to take his stepbrother's call. It wasn't about her rejecting him, Jack told himself. He could handle rejection. If a woman wasn't into him, that was fine. He certainly didn't lack for female company and finding a woman willing to share his bed had never been a problem. Hell, Laura had been more than willing to share his bed. She had been as hot and eager for him as he had been for her.

Until Peterson had called.

When given the choice, she had walked away from him for Peterson. The son of a rich man, the golden boy that people flocked to, the one his own mother had adopted as her son all those years ago and had preferred over him. The fact that Laura had chosen Peterson over him fed his anger. But beneath that anger there was something else—an ache that felt dangerously close to hurt.

Enraged with himself that he had allowed Laura to affect him so deeply, that he had somehow given her the power to cause him this hurt, Jack stormed through the suite. He pushed open the door to the bathroom, went to the sink and doused his face with cold water. It hit him like a slap and helped clear his head somewhat.

Grabbing a towel, he dried his face and shoved the hair from his eyes. He braced his hands on the sink, drew in a breath. Satisfied he had his emotions under control, he hung the towel on the rack beside the counter. As he did so, memories of Laura flashed through his head. Laura staring at his naked chest, unknotting the towel at his waist. Laura looking at him, her eyes dark with desire, her mouth hot and hungry as she kissed him. Then suddenly it wasn't him Laura was looking at. It wasn't him she was kissing. It was Peterson she was clinging to, Peterson whose name she was gasping.

All the anger came rushing back. Furious with her and with himself, Jack turned away and stalked back into the living area. He headed straight to the bar where he snatched a glass and poured himself two fingers of whiskey. Wrapping his fist around the glass, he brought it to his lips and was about to toss it back when he realized what he was doing. He slammed the glass down on the bar untouched, sending liquor sloshing over the rim. He would not use liquor to numb the anger and pain the way his father had done.

Instead, he did what he always did. He took refuge in his work. Jack wasn't sure how long he worked. Long enough for him to plow through a mountain of e-mails and reports from his various holdings. Long enough for his shoulders to become stiff. Long enough for his stomach to remind him that the minibar snacks he'd fed it during his infrequent breaks weren't doing the job. But the thought of venturing out to dinner held no appeal. Besides, he was on a roll, Jack told himself.

Retrieving his cell phone, he punched in his assistant, Dotty's, home number. The second she answered, he barked out, "I want you to call Jardine's office and tell them to make sure they have everything ready to close on this deal," he said, referring to the attorney handling the sale. "And the minute the thirty days in that default clause are up, I want the deal closed." When she didn't respond, he asked, "Dotty, did you hear me?"

"I heard you," she said. "But if it's okay with you, I'll wait until morning and call Ms. Jardine at the office because I'm guessing she and her family might be getting ready for bed about now."

The sarcasm in her voice wasn't wasted on him. "It's not that late," he told her. But a glance at the clock on the bedside table proved him wrong. It was after ten o'clock, which meant it was even later in New York. The silence that followed was telling. "All right, it is late," he conceded. "And I'm sorry if I disturbed you. But I want you to call first thing in the morning and tell her—"

"I know. You want the deal closed ASAP. I'll call Ms. Jardine's office in the morning and make sure everything's on track."

"Good. I also want you to make some calls and find out exactly where Laura Spencer stands on raising that money. I know her mother and stepfather are trying to refinance the nightclub in Paris. Find out where they are on that." He filled her in on what he already knew. Namely that Chloe had signed over her stock to her sister and Laura had pledged it and her own stock for a loan. He also knew that she had cashed out her stocks and savings. What he didn't know was if Peterson had loaned her the money. "Give Sean Fitzpatrick at Fitzpatrick Investigations a call, too. Have him see if Matt Peterson or his family have made any large cash transactions."

"Jack, you never said anything about your stepbrother being involved in this deal," Dotty told him and he didn't miss the worry in her voice.

"I don't know that he is. But he and the Spencer woman are close friends and I don't want any surprises."

"All right," Dotty told him. "And since I've got you on the phone, what do you want me to tell the people at City Park about that donation you made to restore the carousel? They're most appreciative and want to have a commemorative plaque installed, acknowledging the donation. They also want to hold a press conference to announce Hawke Industries' generosity."

Jack hesitated a minute, then recalled the night Laura had shown him the Carousel Gardens and told him about her grandfather taking her there for the first time. "Tell them the plaque should read In Memory of Oliver Jordan, Hotelier."

"And the press conference?"

"Tell them I want to wait until after the first of the year and have the Contessa Hotel listed as the donor. List Laura Spencer as their contact person."

"Got it," Dotty told him. "Anything else?"

"That's it. Just make sure our people are ready to come in here and get things rolling once this goes down so I can get started on the Henderson's Plastics deal," he said, referring to a company he'd been eyeing in California.

"So you won't be sticking around New Orleans?"

"No. There's no reason for me to stay here once things are under way. Besides, my home is in New York."

"You live in a hotel suite," she reminded him.

"Which has a laundry, a housekeeper and twenty-four-hour room service."

"That's not a home, Jack."

"It's the only home I need. Good night, Dotty." He hit the off button on the phone. Annoyed by his assistant's remark,

Jack went over to the minibar, grabbed a can of nuts and a bottle of water. He popped the top on the can of nuts, ate a handful and then washed it down with water. As he munched on the snack, he looked around the luxurious room.

There wasn't a thing wrong with living in a hotel, he told himself. Living in a hotel suited him just fine. There was no fuss, no maintenance, no lawn to cut and a hot meal was only a phone call away. If it felt a little empty or pristine at times, so what? Besides, he wasn't there all that much anyway.

Polishing off the rest of the nuts, Jack walked over to the window and drew open the drapes to look out at the city. The threat of rain that had lingered all day had finally arrived and fell steadily on the streets below. The sky was starless thanks to the dark clouds. Even the moon struggled to be seen through the rainfall and clouds. The streets below were nearly empty, save for an occasional car. Jack suspected that the lack of traffic had more to do with people's lingering fears of flooding in the aftermath of Hurricane Katrina than it had to do with the actual threat of a rainstorm. He couldn't help feeling empathy for the people who had lived through the nightmare and had bravely returned.

Since the stormy weather suited his mood, Jack left the drapes open. After trading his dress slacks and shirt for a pair of jeans, a shirt and sweater, he returned to the table and his laptop where he went back to work. He was knee-deep in the projected operating budget for the hotel when he looked for the report that detailed the operating expenses for the prior five years and realized he didn't have it. Evidently, he had left it in Laura's office when he'd stormed out that afternoon. Still too restless to call it a night, Jack took the elevator downstairs to the executive office to retrieve the report.

Exiting the elevator, he started down the hall toward the office. He had the key to the door in his hand when he reached the suite of offices and found it unlocked. When he entered the reception area, he spied the light shining from Laura's office. The door was ajar and he could hear her speaking to someone.

"Yes, I know," she said. "I know that, too."

She was on the phone, he realized, and felt that punch in his gut again as he remembered who she had been speaking to when he'd left her this afternoon. Refusing to allow himself to go down that road again, Jack reminded himself he was there to get a file. He pushed the door open and walked over to the table.

Laura turned as he entered and there was no mistaking the surprise on her face. Lightning flashed outside the window behind her, illuminating her face. Her skin was pale, her eyes huge. She'd repaired the damage to her hair and lipstick that he'd done earlier, but it did little to disguise her fatigue.

"I'd better go, Mother. It looks like this storm is turning nasty. I should probably head home before it gets worse," Laura said.

It was her mother, Jack realized. Annoyed with himself because he was pleased that it hadn't been Peterson she was talking to, he began searching through the files for the report he needed.

"Yes, I understand. Just let me know as soon as you hear."

So her mother still hadn't been able to get the refinancing on the nightclub, he surmised. Did that mean Peterson hadn't come through for her yet? Even if his stepbrother didn't have that kind of money himself to lend her, his parents certainly did. It would take moving some stocks or pledging other assets, but Edward and Nicole Peterson were very wealthy people and they had never denied his son anything. Too bad the same couldn't be said for her son. But then, Jack had stopped being Nicole's son a long time ago, he reminded himself. All he was to her was a reminder that she had once been married to a loser.

"I will, Mother. Yes. I love you, too," Laura said and hung up the phone. After a moment, she said, "Jack, I'm sorry about…about earlier."

"Don't sweat it. I didn't," he told her and continued rummaging through the files.

"No, I guess you wouldn't," she tossed back.

There was something in her voice, a weariness beneath the sharp retort that caused him to look over at her. She looked sad and confused and vulnerable. But it was the sadness that touched something inside him, something he didn't want her to touch. And because she had the ability to make him feel, he resented her for it. Unable to locate the report he wanted, Jack dumped all the files into the briefcase he had left on the table. He'd take them all back to his suite and look for the one he needed there, he decided. Another bolt of lightning streaked through the sky. Thunder boomed. The lights flickered and he jerked his gaze up. "How good is the backup generator?"

"Good enough."

"When was the last time it was serviced?"

"I don't know the exact date. But it was sometime last year, shortly before I took over management," she told him as she began shutting down her own computer system. "We haven't had a major storm since Hurricane Katrina."

But he knew that the backup generator was old. In fact, according to the records, it had been retired and designated as the backup more than ten years ago when a new generator had been purchased. Given the difficulties experienced in restoring power to the ravaged city, he wasn't sure that either generator could sustain a minor storm, let alone a major one. And this one sounded like a big one if that last blast of thunder meant anything. "You may want to rethink trying to get home in that mess and take a room here for tonight."

"I'll be fine," she assured him as she switched off her desk lamp and gathered her briefcase and purse. When she reached the door, Jack allowed her to precede him and then he followed her out. After locking up the offices, they walked in silence down the corridor to the elevator banks. Jack punched the up button. She pressed the one for down. And they waited.

And waited.

She punched the button again. So did he. But according to the floor indicator, both elevators continued to move at a snail's pace. "I'll just take the stairs," he told her.

"Jack, wait," she said when he started for the stairwell door. "That's a lot of stairs. I'm going to take the freight elevator. If you don't mind riding down to the first floor with me first, you can use it to go up to the penthouse."

"Sounds good to me," he told her and followed her down to the far end of the hallway where the elevator the staff used for servicing the guest floors was tucked in a corner. Within moments of pressing the button, the elevator doors opened and they stepped inside.

Laura hit the down button for the first floor and the elevator started to descend.

Jack watched as the car lumbered down, passing the fifth floor, then the fourth floor. And then the elevator slammed to a halt, nearly knocking Laura off her high heels. Jack caught her arm to keep her from falling forward.

"Thanks," she murmured as she straightened herself. Then she hit the button for the first floor again.

Nothing happened.

When she tried three more times and the car failed to move, she said, "What in the devil's wrong with this thing?"

Jack frowned. "What's wrong is it's stuck. And so are we."

Eight

Stuck?

They couldn't be stuck, Laura told herself. The elevator was just having a little hiccup. That was all. No way was she stuck in this elevator with Jack. "It'll start again in a minute," she said more to herself than to him. She set her briefcase and purse down on the floor and punched the floor buttons—all of them.

Nothing happened.

"I told you, it's stuck. Try pushing the emergency lever."

She tried. But still nothing happened. She pulled open the door to the red emergency box that contained the phone only to find that someone had cut the phone cord. Laura could feel her heart begin to race. Telling herself there was no reason to panic, she snatched her purse from the floor. "I'll just call the front desk on my cell phone," she said and began digging through the handbag. When she located it, she flipped it open. "No signal," she told him. "Either the storm took out the satellite or the walls of the elevator are interfering with the reception. You'll need to call the hotel on your phone."

Jack reached for the clip on his belt, but it was empty. "I left it in my suite."

Her stomach sank at the news. She was in trouble. She was alone with Jack in a space the size of a small closet. And no one even knew she was there. Not Chloe. Not her assistant, Penny. Not any of the hotel staff. The realization sent a wave of panic rushing through her. She had to get out of here. She had to, Laura told herself and she began slapping at the buttons again.

"Hey, take it easy," Jack told her as he caught her hands, holding them in his fists. When she started to struggle, he narrowed his eyes. "What's wrong? Are you claustrophobic?"

"No," she responded. But as she looked around, noting just how small the elevator was, she felt even more trapped. The air suddenly seemed thin, as though she were on a high mountaintop. "At least I wasn't until you mentioned it," she told him, both annoyed and scared. Pulling her hands free, she tried her phone again.

"It's okay," he told her.

Laura ignored him. Struggling to breathe, she tried to fight off the growing panic while she continued to hit at the buttons on the panel. She had to get out. She had to get out. She repeated the words silently like a litany.

"Laura," he said.

When she failed to respond, he stepped in front of her. But with the tide of panic sweeping through her and her breathing growing more difficult by the minute, she struck at him. Her blows seemed to bounce off his chest, but still she continued to fight him to get to the control panel. She needed to get the door open. She needed to get out of the elevator.

Jack caught her fists, sandwiched them between his palms and held them. "Laura. Laura," he repeated her name softly. "Breathe. Try to breathe."

It was the gentle way he had said her name that eased some of her panic. No longer struggling, she drew a deep breath, released it. As her heart rate slowed, so did her breathing. She looked up at Jack, stared into blue eyes that were warm, caring, concerned.

"It's okay," he told her gently.

But it wasn't okay. It might never be okay again, she thought. She was running out of time to get the money and her mother's attempts to refinance the nightclub had been turned down by two banks already. Her hopes of retaining the Contessa were on the verge of sinking and had a great deal to do with her stressed-out state. The ugly conversation with Matt and the realization that their relationship was nearly over had only added to what had turned into a lousy day. But it was the knowledge that she was swimming in dangerous waters on a personal level where Jack was concerned that worried her the most. She didn't want to be attracted to him. She didn't want to want him. And she didn't want to like him, to care about him. Even if the Contessa was not an issue between them, the emotional risks were far too great. Jackson Hawke was not a man who believed in love and commitment. He'd made that abundantly clear. And she… She was a woman who believed in and wanted both. To be trapped in an elevator with him was only asking for trouble that she didn't need, that she wasn't sure she could handle. That night in his hotel suite had proven that. So had this afternoon in her office. Had it not been for Matt's call, she wasn't at all sure she would have called a halt to things.

"Better?" he asked.

She nodded, drew another steadying breath. "You can let me go now."

He hesitated a moment, then released her. "I don't think it was a power outage. The light in here is still working. It's probably just the elevator."

Thinking more clearly, she noted that the light was indeed still working and told herself that was one thing for which she could be grateful. Otherwise, they would be trapped together in the dark. She waited, expecting him to remind her what poor condition the entire elevator system was in, but he didn't. Probably because he knew that she was well aware of it already. "It still doesn't change the fact that the car is stuck."

"No. But it means the rest of the hotel has power. The next time someone goes to use the service elevator, they'll discover it isn't working and report it to the maintenance department. Once maintenance is aware there's a problem, they'll correct it and get the car running again. Then we'll be able to get out."

"That would be fine except for the fact that no one's likely to discover the elevator isn't working until morning. It's after eleven o'clock. Room service stopped fifteen minutes ago and most of the housekeeping staff are gone for the day," she explained. "The chance that anyone will even try to use this elevator before morning is very slim."

"Maybe. Maybe not," he conceded. "The front-desk staff know you're still in the hotel. They might be used to you keeping long hours, but when you don't leave, someone's bound to come looking for you."

Laura shook her head. "There was a shift change two hours ago. I doubt anyone knows I'm still here. If they do, they'll think I just decided to spend the night on the couch in my office. I've done that before."

"What about Chloe? She's staying with you, isn't she? She'll come looking for you when you don't come home," he reasoned.

Laura would have laughed if she hadn't felt so dismayed. "Her stepsister, Meredith Grant, was arriving this evening for that meeting Chloe conned you into taking to discuss Meredith's company. Tonight Chloe was introducing Meredith to the city's nightlife. Knowing my sister, her chance of getting in before dawn is about as good as my chance of winning the lottery."

"What about your friend Peterson, the one you had to take the call from this afternoon?" he asked, an edge in his voice. "Won't he get worried when he calls you tonight and can't reach you?"

"Matt won't be calling me," she said firmly. Knowing Matt as she did, he would see nothing wrong in what he'd said and would expect her to make the next move by apologizing to him. "So unless someone is expecting you, no one knows we're missing."

"No one's expecting me," he told her, and Laura could have sworn the hardness that she'd detected a moment ago was gone.

"Then that means we're stuck here for at least…" she

glanced at her watch and continued "…the next five hours, maybe six, depending on when someone needs to use the service elevator."

"In that case, I suggest we make ourselves comfortable."

"What do you think you're doing?" she asked as he sat down on the floor and leaned against the wall.

"I told you. I'm getting comfortable. So should you."

"Aren't you going to at least try to get us out of here?" she asked, wondering if the man had lost his mind. Didn't he realize they were trapped in an elevator and no one knew they were there?

He glanced up at her. "And just what is it you expect me to do? The alarm on this thing is shot. I don't have my cell phone and yours won't work. And you said yourself that we're going to have to wait until one of the staff comes along and discovers the elevator is broken."

"But that won't be until morning," she pointed out.

"Precisely. That's why the smart thing for both of us to do is to try to get comfortable while we wait," he said and stretched out one leg while he bent the other. Leaning his head against the wall, he closed his eyes.

Irritated with him and frustrated by the situation, Laura looked around, then up at the tiled ceiling of the car. She knew that there were pulleys on the elevator car that were checked whenever the system was serviced. Through the ceiling, they could also get access to the next floor.

Opening his eyes, he followed the direction of her gaze. "You've got to be kidding," he said, sitting up.

"Why? If you get up on top of the car, you can crawl up to the next floor and get out through one of the vents in the elevator shaft." At his look of skepticism, she added, "It's done all the time."

"In the movies, maybe. But not in real life. Forget it. No way am I going to climb around in that elevator shaft and risk falling and breaking my neck. I can wait until morning for someone to find us."

"Well, I can't wait," she told him. But there was no way she could make it up to the ceiling without help. "All right. I'll do it. You just need to give me a boost up so I can reach the ceiling."

He looked at her as if she'd lost her mind. "In that outfit? You've got to be joking. That skirt isn't exactly made for climbing."

He was right. The skirt's straight cut was designed to showcase her legs, not for climbing around in an elevator shaft. "Then you go."

"No." He said the word firmly.

"Why not?"

"Because I don't like heights, okay?"

The admission stunned her. Jack had struck her as a man who feared nothing. Learning he had a fear of heights made him more real somehow and reminded her of the tender man she'd spent time with in the park. "I'm sorry. I didn't realize. I'll do it then. All you have to do is help me get up there."

He muttered something about stubborn women and pushed himself up to his feet. "You know, I should let you do it and just sit back and enjoy the view. But I'd hate like hell seeing you break your pretty neck and cheat me out of that night of sex you're going to owe me."

Ignoring the reference to their bet, she said, "Jack, I said I'll do it."

He pulled off his sweater, handed it to her. "Hold this."

Feeling unfair to have pressured him if he actually was afraid of heights, she said, "Really, Jack. Maybe you should let me go up."

"I said I'd do it," he told her. He stared up at the ceiling tiles for several months, then down at her briefcase. "How sturdy is that briefcase?"

"Very," she said.

"I'm going to need you to hold it as steady as you can while I stand on it so I can reach the ceiling. You wouldn't happen to have a flashlight in there, would you?"

"No, but I've got a penlight," she said, which she retrieved from the key ring in her purse and handed to him.

"Thanks," he said and slid it into his pocket. He tested his weight on the briefcase. Once. Twice. Then he turned to her. "Ready?"

"Ready."

Jack stood on top of the briefcase again and, stretching upward, he pushed on the cover tile in the ceiling that led to the elevator shaft. Once he had managed to nudge the tile aside, he looked down at her for a moment. "All right. Here goes."

"Jack." When he looked back down at her, she said, "Be careful."

"Don't worry, Laura. I intend to collect on that bet." Then he jumped and the tips of his fingers caught the edge of the opening in the ceiling. He clung to it for several long seconds.

Laura let go of the briefcase and moved beneath him so that she could hold either side of his legs. He glanced down at her. "It's okay," she said at his questioning look. "Use my shoulders to brace your feet."

Jack said nothing. And instead of using the leverage she had offered, he tightened his grip and pulled his body up until his shoulders were inside of the opening. Bracing himself on his elbows, he climbed through the rest of the way. For several moments he just seemed to stay where he was, hovering near the opening.

"Are you okay?"

"Yes," he told her and then he moved.

Laura tried to see inside the opening, but it was too dark. She did see a sliver of light occasionally and assumed it was her penlight. Trying to be patient, but finding the wait interminable, she asked, "Jack? Can you see the air vent yet?"

"Yeah," he yelled. He came back to the opening, knelt on one knee and looked down at her. His expression was grim and there was an odd look in his eyes that quickly turned to one of determination. "It's dark as sin inside this thing. But it looks like we're caught between floors. The nearest vent that I can see is a few yards above us. I'm going to see if I can get to it."

"Be careful," she repeated her earlier warning, but she wasn't sure Jack heard her because he had already disappeared back into the dark shaft.

It seemed as though an eternity passed, during which she heard Jack swear twice. Her heart stopped a moment when she heard something fall down the shaft before she realized that it must be the penlight. Finally, he returned to the opening and lowered himself down into the elevator.

"I'm sorry. I tried, but I couldn't get the thing opened. It's sealed tight," he told her as he brushed off his clothes. He sank to the floor, pressed against the wall. His jeans were dusty. His shirt was torn, his hair mussed. "And I owe you for the penlight. I dropped it."

"Forget about the penlight," she said, too worried by the sight of the gash on his forehead to recognize that he was being facetious. She didn't care about the penlight. She didn't even care about them being stuck in the elevator. What she did care about was the fact that Jack was hurt. "You're bleeding," she told him then grabbed her purse and dug through it for the packet of tissues she always carried.

He touched his forehead, looking surprised when he saw the blood. "Must have hit my head harder than I thought. I couldn't see much after I dropped the penlight."

Laura pushed his hand away and dabbed at the cut with a tissue. She was relieved to see that it wasn't as bad as she had first thought. She held the tissue for several moments to stem the bleeding. When she lifted it again, the flow of blood had lessened. "I've got a couple of Band-Aids in my briefcase. Hold this," she said and took his hand to place it on the wad of tissues. "Try to keep pressure on it while I get them."

"If you happen to have a couple of aspirin in there, I could use them. I've got a killer headache."

She did have aspirin, which she gave to him, along with the bottle of water she had tucked in her purse. Once she had cleaned the cut as best she could with the water and tissues, she placed a bandage over it. Sitting back on her heels, she said, "You've got a knot on your forehead and you're probably going to have an ugly bruise, but I don't think you need stitches."

"So I don't need to worry about looking like Franken-stein, huh?"

She knew the comment was meant to be funny. But she didn't feel the least bit amused. What she felt was guilty because he could have been seriously hurt. "I'm sorry. I should never have insisted you climb into that shaft."

"Hey, you didn't hold a gun to my head," he reminded her.

"I might as well have. The only reason you went in there was because of me." And it was knowing that, realizing it was her fault he was hurt, that he could very easily have fallen or worse, that made her feel even more guilty.

Jack tipped up her chin with his fingertip. "It's just a little scratch, Laura."

"But—"

He pressed his fingers against her lips, silencing her. "I'm fine."

"Are you sure?" she asked him.

"I'm sure," Jack lied. The truth was his head felt as if someone had hit him with a sledgehammer. But Laura looked so worried and guilty, he knew telling her so would make her feel even worse. In an effort to distract her, he said, "Any chance you've got some candy stashed in your purse? My dinner consisted of a raid of the minibar in my room, so I'm starving."

She didn't have any candy in her purse, but she did have some in her briefcase. It was her emergency stash, she explained to him as she divided the cache of chocolate-nut bars, peanut-butter cups and chocolate-covered wafers between them.

"I don't have any cups. I don't mind sharing, if you don't," she told him and offered him the bottle of water. He took it. For the next several minutes they ate in silence and as the silence grew he could see the nerves and guilt settling in again. To distract her he asked, "What's it like having such a big family?"

"Crazy. And wonderful," she told him.

As he hoped, she began to relax as she told him about her large, extended family and spending her summers in New Orleans with her grandfather at the Contessa. "It sounds pretty chaotic, all the moving around, people in and out of your life."

"It was, but in a fun way. Chloe used to say we were gypsies and had relatives in every state. But I didn't mind. I always wanted to be part of a big family and every time one of my parents remarried, I inherited another set of relatives."

"What about when they divorced?" he asked. "Didn't it hurt to lose all those new relatives?"

She grinned. "But I didn't lose them. Chloe and I decided that just because our parents got divorced didn't mean we had to. So we just kept the relatives. At last count I had fifteen grandparents and eleven brothers and sisters."

"That's a big family, all right."

"What about you?"

"My father died about ten years ago," he told her. But, in truth, Samuel Hawke had died long before then. He'd died the day his wife had left him for Edward Peterson.

"What about your mother?"

"She walked out on us when I was six. She's remarried now and has another son. I haven't seen much of her since the divorce."

"What about your brother? Are you and he close?"

"Hardly," Jack said, a wry smile twisting his lips as he thought of Matt Peterson. "He's my stepbrother. And there's never been anything that even remotely resembles family love between us. In fact, it's just the opposite. He detests me as much as I detest him."

"But why?"

Jack sighed. "I guess a lot of it had to do with my parents' divorce. It was a pretty ugly scene and watching people you love hurt each other, make selfish decisions you don't understand, isn't easy," he said, recalling his devastation back then.

"If you'd rather not talk about it, I understand," Laura told him.

Normally he wouldn't have told her about it. He seldom talked to anyone about that time in his life when his entire world seemed to have fallen apart. But looking at Laura now, recalling how she had shared the Carousel House with him that night, told him about her dreams, it felt somehow right to tell her. "My father had a construction business. Nothing big or fancy, but it supported our family. Then he landed a big contract to build a couple of office parks and hotels. It was great and there was the potential to make a lot of money on the deal. It would have made us rich. But he needed money to get the insurance and bonding. So he turned to an old friend who had hit it big in the real-estate business. He agreed to put up the money my Dad needed in exchange for half of the company."

"So your dad agreed," she added.

"Yes. Everything seemed to be going well for about six months or so. But my dad was gone a lot, busy with the business. And my mother wasn't the type of woman who liked being alone. Anyway, my dad's partner was around a lot and after a while I guess he wasn't content with just half of the business. He wanted my dad's wife, too. And my mother apparently didn't need much persuading. She was more than willing to swap what she considered a life of loneliness and pinching pennies for a life of fun and luxury."

"But what about you?" Laura asked. "She just left you?"

"I didn't want to leave my dad. He needed me," Jack explained as he recalled how difficult those first few years had been. "Besides, her rich new husband was a widower with a young son just a little older than me. Even when she was still married to my dad, she paid a lot of attention to him because he didn't have a mother," he told her, using the explanation his mother had always given him for her doting on Matt. "Anyway, once they were married, she adopted his son. So I guess you could say she traded me for him."

"But you were still her son," Laura said, her outrage clear.

"My stepbrother didn't think so. Whenever I'd go to visit, it was clear he didn't want me around. And the truth is, I didn't like being around them anyway. I didn't fit in. I just didn't belong." A fact that Matt had made sure he knew, Jack recalled. "After my dad sold his share of the business to them, he and I moved to New York. The visits grew fewer and fewer and eventually they stopped altogether. We haven't seen or spoken to each other in years."

"I'm so sorry, Jack," she said and reached out to touch his hand. "Your mother leaving you and your father like that for someone wealthy, she's the reason you said you wanted to be rich."

"Yes," he admitted. "I thought if I could find a way to make a lot of money and become rich then my mother would come back to us. Pretty stupid thinking, huh?"

"No. It was pretty smart thinking for a six-year-old," she

told him. "And I guess it's served you well. Because you are rich now."

Yes, he was rich, Jack thought to himself. Yet, lately, he had felt just as lonely and poor as he had been at six. He looked at Laura, thought about her crazy family, how her mother's selfishness and irresponsibility threatened to take away the hotel Laura loved, how she was willing to risk everything she owned to save something created by her family. Despite all the turmoil and financial strain, it was clear that she felt rich and was confident in her family's love. When she stifled a yawn, he suggested, "We probably ought to try to get some sleep. It's nearly one in the morning."

"Do you think that's a good idea? I mean, you have a head injury. You're not supposed to let someone with a head injury go to sleep."

He half smiled. "I don't think a little bump on the head qualifies as a head injury."

She frowned. "You were bleeding and you've got a knot on your head. As far as I'm concerned, that qualifies as a head injury."

When she stifled another yawn, he said, "All right. I do. But I read somewhere that when someone has a head injury, they can go to sleep. You just need to wake them up every hour to make sure they're okay. So why don't I set the alarm on my watch to go off in an hour. If I don't hear it when it goes off, you will and you can wake me up. How's that sound?"

She seemed to consider that. "I guess that would be okay."

So he set the alarm. Already stretched out on the floor, he leaned his head back against the wall and shut his eyes. She, on the other hand, couldn't seem to get comfortable.

He opened one eye, watched her stretch out her legs and put her head back against the wall the way he had. She tried tucking her feet beneath her and crossing her arms over her chest. She tried lying flat on her back and then curling into a ball on her side.

"Come over here," he told her.

Laura flushed. "I'm sorry. I didn't mean to wake you. I don't seem to be able to get comfortable and it feels like it's getting colder."

"Here, put this on," he said and tossed her his sweater.

"What about you? Aren't you cold?"

"Just a little. But I imagine it's going to get colder before the night's over. We might as well use our body heat to keep us both warm. So come on over here." When she hesitated, he said, "You don't have to worry, Laura. Being stuck in a cold elevator with a monster-size headache has pretty much put any thoughts of me having sex with you on the back burner for now."

Evidently taking him at his word, she scooted over to his side of the elevator. And when he opened his arms, she settled her head against his chest. Within moments, she was asleep.

But for him, sleep was a long time in coming. There was no need to reset the alarm on his watch when two o'clock rolled around because he was still awake. He was also still awake at three o'clock and four. And his inability to sleep had little to do with his using the floor as a bed and more to do with the woman whose shapely bottom was pressed against his arousal.

Laura stirred against him, adding to his torment and pleasure. He ached to slide his hand beneath her blouse, to feel the heat of her bare flesh against his palm. But to do so now when she was so vulnerable wouldn't be right, he told himself. He'd promised her she was safe. Besides, how would she feel if he slept with her and then foreclosed on the hotel? She already saw him as her enemy. Would she view her actions as a betrayal to herself and her family? Something told him that she would.

There was also the problem of Matt Peterson. How would she feel if she slept with Jack and then discovered that he was Matt's stepbrother, that he had considered bedding her for revenge? It would devastate her. Ashamed that he had ever thought of using her that way, he promised himself she would never know.

Still restless, she turned so that she was facing him, which drove all thoughts of Matt Peterson from his mind. Jack watched her. He noted the sweep of dark lashes that shielded her eyes, the gentle curve of her cheek, the way her lips parted ever so slightly in sleep. He remembered how soft and warm those lips had felt when he'd kissed her, the way she had tasted of both innocence and sin. The memory sent a sharp stab of desire through him, making him painfully aware of why he had been unable to sleep despite his own exhaustion.

She shifted again, adding to his discomfort. This time when she settled, she placed her hand trustingly against his chest. And then she opened her eyes.

Nine

Laura wasn't sure what had awakened her. One moment she'd been dreaming about riding on the carousel and the next moment she'd been under the oak trees in the park with Jack. Then his arms had been around her, pulling her close, engulfing her in the most delicious warmth. And when she had tipped her face up to him, desire had pooled in her belly as he'd watched her out of deep blue eyes that were hot, hungry.

Opening her eyes now, she stared into those same hungry blue eyes. His arms were wrapped around her with one of his hands cupping her rear and one of his legs resting between her thighs. A hard warmth pressed against her belly and heat spread through her like lava as she realized it was Jack's arousal. Suddenly the events of the previous night came rushing back. Being trapped in the elevator. Her panic. Jack soothing her and sharing with her painful memories about his past. Something told her that Jackson Hawke was not a man who shared much of himself with anyone. That he had shared it with her touched something deep inside her.

"Good morning," he said.

"Is it morning yet?" she asked and was surprised how rusty her voice sounded.

Without removing his arm from around her, Jack slanted a glance at the watch on his wrist. "Technically, it is. It's just after six. But the sun probably won't be up for at least another hour. You sleep okay?" he asked.

"Yes," she admitted, surprised by just how soundly she'd slept. Then she remembered the alarm. "I didn't hear the alarm."

"I did," he assured her. "I dutifully reset it for an early hour."

"Did you sleep at all?"

"A little."

But she suspected that wasn't true. There were shadows under his eyes and a tension in his body that told her he'd probably not slept at all. Whiskers darkened his jawline and an ugly bruise spread from beneath the bandage. "How's the head?"

"The jackhammer that was beating in it stopped a couple of hours ago."

She reached up, tested the area around the bandage with her fingertips. "It doesn't look as swollen. But you definitely have a bruise and probably a concussion," she told him. "You should have a doctor look at it once we get out of here."

"I will," he promised.

A wave of tenderness washed through her. She hadn't wanted to desire this man. She certainly hadn't wanted to care for him. He was her enemy, the man who threatened the hotel she loved so dearly. And yet she did want him with an intensity that shocked her. Worse, she was beginning to care for him—more than she should. More than was safe.

But then she had never been one to play it safe, Laura reminded herself. She didn't want to play it safe now. She smoothed her fingers down his face, felt the prickle of his whiskers against her skin, heard him draw in a breath. When he caught her fingers, a thrill went through her as she realized that her very touch had excited him.

"We've probably got at least another hour before someone discovers the elevator is out of commission and finds us. Why don't you try to go back to sleep?"

"I don't want to sleep," she told him. "Do you?"

Heat flashed in those blue eyes. "No."

"Then what do you want to do?"

"This," he said and kissed her mouth.

Excitement swept through her at the feel of his mouth on hers. Her skin burned everywhere his lips touched. He tasted of heat. He tasted of danger. He tasted of need.

When Jack's hands sloped her body, cupped her breasts, Laura thought she would explode. And the more he kissed her, the more he touched her, the more she wanted him. She couldn't get enough of him. Judging by his groan when she stroked his manhood, he couldn't get enough of her, either.

He flipped her onto her back, kissed her again. Harder. Deeper. Her tongue matched his, stroke for stroke. Needing to get closer to him still, she pulled at the buttons on his shirt and when his chest was bare, she pressed her mouth to his chest. When she flicked her tongue over his male nipple, she felt his body quiver.

Then his hands were on her again. "I want you naked," he told her and made short work of the buttons on her blouse. He unhooked the front of her bra, bared her breasts. And the look in his eyes sent a shiver through her. "I've dreamed of seeing you like this, of doing this," he said as he lowered his head and took her nipple into his mouth.

Laura gasped. She speared her fingers through his hair. Desperate to have him inside her, she reached for her belt. "Not yet," he whispered as he laved the nipple with his tongue then moved to the other breast and started the process all over again. The sensations were exquisite and maddening. But still he refused to hurry.

While his mouth enjoyed her breasts, he smoothed his hand down her waist, over her hips and beneath her skirt. By the time he slipped his hand inside her panties and cupped her, Laura was quivering with need. When he eased one finger inside her, she could hardly breathe.

He took his time. He stroked the nub of pleasure at her center slowly at first and with each stroke, Laura could feel the need build. She could hear her breathing quickening. He increased the pressure, quickened the pace. And she could feel his own need mounting, hear it with each ragged breath he drew.

"Jack," she cried out as she felt the orgasm building. She pulled his mouth to hers. She kissed him hungrily, greedily, wanting to send him over the edge as he had sent her. Then suddenly the orgasm hit her.

Pulling her mouth free, Laura clutched at his shoulders. She dug her nails through his shirt and into his skin.

Closing her eyes, she tipped her head back and shuddered as she reached the crest and went over. Just when she started to settle, Jack took her up again and again.

But it wasn't enough. Keeping her eyes on his, she reached for him. She heard his breath catch, felt a thrill of power go through her at his reaction to her touch. The feel of the large bulge in his pants sent another wave of desire through her. She fumbled with his belt, got the button of his jeans open. She had just started to ease down his zipper when the elevator jerked to life and they began moving.

Jack didn't know whether to be grateful or seriously ticked off when he realized the elevator was moving and that they were about to be rescued. He'd been moments away from making love with Laura on the floor of the elevator and a part of him was tempted to hit the stop button on the car and finish what they had started.

But then he thought of Laura. Her hair was tumbled and wild-looking. Her eyes were dark and smoky with desire. Her lips were swollen from his kisses and whisker burns were visible on her pale skin. Her skirt was a rumpled mess and she was struggling to button her blouse. She would be mortified for anyone to find them like this, to see her disheveled appearance. And for the first time in a long time, someone else's needs mattered more than his.

"Here," he said, handing her her jacket.

"Thanks," she murmured and slipped it on.

Quickly, Jack buttoned his shirt. When he realized some of the buttons had been broken in her haste to rid him of his shirt, he grabbed his sweater from the floor and pulled it over his head.

Laura had just managed to smooth her hair when the elevator doors opened. And madness ensued.

"Ms. Spencer, are you all right?" the building's maintenance engineer asked.

"What happened?" the housekeeping supervisor asked, concern in her voice.

"I'm fine," Laura said. "The elevator shorted out in the storm."

"Laura, for heaven's sake," Chloe exclaimed as she muscled her way to the front of the elevator and blocked the door. "I was worried sick about you when you didn't come home last night."

"I'm surprised you got home that early," Laura said.

Chloe scowled at her. "Funny."

"What are you doing here at this time of morning, anyway?"

"Looking for you. When you didn't come home and didn't answer your cell or office phones, I was worried. I thought something bad might have happened to you."

"Something bad did happen," Laura replied. "I got stuck in an elevator."

"Is that Mr. Hawke with you?"

"Yes," Jack replied in answer to the hotel bellman's question.

"The front desk has been trying to reach you since last night," he explained. "I think they had an important message for you."

"Thanks. I'll check with them," Jack said.

"What happened to your head?" Chloe asked him.

Jack pressed his fingers against the bandage, but before he could respond, Laura said, "Mr. Hawke tried to get us out of the elevator by climbing up into the elevator shaft, hoping he could reach the next floor through a vent and get help. Unfortunately, the vents were sealed shut. But in the process, he injured himself."

"Pretty brave of you, Jack," Chloe remarked.

"It *was* brave of him," Laura fired back. "But it was also very foolish." She looked at him then, remorse and concern filling her eyes. "We're lucky he didn't fall and seriously injure himself or worse."

"It's just a scratch," Jack replied, more for Laura's benefit than anyone else's.

"You still should see a doctor," she told him.

"I will," he promised. Aware of the curious eyes watching the exchange, Jack wanted to spare Laura any more awkwardness with her staff or her sister, so he cleared a path by saying, "Now, if you'll excuse us. I think you'll all understand that after spending the night on the floor of a hard, cold elevator, Ms. Spencer and I could both use a hot shower, something to eat and some sleep."

Taking the hint, the people began to disperse—everyone except Chloe, who followed them both to the main lobby. "So you two were stuck in that little old elevator together all night, huh?"

"Yes," Laura said, but Jack noted that she didn't look at her sister. Nor did she look at him. Instead she kept her gaze focused on the floor numbers above the main elevator.

Chloe looked at him and then at her sister. "What did you two do all night?"

"Waited," Laura replied.

Chloe moved a step closer to Laura. "What's that on your face?"

Laura touched her cheek where his whiskers had left their mark. "Nothing. Probably from lying on the floor."

"Doesn't look like a mark from the floor tile to me." She got even closer. "Looks more like whisker burns. Wonder how they got there?"

Laura flushed and Jack expected her to deny it. Instead, she surprised him by turning to her sister and saying, "Probably the same way you got that hickey on your neck the night you went out with Bobby Connors and his car broke down during your senior year in high school."

"His car did break down," Chloe assured her, color creeping into her cheeks.

"And the elevator did get stuck," Laura countered.

Jack wasn't sure if the argument had continued or not because just as the elevator arrived, the front-desk clerk spotted him. "Mr. Hawke," she called out. "I have your assistant on the line again, sir. She says it's important."

"Tell her I'll be with her in a moment," he told her. Then he turned to Laura, touched her arm. "We need to talk later."

She nodded. "Be sure to have someone take a look at that cut."

"I will," he promised again.

"And when you two finish your 'talk,' don't forget you're supposed to meet with Meredith this afternoon," Chloe reminded him.

Jack didn't miss the knowing look in Laura's sister's eyes. But he didn't shy away from it, either. "I won't forget," he assured her. Once Laura and her sister disappeared into the elevator, Jack headed to the house phone to take Dotty's call, wondering what was so all-fired important.

What was so all-fired important, he soon discovered,

was that his stepbrother's father had just initiated a series of stock sales and transfers that, when complete, would net him a cool fifteen million dollars. The exact amount needed to pay off Laura's mother's note, cure the default and stop Jack from foreclosing on the Contessa. Jack had never believed in coincidences. He didn't believe in them now.

Laura didn't believe in omens. She'd never believed that spilling salt, walking beneath a ladder or having a black cat cross your path were signs that something bad was about to happen. But she was beginning to seriously reconsider her decision. After that night she and Jack had spent in the elevator, the main heater in the hotel had died, the sous-chef had quit and a group scheduled to take thirty of the hotel's hundred rooms for a week had canceled due to crippling snowstorms in the north that had shut down the airports. But it was the fact that she had neither seen nor heard from Jack for nearly two days that worried her the most.

When he'd said they needed to talk, she had agreed. While she would have liked nothing better than to go with him up to his suite right then and there, it hadn't been possible. She'd had Chloe itching to hear details, a staff with a million decisions that needed to be made, and she'd been in serious need of food and a bath. But from the way Jack had looked at her, the tender way he had touched her arm, she had been positive he had wanted them to finish what they had started as much as she had.

She still didn't know what the important business was that had caused him to leave abruptly that morning. Nor did she know why he hadn't told her he was leaving. Had it not been for Chloe mentioning that he'd had to cancel the meeting with Meredith for that afternoon, she wouldn't have known he'd left town. But he was back now. She knew from Alphonse, the doorman, that he had returned late that afternoon. So why hadn't he attempted to see her? They had almost been lovers, for pity's sake.

Lovers.

Just the word sent a thrill through her. She wasn't an innocent young girl. She was a grown woman who had made love before and had enjoyed it. But never, not ever, had she experienced anything close to the pleasure that she had experienced in Jack's arms.

At the mere memory, a ripple of heat swirled through her body. Lifting her hand to her throat, Laura recalled with vivid clarity the feel of his mouth, hot and eager, on her breasts, the feel of his hands, so strong and yet gentle, on her skin. She had no doubt that had it not been for the untimely rescue, they would have made love completely that morning. It was what they both had wanted, what they had been heading toward for weeks now, she admitted.

So why, two full days later, had they still not made love?

Was it possible that she had been mistaken about how much he wanted her? Had those hours they'd spent together really meant nothing to him?

It was imperative she discover the truth. Because somewhere between fighting to stop his takeover of the hotel and lying half-naked in his arms, she had fallen for Jackson Hawke. She'd known him less than a month, had resented the threat he represented to her beloved hotel and she was starting to fall in love with him.

Laura was still digesting the fact that she had feelings for a man who, for all intents and purposes, was her enemy when her cell phone began to ring. Grabbing her purse, she dug into the leather bag and hoped it was Jack. But when she located the phone, she saw her mother's number instead. "Hello, Mother."

"Laura, darling. You'd better sit down."

He was in a foul mood, Jack admitted as he walked over to the window and looked out over the city. Night had fallen. On the streets below he could see people scampering, their arms most probably laden with shopping bags and wrapped packages. Everywhere he'd turned over the past two days, people were in a cheerful, holiday mood.

Not him.

He was angry, Jack acknowledged. He was angry with Matt Peterson. He was angry with Laura for lying to him. But most of all, he was angry with himself. He'd allowed himself to become distracted. He'd allowed his emotions to interfere with business. He'd allowed his attraction to Laura to distract him. And because he had, he was on the verge of blowing a fifteen-million-dollar deal.

Peterson was going to bail her out. Unless Jack found a way to foreclose before Peterson could get his funds in place, his deal was dead and Laura would keep the hotel. And Peterson would keep Laura. He didn't like losing. But he'd lost deals before and probably would again in the future. He wouldn't have even minded losing to Laura and seeing her win their bet. What he did mind was losing to his stepbrother. Losing *Laura* to him.

He didn't want her to matter. He didn't want to care about her. But it was because he did care for her that he hated like hell to see her with someone like Peterson. She deserved better than his stepbrother. Hell, she deserved someone better than *him*.

Caught up in his musing, it took Jack a moment to register that the pounding he heard was coming from the door. Turning away from the window, he strode through the suite and opened the door to Laura.

He knew instantly that something was wrong. Her eyes had a wild look to them. Her dark red hair, a tangled mass around her face and shoulders, looked as though she'd been running in the wind. Her eyes were dry, but there were tear streaks down her cheeks. "What's wrong?" he demanded.

"I guess that depends on who you ask," she told him and pushed past him into the suite.

Jack closed the door and followed her. "Since you're the one who came barging into my suite, I'm asking you. What are you doing here?"

"I'm here to pay off on our bet," she told him and stepped out of her heels.

Jack narrowed his eyes. Keeping his voice even, he said, "You're a little early. You've still got another five days."

"Five days or five months. It won't matter," she informed him. "My mother came up two million short in the refinancing. You've won, Hawke," she said, her voice cracking. "The Contessa is yours and I'm here to deliver on my end of the deal."

What was she talking about? Didn't she know Peterson was going to give her the money? But if she knew, she wouldn't be there. She would be with Peterson. "As much as I'd like to collect on our bet," he began with a casualness he didn't feel, "you might want to hold off. The rest of the money could still turn up."

"It won't. And I want to pay off now."

"Laura, you don't have to do this," he told her. "You don't want to do this."

"Sure I do." She pulled her sweater over her head. "We had a bet and I lost. I'm here to pay off the debt."

Jack's mouth went dry at the sight of her in the black lace bra. He was rock hard in an instant. Fighting the desire clawing at his gut, he told himself he shouldn't do this. He would not do this. He would not take advantage of her when it was obvious that she was upset and apparently didn't realize that Peterson was going to come through for her. When they'd started this thing, there had been a part of him that had wanted to bed her, had deliberately planned to do just that, to get back at his stepbrother. But that had changed and he knew he could never use her that way. He refused to do so now. Snatching up her sweater from the floor, he threw it at her and walked over to open the door of the suite. "Go home, Laura," he said through a voice that had gone hoarse with need.

He didn't expect the flash of anger in her eyes. She threw his sweater back on the floor and followed him across the room where she slammed the door shut. Then she turned to look at him. Taking his face in both of her hands, she kissed his mouth. When he didn't respond, she ran her tongue across his lips. Lifting her head, she looked up at him and said, "I'm not going anywhere, Hawke. Not until I've paid off my debt."

His body trembled with need. He wanted to haul her into the bedroom and make love to her until neither of them could remember their names. He wanted to feel her body shudder and clench around him when he filled her. He wanted to hear her call his name and cling to him as he took them both over the edge.

But he didn't.

He couldn't.

Not now. Not when she was so vulnerable, when she was still reeling because she thought she'd lost her hotel. Not when he knew that his stepbrother was going to bail her out even if she did not. He couldn't make love to her with the lie between them. If he did, she would hate him. And the idea that Laura would look at him with disgust and hatred hurt far worse than he ever imagined it would.

With a strength he hadn't known he possessed, Jack caught her hands and ended the kiss. "I was never serious about the bet. It was just a joke," he lied. "Go home, Laura. Before you embarrass us both."

He braced himself, sure he would see shock and hurt in her eyes. Instead he looked into the green eyes of a siren. "So you're saying you don't want me?"

"That's right."

The smile that curved her lips was pure sin. She stepped into his space, stroked his arousal through his slacks. "Liar."

Jack groaned. Unable to resist her, he pulled her into his arms and kissed her with all the hunger, all the need that had been building inside him from the first time he'd laid eyes on her. Tonight, he told himself, tonight she was his. Lifting her in his arms, he carried her into the bedroom.

Ten

Laura could feel the coolness of the silk sheets on her heated skin as Jack placed her on the bed. The contrast served to sober her for a moment. She'd come to him in a frenzy of despair and hurt following her mother's phone call. Those feelings had soon given way to anger. Anger at herself, her mother, her grandfather for not trusting her with his hotel. And anger at Jack for taking the hotel. At Jack for making her love him and then turning away. So she'd come to him. One look into those cool blue eyes and she'd known he was shutting her out. She didn't know why he had turned away from her. She didn't understand why he would deny what was between them. She only knew that she needed him to feel as she was feeling.

He stood beside the bed looking down at her. He wanted her. She could see it in his eyes, etched in the rigid way he held his body. But she could also see he was struggling with the decision to make love with her as he wanted, as they both wanted.

Determined not to let him deny them both, she took his hand and brought it to her breast, held it there. Desire flared in his blue eyes as he squeezed her sensitive flesh through her bra. "Make love with me, Jack," she whispered.

"Laura, you don't need to do this."

"Yes, I do. I want you, Jack. And I know you want me."

This time he didn't deny it. And when she reached for him, he came to her. The feel of his body against hers drove all thoughts away save for the feel of him, the taste of him, the ache at her center that grew stronger with each stroke of his tongue. In a frenzy to be one with him, Laura reached for his zipper.

He tore his mouth free and captured her fingers. "No," he told her. "I'm not going to let you rush this. I'm going to make love to you slowly and enjoy every inch of you. And when I finish, I'm going to start all over again. I want you to remember tonight, Laura. I want you to remember me."

She started to tell him that she doubted she would be able to forget him if she tried, but then he was kissing her again and she forgot what she wanted to say. All she knew was that her body was taut with need and awash with sensation as Jack moved his mouth from her lips to her jaw. From there he worked his way down her neck to her shoulder. He veered left and without removing her bra, he closed his mouth over the tip of her breast. When his teeth closed around her nipple, Laura nearly came off the bed at the exquisite sensations that rolled through her.

He unhooked her bra, bared her breasts and took them

in his hands. Laura moaned as he kneaded and kissed and plucked at her nipples. Then his clever mouth kissed a path down her rib cage to her belly. Her stomach quivered as his tongue circled her navel. By the time he pulled off her skirt and panties, tossing them aside, Laura was frantic to feel him inside her. She reached for him, fought with the buckle of his belt. "You're wearing too many clothes," she complained.

Between them, they made short work of his shirt and slacks. His groan as she freed him from his briefs sent a thrill of excitement through her. But excitement turned to white-hot need as he moved down her body and parted her thighs. "Jack, no."

"Yes." Opening her, he kissed her.

The first stroke of his tongue sent an explosion of sensation through her. When he repeated the process, she gasped. He continued to kiss her, to taste her, to nip her with his teeth. And with each flick of his tongue she could feel the pressure building. Just when she thought she couldn't stand the pleasure another second he increased the pressure and Laura felt the world explode.

"Jack," she cried out, reaching for him.

Then he was inside her. One smooth, slow stroke after the other, moving in and out. In and out. Nearly withdrawing, then filling her again. Then he started to move faster and faster still as he pushed her, pushed them closer and closer to that precipice.

"Look at me, Laura," he commanded.

She looked at him, stared into eyes that had gone dark with need. And desperation. She wondered at the desperation, wanted to ask him what was wrong. Then he entered her again, and the room around her shifted, shattered. And then she was tumbling into space.

Wave after wave shuddered through her, stealing her breath, stealing her ability to think. All she could do was feel. When the orgasm ripped through Jack, it sent her free-falling again. Driving into her one last time, he cried out her name. As his body convulsed, she held on to him, felt each spasm as it hit him before it rolled into her. Finally, when the shudders stopped, they continued to cling to one another.

For a long time, she said nothing. Neither did he. She contented herself with the feel of his body next to hers, the strength of his arms wrapped around her. She didn't allow herself to think beyond the moment. She didn't know where they went from here, if they went anywhere at all. Jack had made no promises. Neither had she. But she knew in her heart that it was promises she wanted.

"We need to talk, Laura. There's something I need to tell you about the foreclosure. You—"

"I don't want to talk about business," she told him. Turning over, she faced him. "What happened between us just now wasn't business."

"But—"

"It was personal, Jack. And I didn't come here tonight to try to convince you not to foreclose on the hotel. I came here tonight because I wanted to be with you. I wanted you. I needed you."

"But there's something I need to tell you. Something you need to know about me," he began.

Laura pressed her finger to his lips. "I know everything I need to know about you. I know that you're smart and arrogant and a tough businessman. I know you can be ruthless, but that you're brave and more caring than you want anyone to know. I know you're a wonderful and generous lover," she said softly as she stroked his jaw.

"I was inspired," he told her, then captured her hand and placed a kiss in her palm.

As impossible as it seemed, she could feel desire curling in her belly again. With a boldness she would never have imagined she possessed, she said, "Maybe I can inspire you again."

Heat flared in his eyes, but his expression grew somber. "You inspire me just by breathing. But you may feel differently when you know the truth about me, about who I am."

"I know who you are, Jackson Hawke. You're the man I'm in love with." When he went still, Laura quickly added, "I didn't tell you how I feel because I expect a declaration from you. I don't. But I wanted you to know the way I feel. I love you."

"Laura, if you knew the truth—"

"The only truth that matters to me right now is that you want me. Do you want me, Jack?"

"Yes," he said, his voice gruff. "I want you…more than I've ever wanted anything or anyone in my life."

"Then show me," she told him.

Jack showed her over and over again throughout the night. With his mouth. With his hands. With his body. And when she awoke in the morning, feeling tender and achy from their lovemaking, he lifted her in his arms and carried her into the bathroom. In the shower, he soaped her body, bathed every inch of her, discovered new pleasure points she hadn't known existed.

"You're so beautiful," he murmured. "So soft," he told her as he worked his way up from her feet to her thighs and the sensitive spot between them. With a slowness that she found maddening, he finally reached her breasts. Then his mouth was on hers, pressing her against the wall while the shower poured over them.

He lifted her onto him and she wrapped her legs around his waist and then he began to move. With each thrust, Laura could feel herself moving closer and closer to the edge of the cliff. And with the water streaming down around their joined bodies, she felt herself begin to fall.

"Jack," she called out, clutching his shoulders as the sensations took her over that cliff.

Moments later, she heard him shout her name as he followed her over the edge.

By the time she exited the bedroom forty-five minutes later, Jack was already dressed in a suit and tie, sitting at the table talking on his cell phone. She noted his briefcase and laptop sat near the door.

"I know it's last-minute, Dotty. But try to set the meeting up with as many of them as you can. If they can't make it, get them to agree to be available for a teleconference." He paused. "Just tell them it's a one-time chance for them to make a thirty percent return on their investment, but I need an answer by tomorrow."

For the first time since she'd shown up at his hotel room door the previous night, Laura felt awkward. They were lovers and she loved him, but she didn't know how he felt. Had last night been a one-time fling for him? Would he want to continue to see her? Or would he foreclose on the hotel and return to New York and never see her again? A sinking feeling settled in her stomach as she realized she didn't have the answers and that those answers may very well not be what she wanted. It also reminded her that Jack had wanted to tell her something last night. Only she had been fearful that whatever he wanted to tell her would ruin what was happening between them, so she had refused. Now in the clear light of day, she realized that might not have been the smartest thing to do.

As though sensing her presence, Jack looked up. "I've got to go, Dotty. I'll see you in a couple of hours." Ending the call, he went to Laura and kissed her. When he lifted his head, he smiled and said, "Good morning, again."

"Good morning."

"I ordered some coffee, croissants, eggs and bacon from room service," he told her and Laura noted for the first time the serving cart piled with silver trays. "I wasn't sure what you liked to eat in the morning."

"Just coffee for now," she said and sat down while he retrieved the silver pot. "Are you going somewhere?"

"I have to go to New York this morning," he told her as he poured her a cup of coffee.

"I see," she said, but she clearly didn't. "Will you be coming back?"

He stopped in the middle of pouring his own coffee at the question. "Of course I'll be back. Why would you think I wouldn't?"

Both relieved and somewhat embarrassed, she said, "I just wasn't sure. I mean, I was the one who showed up here last night and refused to take no for an answer."

He caught her hands, pulled her to her feet. "And I'm glad you did. I meant what I said last night. I've never wanted anything or anyone as much as I wanted you. As much as I *still* want you," he added.

Laura went into his arms, laid her head against his chest. As she breathed in his scent, reveled in the feel of him, she asked, "Do you really have to go to New York now?"

Taking her by the shoulders, he gently set her from him. "I'd like nothing better than to take you into that bedroom and make love to you again. But there's something I have to do first, something I have to fix. Once I've made things right, I'll be back."

"How long will you be gone?"

"A day, maybe two tops. And when I get back, we'll talk."

"About the foreclosure," she said, realizing he would be back right before the scheduled foreclosure on the hotel.

"Yes, we'll talk about that. And about us."

It took a lot longer to fix his situation than he'd anticipated, Jack admitted as he sat across the table the next afternoon with the signed documents in hand. It had also cost him an additional million dollars to sweeten an already very sweet deal. But he'd done it. The foreclosure on the Contessa Hotel by Hawke Industries was now officially canceled. In turn, the investors he'd originally sold the idea to were enjoying a hefty return for their initial investment. And he was now the sole owner of the promissory note and the foreclosure was called off. The entire process had been tricky at best and he'd had to tiptoe around the legality of his actions because of the potential conflict of interest. Fortunately, the attorneys had hammered it out.

Standing at the door, Jack shook hands with each investor and bade them goodbye. "Thanks again, Carlton," Jack said.

"Anytime, Hawke," the other man said and shook his hand. "You call me again the next time you're willing to offer these kind of terms on a deal."

"Me, too," one of Carlton's cronies said with a laugh.

Everyone left but his final investor and his father's old friend, Tom Ryan. "Thanks for coming, Tom."

He nodded. "You know, son, I've known you since you were knee high. I watched you go through your parents' nasty divorce and your father's bout with the bottle. I watched you grow into a fine young man, but a hard one, a man who never allowed himself to feel anything deeply or look at anything beyond the bottom line. For you, everything has always come down to money. I suspect a lot of that had to do with what happened with your parents. And I understood it, but I worried about you."

"Is there a point here somewhere, Tom?" Jack asked, not particularly happy with the portrait he'd heard painted of himself.

"The point is that today you made a business decision that I suspect had nothing to do with the bottom line. Unless I miss my guess, you just blew several million dollars for personal reasons."

Which was true, Jack admitted silently. Feeling somewhat defensive, he said, "What if I did? You and the others certainly profited from it."

Tom smiled, his brown eyes twinkling. "Yes, we did. And I wasn't being critical, son. Hell, I'm pleased about it because I was worried you were going to end up a rich but lonely man."

And he just might have, Jack realized. Had it not been for Laura. Laura had changed all that. Laura had changed him. "Glad I could make you happy," Jack said. "But if you don't mind, I've got a plane to catch."

"Just one more thing, Jack. Tell me. Was she worth it?"

Jack smiled for the first time since he'd left New Orleans two days ago. "Yeah, she was."

And as he dashed from his office to the waiting limo for the airport, all Jack could think about was that Laura had been worth not only the millions it had cost him on this deal, but she had been worth everything he had and more. Now all he had to do was hope that she would forgive him for not telling her right from the start that Matt Peterson was his stepbrother and convince her that a future with him was worth the risk.

"Thank you. Yes, I'll get back to you about the date for the press conference," Laura said then hung up the phone with the business office at City Park.

Jack. Jack had done this for her.

Picking up the letter from the park's Celebration in the Oaks Improvement Committee, she reread the words of thanks for the donation to restore the Carousel House. She skimmed the remainder of the letter, asking her to confirm the wording on the commemorative plaque that would grace the Carousel House in her grandfather's name. Her heart swelled. Jack had made the donation before their night together. Surely for him to do such a thing had to mean he felt something more for her than lust, she told herself.

She thought of his phone call earlier, telling her he was on his way back and would meet her at her house. He'd said he had something to tell her. Was this what he'd wanted to tell her earlier? Then she'd let him surprise her and after he did, she would show him just how much she appreciated what he'd done.

"That's an awfully dreamy expression for a woman who's supposedly working. Don't you agree, Meredith?"

Laura opened her eyes and looked over at the doorway where her sister stood with Meredith Grant. The daughter of a Boston blue blood and an opera diva, Meredith had been Chloe's stepsister during the brief marriage of Chloe's father and Meredith's mother. As in Laura's own case, divorce had not severed the family bonds. Laura smiled at the two of them.

"I think she looks like a woman who's working at dreaming up some wonderful new marketing plan for her hotel," Meredith offered diplomatically, a hint of her Boston roots in her voice.

"Thank you, Meredith," she said and couldn't help but notice the contrast in the two women. While her sister, Chloe, was striking, in-your-face sexy and fun, Meredith was a quiet beauty with an abundance of grace and poise. And where her sister's style was up-to-the-minute chic and bold, Meredith's was elegant.

"You're quite welcome," Meredith told her politely.

"So what are you two doing here? I thought Chloe was dragging you off to some party tonight."

"Not some party," Chloe corrected. "It's a party being hosted by the director of the new action/adventure movie they're planning to shoot here. Oops," Chloe said as her cell phone started to ring. She glanced at the number. "I need to take this," she told them and exited the office.

"Your sister seems to think there could be a few potential clients for me among the Hollywood South set,"

Meredith explained, referring to the name many were now calling New Orleans's fast-growing movie industry. "Laura, I hope you don't mind, but Chloe told me about your situation with the hotel. I have some money in a trust fund I could borrow against and lend you if it would help."

Moved by the gesture, Laura reached out and squeezed the other woman's hand. "I can't tell you how much I appreciate the offer, Meredith. But I can't accept. I've pretty much resigned myself to the fact that come Monday, Hawke Industries will be the majority owner of the Contessa."

"I'm sorry," Meredith told her.

"So am I." She sighed. "But I guess the one good thing that's come out of all this is that I met Jack."

"Oh. I didn't realize the two of you were…involved."

Laura frowned, not sure what to make of Meredith's reaction. "Is there any reason I shouldn't be involved with Jack?" When the other woman remained silent, Laura pressed, "Please, Meredith, if there's something you think I should know, tell me."

The clear blue eyes that looked at her were filled with concern and empathy. "It's just that…in my business I try to keep up with the society columns and based on what I'd read and things Chloe said a while back, I was under the impression that you were involved with Matthew Peterson. In fact, I thought it was rather serious."

"Matt and I did date for a while," she confessed. "And for a short time, I thought it might become more serious. But when I moved back to New Orleans, we agreed to take a bit of a break. We have sort of had a long-distance relationship since then. But it isn't serious. At least not anymore," she told her, which was something she realized she still needed to make clear to Matt. Now with Jack in her life, she could see even more clearly that what she shared with Matt was not real love and to allow him to believe otherwise would not be fair.

"Does Jackson Hawke know that? I mean, does he know that you and Matthew Peterson are no longer a couple?"

"I'm not sure. But then I'm not sure he ever knew Matt and I were involved in the first place. Why? What difference does it make?"

Meredith clasped her hands in that way well-bred women do when they need to compose themselves. When she looked up at Laura, her gaze was steady and her voice gentle as she said, "It might make a difference because Matthew Peterson and Jackson Hawke are stepbrothers."

The news hit Laura like a blow.

"You didn't know." It was a statement, not a question.

"No, I didn't."

"I guess it's not surprising that he didn't tell you," Meredith said. "From what I'm told there's a lot of bad blood between the two of them. It goes back to when Hawke's mother left him and his father for Matt Peterson's dad. I understand Matt Peterson doesn't even acknowledge there's any family connection between the two of them, even though it was Hawke's mother who adopted Peterson. And before you think I'm some terrible gossip, the only reason I know all this is because my mother is friends with Nicole Peterson. She performed at some charity event Mrs. Peterson was chairing."

"I don't think you're a gossip at all," Laura assured her. "Is there… Is there anything else I should know?"

Again, Meredith hesitated. "Just that the rivalry between

Jackson Hawke and his stepbrother has only gotten worse as they've gotten older. In fact, when I was having such a difficult time getting an appointment with Hawke to discuss my business proposal, my assistant went so far as to suggest I approach Matt Peterson with the proposal because the chance to snatch a deal from his stepbrother would be a sure way to draw Hawke's interest. I'm ashamed to say I actually considered it."

"No one would have blamed you, if you had," Laura said absently.

"I would have blamed me. That's not how I do business," Meredith explained. Then her expression softened again. "I'm so sorry, Laura."

"Me, too. I just still can't believe that Jack didn't tell me he and Matt are stepbrothers."

"Maybe he didn't know about you and Matt Peterson," Meredith offered. "I mean, I read the gossip and society sections because of my business. It's possible Hawke doesn't pay any attention to them and never realized you had been involved with his stepbrother."

Had Jack known about her involvement with Matt? Of course he would have known. He'd had her investigated. Her personal relationships, particularly a long one with a wealthy and well-connected businessman would have been noted. Suddenly memories came flooding back—of the night in her office when Matt had called and Jack had left abruptly in a surly mood. She also remembered his odd remark about what would Peterson say when he called for her and she wasn't home. Yes, Jack had known about her relationship with Matt. What she didn't know was if Jack had really wanted her, or had he only wanted what he thought belonged to Matt?

As though sensing her turmoil, Meredith said, "Laura, if he did know about you and his stepbrother and didn't say anything, he might have had a good reason."

"Can you think of a good reason?" she asked.

"No, but if I were you, I would talk to him and find out what his reasons were."

"I intend to," Laura told her. And she prayed that when she did talk to Jack, the answers he gave her wouldn't break her heart.

"Good luck, then."

"Thanks," she said. "And thanks for being honest with me. I know I put you on the spot."

"I just hope that when you talk to Hawke that you get the answers you want."

"So do I," Laura said.

Eleven

Jack spied the flashing police car lights behind him and breathed a relieved sigh when the officer whizzed past him. He had no doubt he'd broken several speeding laws in his race from the airport to Laura's house. Reminding himself to send a donation to the policemen's fund as atonement and thanks, he exited Interstate 10. As he waited for the light to change, he turned on the radio and found himself listening to the Christmas carol about being home for Christmas. Jack smiled, realizing that in a manner of speaking he was coming home—to the first home he'd had in a very long time. And for the first time in even longer, he was actually looking forward to Christmas.

Because of Laura.

His heart seemed to swell in his chest as he thought of her, remembered the feel of her, the scent of her, the sound of her telling him she loved him. He wanted to see her face, hold her close and hear her say those words to him again. And she would, he told himself. Once he told her that the foreclosure on the Contessa had been canceled, it would no longer stand between them. She would no longer need to worry about losing her beloved hotel and he would no longer have to worry about Peterson injecting himself into Laura's life.

Later, he would tell her about Peterson, explain their connection and hope she would forgive him for not telling her about it earlier. But no matter what happened, she would never know that he had even considered seducing her to get back at his stepbrother. That he had thought of doing so still shamed him. He could live with his shame, but he couldn't live with the hurt that it would cause Laura. Whatever it took, he would keep that truth from her.

Deep in thought and eager to see Laura, Jack didn't even see the man standing on the stairs in front of her house until after he had parked and exited the car. Even though his back was to him, Jack recognized the tall figure in the black overcoat sporting his two-hundred-dollar haircut. Jack also recognized the voice talking on the cell phone.

"Laura, it's Matt again. I've got a surprise for you, babe. Give me a call."

Jealousy and anger gripped Jack by the throat and refused to let go. He balled his hands into fists. And when Peterson turned around, he didn't look at all surprised to see Jack there.

"Hello, Hawke."

"What are you doing here?" Jack demanded.

"I could ask you the same thing. This is Laura's apartment, after all. And she is *my* girlfriend. Not yours."

"She might have been your girlfriend at one time, but she's not anymore," Jack told him.

"Are you sure about that?" Peterson asked. He leaned back against the door, a smug look on his face. "Laura and I have been seeing each other for more than a year. In fact, Mom and Dad adore her and they're eager to welcome her into our family."

The mention of his mother and the insinuation that Laura would be marrying Matt infuriated Jack. But he forced himself not to give in to Peterson's baiting. It had been a mistake he'd made far too often in their youth. As a result, he'd ended up being the one getting the bad rap and Peterson had come out smelling like a rose. "Give it up, Peterson. Laura's done with you."

"I don't think so."

Jack couldn't help noticing that his stepbrother had made the statement with the same confidence he'd possessed as an eight-year-old when he'd told Jack that his mother wouldn't be coming back for him. Peterson had been right. His mother hadn't come back for him. She had started a new life with a new son. But Peterson wasn't right this time, Jack told himself.

When he didn't respond to the provoking, Peterson continued, "As a matter of fact, I'm so sure about Laura that I'm planning to announce our engagement at Christmas. She'll make the perfect candidate's wife, don't you think?" He paused. "After all, she is the whole package. Smart, beautiful and of course, there's that sexy little body of hers."

"Shut up," Jack warned.

Peterson smiled, his lips twisting malevolently. He was clearly enjoying himself. "What do you think she's going to say when I give her the check to pay off her mother's loan and stop you from foreclosing on that hotel that she loves so much? I've got it right here," he said, patting his pocket. "I imagine she's going to be very grateful and I certainly am looking forward to letting her show me her appreciation."

Jack wanted to plant his fist in Matt's face. Instead, he took a step forward. "I said to shut up!"

"Why? Don't like the idea of Laura showing me her gratitude with that sweet little body of hers?"

"Don't hold your breath, Peterson. She isn't going to show you anything but the door because the foreclosure was canceled. I bought out the other investors. So you see, Laura doesn't need your money or you. Now why don't you go hop on the plane and go back home to mommy and daddy."

Peterson laughed and the sound did nothing to ease Jack's temper. "Come on, Hawke. Do you honestly believe that given a choice Laura would choose you over me? Face it, you're a loser. Just like your old man was."

Jack wasn't sure if it was hearing Peterson tag him as a loser again or if was the seed of uncertainty that Laura might indeed choose his stepbrother over him, but something inside of him snapped. Grabbing Peterson by the lapels of his coat, Jack hauled him up to get right in his face and said, "Since it's my bed Laura's been sleeping in and my name she screams when I'm buried inside her, I'd say you're the loser this time. Not me."

At the sound of a gasp behind him, Jack spun around and saw Laura standing there on the sidewalk. In the streetlight, her face was the color of chalk and her green eyes were the size of quarters. But it was the look in those eyes, the shock, the hurt, that ripped at him now. Releasing Peterson, he started down the steps toward her. "Laura—"

"Don't," she said, holding up her hand.

"I can explain," he told her, desperate to wipe that shattered expression off her face. "It's not what it looks like."

"Isn't it?" she asked, her voice flat, cold.

"No," he told her firmly. "It's not."

"Don't listen to him, Laura," Matt said as he straightened his coat. "It's exactly what it looks like. Hawke has hated me from the day his mother left his old man and him to be with me and my father. He's always been jealous that his mother chose us over him and what he hated most was that I was the son she really loved, not him. He'd do anything to get back at me for that."

"Including using me," Laura remarked, but her eyes remained fixed on Jack.

"No," he told her.

"That's exactly what he did. It's all a game to him," Matt assured her. "He found out about us, knew that I was in love with you and he devised this elaborate scheme to try to hurt me by taking you from me. Why do you think he bought your mother's note? He knew the threat of foreclosing on the hotel would make you vulnerable to him. He even went to the trouble of getting the foreclosure canceled just so he could play hero and make you indebted to him."

"And what about you, Matt? Why are you here? To play white knight for me, so that I'll be grateful to you?"

"Babe, I'm here because I love you. I knew something was wrong the last time we talked. As soon as I found out what was going on here I knew that Hawke had to be involved. And I'll admit, I did get the money you needed but that's because I know how much that old hotel means to you."

"Or maybe you got the money so that I would be indebted to you instead," she countered and there was no mistaking the cynicism in her voice.

"I did it so that you would see how much you mean to me. I want a lifetime with you, Laura, not a few nights of cheap sex. Because that's all it was to him," Peterson told her. "You heard him yourself. He bragged to me that he'd slept with you just to get even with me."

"That's a lie," Jack insisted.

"Is it, Jack?" Laura asked. "Did you know about me and Matt?"

"Yes, but—"

"Don't listen to any more of his lies, Laura," Peterson told her. He came down off the steps, stood before her and reached for her hands. And the sight of Peterson touching her was like a knife in Jack's heart.

"I love you," Jack told her, saying the words he'd never said to anyone since he was a six-year-old boy, pleading with his mother not to leave him. "And that's not a lie. It's the truth. I may not have been honest about anything else, but that much is the truth. I love you."

"I'm afraid that's not enough," she told him and pulled her hands free from Peterson. "Now if you'll both get out of my way, I'd like to go inside my house."

"Laura, please let me explain," Jack said as she brushed past him and climbed the stairs.

"It's a little late for explanations," she told him. "You'll have my letter of resignation in the morning."

"What about your staff?" he asked, hoping her loyalty

and concern for her employees would persuade her to re-consider and give him time to somehow convince her that he hadn't meant to hurt her, that he loved her.

"I'll draft a statement and speak with them individually. But under the circumstances, I won't be giving the customary two weeks' notice because I'll be leaving town." She unlocked the door, paused and turned. "Oh, and if you still want to buy my stock, Jack, it's yours."

"You've made the right decision, Laura," Peterson told her, triumph in his eyes as he started to follow her. "We'll go back to California and put this whole ugly thing behind us."

Laura blocked him at the door. "You'll go back to California, Matt. You and I are done."

"You can't mean that," he countered.

"Oh, but I do mean it. I'm not in love with you, Matt. I don't think I ever was. So I guess you were right, Jack. Matt is the loser this time. But so are you. Because I loved you, but I'll never forgive you for what you've done."

"Come on, Laura. It's Meredith's last night here. You have to come with us," Chloe all but whined as she followed her out of the house to her car.

Laura loaded the empty cardboard boxes into her trunk and closed it. "I told you, I have too much to do. I've got to clear out my desk, make a list of personal items at the hotel that belong to the family, draft a statement for the employees and update my résumé. I don't have time to go to the Celebration in the Oaks. You and Meredith will just have to go without me."

Besides, Laura thought as she walked around to the front of the car and unlocked the driver's-side door, she didn't know if she could face seeing the lights in the oaks with the memory of her evening there with Jack still so fresh in her mind. She'd spent the remainder of Friday evening and the better part of Saturday alternately crying and cursing Jackson Hawke. But nothing she had done had assuaged the ache in her heart over what he'd done.

"But it's Christmas," Chloe continued, refusing to give up. "This will be my first time going to see the lights since Granddad died. And who knows, it might be my last time to see it. And it might be yours, too, if you insist on selling your shares of the Contessa to Jack and leaving New Orleans."

Her sister was right. She didn't know if she would come back again. With her grandfather gone and the Contessa belonging to Jack now, there seemed little reason for her to return to New Orleans. The realization sent another swirl of sorrow through her. New Orleans had always been the one place to which she'd returned. It was her anchor. It was her home.

"Oh, do come," Meredith urged in that perfect diction that Laura found so lovely. "I've heard so much about this Celebration in the Oaks and the antique carousel. I can't wait to see it and Chloe tells me you're a fountain of information about it."

Feeling as though she were being double-teamed, she said, "I'd hardly call the few facts and figures I know a fountain. And as much as I'd like to go, I really am too busy."

"Don't you want to see the Carousel House one last time? Say goodbye to Pegasus?" Chloe asked.

"Pegasus?" Meredith repeated.

"Her favorite horse on the carousel," Chloe explained.

But mention of the horse brought tears to Laura's eyes.

She thought of her visits to the Carousel Gardens with her grandfather, the young dreams and fantasies she'd spun while riding on that horse. She thought of telling Jack about those dreams and fantasies, of the tender way he had looked at her while he'd listened, of that first time he'd kissed her under the trees in view of the carousel. Then she thought of the donation he'd made in her grandfather's name to restore the antique ride. An act of love, she had thought at the time. Only she had been wrong. Instead of an act of love, it had merely been part of his great plan to seduce her as a means of revenge against his stepbrother.

Evidently taking her silence as refusal, her sister decided to change her tactics and said, "It's because of Jack, isn't it? He's the real reason you won't come with us."

"He's part of it," Laura admitted. A big part, she added silently.

Chloe planted her hands on her hips, flattened her lips in a disapproving line. "I get that you love him and he hurt you. I even get that you're willing to let him take the Contessa from you and leave town because of what he did. What I don't get is why you would let him steal all the good memories you have of that carousel and the Christmas lights in the oaks."

"I'm not."

"Aren't you? I know how special that old carousel is to you, how much you looked forward to going to see it and the lights each Christmas. It's all you talked about from the moment you saw October on the calendar. You couldn't wait to come home to see the lights and ride your horse on the carousel. But you won't even go now to take a look at it and share it with me or Meredith and it's because you went there with Jack." She paused. "He stole your heart and broke it, Laura. Don't let him steal all your precious memories, too. Say you'll come with me and Meredith tonight."

"All right. I'll come with you," Laura said.

Chloe all but beamed and Laura didn't miss the satisfied smile she sent Meredith's way. "Great."

"You won't be sorry, Laura," Meredith told her. "Tonight you'll make a new memory, a happy memory."

Although she thought the remark odd, Laura shrugged it off. "I'm not going to be making any memories at all if you two don't let me get out of here so I can get to the office and pack."

Both stepped back from the car while Laura got in behind the wheel. "The gates open at dark, which will be around five, but I'll probably be lucky to be finished before six. Why don't I just meet you guys there for around seven," she suggested.

Chloe's smile faded. "But I thought we'd all go together and get there when it opens."

Laura considered all she had to do and the already late hour. She didn't want to let clearing out her office drag on to the next day. Her plan was to go into the office in the morning, speak with Penny and a few of the other longtime employees before making her announcement and leaving.

"Won't it be especially crowded if we wait that late?" Meredith asked.

Meredith was right. On the weekend before Christmas, attendance was highest. "The best I can do is six-thirty," Laura said.

"Six," Chloe insisted. "Six-thirty is when all the people who went to early dinner will be stopping to tour the lights."

"All right. Six o'clock," Laura relented.

"And we'll pick you up at the hotel," Meredith informed her. At Laura's querying look, the other woman simply explained, "I understand parking is a problem. Best to not have to worry about two cars."

"All right. I'll see you at six."

By the time six o'clock rolled around, Laura was emotionally and physically exhausted. After loading the boxes into her car, she returned to the office for one final look. She had known that packing up her office would be difficult. She had also known that packing away family mementos like the photos of her grandfather and great-grandfather would be bittersweet. She had even known that losing the Contessa would hurt. She had had so many dreams about running the hotel, continuing her grandfather's legacy. What she hadn't known was that losing her dream of a future with Jack would hurt even more.

It wasn't meant to be, she told herself and sighed. She looked around the office, ran her fingertips across the old mahogany desk one final time, then she shut the door and went downstairs to meet her sister and Meredith.

When Laura exited the hotel, she wasn't surprised to see a limo parked out front. Limos were as common as taxis it seemed. What did surprise her was Alphonse, the doorman, informing her that the limo was for her. Wary, Laura approached the sleek black vehicle and when the driver opened the back door, she was equally surprised to see her sister and Meredith. Chloe was dressed in an eye-catching red leather skirt and boots and Meredith in chic mocha-colored suede slacks with matching jacket. But it was the red Santa hats, champagne glasses and the ear-to-ear grins that caused her to do a double take. "What's going on?" she asked.

"Hurry and get in," Chloe insisted. "You're letting all the cold air inside."

Laura climbed into the backseat. "All right, what's with the limo? Did you to hit the jackpot at Harrah's?" she asked, referring to the city's only land-based casino.

"Actually, we're celebrating," Chloe said and poured her a glass of champagne.

Laura took the glass, but didn't drink. "Just what is it we're celebrating?"

"I landed a contract with Hawke Industries yesterday to act as a matchmaker between businesses," Meredith told her.

"That's wonderful, Meredith. Why didn't you say something earlier?" Laura asked. "We should have celebrated last night."

"Given the situation with you and Jack…Mr. Hawke," she amended, "I didn't feel it was appropriate. But Chloe insisted I tell you. She said you would be happy for me and want to celebrate my success."

"She was right. I am happy for you," Laura told her honestly. "Just because things didn't work out for me and Jack personally is no reason for you to pass up a good business opportunity. I wish you every success," she added, clinking her glass with theirs in a toast.

"He was quite remarkable, you know," Meredith told her. "He had some wonderful ideas, ones I had never even thought of."

"I'm not surprised. He's a brilliant businessman," Laura remarked.

While Meredith and Chloe chatted, Laura fell silent. She stared out the window of the limo, but her thoughts remained filled with Jack. She had half expected to see him at the hotel when she'd gone to pack. If she were honest, a part of her had even hoped she might see him. The truth was now that the initial shock and hurt had subsided some, she wanted to believe that he hadn't meant those things he'd said to Matt, that he hadn't used her. She wanted to believe that what they had shared hadn't all been a lie.

She'd refused to speak with him when he'd tried to talk to her that night. She had ignored each of his calls and not even Chloe's urging her to speak with him had made her relent. But she'd known he'd been outside her apartment most of the night. Between bouts of crying and anger, she'd looked out the window and seen him standing there next to his car. With his arms folded, seemingly oblivious to the bone-chilling cold that was part of New Orleans's winter, he had stood there watching her house window. And each time he'd seen her at the window, he'd straightened and started toward her. So she'd pulled the drapes closed and walked away. She'd almost expected to find him there in the morning. But when she'd awakened, he'd been gone. And there had been no more calls, no more attempts on his part to see her. The memory brought on another wave of hurt and longing.

"We're here, ladies," the driver announced.

"Oh my, look," Chloe exclaimed.

Shaking off her sad thoughts, Laura set her untouched champagne glass down and exited the limo. And she stepped into a winter fantasy. There on the ground at the entrance to the park were mounds and mounds of white snow. "I don't understand," she said as she walked over to join her sister and Meredith.

Kids were squealing all around her, frolicking in the mountains of white. Even the adults were laughing and carrying on like children who were seeing snow for the very first time.

Stooping down, Laura picked up a fistful of white, let it fall from her fingers. "It's snow. It's really snow," she said and when she looked up, she saw Jack. He looked so tall and handsome and wonderful standing there. But it was the look of longing and fear in his eyes that made her heart skip a beat.

"Technically, it's called artificial snow," Meredith told her. "It's made with machines called snow canons by spraying water and using air pressure—"

"I'll take it from here, Meredith," Jack said as he approached her.

She shot a glance at Meredith and her sister. "You knew about this?"

Chloe made a show of being fascinated with the snow. Meredith smiled and said, "I actually made two deals yesterday. One with Hawke Industries for business and one with Jackson Hawke personally."

"You may have to give a refund on that last one," Laura told her, still not sure she was willing to trust him with her heart again.

"All I guaranteed him was that I'd get you here so you could listen to what he has to say. I told him getting you to believe him was up to him," Meredith said. "But personally, Laura, I'd listen. I've made enough matches to know when two people have found something special. It would be such a shame to walk away from that without being absolutely sure."

"All I'm asking for is ten minutes, Laura," Jack said. "Listen to what I have to say and if you still can't forgive me and want me out of your life, I'll sign over the Contessa to you and never bother you again."

A part of her was afraid to listen. She was afraid because she wanted to believe that what they'd shared had been real and that she would fall for more lies now.

"Please, Laura. Ten minutes. It's all I ask."

"All right," she said.

"This way," he told her and led her through the gates of the park to a waiting horse and carriage.

"I don't understand," she said as he helped her into the carriage where he settled them both under a bright red throw and nodded for the driver to leave. "How did you manage this? The park is closed to all vehicles. It's walking tours only since Hurricane Katrina."

"Meredith arranged it. And the snow," he told her.

The horse's hooves made a clip-clopping sound as the carriage drove along the winding path through the huge oaks glittering with white lights. Everywhere she looked, there were mounds and mounds of white snow lining the paths, turning the park into a winter wonderland. "But why?"

"Because that night you took me to see the lights, you told me about your snow-deprived childhood here."

That he had remembered softened something inside her, made Laura hope. And because she felt herself weakening, she made a point of looking at her watch. "Seven minutes."

"I also remembered you telling me about thinking the carousel was enchanted. Unfortunately, Meredith couldn't come up with a way to arrange that so quickly."

Laura remained silent; she was moved that he had remembered what she'd told him. As the horse continued on its way amid more snow, she said, "All of this… It must have cost a fortune."

"I considered it a small price to pay to get you here."

When they reached the Carousel Gardens, the horse stopped and Jack said, "I thought we'd walk from here."

They exited the carriage and when Jack helped her down, he held on to her for several seconds. When she stepped back, he released her. For the next few minutes, he said nothing and when they reached the Carousel House, they stopped.

"I got the letter telling me about the donation you made to restore the carousel in memory of my grandfather." She turned to him then and asked the question that had plagued her. "Why did you do that, Jack?"

"I made the donation after you took me here. I could see how much that carousel meant to you. And you taking me here, sharing it with me, meant a lot to me. I think it's when I fell in love with you."

Laura looked away, wanting to believe him, afraid, too. "If you loved me, how could you use me the way you did?"

"I didn't."

"I heard what you told Matt. I heard the way you told him, about us making love, about how he was the loser now because you'd taken me from him." Even now, the memory of his words made her feel raw inside.

"I never meant to hurt you, Laura. It was anger and years of bitterness that caused me to say those things."

"If you're saying you didn't know about me and Matt, I don't believe you."

He frowned and she thought she could detect a trace of

temper as he insisted, "I *didn't* know about the two of you.
At least not at first. And I'll admit that when I found out
and we made that bet, I did think about seducing you to
get back at him. But that plan lasted about a minute because
as hard as I tried to convince myself that I was pursuing
you because of Matt, it didn't work. Matt was the last thing
on my mind when we were together." He caught her by the
shoulders, turned her to face him. "He was the last thing
on my mind when I kissed you, when I held you, when I
made love to you. Because I fell in love with you, Laura."

"Then why didn't you tell me about Matt being your
stepbrother after we became lovers? Why let me think you
didn't even know him?"

"I wanted to tell you. I started to tell you that night in
my hotel suite. But then you were upset about losing the
hotel and were insisting you pay off on our bet. I wanted
you so badly that night and then once we made love, I was
afraid to tell you because you would think that I'd used
you. I also was afraid that Matt would come through with
the money to pay off the note and I would lose you to him."

"You should have trusted me, Jack."

"Yes, I should have. But at the time, I was in a panic. All
I could think of was that I didn't want to lose you to him
the way my father had lost my mother to Peterson's father."

"I'm not your mother, Jack. And you're not your father."

"Don't you think I realize that now?" he demanded.
"I'm sorry I hurt you. I'd sooner cut my heart out than hurt
you. Don't you think if I could take it all back, take all those
horrible things I said back that I would?"

"I don't know, would you?" she asked, but she already
knew the answer, Laura admitted as she felt her heart lighten.

"Yes, I would, dammit. But I can't. All I can do is tell you that I love you. And hope that you still love me enough to give me another chance. Will you give me another chance?"

Laura heard the plea in his voice, saw the care shining in his eyes. She slid her arms around his neck, and, smiling up at him, she said, "Yes, I'll give you another chance, Jackson Hawke, because I love you, too."

Epilogue

December, one year later.

When the car turned onto the exit for City Park, Laura looked over at her husband and said, "Jack, I thought we were going to dinner."

"We are. But there's a little stop we need to make first," he told her as the car pulled to a stop at the entrance to City Park.

After Jack helped her ease her very pregnant body from the vehicle, Laura couldn't help but notice there were no lines stretched around the block to view the lights in the oaks as there normally would be just days before Christmas. "Please tell me you didn't rent the park just for us."

"Only for an hour," he assured her as he led her to the gate.

"But it's Christmas, Jack. The children—"

"Will see the lights for free tonight. Everyone will. It's part of the deal I worked out with the park. But there's something I want to show you first."

"Another surprise?"

"Yes," he told her and, cupping her chin, he brushed his lips against hers.

In the ten months since she'd married Jack, her life had been filled with one surprise after another. After funding the initial improvements for the Contessa, Jack had turned over the hotel to her completely. He hadn't interfered or offered advice unless she'd requested it. She'd implemented her marketing plans and the Contessa was doing remarkably well. Her marriage to Jack had proved equally surprising. They had merged their lives, as well as their hearts. He sought her opinions, shared his thoughts and feelings with her as she never dreamed he would. While his relationship with his mother and stepfamily remained strained, the bitterness seemed to have waned and he'd grown more comfortable being part of her family.

To her surprise the passion between them remained just as powerful now as it had a year ago—despite her watermelon-size belly. But it had been the life growing in her belly that had come as the biggest surprise. She wasn't sure who was more thrilled about the baby—her or Jack. What she was sure of was that she had never felt more loved or cherished or happy in her life.

"Good evening, Mr. Hawke. Mrs. Hawke," the clerk at the gate said.

"Evening," Jack said. "Everything ready?"

"Yes, sir. Everything's ready."

"This way, Mrs. Hawke," Jack told her.

Rather than surprised, Laura was deeply touched by the sight of the horse and carriage. After Jack assisted her into the carriage and covered her with a throw, she rested in the comfort of his arms as the driver took them through the park. The horse and carriage made its way along the winding path through the oaks glittering with white lights. Laura couldn't help remembering a similar ride with Jack in the park last December and her shock to discover he'd had snow pumped along the roads to give her the white Christmas she'd dreamed of as a child. A gust of wind whipped through the trees and set the lights to shivering. Laura shivered, too, and burrowed under the blanket closer to Jack.

"If you're too cold, we can go back," Jack offered.

"No, I'm fine. It's just the humidity," she explained to him. "It makes it seem colder than it is."

When they reached the Carousel Gardens, the carriage stopped and Jack helped her from the carriage. He frowned and looked up at the sky. "I swear it's dropped ten degrees since we got here. And if I didn't know any better, I'd swear those were snow clouds."

"I wish," she said and she did. Snow in New Orleans was a rare thing indeed.

"You sure you're not too cold?"

"Quit fussing, Hawke, and show me the surprise."

Taking her hand, Jack led her down the path toward the Carousel House. As they made their way to her favorite part of the park, Laura felt another wave of love for the man she'd married. Thanks to Jack's donation, the antique carousel that she adored was on its way to being fully restored. Unfortunately, the expertise needed and painstaking detail could not be rushed. As a result, the carousel was still inoperable for this holiday season.

When they turned the corner, Laura heard the music and smiled at the familiar sound. "The calliope is working."

"Yes," he told her and guided her along the next curve of the path.

And then she saw it. Her beloved carousel aglow with lights, music playing, horses weaving up and down as it turned in a circle. "But I thought it wasn't finished. The restorer said it would be another month," she exclaimed.

"They managed to finish ahead of schedule," Jack told her.

Laura looked at her husband. "How? By working around the clock?"

Jack's cheeks darkened slightly. "Trust me, they were well compensated. Wait here a second," he told her and hopped onto the carousel. After disappearing inside the maze of mirrors for a moment, the carousel slowed to a stop. Returning to her, he offered his hand and said, "Come on."

He helped her up onto the carousel and once she was on, she went straight to Pegasus and lovingly stroked the horse. "It must have cost you a fortune to do all this."

"It was a small price to pay to see that look on your face. Do you like it?" he asked.

"I love it. And I love you, Jackson Hawke," she said, wrapping her arms around his neck.

"Not half as much as I love you, Mrs. Hawke," he responded and covered her mouth with his. When he slid his hands down her body, cupped her bottom and pulled her to him, Laura thrilled at the feel of his arousal. Knowing that he wanted her so much even now fed her own hunger for him.

Another blast of wind sent her scarf and coat whirling

around her and Jack ended the kiss. He tugged the scarf around her neck and there was no mistaking the love and desire in his eyes as he looked at her. "I think I'd better get you out of this cold, Mrs. Hawke," he said.

But Laura barely heard him as she spied the white flakes beginning to fall. Surprised and delighted, she said, "Jack, look. It's snowing."

"I'll be damned," he said, laughter in his voice. Scooping her up into his arms, he stepped off the carousel and began walking back to the carriage. "Looks like you're going to finally get your Christmas fairytale," he told her.

Oh, but she'd gotten so much more than her Christmas fairytale, Laura thought as she reached up and brushed snow from his brow. She'd gotten the whole fairytale when she'd gotten Jack's love.

* * * * *

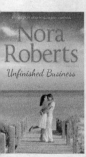 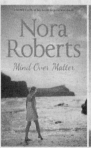 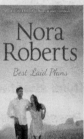 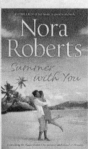

MILLS & BOON®
By Request

RELIVE THE ROMANCE WITH THE BEST OF THE BEST

A sneak peek at next month's titles...

In stores from 17th April 2015:

- **Forbidden Seductions** – Anne Mather, India Grey and Kimberly Lang

- **Mistress to the Magnate** – Michelle Celmer, Jennifer Lewis and Leanne Banks

In stores from 1st May 2015:

- **Untamed Bachelors** – Anne Oliver, Kathryn Ross and Susan Stephens

- **In the Royal's Bed** – Marion Lennox